WIT

D0175624

Andrea Schicke Hirsch

SASQUATCH

**SPENCER
HILL
PRESS**

Spencer Hill Press

Contact: Spencer Hill Press, 27 West 20th Street
Suite 1102, New York, NY 10011

Please visit our website at www.spencerhillpress.com

First Edition: July 2015
Hirsch, Andrea Schicke, 1957

Sasquatch : a novel / by Andrea Schicke Hirsch - 1st ed. p. cm.
Summary: Sixteen-year-old boy is certain that the mythical Sasquatch not only
exists, but is living in the wilderness just beyond his backyard fence, and he is
determined to prove it.

The author acknowledges the copyrighted or trademarked status and trademark
owners of the following wordmarks mentioned in this fiction: Academy Award,
Advil, Apples to Apples, Amazon, Batman, Best Buy, Beefaroni, Bilco, Boston
Marathon, Boy Scouts, Butterball, Cadillac, Campbell's, Coca-Cola, Coors,
Days Inn, Discovery Channel, DMB, Dumpster, Facebook, Fig Newtons, The
Flintstones, Ford Mustang, Formica, Girl Scouts, Green Day, Greyhound,
Harry Potter, Harvard, Honda, Grand Hyatt, iPod, Ivy League, Jackass, Jell-O,
Jeep, Karmann, Kit Kat, Lake Compounce, Lexus, Lysol, Magnum, Maroon 5,
McDonald's, Men in Black, Metropolitan Opera, Mustang, Niblets, Obie Awards,
Oreo, Photoshop, Pledge, Range Rover, Reese's Pieces, Rice-A-Roni, Southern
Comfort, Stop & Shop, Thermos, Three Stooges, Tony Awards, Tropicana,
Twinkies, VISA, Volkswagen, Walmart, YouTube

Cover design by Lisa Amowitz
Interior layout by Jennifer Carson

978-1-939392-47-3 (paperback)
978-1-939392-54-1 (e-book)

Printed in the United States of America

FOR ETHAN

CHAPTER 1

What the hell was that?

A hollow, metallic crash sent me shooting up out of bed like I had been blasted from a cannon. The splintery boards were cold under my bare feet. Hard to believe it was July. Listening intently, I fumbled for the lamp, knocking a book off the night table. Its hard corner stabbed my left baby toe before it hit the floor. I yelped in pain, then sucked it back in, hearing more commotion outside.

The crashing had changed to thumps and rustles and a weird, high-pitched chittering.

Sweeping the flat of my hand across the wall, I found the switch for the overhead fixture. Once the room was flooded with light, I yanked the door open.

"Dad!" I called down the stairs in a low, harsh whisper. "Dad!"

My heart sank when I heard a distinct snort and rumble, followed by the flapping of wet, fluttering lips—the unmistakable rhythm of my dad's snoring.

How could he be sleeping through this midnight assault? I went to his room and opened the door. He was lying on his back, mouth wide open, eyes definitely shut. "Dad," I said loudly. "Dad, there's something outside."

In response, he emitted a throaty gurgle before he rolled over. Then I noticed the soft gleam of two silver beer cans sitting side by side on the night table. He'd drunk three already with dinner. I was just going to have to deal with the situation on my own, so I darted back to my room and grabbed my baseball bat.

Taking a deep breath, I plunged down the stairs, making as much noise as I could and turning on every light along the way. If I was lucky, whatever was outside would be scared off before I had a chance to meet it face-to-face.

The noise had come from the backyard, so I headed straight to the kitchen door. Hand on the latch, I stopped to listen.

It was still out there, snorting and snuffling. A ten-foot-high fence constructed from a crazy assortment of salvaged planks and boards surrounded the house. I wished I had thought to close the gate when I locked up.

One…two…three… I threw on the floodlight and slammed open the door so hard it cracked like a shotgun report. Raising the bat over my shoulder, I peered into the inky darkness. My heart was pounding.

The garbage can had been raided. It lay on its side halfway down the walkway, a mess of coffee grounds, eggshells, and soggy paper towels littering the grass.

"Damn." I dropped my weapon and stepped down the damp concrete steps to clean up the mess. I was laughing a little when I picked up the garbage can. It was deadweight heavy, like we'd thrown away a frozen Butterball turkey. I shook my head at my ridiculous behavior—what had I been expecting, the boogeyman?

A head popped over the metal rim—hard little eyes glittered like black diamonds. I yelled. Dropping the can with a clatter, I turned and ran. It wasn't until I was on the top of the back stoop that I dared to turn around and identify the marauder.

A stupid raccoon had the nerve to still be all bristled up and spitting mad on the lawn—chittering away like he was telling me off for disturbing his midnight snack. I rushed at him, flying back down the stairs and pausing long enough to pick up a loose stone, which I heaved in his general direction.

"Get out of here!" I shouted. The rock fell way short of its mark, and the little stinker melted into the night.

Without a chance of getting back to sleep anytime soon, I made a PB&J and settled down in front of the computer. There was no television in that dump, but we were online. Dad needed to be for work. After a little aimless surfing, I opted to watch a DVD and chose *Night of the Living Dead* from my collection.

Five minutes into the film, I knew I had made a bad decision. I think I'm the only person George Romero has ever brought to tears from sentiment, not fear. I directed a zombie movie too. Not all that original, I admit, but when you have to recruit your buddies to help you make a movie, no one wants to make a film about adolescent angst. But just about anyone will paint a little blood on his face and shuffle around groaning. That was for my video production class at my old school. I doubted I would ever be going back.

Divorce sucks.

CHAPTER 2

The coffeemaker was sputtering its last burst of steam when my dad lumbered into the kitchen.

"Morning, Jake," he mumbled.

"Hey," I said. "Pour you a cup?"

"Sure." Dad fell heavily onto a chair at the table. "I think my stomach can handle it." He dropped his face into his hands and started to rub his eyes and cheeks hard, as if the pressure might force him awake.

Putting the chipped mug in front of him, I said, "You missed the excitement last night."

"Yeah?" Dad wrapped his hands around the cup. His eyes were bloodshot, and his brown hair was a mess, sticking up in greasy clumps. *You need a shower, dude.*

I put a laugh in my voice. "Yeah. Scared the crap out of me. I think I might know why Horace put up that weird fence."

Dad sat up a little straighter. Was that actually a glimmer of parental concern putting a steely glint in his eyes? "What happened?"

"Well, from the way it sounded, I thought we were being attacked by aliens."

"What was it?" Dad's voice was sharp. "Did you see anything?"

"Just a raccoon."

His shoulders slumped; the gleam of interest faded. "Oh. I hate those little pests. They make such a mess."

"Tell me about it," I griped, pouring myself a cup. "You want something to eat?"

"Nah. Coffee's good."

"Right." I took a sip, burning my tongue. As far as I could tell, he wasn't eating much lately. Just drinking a lot of beer. "You know, we're getting low on supplies. We should take a run into town today."

Something shiny flew through the air toward my head. I put my hand up—really to protect my eyes—and caught my dad's keys. They were still warm from his jeans pocket.

"You go," Dad said. "I'll give you some money."

"Dad," I protested. "I don't have my license. If I get caught, they'll never let me get one."

"Who's going to catch you?" Dad took a slurp of coffee, looking at me over the rim of his cup. "It's not like we're in Norwalk where there's a cop on every corner. Just be careful and don't make any mistakes—no one will know the difference."

It was tempting. I loved driving the Jeep, but it didn't feel right. "You're out of beer," I pointed out. "Even if I don't get arrested for driving without a license, no one's going to sell me beer." Not that being out of beer was a bad thing.

"You got a point there, Jake." He stretched and yawned. "I'll tell you what…let me get some work done this morning and we'll go after lunch."

"Work? As in, on the computer?"

"Yes, on the computer. I have to track that shipment from Guatemala."

"What am I supposed to do?" I was pissed. It would have been nice to have an hour or two to catch up on my email and check out what was new on YouTube.

He stood up, scratching his belly. "How the hell do I know? Read a book. Go for a hike. Take that camera of yours and start making a documentary about Connecticut wildlife."

Uncle Horace's property backed up onto a huge state preserve—thousands of acres of wilderness. A trail was clearly marked every few hundred feet by big daubs of yellow paint smeared on tree trunks. I tramped over hills and slogged through a swamp. I came across a couple of deer and nearly had a heart attack when a big old tom turkey stuck his warty red head out of a bush.

To be honest, I wasn't too comfortable about hiking alone. Sure, it was fine being in the great outdoors—but what if I fell and broke my leg? Even if I had my cell—which I didn't because you couldn't get a signal out there anyway—I wouldn't know how to describe where I was. I hadn't even brought a water bottle. A guy could die out here.

I'd thought about Uncle Horace a lot since my dad and I got here. Funny, I'd never met the guy—never even knew he existed—and here I was living in his house. What kind of weird life had he had, way out here, not a neighbor for miles? He must have been a regular hermit.

Still, Dad was grateful to the crazy old guy. Inheriting the beat-up cottage surrounded by the homemade fence came just at the right time, because Dad was running out of cash and didn't know how he was going to pay the next month's rent.

My face got all hot as anger shot through me, fresh as ever. I was still mad at my mom. She dumped my dad and married someone else. No way was I ever going to make life with her new husband easy.

The path headed up another incline, curving around a huge outcrop of boulders that rose at least twenty feet straight up. As I turned the bend, I was forced to stop. A bunch of skinny tree trunks, at least six or seven of them, stripped bare of branches and bark, were propped against each other across the path, the clumsy teepee barring my way. At first glance the arrangement seemed haphazard, like some freak storm had swirled through. But on closer inspection, the placement looked deliberate, which made me think there was nothing natural about the obstacle.

If I wanted to keep going, I would have to swing off the trail into dense brambles, which were crawling with ticks for sure. Catching Lyme disease was the last thing I needed. Scaling the barrier was an option, but then I would be risking a broken neck.

I had just about made up my mind to give up and head home when the hairs on the back of my neck stood on end. The woods around me were completely silent—not one bird sang. Even the insects quit buzzing. For a few seconds, I was frozen, unable to move forward and afraid to turn around. A cloud moved across the sun, making the shadows deepen.

A breeze tickled the back of my arms, touched the nape of my neck like a cold breath. I got a whiff of a weird smell, deep and rank, like rotting eggs. Sulfur—I remembered that smell from a science lab experiment a couple of years ago. But there were other odors mixed in—meat and mud, the decay of wet leaves. The smell wasn't strong, but it wafted along on the breeze like a warning.

Then the cloud passed, and it grew light again. The stench disappeared on the tail end of the breeze. I took a deep breath. It was the first one I'd inhaled in a while, and I looked over my shoulder to make sure nothing was following me before jogging back home.

CHAPTER 3

"**Y**our mother called again," Dad announced as I walked in the door. He was hunched at the computer, his nose practically touching the screen. He probably needed glasses.

I didn't answer. Because I didn't care.

"Did you hear what I said?" Dad asked.

I grunted to let him know I heard him and that I didn't want to get into it. No such luck.

"You should give her a call." Dad turned around to give me one of his meaningful looks. I ignored him. "If you don't, she'll just blame me. Accuse me of poisoning your mind against her."

So that's what he was worried about. He didn't want Mom bitching at him. Well, I certainly didn't want her bitching at me. He was the grown-up. He could deal with her.

"At least call your sister. I'm sure she misses you."

Megan. Thinking about her did give me a twinge of guilt. Just a twinge. She made her decision and I made mine. If she wanted to live in the big, fancy house with Mom and her creepy new husband, she couldn't expect everything to be all hunkydory between us. But sometimes I did miss her.

Dad pushed himself away from the computer with a sigh. "I'm starving. What's for lunch?"

"That's what I've been trying to tell you," I said. "There's nothing."

"Well then, I guess we have to go into town," he said. "You drive."

It was pretty laughable, calling three stores, a small library, and a post office a town. There wasn't even a school. I was registered to go to some district high school that was, like, ten miles away. I wasn't sure if we would even have to stay there that long, though. Everything depended on whether or not Dad could get his business back on track. If he could, we might be able to return to civilization.

I actually liked the food market—it felt like a general store in an old Western. It managed to have everything you needed plus a few extras, like an ATM. Dad and I split the list and headed in different directions. I loaded the guy food into the cart—hot dogs, hamburgers, spaghetti, bananas, peanut butter, and white bread. In a salute to good health, I tossed in a bag of salad greens and a bottle of dressing. As I reached for a box of frozen chicken nuggets, I thought of Mom's roast chicken, how its rich smell filled the house. Sighing, I threw the nuggets into the cart.

After grabbing a few rolls of paper towels and a package of toilet paper, I scouted around for Dad. He was at the front of the store, talking to some guy with a bald head and a big belly.

"So, you're in Horace's old place," the man was saying.

"That's right," my father answered. "My uncle. He left the place to me."

The man shook his head, looking down at the floor. "Odd fellow, Horace. He had some funny ideas."

"Every family has their eccentric." Dad gave a fake laugh. "I guess Horace was ours. He never did anyone any harm, though."

"Well, things he talked about gave some people around here the jitters."

"As far as any of us knew, he was just a nutty old science teacher with a vivid imagination." My father raised his chin, his shoulders stiffening.

"Living way out there on your own, I guess it would affect you." The man crossed his arms and took a breath, like he was considering what he was going to say next. Then he looked at my father. "Have you seen Samuel around the place?"

"Samuel?" Dad repeated.

"Samuel Baldwin. He's another old codger that lives up there on the ridge. He and Horace were tight."

"Can't say we've seen him."

"He's squatting in an abandoned ranger station, about a mile up the old logging road. Don't know how he gets by. But if you're ever up that way, you might look in on him, see how he's doing. We try to look out for each other around here."

"Sure thing."

The man's gaze shifted past my father, and he finally noticed me standing there. "This your son?"

"Yes, this is Jake," my father said.

"Nice to meet you." The man offered me his big, beefy hand. "Dave Pelletier. I own this place."

"Hey." I stepped forward and shook his hand.

Pelletier let go, eyeing me with interest. "Nice to have new young people in the neighborhood. How old are you?"

"Sixteen."

Pelletier smiled at me, showing the glint of a gold tooth under his mustache. "I don't suppose you'd be interested in a job?"

CHAPTER 4

I took the job at the grocery store. Why not? We needed the money, I got an employee discount, and what else was there to do?

And now I was being rewarded for my selfless decision to join the workforce.

Nell Davis was training me.

"So, every time you begin your shift at the register, you'll start with a new cash drawer and you have to enter your ID code."

Concentrating on the lesson wasn't easy. All I could think about, as we stood behind the counter together, was Nell's height—that if she ever let me get close enough, I could just rest my chin on the top of her head. A perfect fit. And her hair—long, dark brown, straight, and shiny—would feel like silk. I knew how good her hair smelled already. She used one of those fruity shampoos that actually made me salivate.

When she turned to look at me over her shoulder, I noticed the long lashes that fringed her wide, dark eyes. Then I realized that the look on her heart-shaped face was annoyance. "Well, go ahead," she said, "key in your ID code."

"Huh?" I tore my gaze away from her pink lips.

"Your ID code," she repeated with an impatient sigh. "Did you forget it already?"

"No, no. I know it. Here, just let me…" When I reached to get to the keypad, my arm brushed hers. She backed away with a graceful little sidestep to avoid any further contact. "Sorry." I could feel my face going all hot.

"No problem. Just enter the code." She shook her head.

Things did get better as the training session went on. Nell was not only one of the prettiest girls I'd ever seen, but she was really smart. Once she realized I wasn't a complete idiot, we both relaxed enough to have a conversation. I even managed to crack her up a couple of times, making up funny stories about the customers.

After an hour or so, it got busy and we took turns—I'd ring while she bagged and vice versa. It was almost noon when a guy about my age came walking by—one of those guys with a bullet head stuck on meaty shoulders. He was tying on a red apron, so I knew he was an employee. When he got close to Nell, he looked at her like he was hungry and she was a hamburger. Then he noticed me.

"Hey, Nell," he said to her as he shot me a dirty look.

"Hi, Barry." I was glad to hear that Nell sounded bored.

"Who's this?" Barry asked with a nod.

I stuck my hand out and looked him straight in the eye. I wasn't going to let this jerk get anything over on me. "Jake Oliver. Nice to meet you, Barry." He didn't do anything— didn't take my hand, didn't say hello, just walked away.

But for the rest of the morning, every time he passed by to stock the shelves or mop up a spill, he gave me a look that could sour milk. Especially when I would get Nell laughing.

Finally, at one o'clock he showed up with a new cash drawer. "Break time," Barry said to Nell, making a point to ignore me.

"Come on," Nell said to me, leading the way. "Let's eat. We get a half hour and a free sandwich from the deli counter. I'll show you the break room."

I picked up a premade turkey on a hard roll from the case near the deli section. Nell had Zack, the guy behind the counter, make her the biggest, bloodiest roast beef sandwich I'd ever seen. She was such a thin girl, I wondered where she was going to put it all. When she saw the look on my face, she blushed. "My parents are vegetarians. I've got to protein-load when I can."

As we settled down with our sandwiches and a couple of sodas, I asked, "So what's Barry's problem?"

"Territorial." Nell's pearly-white teeth chomped neatly into her big, fat sandwich. It took a few munches before she could say, "He doesn't like competition."

"Competition? Who's competing?" I took a more civilized bite out of my sandwich—didn't want to spit anything out while I talked.

"Just because we're the only two people in the immediate neighborhood under the age of forty, Barry thinks he's my default BFF."

I was afraid to ask. "Are you…you know…together?"

She rolled her eyes and dropped her sandwich. "Please."

I shrugged. "Well, he's blond and jocky-looking. I thought girls liked guys like that."

"Some girls actually prefer brains over brawn." She tore off another hunk of sandwich. I think I managed to hide my smile. She chewed, then daintily picked a wedge of meat from between her teeth with her pinky. "So, anyway. I know old Horace was your uncle or something. But that doesn't explain why you moved here."

"Let's just say my dad is going through a transition period."

"And your mom?"

I put down my sandwich, losing my appetite. "My mother's period of transition has taken her in a different direction."

"Oh," Nell said. "Divorce, huh?"

"Yep." I was going to leave it at that, but there was something about the way Nell sat next to me, so quiet and patient. My voice came out low and rough. "My mom's a nurse. She met this rich old doctor at work who only cares about money and golf. She dumped my dad to be with him in his big show-off house. Then she just expected us to abandon Dad, to be happy about all the changes."

"Us?"

"Me and my little sister, Megan. Megan's with Mom." I felt myself blushing. Great way to impress a girl, right? Geez. I forced a hearty voice. "Anyway, that's the story. What about you? Did you grow up here?"

Nell finished chewing the last hunk of her sandwich, ending with a big swallow. "We moved up here about eight years ago from New York City, if you can believe it. Talk about culture shock. My dad's a set designer. He commutes down whenever he's got a project going. My mom used to design costumes, but now she does all kinds of crazy things."

"Like what?"

"We have a farm, kind of. Right now she's raising a couple of llamas, a small herd of goats, and a flock of exotic chickens. She weaves and makes cheese and grows herbs and whatever nutty old hippie idea comes to her."

"Sounds interesting."

"You could call it that." Nell crumpled up her sandwich wrapping and napkin, tossing the wad neatly into the trash can. "Back to work."

CHAPTER 5

Why had I thought riding my bike into town was a good idea? Dad had offered to drive me, but I declined, not knowing what time I would be getting out of work. After standing on my feet most of the day, it didn't help that the trip home was mostly uphill and it was late. Mr. Pelletier had come up to us at the end of our shift and said that Myrna had called in sick, and would anyone be interested in putting in a few extra hours? Both Barry and Nell got all shifty-eyed at the question, so I'd decided to be a good sport and volunteered.

Though it was still a couple of hours until sunset, the shadows were getting longer, and it might have been cooler if the heat that had baked into the pavement all day wasn't radiating back up. Not a single car had gone by in at least twenty minutes. As I pedaled along, my thighs aching and sweat running off me, I wished my dad would come along in the Jeep.

Mom would have. She would have been worried because I was three hours later coming home than she expected. After she found me and helped me load my bike into the back of the car, she would bring me home, where dinner would be waiting.

The *old* mom would have, anyway. The nurse that worked sixty hours a week but still managed to spend time with her kids—not the skinny, tanned woman married to Dr. Old Fart who played tennis and dined at the club.

My stomach was so empty it felt like that lunch break had happened yesterday. And I was sure that the lettuce and tomato on my turkey sandwich were the closest thing to a serving of vegetables I was likely to get. I never could figure out what my father had against broccoli. I must have been suffering from a serious vitamin deficiency if I was thinking about vegetables.

A little bit of a breeze to stir up the air would have been nice. I might've been able to catch a breath. I was thinking about wimping out, jumping off my bike to walk it up the crest of the next hill, when I heard something that caused me to come to a full stop.

A roar, deep and guttural—but not like a lion. A scream, almost. I slammed on the brakes, skidding, nearly falling.

It was a far-off, quavering bellow that rang out over the treetops, the scariest and weirdest noise ever. And sad. My heart pounded. My breath came in jagged rasps even as I strained to listen, trying to identify the animal that could produce that cry. Minutes passed without another sound—as if every bird and tree frog was waiting to hear it again too.

For a second, I thought the noise came completely from inside my own head, that by letting myself think about how I felt about Mom and our family being ripped to shreds and losing everything that was safe and familiar, I'd caused that eerie sound to echo in my skull.

But—that was just crazy. I heard something all right. Something strange, unearthly. But I was in Connecticut, riding my bike on a hot July evening—a normal kid doing a normal thing. I had never in my life heard anything like that. Maybe it was a bear. What kind of noise do bears make? I knew there were black bears in this part of the state.

I stood still for a while, listening for that weird sound again, but the only thing I heard was the rustle of leaves caused by a light wind that finally began to move the stagnant heat. The tree frogs resumed their shrill chorus. Insects buzzed and clicked. There were countless creatures, hunters and prey, living in the woods. Many of them only stirred awake now that night was falling. How many were watching me, standing exposed in the center of the deserted road?

With the cooler air and having the unexpected opportunity to rest my aching legs, I got my second wind—fear is energizing—and pedaled the rest of the way home as fast as I could go.

CHAPTER 6

I had just stacked the last couple of pints of native blueberries and was about to bring out the banana crates when Nell asked, "What are you doing tomorrow?"

"Huh?" With clever dialogue like that, it was a wonder this girl kept talking to me.

"Tomorrow. Do you have any plans?" She was picking through the peaches, taking out the bruised specimens and making a display with the good ones.

"No, not really." I shrugged. I had been hoping I could get my dad to drive me somewhere closer to civilization, where there might be a multiplex or a Best Buy. Maybe get in a driving lesson and continue the discussion about taking my driving test. I'd finished Driver's Ed, I was ready, but Dad was worried about the increase in car insurance he would have to pay. He refused to ask Mom for financial help. But to be fair, I didn't want to ask her for anything, either.

"I'm open to suggestions." I hoped that sounded smooth.

"Well, I bet I know something you don't know." Nell surveyed her peach arrangement with a critical eye.

"I'm sure you do." I'm sure she knew a lot more about everything than I did. She was that kind of girl.

"Did you know the best place to swim around here is a short hike from your house?"

"No, I didn't," I confessed.

"It is. And tomorrow is supposed to be the hottest day of this heat wave we're having."

"Too bad I don't know how to get to that swimming spot."

"Funny you should mention that." Nell looked at me with a smile. "How about I meet you at your place around noon?"

"I'll pack us a lunch—with lots of meat."

Nell showed up the next day in a rusted-out old green VW Karmann Ghia. I took her inside to introduce her to my dad, but he hardly noticed her. He'd never thought much of my girlfriend Kendall, back in Norwalk. What happened between us was a whole other story, but how could you not sit up and pay attention when Nell Davis walked into the room? Yet, there he was, eyes riveted on the monitor as usual, not even bothering to give a little wave. He had spent the whole week hunched over the computer, still trying to track that shipment from Guatemala. I had a feeling that every dime he had was tied up in the deal.

Embarrassed by my dad's rudeness, I grabbed the cooler full of sandwiches and lemonade, hesitating for a second before grabbing my camera bag. We set out, Nell leading the way along a narrow path. She was wearing a T-shirt and cutoffs, and I could barely take my eyes off her long, brown legs. We were following a trail I hadn't explored yet, marked with blue paint.

"So, what was your dad working on?" Nell asked over her shoulder.

"He runs an import business. He travels all over the world buying up cheap, handcrafted stuff made in third-world countries that ends up getting sold in chain stores over here."

"*Ow!*" Nell spun around and shot me a hot glare.

"Are you okay?"

"That wasn't funny!" She rubbed a spot just above her right elbow. "What was that? An acorn…a pebble?"

"What?"

"Didn't you just throw something at me?"

"Why would I do that?" I was confused and kind of hurt that she thought I would throw something at her. "Let me see."

She flinched away. "Never mind. Maybe an acorn did fall off a tree."

"I didn't see anything." As a matter of fact, I had been literally watching my step because the path was full of roots and I didn't want to trip.

We started walking again, the trail passing through a little valley between two hills covered with huge rocks that pushed out of the earth.

"Yow!" Something sharp and stinging pinged off my right temple. I put my hand up to the spot, rubbing hard to soften the pain.

"What?" Nell stopped and turned.

"I just got hit too. And not by an acorn." I scanned the top of the hill. "Not unless acorns fall off trees horizontally and really fast." I craned my neck, looking up over the rocks into the branches of the high trees for our assailant. The woods were still; the heavy air surrounded us like a wet blanket. I experienced an uncomfortable prickling sensation down the back of my neck.

Another small missile zoomed through the air near us, hitting Nell's backpack before it dropped to the carpet of brown leaves at our feet. I picked the object up to examine it. Exactly what I thought it would be—a small pebble, about the size of a chickpea. I fisted my hand tightly around it, looking up over the ridge. "Okay, very funny. Who's there?" The only response was a scurrying chipmunk startled by the sound of my voice.

I met Nell's eyes and saw right away that she was more pissed than scared, which was pretty much how I felt. I said in a low voice. "Probably just a couple of kids fooling around."

"If we keep standing here, we'll only continue to be targets. Let's keep going. We're almost there."

We picked up our pace and soon came to a crossroads where tree stumps and a metal fence obstructed one path. Beyond the barrier, "No Trespassing" signs were pasted on the tree trunks every few feet. So, of course, that was the way we went. Climbing over the roadblock, I asked, "And we're going where we're not supposed to go because…?"

"Because that's where the swimming hole is," said Nell, cheerfully matter-of-fact. "We're not supposed to swim there because it's part of the reservoir system, that's all."

After we'd walked a couple hundred more feet, the woods opened into a wide lake. Nothing but water, trees, and sky stretched off into the horizon.

"Wow," I breathed.

"Told you it's a pretty spot," said Nell.

"And no one cares if we swim here?"

"Oh, they would care if they caught us, but no one will." She shrugged.

We took our sneakers off as soon as we reached a smooth slope. Leaving our lunch in the shade of a huge pine tree, we stripped down to our bathing suits—I couldn't help but notice how hot Nell looked in that blue bikini—and plunged into the cold, green depths of the water.

We swam and dove, splashing and tagging each other until we both got tired enough to rest on the towels we had laid out to warm in the sun.

The blazing sun and the cool dampness on my skin at the same time felt good. Nell was lying on her back, completely at ease, eyes closed. Quietly, I reached for my backpack and took the video camera out, trying not to make a sound, keeping half an eye on Nell to make sure she didn't move. I wanted to get a shot of her just like that, the bright light and soft shadows sculpting the planes of her face.

The camera emitted the tiniest whirr when I turned it on, which was enough to send Nell shooting up into a sitting position. "What the hell?" She raised her arm to shield her face from the lens.

"Nothing." I dropped the camera onto my lap. "Just wanted to capture the moment." Her reaction surprised me. Everyone who knew me well knew I was likely to have my camera and might start filming when inspiration struck. I'd never thought of it as an invasion of privacy.

"Well, you can't go around filming people without warning them." She raked her fingers through her wet hair. "I look like hell."

"No, you don't." She was beautiful.

She slipped her T-shirt over her head. "Do you always carry that thing around?"

"No. Only if I think something interesting might happen." I put the camera away before grabbing the sandwiches and drinks. I tossed a sandwich onto Nell's lap. "Sorry, tuna salad was the best I could do. We were out of sides of beef."

"Ha-ha. Who knew you were such a funny guy?" For a second, I thought she might really be mad at me. Then I saw her lips curl into a little smile as she took a healthy bite of her sandwich. "At least it's on processed white bread." I handed her a bottle of lemonade, and when she took it from me, the tips of her fingers touched mine. They were still cool from the swim. "So, that's a pretty impressive camera."

I winced inwardly. It was a nice camera, top of the line. A fact that never stopped making me uncomfortable. My mother had given it to me for Christmas. I wasn't going to accept it—it felt too much like a bribe. Anything that expensive had to have been paid for out of Dr. Old Fart's deep pockets. In the end, I couldn't resist opening the box, and once I held it, I couldn't bear to put it back. Every time I used it I had the same creepy reaction—a zap of emotion that made me queasy and happy all at the same time.

"What kind of movies do you like to make?" Nell was asking me, munching on her sandwich. I found the jar of pickles and offered her one.

"Everything, anything. I haven't really started a big project. I've made a couple of short films. One about zombies and a comedy about a guy who loses his shoes. For a while, I was the cameraman for my school news broadcast."

"That's cool," Nell said, then added kind of shyly, "I write."

"Yeah? Like what?"

Now she shrugged. "Oh, poetry, short stories. But I have an idea for a play. Maybe it could be a screenplay."

I smiled. "We could collaborate."

"Maybe." She looked at me in a way that made my head swim, like she really thought I was interesting. I was just about to ask her what her idea was, when a rustling in the woods startled us both. Then Barry came stumbling out from behind some bushes.

"Nice of you to invite me to your little party," he sneered.

"We're not having a party, Barry." She sounded bored. "Just taking a swim."

He took in the sandwiches and lemonade. "It sure looks like a party."

"Well, it's not," Nell insisted. "So you're not missing anything. You can move along now."

"Have a heart," whined Barry. "I just came up here for a swim myself. I didn't know you could make private reservations."

"Well, behave yourself, then," said Nell, in a teacher kind of voice. "Don't ruin the afternoon by being a jerk."

"I'll take one of those." Barry helped himself to a sandwich.

At that moment, I wished that guy was a thousand miles away. After he grabbed the food, he stepped away to kick off his sneakers.

Nell and I exchanged a look, and I could tell we were thinking the same thing—was Barry the mysterious pebble-thrower?

"So, Barry," Nell said. "How long have you been out here?"

"I just got here." He sat on a fallen log and unwrapped the sandwich.

"You didn't follow us up the trail?" I put a challenge into my voice.

"What are you talking about?" Barry said.

"We're talking about some jerk who was throwing things at us," I said.

Nell put her fists onto her hips. "As I remember, you have a pretty good arm."

"You guys are crazy if you think…" Then he paused, looking at me. "Well, maybe not both of you. But you could be, Oliver. Crazy runs in the family, right? Maybe your uncle's spook was throwing shit at you."

"Shut up, Barry," said Nell.

"What's that supposed to mean?" I asked.

"That uncle of yours. Bigfoot Hunter Horace."

"Bigfoot?" I scoffed.

"Yeah. Didn't you know?" Barry said, laughter in his voice. "Old Horace was always tracking 'mythical beasts' in the woods."

"You don't know what you're saying."

Nell glanced up at me, looking a little sheepish. "Jake…it's kind of the truth. My parents used to see him in town sometimes. He was always talking about his important research."

Oh boy. That was crazy. Couldn't deny that. "He was a retired science teacher. My dad said he was like an absentminded-professor type."

"More like out-of-his-mind type," Barry said nastily.

"You know, Barry, there are other people who believe there is something out here," said Nell.

"Oh, yeah, right." Barry took another bite of his sandwich. "I forgot about Samuel. He believes in those bullshit fairy tales too." I remembered Mr. Pelletier mentioning that Samuel was my uncle's buddy.

"Not just him."

Dense clouds darkened the sky. We sat in silence for a couple of minutes—Barry chomping away, Nell starting to tidy up our picnic. Me, I was trying to keep my face from going beet-red with embarrassment. Nothing like trying to make a new start somewhere—only to find out you're related to the local crackpot.

But then I started thinking—it's not like everything around here had struck me as absolutely normal. There were plenty of things about these woods creeping me out. Maybe Horace wasn't crazy. Maybe he was on to something. And what would happen if you could prove there was a Bigfoot out here? My heart started pumping with excitement.

A big plop of rain hit me on the nose. Another hit Barry. The air grew chill. "There goes the party," he said.

Nell looked overhead. "It's going to get bad." As if on cue, the wind whipped up, tossing the treetops around. Lightning seared the sky. We all jumped up and I started shoving everything into my backpack.

"My car's pretty close," Barry called over the wind and increasing rain. "You guys better come with me. I'll give you a ride back to Oliver's house."

CHAPTER 7

Nell rode up front with Barry, but I didn't mind. My brain was racing. I only wished I could tell Nell what I was thinking, because I knew I would need help with the idea I was hatching. It was probably just as well, though. I wanted to take a look through Horace's stuff. When we moved in, we kind of just pushed the old man's belongings aside to make room for our own. We'd never really gotten around to digging into his drawers, taking a look at the books he had on the shelves. Maybe because Horace was such a stranger to us both. We were adjusting to so much disruption and change in our lives; it seemed pathetic and sad to sift through his life when we were already feeling sad enough about our own.

By the time Nell and Barry drove off in their separate cars, the storm was cranking. I burst through the front door to find Dad tossing a pile of clothes into his old canvas rucksack. The air in the room was hot and close. I was breathing hard, the rainwater puddling around my feet. "Dad, it's really cooling off out there. We need to open some windows."

Dad's expression was dazed. A clap of thunder cracked right over the house, shaking the window frames. "It's raining."

"No kidding." I threw open the window nearest me, not caring if the rain spattered in. A rush of cool dampness moved through the stifling room. It felt good. I missed air-conditioning and was glad the weather was finally breaking. "What's with the duffel bag? Are we doing the laundry early this week?"

"Laundry? Uh, no." He reached down and picked up his hiking boots, dropped them into a plastic bag, and shoved them into the rucksack. "That shipment is lost. I've got to get down to Guatemala and track it myself."

"When are you leaving?" I shivered as a spray of rain blew in.

"I've booked a flight for tomorrow. You have to drive me to the airport in the morning." He was counting underwear and socks as he threw them in the bag.

Running my hands through my wet hair, I protested, "Dad, I can't. I don't have my license. If you'd just let me make an appointment for the test—"

"Quit worrying so much, Jake. You're a good driver. You'll be fine."

"What am I supposed to do while you're gone?"

"You'll have the Jeep. Come back here. Go to your job. Hang out. How do I know?"

"I don't suppose I could come with you?"

He looked at me, and I could see he was getting pissed. His voice was sharp. "Are you kidding? I'm tapped out. If I don't get that shipment up here, I'm finished. I barely had enough credit left on my Visa to buy one ticket." He glanced away, scanning the room for things he still needed to pack, and mumbled, "You don't even have a passport."

Like not having a passport was my fault. "I don't feel comfortable staying out here alone."

"Then go stay with your mother," he snapped. "I'm sure she'd love to have you." He squeezed his leather toiletry bag in before pulling the zipper closed.

"You know I don't want to do that." Now it was my turn to get pissed. "But she would freak out if she knew you were leaving me here alone."

Dad's face went red. "You think I give a rat's ass if she freaks out? She's the one who screwed everything up. She's the one who walked out." His voice rose to a shout. "She dumped me for some rich old jerk, and still the judge gives her practically every last nickel. Explain that one to me!"

His angry words felt like punches to my gut. I crossed my arms over my stomach and tucked my chin down. Looking at the floor, I said, "Because she was the one who earned the money."

Out of the corner of my eye, I saw my father raise his hand to smack me. *Go ahead*, I thought, *just lay into me*. He froze, then dropped his arm. "Look." His voice was low, rough. "Do what you want, but it would be great if you could hold the fort here. I shouldn't be gone more than a week—two at most. You're sixteen, Jake—you don't need a babysitter...or your mommy."

"I know." I looked up at him, wary. "I'll be fine. You just caught me by surprise, I guess." I could tell by the way his shoulders slumped that he was sorry for losing his temper. "Just promise me I can get my license when you get back."

"If I find that damn shipment, we'll be fine. We'll be able to do whatever we want." He reached for me, patted my cheek gently with the flat of his palm. "I'm getting hungry. Why don't you see what we have for dinner?"

Finally, over fish sticks and canned corn, and after he drained his third beer, I got up the nerve to ask my dad about Horace. "So, anyway, Dad," I started as he popped the tab on can number four. "I've been talking to my friends, and it seems old Horace was kind of a strange guy."

"Yeah?" Dad shoveled a forkful of corn into his mouth. A kernel escaped his bottom lip and stuck to the stubble on his chin. His eyes were bleary. It was going to be a long trip to Guatemala. "Don't believe everything you hear. Especially in a hick town like this."

"Well, why don't you tell me what you know about him?"

He took a slurp of beer, considering for a few seconds. "Okay. This is what I know. Horace was my father's older brother. Went to Harvard or Princeton…one of those Ivy League schools. He was some kind of science genius." He burped, then munched on some fish.

"What did he study?" I asked.

"I have no idea. All I do know is when he was working on his PhD, he had some kind of mental breakdown and dropped out. Wound up with a job teaching biology at a fancy prep school around here someplace. Did that for like thirty years."

"How'd he end up in this dump?"

My father stared at his plate. "How does anyone end up anywhere?"

"I mean, is there a reason he picked this area?"

Dad was getting exasperated. "I don't know. Nobody knows. He wasn't close to his family. My father barely knew him. What are you driving at?"

"Well…" I took a gulp of air. "Someone told me Horace thought there was a Bigfoot around here."

After a moment of dead silence, my father roared, "That is the biggest piece of crap I ever heard!" He threw his fork down on his plate with a clatter. "That's just what I mean. Stupid backwater places like this… Some poor old dude with a little bit of a mental problem moves into the neighborhood… and the ignorant local yokels start saying all kinds of crazy shit." He pushed away from the table, swaying a little bit. Right then, I was glad he was going away for a while. Pointing his finger at me, he slurred, "Like I said…don't believe everything you hear."

I knew it was pointless, but I couldn't let it go. "Wait, Dad, listen. Since we moved here, I've noticed some weird stuff."

"Like what?" My father laughed skeptically. "Raccoons in the garbage?"

"Like branches blocking trails in the woods and a horrible smell. The other night, when I rode my bike home—I heard the eeriest cry. And this afternoon, when I was with Nell—something was throwing rocks at us."

My father crossed his arms and gave me a disparaging look. "So, if all this weird shit is going on all the time, how come this is the first time you mention it to me?"

I watched his face, reading his resistance to believe me in his half-closed eyes, the slackness of his mouth, the way he clutched the beer can in his hand. "Because you haven't been the easiest person to talk to lately." I stacked the dirty plates and picked up the crumpled napkins. "Never mind. Forget I said anything."

CHAPTER 8

After my father lumbered off to bed, I cleaned up the kitchen and made sure I set the alarm clock in time to get him to the airport.

I lay on my bed for a while, thinking about Horace, imagining what it was going to be like living all on my own for a few weeks. I'd never lived by myself before. It was going to be strange. But it would also give me a chance to dig through Horace's stuff and spend some serious time online. I had research to do.

The storm had blown all the muggy air away, and a cool breeze moved my bedroom curtains. Finally, good sleeping weather.

I must have dozed, because suddenly I was awake, and confused, sitting bolt upright in my bed, surrounded by darkness. Listening for—something.

There, that eerie wailing. It was like the call I heard the other night. An aching bellow echoing through the night. And it was coming from somewhere close. It sounded like whatever was making that call was in the backyard, just beyond the fence. It didn't sound human, but it wasn't like any animal that I knew of, either.

There. Again. Close. But somehow a thinner sound than the other day, less throaty, more nasal. But still sad.

I jumped to the floor and was at my father's room in two strides. "Dad, wake up!" I shouted. I could see from the moonlight spilling in through his window that he was dead to the world. At his side in a second, I grabbed his shoulder, shaking him awake. "Dad, I'm telling you—something's outside!"

He groaned and mumbled something, but at least he stirred.

The cry sounded again—a wavering question that seemed to hover like mist over the ridge.

"What the hell was that?" Dad's voice was thick with sleep.

"That's what I want to know."

Dad sat up, planting his feet firmly on the floor, rubbing his face. He slapped his hands onto his thighs as he stood. "Well, let's go find out."

We were down the stairs and out the back door in a flash. Somewhere along the way, my father had grabbed that old baseball bat.

I'm not sure how we even got there, but suddenly we were standing side by side, bathed in the blue light of the moon, in that bare patch of dirt that we called the backyard, looking up at the sky over the jagged edge of Horace's homemade fence. The air was still chill and damp after the rain. It smelled of moist earth and pine.

We heard the call again. I was sure my father heard it when I saw the white gleam in his eyes as they locked with mine. Instinctively, we moved closer to one another. Then we heard the commotion of something crashing clumsily through the brush, snapping branches as it moved along.

"It's just on the other side of the fence." Dad's breath came in rasps.

"I'll go out there if you go out there."

"Let's do it."

My father and I marched out together shoulder to shoulder. Beyond the perimeter of the fence was a wide expanse of meadow that shimmered silver in the moonlight. There, in the center of the field, not ten feet from us, loomed the black silhouette of a tall figure.

Dad shouted a challenging whoop that sent a thrill of excitement through me. He brandished the bat up over his shoulder, ready to swing. Remaining close to one another, we approached, moving with more caution, straining our eyes to make out what we were looking at.

The figure remained motionless at first, but I could sense its quivering tenseness, like a deer deciding whether or not to bound off. I could barely breathe and didn't know where I was finding the courage to put one foot in front of the other. It helped that my father's tread was so solid, unwavering.

The figure raised its arms in a gesture of surrender. Dad stopped, peering intently. "Oh, for Christ's sake." He lowered the bat.

"How do," said the alleged Bigfoot. "You must be Horace's folks."

"Let me guess," Dad said. "Samuel, right?"

CHAPTER 9

To my surprise, my father invited Samuel in for a cup of coffee. Maybe it was because he was such a scarecrow of an old man, even Dad took pity on him. Or maybe he remembered the promise that he'd made to Mr. Pelletier to look out for his uncle's old friend. Anyway, five minutes after almost braining him with a baseball bat, my father was asking Samuel how he took his coffee.

"Milk and sugar," said Samuel in a gruff voice. "Light and sweet." He sat straight-backed at the kitchen table, his gnarled hands folded, the frayed cuffs of his old flannel shirt nearly covering his swollen knuckles. Thank God he'd taken off the headlamp he was wearing when we first met him. Even though it was unlit, the way the moonlight reflected off the lens made old Samuel look like he had a third eye.

When my father placed the steaming mug in front of him, Samuel reached for the sugar bowl with eagerness, spilling in several heaping spoonfuls before stirring in the milk. I found a box of chocolate chip cookies and shook some out onto a plate. Samuel could barely wait for me to offer him one. I wasn't surprised. Sickly thin, with a grizzled beard covering his weathered face, Samuel looked starved. He tucked his long, gray hair behind his ears before he dunked the cookie into his coffee, slurping it into his mouth.

My father took a seat across from Samuel, watching him with curiosity. "I know you were a good friend of Horace's. I'm sorry for your loss."

"Thank you," Samuel said with a swallow, his prominent Adam's apple bobbing up and down. He sighed. "Old Horace and I spent a lot of time tramping through these woods together all right."

"It seems you tramp through the woods at all hours of the day and night." My dad crossed his arms, never taking his eyes off the old man.

"Sometimes in the day. Sometimes at night." Samuel reached for another cookie. I noticed an unpleasant odor rising off the man—old sweat, unwashed hair, and something sour like rancid vinegar. The smell made my eyes sting. I wondered how long it had been since old Samuel had a hot bath.

"Can I ask you what all that caterwauling was about?" Dad asked. "Because I have to tell you—Jake and I were sound asleep. You woke us up. Gave us quite a scare."

"Just tracking Sassy." He took a long glug of his milky coffee.

"Excuse me?" Dad said.

"Tracking Sassy," Samuel repeated, like he was talking to a dense kindergartner. "Good night for it—full moon just after a soaking rain. Sometimes you can get him to answer a call."

"I'm afraid I don't understand what you're saying," my father said.

My heart began to pound, and my head was full of questions that I couldn't get out of my mouth. Samuel looked at me, his eyes a pale, opaque blue. "The boy here knows what I'm talking about. I can tell by the look on his face."

"Why don't you just go ahead and tell me," my father insisted.

Samuel popped another cookie into his mouth and crunched happily away. "Go ahead, boy. Tell your old man what I'm driving at."

"Sasquatch, Dad," I said, my voice a croak. "Bigfoot. Like I told you."

"Oh, for God's sake." My father pushed out his chair and stood. "You both must be suffering from some kind of collective delusion." He snatched the milk carton from the table and practically threw it into the refrigerator, swinging the door so hard the bottles and jars inside clinked and rattled.

Samuel continued, his eyes still locked on mine as if my father hadn't spoken. "When the ground's wet, you might actually find a footprint. When it's hot and dry, like it's been, it's tough to track 'em. Even an elephant wouldn't leave much of an impression on them dry leaves and hard ground."

For a second, it was like an electric current sparked between the old man and me, and I was filled with an excitement I'd never experienced before. Somewhere, right out the back door of this crummy old house, was something ancient and mysterious, rare and amazing. And it was mine to discover. "Did you find any tracks tonight?" I managed to ask, which was hard considering I could hardly catch a breath.

"What do you think led me here?" Samuel replied.

"You know, Samuel." My father moved abruptly to the back door. "You certainly have an interesting hobby, and I know that Uncle Horace was your fellow enthusiast, but..." He opened the door, ready to give Samuel the bum's rush.

"I think he was on his way to a big patch of blueberry bushes about a quarter of a mile from here." Samuel was oblivious to my father's growing annoyance.

"He eats blueberries?" I asked, surprised.

"Oh, he eats just about anything. Omnivore—like a bear. And like humans, of course."

"Do you know where he lives? Does he have a lair or a nest or—"

"Hey, Sam, Jake," my father interjected. "This is all very fascinating, but fellas, it's the middle of the night. Jake, we got to get up early in the morning."

"But, Dad—"

"Samuel, it was nice meeting you, and I hope to see you soon, but really, man, it's time we got some sleep." Dad opened the door to hasten his departure.

Samuel rose, his long, gangly limbs opening up like one of those folding rulers. "I understand." He looked at me and winked. "We'll continue this conversation another time."

"I don't think so," my father said firmly. "We look forward to being neighbors, and if you need anything, let us know. But I don't think Jake and I will be getting involved in your hobby. And in the future, I would appreciate it if you kept your calling to the daylight hours. We like to sleep at night around here."

"Hobby?" Samuel was indignant. "Studying Sassy is not a hobby. It's my life's work. It was your uncle's too."

"Whatever." My father sighed.

As Samuel moved to the door, I stood as well, ready to say good-bye. Before Samuel passed my father, he stood close to me, his sour smell making my nose and eyes sting. "Find me, boy," he said low in my ear. "When you can. At the old ranger station."

CHAPTER 10

I had never thought about it, but it turned out the last few weeks I'd spent with my dad had been great training for living solo. I cooked my own meals, didn't need anyone to tell me when to brush my teeth, and was careful to lock all the doors and turn out the lights before I went to bed.

That first night I spent alone, I made myself go outside. Settling in one of the old aluminum lawn chairs, I just listened. The peepers were singing like crazy. I loved the chorus of the little green tree frogs. With the bullfrogs hitting the bass notes from the lake up the trail, and the crickets in the tall grass sawing their creaky rhythms, it was a regular summer symphony. Though I could have done without the mosquitoes' whiny soprano.

It was a clear night and the moon was full. I identified the few constellations I recognized, but Horace's fence limited the view. Looking at the sky from that closed-in backyard was like looking out of some creature's dark mouth, the spiky tips of the fence its snaggly teeth. It was so ugly and badly cobbled together, I wondered why the town hadn't made him tear it down. I guessed the property was so far away from anything else that nobody cared. A shiver ran through me when I thought about what Horace was trying to keep out.

But if I was afraid of what was out there, I would never find it.

I got up and opened the back gate, stepping into the silvery meadow where we'd met Samuel the night before. Beyond the field, the trees formed a dense curtain, so black the woods seemed impenetrable. Along with the orchestra, I heard the loud rustles of a large animal moving through the underbrush. Probably only a deer, but it could have been something else.

I didn't hear any wild, lonesome cries, though, so I turned back to the house. I planned to spend a couple of hours going through Horace's papers before turning in.

"There you are," I said when Nell showed up in the break room. I had come in to work early, itching to talk to her. So, of course, she was late.

"Where else would I be?" She threw her purse in her locker and slipped an apron on over her head. She slammed the metal door shut with a *clang*. As she reached around her back to tie the ends of the apron around her waist, she looked at me with an expression I couldn't read. "What do you want?"

"Uh, nothing." Actually, I wanted a lot. After spending hours trying to make sense of the chaos of Horace's notes and journals, I'd gathered enough information to think he might actually have left me clues to follow. I had a plan, but I needed help. And I wanted Nell to be on board. Sensing her present mood, I had to approach her delicately. Living with a mother and sister could teach you a lot about the dangers of girls' moods, if you're smart enough to pay attention. I don't think my dad ever was.

Nell didn't become approachable until our lunch break. She sat down at the table with a big Italian grinder stuffed with cold cuts in front of her, an expression of dreamy anticipation on her face. We didn't talk much while she made the first ravenous dents in her sandwich, but after a few minutes she sighed and seemed to rest a moment.

"Hey, I've been thinking…"

"About what?" Nell dabbed away the glistening trail of oil that was trickling down her chin.

"Remember we talked about working on a movie together?"

"Sure." She sipped her iced tea.

"Well, I've come up with an idea I'd really like you to help me with."

"What is it?" Her eyes met mine, alight with interest. She was so interested, she actually seemed to forget her sandwich.

I leaned toward her. "This Sasquatch thing. It really has me intrigued..."

Just then the swinging door banged open and Barry trod heavily into the room, stomping through on his way to the men's room. "Hey."

It wasn't until the bathroom door closed behind him that I continued. "I really want to talk to you about it, but not here. Could you come over to my house after work?"

"I don't know," Nell said. "Would that bother your dad? He seems to be so wrapped up in his work."

"We wouldn't be bothering him," I said, though why I didn't tell her that he was gone for who knows how long, I didn't know.

"Why don't you come to my house?" she suggested. "Stay for dinner." A blush rose in her cheeks. "My parents have been wanting to meet you anyway."

"Really?" Her parents wanted to meet me? That meant she'd talked about me. The thought of that made me ridiculously happy. "That would be great."

"Good. I'll call my mom and tell her you're coming. I hope you don't mind eating vegetarian."

Mind? Vegetables? She had to be kidding! "No, no, I don't mind."

CHAPTER 11

Driving the Jeep with insane caution, I followed Nell to her house. The driveway ended at a gleaming white farmhouse with several outbuildings behind it.

"That might be the cutest thing I've ever seen," I said. A tiny goat approached us with a jumping little gait that could only be described as happy.

"Oh, this is Paco." Nell dropped to one knee to hug the little fella.

"Isn't he kind of little to be away from his mother?"

Nell looked at me with surprise. "Haven't you ever seen a pygmy goat before?"

"Nope. This is my first."

Nell stood and walked toward the house, acting like everyone had a pygmy goat hanging around. Little Paco fell into step behind her like a puppy, giving a little head-butt of a nudge to the back of her calves every few feet. "For some crazy reason, he thinks I'm his mommy."

Just then, I heard a soft, high whinny before a minuscule palomino horse trotted out from behind a shed, followed by a slightly bigger, but very petite, donkey. "You got Munchkins around here too?" I had a hard time believing what I was seeing. "Maybe a couple of circus midgets?"

Nell snorted. "No. Not yet, anyway. My mom's just obsessed with miniature things." She stopped, and the elfin parade came to a halt with her. "This is Callie, the miniature horse." She rubbed Callie between her ears, then turned to the donkey. "And this guy here is Algebra. He thinks he runs the whole show." I swear to God, the little donkey made eye contact with me and grinned.

A piercing rooster's crow sounded right behind me, making me jump.

"And now you've met Chickabod." Nell laughed at my reaction. "He really *does* run the place."

I leapt back as a tiny, brightly plumed rooster came at me like he was going to peck my bare ankle with his bright yellow beak.

The funny little interspecies family trailed after us right up to the steps of the house's wide porch.

"Hey, Ma! We're here." Nell announced our arrival with a shout and a clattering entrance. A wild yapping started somewhere in a back room and grew louder until a tiny Yorkshire terrier came skidding around a corner, its little claws scrabbling against the polished hardwood floor. Nell dropped to a knee. "Hello, Chia," she said before kissing the dog on the nose and rubbing its ears. The Yorkie turned an assessing eye at me, sniffing at my dirty sneakers with disdain.

Inside, the house was welcoming, with tons of windows and skylights that let in the late-afternoon sun. I got the general impression of comfortable furniture covered in colorful materials and lots of plants as Nell pulled me through the living room into the kitchen.

Mrs. Davis looked up from slicing carrots at a long worktable piled high with an assortment of fresh vegetables. Nell didn't take after her mother. Her mom was short and kind of chunky, dressed in a flowing, brightly colored dress. She had blonde hair piled on top of her head, showing off her long, beaded earrings. Her smile was welcoming enough, but I noticed the sharp interest in her bright blue eyes as she sized me up. "Well, it's nice to meet you, Jake. We've been hearing a lot about you."

"Thank you for inviting me."

"Always nice to have company for dinner. Eleanor, have you shown Jake around?"

Eleanor? I had never thought what *Nell* might be short for.

"Dinner will be ready in about ten minutes," Mrs. Davis continued. "Why don't you go collect your dad now so he'll have a chance to wash up?"

"Sure." Nell tugged at the bottom of my T-shirt. "Come on and see the studio."

We passed a hydroponic greenhouse, a vegetable garden, and a shed for the regular-sized goats. If I thought the house was nice, and the little critters were cute, it was nothing compared to what I thought about Mr. Davis's studio. He had remodeled the barn and installed huge skylights in the high ceiling. There were computer stations, paints, easels, and worktables. A corkboard wall had sketches and clippings pinned all over it. One corner seemed to be dedicated to carpentry, with a table saw and tools. Sawdust mounded on the floor.

As soon as we entered, Mr. Davis stood to welcome me. Dressed in worn jeans and a denim shirt, he was dark, like Nell, and he looked like he hadn't thought about getting his graying hair cut in a while. From behind his wire-framed glasses, he gazed at me with the same kind of intimidating, intense curiosity as Mrs. Davis, but his handshake was firm, and I liked his smile.

"Dinner's almost ready, Dad," said Nell. "Mom wants you to come and carve the tofu."

"Very funny." Mr. Davis gave Nell's nose a tweak. "I'll be along in a couple of minutes."

Everything Mrs. Davis served was delicious. The salad was made from greens and cucumbers from her garden. Fresh herbs gave everything a bright flavor. She had grown the eggplant, squash, and tomatoes in the ratatouille. The bread from a local bakery was dense, chewy, and slathered with cheese made from the milk of the goats I had met in the shed.

There was lots of joking and chatter, her parents peppering me with questions about my family and interests. The Davises were so at ease and happy, it made me sad. Sitting in the soft light, listening to their laughter and conversation at a table laden with delicious food, reminded me of the dinners my family used to share. Their home, full of light and energy and creativity, was so different from the cramped, closed shack Dad and I were living in, where every thought seemed to be shaped by worry and disappointment.

After the peach cobbler was consumed, I started making moves to clear the table, but Mrs. Davis shooed us away and Nell dragged me off.

"This is okay?" I asked as Nell closed her bedroom door behind us.

"What do you mean?" she asked.

"Your parents don't mind us being in here with the door closed?"

"Why should they?" Nell laughed. "Are you going to jump my bones?"

Actually, that's just what I'd have liked to do. But I knew better. "No," I said. "It's just—Oh, nothing." How could I explain the strict rules Kendall's parents had about boys in the house?

Nell flopped on her bed. The whole wall behind her was floor-to-ceiling, wall-to-wall bookshelves, crammed full. I could guess what she did in her free time. "So. Finally. What's your idea?"

I pulled out the chair at her computer table and sat down. "I've been thinking about all that crazy Sasquatch stuff, and going through old Horace's papers."

"Yeah?" She was leaning back on her elbows.

I had to present my scheme to her carefully. I didn't want to convince her that insanity ran in the family. "Well, if you read some of his notes, there might be actual evidence of truth behind the rumors." Nell started to roll her eyes. "No...just listen. I'm not saying I absolutely believe there's some big hairy man-beast roaming around out there—I'm just saying, what if there is? And what if we could prove it?"

"I guess every TV network in the world would descend on our little town," said Nell.

"And we'd be famous."

"That's not always such a good thing."

"But being rich and famous would be good," I offered. "And I can tell you, the rich part would make a difference to my dad and me these days."

"Where does the rich part come in?"

"If we got all those television networks to buy our video documentation."

"Come on, Jake," Nell said. "I watch all those shows. There's a ton of guys out there looking for proof that Bigfoot exists. And they're all looking in the Pacific Northwest—nowhere near Connecticut. What makes you sure we would succeed where everyone else has failed?"

"They don't have Horace's information. And they don't have a guide."

"A guide?"

"Samuel. He's probably out there tracking it right now."

"That's the problem, Jake. He's just looking. And he's been looking forever. No one knows if he's ever actually found anything."

"I'm not promising that we're going to find anything, either. That's why we're not going to tell anyone what it is we're up to."

"And what exactly are we 'up to?'"

"If there's something out there, we're going to find it. But because everybody will laugh at us if we tell them the truth, we're going to tell them that we're making a documentary about local legends."

"And what local legend is that?"

I leaned forward, eager to tell her what I learned from going through Horace's books. "Going back a hundred years, there are stories about sightings of a creature called the Leatherman that fit the description of a Bigfoot."

Nell shook her head. "I don't know, Jake."

"We might not find anything. And if we don't, we have fun hiking around the woods making a movie. If we do—well, it will be incredible."

Before Nell could give me a hint if she was into the idea or not, her father called up the stairs and insisted that we join them for a game of Apples to Apples. I suspected Mom and Dad weren't so completely cool about our being alone in that bedroom after all.

By the time I left, it was late and I was tired. The night was cool, and I opened the Jeep windows wide, enjoying the fresh air. I cranked Green Day on the stereo. Always conscious that I was an illegal driver, I made sure I didn't speed along the deserted roads. And it paid off. As I was going around a blind curve, a buck bounded in front of the Jeep, its panicked eyes shining in the glare of the headlights. I slammed on the brakes, the car swerving wildly before coming to a stop, only inches away from a huge pine tree. I could smell the burn of the brakes.

Breathing heavily, I turned off the music, trying to calm myself. It had been a close call. I could have creamed the deer, totaled the car, and killed myself all in the space of a few seconds.

Then I heard clumsy crashing in the woods. I focused where the buck had first appeared and saw a huge figure emerge. I could see that it was tall—close to nine feet and covered with fur. And I smelled it. That horrible odor that was familiar, but stronger this time—putrid meat, shit, rotting teeth, sour milk, and wet dog all rolled together—the worst stink you could imagine.

For seconds that seemed like hours, both of us froze—exchanging stares, trying to make sense of each other in the dark. In the indirect reflection of the headlights, its face was a blank mask. But its eyes were red, seeming to burn like lasers through the Jeep's windshield.

Then the creature disappeared, returning to the black denseness of the woods.

CHAPTER 12

I was literally petrified—so scared I felt I'd been turned to stone. How long before I took a breath? I don't know. The engine was still idling. Another song came on the radio— something about a cherry tree and a horse. What animal had I just seen? I didn't know what to do. I wanted to peel out of there pronto. But I forced myself to stay, finally taking a deep gulp of air. I needed oxygen if I was going to think. If I ran away now, what was the point of daydreaming about fame and fortune? I'd just seen my Holy Grail, my pot of gold. It was real. Sasquatch was real.

Now all I had to do was prove it.

And I wasn't going to do that by running home and throwing the blankets over my head.

My hand was shaking as I lifted it to switch off the ignition. I paused. Should I turn the car off, or keep it running for a quick getaway? A crazy vision popped into my head— the monster jumping out of the bushes and stealing the Jeep, driving off with squealing tires, and leaving me stranded by the side of the road. Then another crazy vision flashed through— the monster jumping out of the bushes and attacking me—all red eyes and white fangs—and as I shot back into the car to escape, I couldn't get it started and I was eaten alive. I was screwed either way.

In spite of my Jell-O hand, I turned off the ignition but kept the key firmly in my grip, ready to slide it back in.

When I got out of the car, the Jell-O effect was also working on my watery knees. It was quiet. The stink still lingered in the air, fainter now, like an old fart that won't fade away. A horrible thought came to me. Maybe the smell was coming from me. God knew I had been scared enough to crap myself. The thought almost made me laugh.

But I was too nervous to make a sound. Forcing myself to put one foot in front of the other, I walked over to the place where the creature had disappeared. Still quiet. Not an owl call or a cricket chirp. Certainly no snapping of branches or crunching of dead leaves being trod on by an animal that had to weigh five hundred pounds. How had it slipped away so silently?

Maybe it hadn't. Maybe it was only a few yards away, watching me.

Note to self—keep a flashlight in the car.

I crouched in the spot where I thought the creature had stood. It was too dark to see anything. I ran my hand lightly over the ground and was pretty sure I could tell where it had stood by distinct indentations. Footprints. Big footprints.

Note to self—buy some plaster of Paris. Horace had written down all kinds of data about measurements of the plaster casts he'd made from prints. Footprints that measured seventeen inches long and eight inches wide. But that was all I had found—just the data, not the casts. I'd just have to make some of my own.

Note to self—keep camera with you at *all* times.

I listened and sniffed until the stench cleared and the mosquitoes started to swarm my head. I thought again about what I'd seen, and it came back to me like snapshots. The buck leaping out in front of the car, its dark eyes shining with fear, nostrils flared. Then the creature appearing seconds behind, only stopping because it was startled by the car. And then it dawned on me—he must have been hunting. He would have killed the deer, of course, but how? Would he have jumped on its back, sinking his teeth into the neck, a spray of blood spurting from its torn jugular as it dropped to its knees? Or would the monster have grabbed hold of the budding antlers with huge, powerful hands to give a sharp snap to the head, breaking its neck? Once the kill was made, would he begin eating right away—or drag the carcass off to a lair somewhere to dine at his leisure?

An icy trickle of sweat worked its way down my spine. Right then, I was glad I didn't know the answers to those questions. Trotting back to the Jeep, I revved the engine and sped back onto the road.

By the time I got home, I had changed my mind about calling Nell in a panic and wished I could get a hold of Dad, but that wasn't an option. The only thing to do was to start putting together an action plan. Horace's notebooks were still on the kitchen table where I'd left them, and I decided to start tracking my own field observations. Out of habit, I turned on the computer, intending to open a Word file, but then thought better of it. Once Dad was back home, I might not have access to the computer when I needed it. I also didn't want him reading my notes. I found a couple of blank, spiral-bound notebooks mixed in with all of Horace's other stuff and decided to carry on his tradition, keeping my notes the old-fashioned way.

First, I quickly scribbled down every detail I could remember from the encounter while it was still fresh. And when I say *scribble*, I mean *scribble*. My hands were still shaking. I thought back to when I first had an inkling that something bizarre was going on—that first day I found the odd arrangement of stripped branches blocking the hiking trail—the first day I caught scent of the beast. Suddenly, I knew how I was going to begin the film.

CHAPTER 13

"Jake, there you are." Mr. Pelletier met me as I entered the employees' entrance. He was a nice guy, but I didn't have time for chitchat. I was in a hurry to find Nell, to tell her about my plans.

"Good morning, sir." I forced myself to slow down.

"Come back here with me for a minute, would you?"

"Of course."

He led me into the huge refrigerated walk-in where stocks of meat, produce, and dairy products were stored. There were piles of cartons stacked by the door.

"These are perishables that have nearly reached their sell-by dates. Once we get them off the shelves, we put it all back here, then I have a couple of charitable organizations that come along and take what they can use."

"That's great," I said. "Do you want me to load the trucks when they come?"

"Oh, sure." Mr. Pelletier cleared his throat. "But, before they get here…"

He seemed to be having a hard time getting out what he wanted to say.

"Yes, sir?"

"Well, when I can, I usually pack up a box for Samuel."

"Oh, that's nice."

"Do you know where he lives?"

"He told me something about the old logging road."

"He told you? You've met him?"

"Yes, sir."

"Oh, well, that's good," said Mr. Pelletier. "I was figuring, since you live out that way, if you wouldn't mind packing up a box and delivering it to him. There're eggs, some nice bread, and a couple of cartons of Tropicana that shouldn't go to waste. I know he likes orange juice."

"Sure, Mr. Pelletier. I'd be happy to do it." And I meant it. It was the perfect excuse to pay the old man a visit. He might be even more open to talking to me if I was bearing gifts.

"Fine, son, thank you." Mr. Pelletier cleared his throat again. "And if you see something you could use, feel free to help yourself. Like I said, I hate to see good food going to waste…and growing boys need their nourishment."

I finally got it. My cheeks burned hot. This was because of the box of macaroni and cheese and the one apple I'd bought a couple of nights before. I hadn't gotten my first paycheck yet, and Dad had neglected to leave me any money. I had really come to appreciate that free sandwich at lunch. Mr. Pelletier must have figured out when he rang up the sale that I was paying for my dinner from spare change I found by scrounging through jacket pockets and under cushions.

"Yes, sir. Thank you." My throat suddenly went tight and dry. I was grateful to him for his kindness but ashamed that I needed it.

Luckily, Mr. Pelletier just patted my shoulder. "I'll leave you to it."

It was a super busy day, and I barely had a chance to wave hello to Nell, let alone call a meeting of the Sasquatch Search Team. We didn't even eat our lunch on the same shift. As I stood at the time clock looking for my card to punch out, the sweet smell of her shampoo alerted me that she was nearby. I turned and smiled at her and a jolt of happiness shot through me when she returned the grin. I must have been standing there with a goofy look on my face, because she said, "Did you forget what your name is?"

"Huh?"

"You seem to be having a hard time finding your timecard. I was just wondering if you maybe forgot what your name is."

"Very funny." I snatched a card from the rack and shoved it into the slot, waiting for the *kerchunk* that told me I was clocked out.

"Good job, Eleanor." Nell laughed.

"Huh?"

"That was my card you punched, doofus."

Ouch. "Oh, sorry," I said.

"No problem." She shook her head. "Let's just find the one that says 'airhead,' and we'll get you out of here."

"Ha-ha. Didn't your parents ever tell you not to make fun of the mentally challenged?"

"Yes, they raised me right." Nell reached past me to grab my card. I was acutely aware of the warm softness of her bare arm as it pressed against mine. "So let me help you with this." She punched my card with a brisk flick of her wrist and more laughter. "They liked you, by the way."

"Huh?"

"My parents. They liked you."

"Oh," I said. "I liked them too. They're cool."

"They're all right."

I was just on the verge of asking her if she wanted to take a ride out to Samuel's cabin to deliver the groceries, when I caught myself. It wasn't just the care package for the old guy that was waiting for me in the walk-in. There was a big box for me too. I was planning on a nice dinner of day-old fried chicken, potato salad, and marinated string beans—leftovers from the deli-counter prepared foods. I needed that food and was glad I had it. But I didn't want Nell to know that I was accepting Mr. Pelletier's charity.

"You coming?" Nell asked, sending my heart thumping.

"No. I left something in the break room. You go on ahead."

She shrugged. "Okay." She slung her purse over her shoulder and turned to go.

"Hey, Nell?"

She paused and looked back at me. "Yeah?"

"Remember that Bigfoot documentary we talked about?"

"Sure," she said, pulling her keys out of her pocket.

"Are you in?"

She smiled. "Of course!"

I smiled too as I watched her leave before I went to fetch my dinner.

By the time I found the rutted old logging road, I was getting excited. My head buzzed with questions I wanted to ask Samuel, the first being, "Where's the best place to start looking?"

But if I thought I was about to get my first lesson in Bigfoot Hunting 101, I was in for a disappointment. Oh, I found the cabin all right—or the shack or the hovel or whatever you wanted to call it—but Samuel wasn't there. The cabin had started out as a ranger station, one of those squat buildings that look like log cabins you find in all the Connecticut state parks. This one had seen better days. The windowpanes had been all busted out and replaced with boards. Shards of glass still glittered in the mess of weeds that grew around the foundation. A rough piece of plywood stood in place of a real door. A padlock and chain provided rough security. The dark brown walls were spray-painted with all kinds of rude graffiti like "crazy bastard" and "loony toon." There was nothing more stupid than redneck hick kids trying to act ghetto.

Even though the cabin was obviously locked from the outside, I gave a knock on the door. The whole place felt abandoned, absent of life. I hoped he was okay. I had the carton of food for him in the Jeep, and there was nothing to do but leave it in the shade of the building's eaves with a note telling Samuel I would be back and that I'd like to talk.

CHAPTER 14

"In the first years of the 21st century, the woodlands of north central Connecticut have seen a great resurgence of wildlife. The countryside teems with deer, turkeys, and Canadian geese. Species that were near-extinct in the region only scant years ago are now sighted regularly, such as barn owls, moose, and the black bear. Fierce predators—bobcats, mountain lions, and roving packs of coyotes—have reclaimed their hunting grounds. Experts even speculate that the wolf may soon reappear."

At this point, as planned, Nell moved from the brightly lit path to stand in the dark, blue-green shade of a huge hemlock. She dropped her voice a half-octave or so, adding an ominous ring. "But there is another creature said to live in this dense wilderness. There are legends of similar creatures in every culture where people eke out their lives in remote, lonely regions. You have heard of these mythical beasts—Yeti, the Abominable Snowman, Sasquatch, Bigfoot. Typically they are described as standing upright to the height of eight to nine feet, with massive limbs, covered in fur, leaving behind a trail of enormous footprints.

"For most of us, these reports are the stuff of campfire tales and scary movies, the boogeyman in a child's closet. But some believe that the Sasquatch is real, and while most commonly thought to inhabit the vast forests of the Pacific Northwest, there are a handful of people who believe these creatures roam the woodlands of the northeastern United

States as well. In fact, there are documented sightings of such beings in this vicinity going back to the 1800s.

"So, who are these people who believe? Those who have had actual encounters.

"We begin this documentary as skeptics, investigating the possibility that such a creature may exist in what is, to us, our own backyard. We will follow the research notes of scientist Horace Oliver in our investigation into the existence of Sasquatch."

I knew it. The camera just loved Nell's face. It's funny—just because you're pretty doesn't mean you'll photograph well. But with Nell, that just wasn't the case. When I saw her through the lens, her dark eyes were bright and intelligent, and I could tell that her voice was going to record well too.

We were out in the woods, on that trail where I'd first found the weird arrangement of tree limbs. I thought this would be the perfect place to start our documentary, as it was the place where my own involvement began. Nell had done a great job writing the introduction. Bathed in the soft, sun-dappled light, she looked like a woodland fairy. I was glad I had persuaded her to be the film's narrator.

"Cut," I said when she was finished. "That was great. I think we can start the next scene." We moved up along the trail. I was relieved to see that the slender trunks were still there, though the branches seemed to have sagged a bit over the weeks since I'd first stumbled across them. Now it was my turn in front of the camera, and as Nell filmed me, I related my own experience as a third-party encounter, describing the smell and conjecturing about the structure without letting on that it had been me that first noticed everything.

Once we were finished with scene two, I suggested we move around the obstruction and continue up the path, maybe find out what we were being blocked from. I was so happy being out in the woods alone with Nell. It was the first time we'd been truly alone since Barry had interrupted our outing at the swimming hole.

We'd met a couple of days earlier at the little diner on the edge of town and started working on how we would begin. And now, here we were, laughing and talking. It was such a perfect Sunday afternoon, I could almost buy our own cover story—that I was making a student documentary about local legends, that we were just two kids and a camera looking for extra credit. I could tell that Nell almost believed it too. Even though I didn't tell her about the stare-down between me and Sassy the other night.

Well, I kind of told her—I told her about almost hitting the deer and realizing that something big was hunting it, but I didn't tell her I got a real eyeful of the critter. I don't really know why—maybe because I didn't want to scare her off. If I did, I wouldn't be able to spend time with her like this. Maybe I didn't want to remember how scared I was, staring into those glowing red eyes.

"You know what I'd like to do now?" I said, after finishing the bit about the barricade.

In a funny Italian accent, Nell replied, "No, Signor Spielberg. I do not."

"Oh, that's hilarious."

"Just trying to play the part." Nell peered at me from behind the camera.

"And what part is that?

"You know, I'm the exotic Euro-trash cinematographer."

"Okay, fine, Fellini. Can we talk about setting up the next shot?"

"Of course, *Signor Directore*."

I sighed, not really annoyed, but trying to make her feel like she was acting like a silly kid. "If you're ready to be serious, here's what I'm thinking." I pointed beyond where she stood. "I think it would be cool if you could climb up to the top of that hill there and film me as I move up the trail. As I walk, I'm going to talk about what I think we might find on the other side."

"Sort of 'a bear goes over the mountain to see what he can see' vibe," Nell said, all mockingly serious.

"You're just a laugh riot today. Really, you're on fire." Shaking my head, I added, "Just climb up to the top of that hill and start shooting."

Nell laughed as she scrambled up the steep grade, stepping over rocks and occasionally grabbing a tree branch with her free hand to steady her balance. Finally, she stood on the uppermost swell, bathed in a shaft of sunlight that broke through the canopy of leaves. "Ready?"

"Yeah." I paused before I said, "Action!" My voice echoed strangely in the silent woods.

I started moving up the trail myself, yammering on about what a Bigfoot lair might look like, and why this part of the preserve would make a good habitat for a large omnivorous creature—a nonsensical spout of crap I tossed off the top of my head from what I remembered from Horace's notes.

Meanwhile, Nell kept the camera steadily on me and behaved herself by not cracking up at my performance. Just as I was getting within a few yards of her, though, she suddenly decided to start backing away from me. Not knowing how the shot looked through the viewfinder, I could only assume that she was going for a better angle or something. Then she dropped out of sight, letting out a little whoop of surprise as she disappeared.

Stunned for only a second, I ran up the incline, the soles of my sneakers slipping on dried leaves, my fingers scrabbling at branches and rocks as I grabbed for purchase. I reached the crest—instead of the gentle, downward plane I expected, the hill ended in a steep grade, as if the backside had been scraped away by a huge ice-cream scoop.

I didn't have much time to scan for Nell's whereabouts. As I stepped along the edge of the cliff, my feet skidded on some moss, and suddenly I was in free fall. The sky and trees spun around like a kaleidoscope. The air was knocked right out of me as I landed on my back with a *whump*.

Before I could catch my breath, Nell was scuttling across the mattress of fallen leaves that seemed to have cushioned our fall. "Are you all right?" I could hear worry in her voice. She hovered above me, those brown eyes shiny with concern.

I brought my hands to my chest, feeling for damage. "I guess so," I said. "How about you?"

"I'm okay," she said. "But that last step is a doozy."

Pushing up on my elbows, I looked around. "Where the heck are we?" It wasn't so much that the hill had been scooped out, but more like we were in the bottom of a large cereal bowl, the brown leaves filling it like cornflakes.

"Weird land formation, right?" Nell said. "Could be anything—the foundation for a house. Something left by glaciers. Maybe a crater caused by a meteor a thousand years ago."

Sitting in the leaves, still a little stunned, we both took a moment to get our bearings.

"Hey, where's the camera?" I asked.

"Oh, the camera…" Nell said. "I must have dropped it as I fell. It has to be here somewhere."

We crawled around, swooshing our hands through the layers of leaves, looking for the camera. My knees and the palms of my hands were getting torn up, scratching against the twigs and acorns mixed in with the leaves.

After a few minutes, Nell cried out, "Found it!"

I stood up and tried to run over to her but couldn't find steady footing in the deep layers of shifting debris. Next thing I knew, I was falling again, and this time I landed right on top of Nell.

We were nose to nose.

"Well, the camera looked okay when I found it, but I can't promise that now," Nell said dryly.

I was so aware of the warm softness of her beneath me. With each word she said, a warm puff of her breath patted my face. Her breath smelled of peppermint and her hair smelled like mangos and she smelled like herself and all her smells were mixed in with the spicy aroma of the leaves. I swear the combination made me dizzy, and I sort of forgot everything but Nell's closeness. I couldn't help myself. I kissed her.

And she kissed me back.

So I kissed her some more. I could taste the saltiness of her skin. She put her hands on my shoulders. I tickled her lip with my tongue and then…

Stars exploded in a churning display before I felt the sickening pain. Nell was gone, slid out from underneath me, leaving me facedown in the leaves, doubled over in pain, clutching my screaming balls and choking back vomit.

Finally, when I could breathe again, I gasped, "What the hell?" But no one heard me. Nell was gone—I could hear the sound of her footsteps crackling and thumping through the woods. She was moving fast. She would be back at the house and driving away in her old Karmann Ghia before I would even be able to stand up.

What had I done to deserve a full-force knee to the nuts? As I waited for the agony to subside, I played that brief moment of bliss over and over, trying to figure out just exactly how I had pissed Nell off so bad. If Nell didn't want me to kiss her, why didn't she just say so? I would have listened. She didn't have to assault the family jewels.

At last I could sit up, and eventually, I could stand. Thank God the camera seemed to be okay. I walked slowly, still sore, as I started to climb out of the pit. Before I got to the top, I noticed a shadowy recess created by an interesting jumble of boulders. The huge stones, three or four of them, rested against each other in a crude lean-to, like something Fred Flintstone might have used as a carport. I moved closer. The hard-packed dirt inside seemed to have been swept clean, as if a camper had used it for shelter not too long ago. I don't know why, but I entered, aware of the cool dampness that came off the stones and the hollow quiet within the walls. Stepping to the rear, where earth, rocks, and the twisted veins of tree roots formed the back wall, I smelled an unmistakable odor, that musty stink of feces, rotting meat, and wet fur.

Too bad you can't capture a smell on film.

How long does a smell last?

When was the last time Sassy had bedded down in here? Suddenly, fear squeezed my chest, making me short of breath. Was it only Nell's retreating footsteps I had heard? Was something stalking her, shadowing her movements?

I clambered out of the pit as fast as I could and jogged my way back to Horace's house, not taking one honestly deep breath until I saw that Nell's car was gone from the driveway. She had made it back safe.

CHAPTER 15

By the time I got to the house, I had started to get mad at Nell. Not to mention that I was humiliated, embarrassed, and hurt by her obvious and violent rejection of me. Like I said, she could have just said no, or laughed in my face—that always works. But no, she had to jeopardize my future ability to father children. Pretty harsh.

Once inside, I filled a plastic sandwich bag full of ice and held it against my still-throbbing crotch as I checked Facebook. Megan had uploaded some goofy pictures. Ham that she was, she loved to mug for the camera. I felt a little sad. I hadn't seen my sister in, like, a month, and already she looked different, older. She'd cut her hair short and put a hot-pink streak through the new bangs that fell across her forehead.

What made me sadder than the changes in my sister was the fact that none of my friends from Norwalk had left any kind of message for me. Oh, there were all kinds of jokey stuff from people I knew, but nothing was specifically posted for me to see.

I made myself check my email. You'd think I'd want to. But I didn't. It was always full of my mom's cheery little messages, begging me to answer. I didn't really read any of them but clicked Reply on the latest one and typed that I was fine before I hit Send. Occasionally, I gave her some real information, like that I was working for Mr. Pelletier. But, as a rule, I left out the important stuff like, "Dad's out of the country and I have no idea when he's coming back." No need to freak her out, right?

As usual, the one message from Megan was a note calling me a jerk. That didn't bother me. What really hurt was that I hadn't gotten any messages from my buddies, Andrew and Kyle, in weeks. Or Kendall. Kendall and I had decided to break up when I moved away, but promised to stay friends. That hadn't lasted long. I guess I'm not so good with the ladies.

But surprise, surprise, at the very bottom there was an email from my dad. My heart started thumping as I opened it. That achy lump rose in my throat. I missed him more than I wanted to admit.

Jake:

Sorry this is the first word I've sent. Had a hard time trying to track down the shipment, but I think I straightened everything out. (Someone was trying to rip me off.) But since I'm down here anyway, I'm trying to pull together another deal, so I might stay for another few weeks. Communicating is difficult. I'm sending this from an Internet café in the first real town I've been in for days. I'm sure you're doing fine.

Dad

Great, Dad, thanks. Yeah, I'm doing fine. The girl I thought I was falling in love with kicked me in the nuts so hard I may never stand up straight again, I'm practically scrounging food from the Dumpsters at work, and I'm just waiting to be arrested for driving without a license, and oh yeah, did you pay the electric bill? But other than that, I'm okay. Just great. Oh gee—forgot to tell you about the big hairy monster I met in the middle of the night. Happy travels.

I had to admit I could see why my mother got so pissed at him.

Living alone sucks.

I made myself scrambled eggs and toast. I was getting pretty sick of eggs. By the time I was done eating, it wasn't even four o'clock. I tried calling Nell on her cell phone, but she didn't answer. There was still plenty of time to go to her house and make sure she was okay. But shouldn't she be checking on me?

The farmhouse looked slightly pink in the late-afternoon light, and as I got out of the car, the quatro amigos—that is, the teeny-weeny goat, donkey, rooster, and dog—came trotting out from the side yard to greet me. All of them were jumping around my knees. I was careful not to step on anybody as I noticed that Nell's car was parked over by the goat shed. An old Range Rover and a Honda Element were parked side by side in the driveway.

I rang the bell and waited. No one came to the door. I rang the bell again, this time listening. All the cars were here; someone had to be inside. How could I find out what had upset Nell so bad if I couldn't talk to her?

Although I was certain I had heard the sound of the doorbell through the closed door, I thought maybe it was broken somehow and they couldn't hear it in the house. But surely the little Yorkie's nonstop yapping had alerted them to the fact that someone was at the door? Just to make sure, I knocked—waited a minute or so—then pounded a little harder. Still no one came. Okay, so I was going to get the silent treatment. Nice. I could imagine everyone huddled in a closet, shushing each other.

I gave up. Turning to leave, suddenly I found myself standing face-to-face with Mr. Davis. The look on his face gave me a jolt of alarm.

He was angry. His mouth was set in a severe frown. His eyes were blazing. The last time I'd seen heat like that coming out of someone's eyes, my dad came close to pounding me. I put my hands up in defense and said, "Mr. Davis, I—"

"I don't want to hear it!" The veins were popping in his neck as he thrust his face so close to mine, flecks of spit hit my face. I flinched and stepped back, bumping into a little table and sending something smashing onto the porch floor.

Mr. Davis jabbed me in the chest—hard—with his right index finger. "I don't know what happened out there in the woods." Jab. "All I know is I don't like the state my girl was in when she got home." Jab. "And she was with you." Jab. "I'm telling you right here and now—you leave my daughter alone!" Jab.

"But…" I started again, afraid he was going to leave off the jabbing and hit me full force. I wanted to tell him what had happened, wanted to tell him I wasn't a bad guy. I wanted to see Nell.

He balled his hands into rock-hard fists and growled through clenched teeth. "Get. Off. My. Property."

"Okay, okay." I kept my hands up as I tried to sidle past him to the Jeep. "I'm sorry. I'm going. Please tell Nell—"

"Get the hell out of here!" Mr. Davis bellowed.

I bolted down the stairs and ran to my car. Looking over my shoulder, I saw Mr. Davis tear into the house, the front door slamming behind him

My hands were shaking. There was a dull ache in the center of my chest where Mr. Davis had poked me, but I managed to start the engine.

A soft tapping sounded at my car window. I nearly jumped out of my skin.

It was Mrs. Davis. She had a worried look on her face and motioned for me to lower the window. My instinct was to floor it and get the hell out of there. What if Mr. Davis saw me talking to Mrs. Davis? I really thought he might kill me. But what could I do? I rolled down the window.

Her voice was low and rushed. "I'm sorry about this, Jake. I believe you're a nice boy. We have a tendency to overreact around here. I don't necessarily think you're at fault. Be patient. I hope we get a chance to talk things out. But you better go now." Then she just turned around and darted into the goat shed, which was probably where she'd been hiding out the whole time I'd been banging on the door.

Hard to believe this was the same cool family I had sat down to dinner with only a few nights before.

CHAPTER 16

I showed up at work the next morning, ready to give Nell the cold shoulder. The more I thought about it, the less I thought I deserved the treatment I had gotten from her dad. But she was way ahead of me. The snubbing I'd planned was nothing to the complete freeze-out I got from her. I was officially a nonhuman. Every time I came near her, it was like I was invisible, like I no longer existed. Considering the fact that I was living alone and hadn't heard from an old friend in weeks, I seriously began to wonder if, somewhere along the way, that Sasquatch had crushed my skull and now I was just a lonely ghost hoping for someone to notice me hanging out in the shadows.

That is, until Barry decided to join me for lunch.

I was munching on my turkey sandwich when Barry plopped down next to me. "So. Made a move on her, didn't you?" He had this knowing smile on his mug that made me want to punch him.

My face went hot and red—how did he know? Did Nell confide in him? I tried to bluff my way through it. "What are you talking about?"

"Oh, I've seen the signs," said Barry smugly—like he knew all about everything. He leaned hard against the back of the chair, stretching his legs in front of him. "So, what'd you do? Try and cop a feel?"

"Nothing happened," I said. "We had a misunderstanding, that's all."

"Sure, right." Barry smirked. "You went for it. Don't get me wrong; I don't blame you. But you can't just go and make a grab for Nell. If you knew her like I do, you'd understand. For now, let's just say she's got issues."

Inside, I was fuming. It killed me that jerkwad Barry knew more about Nell than I did. Never mind that he'd known her for years and I'd only met her a few weeks ago. Half of me wanted to get up and stalk out of the room; half of me wanted to beg Barry for some insider info on Nell. Either way, there wasn't a chance in hell I was going to be able to finish eating my lunch. I couldn't decide what to do. Fortunately, I was rescued from my dilemma when Mr. Pelletier entered the room.

"Oliver," he said. "There's a young lady here to see you."

"Me?"

"Yeah, you," Mr. Pelletier said. "She's waiting for you at the customer service desk."

Leaving my sandwich and idiot Barry behind, I made my way through the store, wondering all the time who could be looking for me.

At first, when I saw that bright streak of pink hair, I was totally confused. I didn't know any midget punk-rocker types—but when that kid cannonballed into my arms, I knew it was Megan.

"Yo, bro!" She grabbed me around my middle, hugging me so hard I couldn't breathe. If she'd clinched me like that under ordinary circumstances, I would have stomped on her foot to get loose. But that afternoon, feeling as low as I did, having someone showing me such full-force affection was great.

Finally, she eased up a little bit and stepped back. "Dude!" she exclaimed in that breathless way she had of talking, like everything was a big deal. "You wouldn't believe what I went through to get here!"

I realized that Mr. Pelletier was standing directly behind me, and everyone else in the whole store was staring at us. Clearing my throat, I introduced her.

Megan stuck out her hand with a bright smile, "How do you do, Mr. Pelletier? It's very nice to meet you."

"A pleasure, Miss Oliver. I'm sure your father must be happy to have you here."

Megan screwed her face up into this annoyed expression. "You'd think, right? But I can't get him to return a call." She turned to look at me. All of a sudden her face went all red and blotchy, like she was dropping her happy mask and might cry. "What's up with that, bro?"

I grabbed her elbow, letting out a nervous laugh. "Oh, you know Dad. So forgetful." Looking around, I noticed that Mr. Pelletier was still watching our little reunion with interest. Barry was too. I guess he had followed me out of the back room. Nell was watching from behind the register. At least she could finally see me.

It was only then that I realized that my mother should have been standing next to Megan. How did she get here if Mom hadn't brought her? "Hey, Mr. Pelletier. My dad let me have the car today, and I'm still on break. Would you mind if I ran my sister home?"

Mr. Pelletier was all blustery and generous. "Of course, of course. Take your time. Get her all settled in."

We were finally alone together in the Jeep.

"Sick! You're driving." Megan wore a big grin on her face.

"Yeah. Sick, all right." I decided not to tell her that I was committing an illegal act. "What the hell are you doing here?"

"Nice to see you too."

"No, really. You never said you were coming."

"You never asked."

"Oh, cut the crap," I said. "You know what I mean. And where's Mom? Was this a drive-by dump?" Even as I asked, a depressing thought struck me. Maybe Mom brought Megan up and she didn't want to see me. Maybe she was afraid I'd dis her in front of everybody. Or maybe she was so tired of my silent treatment, she'd decided to quit trying to get through to me.

"Mom?" Megan said vaguely as she looked out of the window.

"Yes, Mom."

"Oh, Mom. Right. She's on Nantucket."

"As in, the island off the coast of Massachusetts?"

"That's the one. She's not coming back until the end of August."

"And why aren't you there?"

"Wasn't invited."

"Not invited?"

"Nope. Three's a crowd. You know. Second honeymoon and all that." Megan's face went blank as she stared straight ahead. Her punky haircut made her seem older, but there was a soft roundness to her cheeks that made me sure she was still my kid sister.

"I still don't get it. Dad's been pretty distracted lately, but I'm sure he'd mention you were coming."

"I didn't tell him. As far as anyone knows, I'm at soccer camp for the next four weeks."

"So why aren't you there?"

"I don't play soccer anymore! I quit last fall."

"So?"

"So—why the hell would I waste a whole month running around a hot field if I don't give a crap about the stupid game?"

"Then why did Mom send you there?"

"Because she hasn't noticed a thing about me since she married Dr. Old Fart. And she didn't know how else to get rid of me."

I softened my voice a little bit. I got why she was pissed. "You still haven't explained why you're not actually at soccer camp—or how you got here."

"They put me on a goddamned Greyhound bus. Couldn't even drive me up themselves. I was supposed to rendezvous with the camp bus in some godforsaken town in Vermont or New Hampshire or somewhere. But I got off in Hartford. Caught a bus headed up in this direction instead. Hitched the rest of the way. Knew where to find you from the emails you sent to Mom. Easy peasy."

My heart thudded thinking about my fourteen-year-old sister alone on the road. It was a wonder she hadn't been raped and murdered. "Megan! There must be an APB out on you! The cops are probably combing New England right now. Talk about your Megan Alert!"

"Amber Alert, bro. Megan's Law—Amber Alert. But relax. I called the camp, pretended I was Mom. Told them there was a sudden change in plans but they could keep the fee. Believe me, as soon as I told them they didn't have to return the money, they were very cool about it."

"What's going to happen when Mom finds out?"

"Finds out what?" Megan laughed. "Mom's going to call me once a week on my cell, and I'll answer. Tell her how I love the place. She'll never know. That is, unless Dad gets all responsible-parenty and blows my cover."

"That's not going to be a problem."

CHAPTER 17

"No way! You have got to be kidding me!" Megan's jaw dropped as she stepped into Horace's shabby little living room. "You've been living here all by yourself?"

I looked around, seeing everything through Megan's eyes. I'd done a pretty good job of keeping the place neat, though a thin layer of dust had settled on the beat-up tables. There wasn't a thing I could do about the dingy slipcovers on the sofa and chair. Everything was wiped down and tidy in the kitchen, I knew. And the bathroom wasn't too disgusting.

Megan dumped her huge backpack down on the floor in the corner before flopping down on the sofa. "This is soooo cool! Where's the TV?"

"No TV. But we're online. The computer's over there."

"Where's the stereo?"

"No stereo."

"I'll take care of that." Jumping up, she started rooting around in her bag. She pulled out an iPod and a little black case. She fiddled with it until the room filled with P!nk's husky vocals. Raising her voice to be heard over the music, Megan said, "Now we're ready to party!"

I picked up the little black speaker case and shut off the noise. "No. No parties."

"Dude! Why not?" demanded Megan. "We got a house and no grown-ups. It looked like a couple of the people at that store would be cool to hang out with. Let's have a party!"

"No way. I don't want to draw too much attention to us. Nobody knows that Dad's away."

"Oh, come on, bro! That blond kid who followed us out to the car looked like a guy who could get his hands on a keg."

"I'm sure he could." My sister could sniff out trouble faster than anyone I knew. Barry was the last person I wanted to know that we were home alone. "Don't be a jerk, Megan. If anybody finds out Dad's gone, you'll be in soccer camp by tomorrow night."

She slumped down against the cushions on the sofa, her arms crossed. "You're right. But what the hell else is there to do around this place?"

"Not much," I admitted. "But I *am* kind of working on a project. And if it goes the way I hope, I might make some money." Now that Nell was out of the picture, I needed a replacement assistant. Megan could be a pain in the neck, but I could usually handle her.

She sat up, suddenly all perky with interest. "Yeah? What's the project?"

I told her everything over dinner. I don't think she really believed I'd encountered the creature that night by the road, but by the time I was done with my story, her interest overcame her skepticism. After finishing the tuna casserole, which Megan couldn't seem to eat without making gagging noises, she said, "So, let's get started."

"Get started on what?"

"Let's go out looking for the boogeyman."

"Now? But it's dark outside." The memory of fiery-red eyes sent a shiver down my spine.

Megan put a hand on her hip and glared at me like I was the stupidest person in the world. "Well, didn't you tell me that Sam guy wanders around looking for him at night?"

"Yeah, but the whole point is to shoot a video."

"I saw that camera Mom got you. It's pretty sophisticated. You could pick up something."

Nothing gets past Megan. She was right. But still, I was tired, and the thought of roaming the unfamiliar woods at night? Frankly, the idea scared me.

Megan could see that I wasn't about to budge. "Oh, please," she whined. "I've been cooped up here all afternoon. At least you got to go back to work. Let's go out and look for Bigfoot."

"Megan, this isn't a joke. I told you. I know there's something out there. I've seen it. We can't just go stumbling out into the dark without a strategy."

"But I'm bored."

"There's always soccer camp."

After we watched a DVD, I finally convinced Megan to go to bed around ten o'clock. She'd never have admitted it, but her runaway adventures had wiped her out. In about ten minutes, she was in dreamland. She was sleeping in Dad's room, and I stood at the door for a minute, listening to her soft snoring. I'd never tell her, but it was nice to have another breathing human being in the house with me—even if it was my bratty sister. Unfortunately, the whole day had left me really keyed up, and I knew that I wouldn't be able to get to sleep for a while yet.

Heading back to the living room, I sat down with Horace's notebooks. I'd found maps of the area and was trying to pinpoint the spots where Horace claimed to have sited the creature. After an hour or so, my eyes were getting blurry. Yawning, I turned off the desk lamp.

Then I heard it. That eerie call, a deep, hollow, sorrowful howl that echoed across the wilderness. I knew right away that it wasn't Samuel this time. There was a deep resonance to the sound that I didn't believe a human could imitate.

Megan was pretty willing to believe my crazy story—always up for excitement—and my first impulse was to run and get her so she could hear it for herself.

I started for the stairs, then stopped. The call repeated, closer now. The hairs on the back of my neck prickled. Megan. Something strange and potentially dangerous was really out there, and she was sleeping peacefully upstairs.

And she was my responsibility.

CHAPTER 18

The next morning, before we'd even left the backyard and hit the trail, Megan was complaining. About everything. The path was too rocky, she was getting a blister (I'd told her to wear sneakers, not flip-flops), bugs were biting her, and she was hungry and bored. She was not exactly my idea of an intrepid assistant. I couldn't help thinking about my day out in the woods with Nell—not only the way we joked around, but the serious planning and discussions about the script, camera angles, and shot sequences. Operation Bigfoot wasn't a collaboration anymore, just me telling Megan what to do and begging her to quit whining.

This wasn't a workday, though—more of a reconnaissance trip. I wanted to give Megan a visual and geographical reference to the experiences I'd already had. Earlier in the morning, I'd dragged her with me to drop another carton of supplies off for Samuel. I had been hoping for a chance to talk with him. I wanted to ask him if I could interview him for the documentary, so I was disappointed when, again, he wasn't anywhere to be found. There were signs that he was still occupying the cabin. The last carton I'd left was sitting alongside the building, filled with the now-empty cans and wrappings of my last delivery, but the little shack was still padlocked and boarded up. After I loaded his trash in the back of the Jeep, I left the new box of supplies in its place with a note reminding him who I was and inviting him to stop by Horace's cabin.

Megan and I tramped around for a while, checking out all the old haunts. By then, time, gravity, rain, and wind had deconstructed the branch teepee I'd stumbled across that first day. All that was left was an unremarkable pile of sticks. The Fred Flintstone lean-to was nearly a mile on, and by the time we got there, Megan wasn't the only one who was cranky. Seeing that large, round hollow where Nell and I had tumbled really rattled me. It was getting close to noon, we were both hot and sweaty, and I was sick of swatting mosquitoes. The rock shelter was just as I'd left it, though some dead leaves had blown in and littered the floor. I stepped under the shade of the huge overhanging boulder, once again feeling the coolness coming off the rocks, smelling the dampness of the earth beneath my feet, but nothing else. Moving farther in, I sniffed the walls, going down on my hands and knees to find out whether the creature's odor still lingered where I imagined it had slept. This time there was nothing unusual—just dirt and damp and moldering leaves.

I stood up, brushing the dirt off my hands, to find Megan staring at me like I'd lost my mind.

"O-kay, bro." Her voice was wary. "So, what's with the bloodhound imitation?"

"I told you, this Bigfoot or Sasquatch, or whatever it is, has a really powerful odor. It was really strong the last time I was here."

"I don't smell anything."

"I know. Me neither. I'm just telling you that I did the last time."

"Is there anything else that'll convince me that there's some monster out here? Because right now, I'm beginning to worry about you."

I was kind of hurt. "But you said you believed me."

"Maybe I'm just too hot and hungry to care right now. Can we go back?"

"Not just yet. But if you're a good girl, there's a treat in it for you." I turned and headed back to the trail, this time taking the route that would lead us to the swimming hole.

We were walking through the valley where Nell and I had been pelted with stones. I slowed down, almost wishing that a rock would whiz by. The path was narrow, and I let Megan take the lead because she sometimes followed too closely and stepped on the backs of my heels. She was listening to her iPod, singing under her breath to whatever dopey love song was pulsing through the earbuds.

I slipped the backpack off my shoulders and took out the camera. I turned it on and trained the lens on her. It's funny how the world gets so small and concentrated when you're looking through the viewfinder. Megan seemed dwarfed by the huge trees looming on either side of her as she trudged along, swinging her arms, swiveling her head to take in the scenery on either side of the trail.

"Youch!" she cried as she stumbled. "Shit!"

"What?" I caught up with her, scanning the ridges on either side for flying projectiles. Note to self—be careful what you wish for.

"I stubbed my toe on a damn tree root." She rubbed her foot.

"I told you to wear sneakers."

"God, you've turned into such an old lady." Megan slid her flip-flop back on and she looked up to see the camera was at my face. "Hey! Cut that out! I've told you a million times, I hate candid shots!"

I laughed. "I got plenty. When you have those buds plugged in your ears, I can get away with anything." I was still filming her, enjoying the fit she was throwing.

She tried to bat the camera away. "Turn it off! Turn it off!"

"No way. Now I can blackmail you."

"What are you talking about? It's not like you caught me on the toilet or anything." She glared at me, hands on her hips.

"Hmm, on the toilet. Good idea. Hadn't thought of that. I'll have to keep it in mind for another time, but what I have now will work. If you take one step out of line, I'll email this to Mom and show her you're not at soccer camp."

Crossing her arms, she stamped her foot and pouted like a little kid. "You are sooo mean!"

I lowered the camera. "Oh, come on. I'm just kidding."

"Erase it!"

"Quit worrying and start walking. We're almost there."

"Where?"

"You'll see."

"You make me so mad sometimes." She spun around and marched away from me.

We had gone a few hundred yards when she snatched the camera out of my hand. Once she got it, she ran like crazy. I gave chase, and when I caught up around the bend, she was rewinding the camera, getting ready to erase the shots I'd just gotten of her.

I almost reached her when she turned and held out a warning hand. "You take one step closer, and I'll smash it on this rock." Her gaze moved from the viewfinder, then to me, then returned to the tiny screen. Her voice changed. "Hey, who's this?"

"Don't erase that. Give me the camera." I moved next to her and glimpsed Nell's face in the viewfinder.

"Hold on." Megan was watching intently. "Hey, didn't I see her at the store?"

"Maybe." I tried to sound indifferent.

"How come you didn't introduce me to her?"

"Never mind. Give me the camera." I made another grab for it.

She twisted out of my reach. "Is she your girlfriend?"

"No."

"Hey, I know where this is! We were just there."

"That's right."

"Is she in on Operation Bigfoot too?"

"Not anymore."

"Why not?"

"To be honest with you, I don't really know."

Megan had a wicked grin on her face. "So, what happened?"

"Never mind, Megan." She was really starting to piss me off. "If you give me back the camera, I'll tell you later. But not now, okay?"

"Okay, but you have to promise to erase me."

As if I could. "Deal."

CHAPTER 19

"So, where's Goshen?" Megan asked, lying on her back, squinting against the sun.

"I don't know." I smeared a little fresh sunblock on my nose. "Something like seven miles south of here. Why?"

"Well, the other day, while I was hitching, I saw a bunch of signs that said there's a carnival in Goshen this weekend. I figured it couldn't be too far away."

"A carnival? You've got to be out of your mind if you think I'm taking you to a carnival." I tried hard not to think about her hitching. When I finally got up the nerve to ask her, she gave a vague story about some has-been hippie stoner in a beat-up old VW bus. She tried to be all breezy about it, but she didn't make eye contact with me.

"Oh my God, Jake!" Megan shot up to a sitting position, smacking me on the shoulder on her way up. "What the hell is the matter with you? Have you turned into some weird old troll, or what?"

"Ow! What'd you do that for?"

"Because you're the biggest party pooper I've ever met. You sure you just turned sixteen, or was it sixty-one? Why can't we go to a carnival?"

I stood up, easing over the slippery rocks and roots to get to the water's edge. Stepping in ankle-deep, I saw the quick shadows of fish investigating my toes, felt their tiny, nudging snouts. I sighed. "Megan. Those carnivals are the biggest money-suckers going. Why don't we just stay home and burn a hundred bucks? Think of the money we'll save on gas."

"Ha-ha, very funny." She joined me at the water's edge, and she smiled as the minnows started tickling her toes too. "So, you're worried about money."

"Duh."

Her smile widened. She pulled at my hand. "Come here. I want to show you something." Leading me back over to our towels, she fell to her knees and dragged her little daypack over. After undoing a series of buckles and zippers, she reached some secret compartment way down at the bottom. "Ta-da!" She pulled something out. Opening her fist, she revealed a huge wad of cash bound with a bright pink rubber band. "That carnival? My treat."

"Jesus, Megan. How much is there? Never mind, I don't want to know." I couldn't take my eyes off the roll. I had to fight the urge to snatch it out of her palm. "What did you do? Rob a bank?"

"This, oh brother of mine, is the fruit of parental guilt. And if you weren't so holier-than-thou, you could have one just like it."

"Mom gave you all that?" I was shocked.

"Yeah, baby. The days of the five-bucks-a-week allowance are a thing of the past."

"What did you do to earn it?"

"It's not what I'm doing. It's more like what Mom knows she's not doing."

"What do you mean?"

"Like the soccer thing. I gave it up, but she didn't know for weeks, because she's not paying attention. She's too busy keeping Dr. Old Fart happy. As soon as she realizes she's being a neglectful mother—bingo!—a couple of hundred bucks falls into my lap."

"There's a lot more than two hundred dollars here."

"Well, she's been screwing up quite frequently. Standing me up for a mother-daughter shopping trip, forgetting to pick me up after school, making me babysit his grandkids—it adds up."

"Quite a racket you got going there."

"That's right, bro. I've got plenty of cash. So, can we go?"

"I don't know." Honestly, I don't really like carnivals. The food is gross—stale popcorn and suspicious hotdogs are not my idea of good eats—rides make me nauseous, and I suck at all those midway games. I'll never win one of those big stuffed animals in my life.

"Please, please, please!" Megan squeezed my right hand, then let go to stuff her stash of cash way down to the bottom of her pack again. "Look, I want to spend time with you, but not in solitary confinement. Let's go have some fun."

Once we were there, I was glad we had gone. After all, it was a beautiful summer night, and I was with my little sister—who, if nothing else, totally got me. The lights on the Ferris wheel glowed against the night sky, and after we parked, Megan and I bought some tickets and shared a cone of cotton candy while we decided where we were going to start. Since it was getting dark, most of the families with little kids were straggling off the grounds, leaving behind packs of roaming teenagers. Seeing those gangs of buddies horsing around and laughing made me miss my friends. I cringed at the thought that anyone might think Megan was my girlfriend, not my sister.

After two rounds on the bumper cars, Megan tugged me over to the monster slide. Just as we got into line, some big doofus came hurtling down the yellow chute, whooping and hollering the whole way, keeping his momentum fast enough to crash through the barriers and plow into the crowd. He missed us by inches. There were screams and cursing, and a couple of attendants rushed to grab the guy, who was rolling around on the ground guffawing like a crazy mule. I could smell beer on him. The ride attendants finally managed to yank him to his feet, and I found myself standing face-to-face with Barry.

A woozy grin twisted his mouth. "Jake! My man!" Barry was shaking the carnival guys off him like they were bugs. He glared at them, warning them away, and they retreated, one guy muttering, "Keep off our ride, asshole," as they went back to their jobs. The lopsided smile returned to Barry's face. This time, though, his eyes were half-closed as he noticed Megan. "And Little Sister Jake." He used a tone that made me want to punch him. "All right! Time to party!" Before I could step away, Barry had thrown his beefy arms around both our necks and started pulling us. Worse than thinking Megan was my girlfriend, all these strangers were looking on in disgust, thinking Barry was my buddy. Bad enough I had Barry's sweaty pits just inches from my nose, but when I glanced at Megan, she was looking up at him like he was Prince Charming.

"So, who're you guys here with?" Barry asked.

"Just us," Megan said. "Boring."

Thanks Megan, love spending time with you too. She had reached up and was holding his hand where it dangled over her shoulder.

"My people are here," he said. Who did he think he was—some rock star with an entourage? "I'll hook you up." He looked around the streaming crowd. "Justin! Michael! Where the hell are you guys?"

Angry faces glowered at us. I was mortified. "Hey, Barry, man. Chill. We'll find your friends. Don't make a scene." It suddenly occurred to me that "his people" might have ditched him.

"Barry! There you are!" A pretty blonde girl emerged from the crowd. "Where've you been?"

Barry stopped, finally relieving Megan and me from the burden of his embrace. "Hey, Katie baby." He swayed on his feet. I could imagine him toppling over like a felled tree. "These are those new kids. Meet Jake and…and…his little sister."

Megan looked at Barry with an annoyed expression. She considered herself a girl who made an impression. "Megan." She gave a little wave of greeting. "How you doing?"

Katie responded likewise, her eyes flickering from Megan to me, then back to Barry. "So are you ready to go?" she asked him.

"Hell, no," Barry declared. "The night's still young, right?"

"It's getting late."

"We still got beer left?"

Katie rolled her eyes and sighed. "I think so."

"Then we still got some partying to do." Barry straightened his shoulders, like he was getting ready for some serious business. "Where is everybody?"

"They're hanging out under the tree."

Barry threw an arm around Megan's shoulders again, and thankfully opted to load Katie with the other one. He started to lead the girls off, and I had no choice but to follow. We wound our way past the games, the food carts, and the ticket booth, out of the glare of the floodlights and bustle and into a quiet, dark field beyond the carnival grounds. Against the night sky, I made out the silhouette of a huge tree. When we got a little closer, I heard voices talking in the shadows. For a minute, it was peaceful, just soft conversation and laughter. That is, until Barry let out a shrieking war cry.

"Yaaooooowww!" Barry threw his head back so far and screamed so loud the tendons in his neck popped.

A hissing chorus of *shhhhh* broke out from whoever was hanging out in the tree's shadow. Someone said in a low voice, "Shut up, man—or you'll get us all busted." It wasn't until then that I smelled marijuana. This was not a cool place to be with my little sister.

Barry laughed. "Someone get me a beer. I'm feeling good! Wanna keep my buzz."

A guy's voice said, "I'll give you a beer if you shut up, man." I heard a cooler lid being lifted, a hand digging through ice. The owner of the voice emerged from the shadows. He was about my height, with long hair. He looked at Megan and me as he handed a can of beer to Barry. He nodded. "How're you doing?" He saw Katie. "You okay?"

"Sure, Justin. Just trying to keep an eye on Barry," said Katie. "This is Jake and Megan."

"Hey," Justin said. "You want a beer?"

"No, thanks," I said as simultaneously Megan said, "Sure."

Barry downed that beer in one swallow and wiped his mouth with the back of his hand. "So. What the hell are we all doing here when the action's out there? Come on, let's go have some fun!" He let loose a deep, gurgling burp.

"Oh, all right," said one drowsy voice, and one by one, a bunch of kids stepped into the glow cast by the carnival lights. As Katie introduced us, I could tell that everyone but Katie was seriously stoned. That is, except the last person to come out of the shadows. Her eyes were clear and bright. When those eyes met mine, I swear my heart really did skip a beat.

"And this is Nell," Katie said.

Blood rushed to my brain, my mouth went dry, and my palms started to sweat. Before I could say hey, much to my horror, Megan was all over her.

Barry laughed. "Oh, they've met."

"I know who you are," Megan babbled. I swear, she'd knocked back her beer as fast as Barry.

"Is that right?" I heard Nell say. "So who am I?" There was a challenge in her tone.

Megan threw her arm around my shoulders. "You work at the grocery. You're the girl in Jakey's video."

Jakey? Did she have to say *Jakey*?

Nell shot me a look. She opened her mouth to say something, but before she could, Barry let out another whoop of laughter. "Video? Somebody making sex tapes?" In a second I was pulled away from Megan, caught in a headlock, my nose ground into Barry's armpit again. The jerk ground the knuckles of his other hand hard into my scalp. It burned like hell.

My head caught against his chest, I twisted and kicked, pounding at his side and belly with my fists to get loose. It was like hitting a bag of cement. I struggled while he laughed. When he finally let go, he managed to pull my T-shirt up over my head and threw it up into the air. It snagged on a lower branch of the tree. "You're full of surprises, Jakey, my man. No wonder Nell's not talking to you."

"You're an idiot, Barry." I ran to retrieve my shirt. By the time I plucked it free and got it back on, I was standing alone. The rest of them had moved off in a pack, returning to the glare of the carnival grounds, their voices drifting back like wisps of smoke.

It took me a while to find anybody. Turned out they'd split up into two groups. I found the girls in the funhouse because I recognized Megan's distinctive squeal among the general high-pitched screams and shouts. It sounded like they might be in there a while, so I decided to get a Coke. That's when I spied the guys gathered at the strong-man game. I hate macho strength competitions—probably because I'm so bad at them. I bought my soda and sidled away to wait at the funhouse exit for the girls.

I didn't get very far. Barry caught sight of me and took me down in a tackle, dragging me over to the game. "Hey, dude. There you are. It's your turn, man. Ring the bell."

"That's okay, Barry. I'll take a pass." I jerked my arm out of his meaty grasp. "You go ahead."

"Come on, man. Don't be a wuss." Barry grabbed the sledgehammer out of Michael's hand. By now the crowd had thinned, and the guy running the game—an old man with grizzled white whiskers and bleary eyes—obviously didn't care that order had broken down. He could see that drunken Barry wasn't worth messing with.

Barry thrust the handle of the hammer in my face. "Go ahead, man. Show us how strong you are."

"I'm not even going to bother, Barry. I'm sure you can beat me."

"Just like I thought, Jakey-boy. You are a pussy. Watch this." Barry heaved the sledgehammer over his shoulder, winding up to slam the head down onto the red-and-white bull's-eye at his feet. When he went to strike, he lost his balance, swinging wildly, almost falling over as the hammer missed its mark.

The other guys laughed, calling Barry names. "Who's the pussy now?" one of them yelled, smacking his lips in loud, sucking kisses. More jokes and insults came from the pack. Barry steadied himself as a bullheaded glower stole across his face. A bad feeling ran up my spine. The other guys knew their pal well enough to anticipate what would happen next, because they took off, darting through the thinning crowd.

Barry swung again—this time aiming at my skull. Though I was slow on the uptake, I managed to step away, arching backward from the sweep of his blow.

Displaced air rushed past as the hammer missed my nose by a quarter of an inch. "What the hell's the matter with you?"

The attendant seemed to wake up just as the girls spilled out of the funhouse. Everyone was shouting at Barry as he wound up for his second attempt to turn my brain into guacamole. He was completely bombed, and experience had taught me how to duck and weave to avoid a physical confrontation. I'm not saying my dad ever came at me full force, but I'd learned to get out of the way of a pissed-off drunk.

The game attendant must have picked up a few moves too. He managed to snake out his scrawny foot just right and tripped Barry, sending him sprawling facedown into the dirt. He landed with a thud and a groan, and the girls were on him in a flash, trying to help him back to his feet. The attendant grabbed the sledgehammer, put up a "Closed" sign, slung a rope across the entrance to his game, and disappeared before he could get more involved.

It was disgusting. Even though he had tried to murder me, the girls—including my own sister—were brushing the dirt from Barry's knees and checking him over like a bunch of EMTs at a crash site. I couldn't take another second of the whole scene. "Megan, stop! I think the patient'll live."

She gave me a dirty look. "What were you guys fighting about?"

"I wasn't fighting anybody. Just trying to defend my life."

"You must have done something to piss him off."

"Are you kidding me? That jerk is drunk off his ass. Any rational brain cells he might have are shut down for the night. Let's go home before he comes to."

It was bizarre, but that nosedive seemed to have knocked all the life out of Barry. It was like someone had cut the strings on a big, beefy marionette. All the fight was gone.

"Come on, Barry." Nell tugged on his arm. "It's time to get you out of here."

The attendant appeared again. "That's right. Get your pal out of here before I call the cops on him." He stood with his arms crossed, looking at us with a mean glare.

"If Barry gets arrested, his father will kill him." Katie was attempting to help Nell get the massive lump off the ground.

"Do you hear that, Barry?" Nell yelled in Barry's ear. "You're going to get in trouble. We'll have to call your dad."

"No way," Barry mumbled. "Nobody call that asshole."

"Well, then you have to get up."

"Can't."

Megan had joined the other two girls. It was like watching ants trying to pull a watermelon to their hill. My sister shot me a scorching look. "Well, come on, Jake. Obviously we need your help."

I crossed my arms, coolly watching their efforts. "Why should I care what happens to Barry? You guys weren't worried about me when he was trying to crush my cranium."

Katie looked up at me, her big blue eyes all cloudy with concern. "That's just the way Barry is sometimes. He didn't mean anything. Please help."

Then Nell looked at me. Really looked at me. Like, for the first time since whatever happened between us in the woods happened. She looked right into my eyes and said, "Please."

For the third time that night, I had my nose in Barry's armpit.

Among the three of us, we—me, mostly—managed to haul, push, tug, and carry Barry back to the big tree out in the field. The other guys had taken off. The only traces left behind were a couple of beer cans and flattened popcorn boxes.

Those baby blues of Katie's immediately flooded with tears. "How could they do that to us?"

"You know Michael—the world's biggest worm—he figured trouble was coming and he didn't want to get busted." Nell was angry.

"I guess I could call my father," said Katie. "But if he sees Barry like this…"

I finished her sentence. "He might not let you hang out with idiots anymore?"

"We'll give you guys a ride home," Megan chimed in.

Great. Barry was slung over my shoulders again, and the ache in my back was starting to feel like a permanent condition. I sighed. "Help me get him to the parking lot."

Barry straightened up, easing his weight off me. "One sec." He grunted, then promptly spurted a stinking stream of puke.

The rest of us jumped out of the splash zone, the girls expressing their disgust in little screams and shrieks. Me? I was just glad he was evacuating the contents of his stomach before he crawled into my dad's car.

We made it to the Jeep, parked alone under a streetlight in the otherwise deserted lot. After we wrestled Barry into the backseat, he was snoring in about thirty seconds. Katie and Megan scooted in on either side of him, leaving Nell to ride shotgun. She was still using the mango-scented shampoo.

Katie gave me directions to Barry's house, somewhere out along Route 63. We rode along in silence that might have lasted the whole ride, but then Nell whispered, "Thanks."

"You're welcome." I turned on the radio and we listened to Maroon 5. Barry was flopping around in the backseat, and the girls started groaning and complaining. Looking in the rearview mirror, I could see Megan trying to shove him into a more vertical position. "I don't get it. Why do you hang out with those guys?"

Nell kept her eyes straight ahead. "They're not always such jerks. And I've known them since I was eight."

"Still, even if Barry hadn't gotten so weird, they were all stoned. You shouldn't be driving around with them."

"I don't, usually. But my car has a flat tire." I could feel her looking at me. "Don't you ever get wasted?"

"I don't like the taste of beer, and I smoked pot once and it made me paranoid." I wasn't about to explain to her how the smell of stale beer makes me sad and anxious. How it smells like failure. "How about you?"

"I'm weird enough as it is."

I laughed, trying to keep the grin on my face from getting too wide. Nell was talking to me. We were having a conversation.

Nell pointed. "Barry's driveway is coming up here on the right."

I pulled in, cutting the lights. We had already decided we'd try to drop Barry off without confronting his father, who apparently was a hard-ass, crew-cut, military type who thought Barry was a total loser. Not that I would argue with the guy, but I really didn't want to meet him while dumping his drunken son on his front lawn in the middle of the night, either.

By the time we wrestled Barry onto a chaise lounge, I was covered in cold sweat, imagining scary Papa Kramer bursting out the front door brandishing a shotgun. Once Barry was deposited, we jumped back into the Jeep, and I peeled out. Once I was sure we'd made a clean getaway, I slowed down. It would suck to get pulled over for speeding now after all we'd been through. We headed to Nell's house.

The girls were giddy with relief and gabbing the way girls do. Megan had snagged the front seat and was running off at the mouth like she'd known Nell and Katie all her life.

When we arrived at Nell's and I stopped the car, I turned to say good-bye. Katie had opened the door and the interior light had popped on. In the dim glow, Nell was looking at me with a thoughtful expression. Our eyes locked for a second before she blushed and looked away. "You girls will understand if I don't walk you to the door."

"Oh, sure. That's okay," Katie assured me, clueless.

I looked at Nell. "I avoided running into one bad-ass father tonight. No sense pressing my luck."

Her blush deepened. I could feel Megan's gaze darting between Nell and me, trying to figure out what we were talking about. "Yeah, sorry about that," Nell said.

"Me too. Whatever happened the other day—I'm sorry about that too."

"I know. See you later." With a smile I could tell was meant just for me, Nell got out of the car and followed Katie up the walk.

CHAPTER 20

Next morning, I woke up crazy happy. I'd never tell Megan, but I had to give her all the credit. If she hadn't made me go to that stupid carnival, I might never have had a chance to patch things up with Nell. The whole Barry mess was even worth it.

It was still early, but the morning was so fresh and cool, I couldn't stay in bed. As I passed Dad's room, I could hear Megan's little sleeping wheeze. The sound made me happy too. Living alone was okay. I'd proved that I could do it, but I slept easier with Megan in the house.

Once the coffee was brewed, I poured myself a big cup and took it out to the backyard. Sitting on a creaky lawn chair, I sipped the hot coffee, watching the bright sunrise warm the clouds, and listened to the birds.

I might just get to like it around here.

It was kind of frustrating, though, not being able to see over that stupid fence. Once I drained the mug, I headed back inside. I fought the urge to call Nell. Looking back on our conversation the night before, I knew we hadn't exactly made up—but we had reached a place where we could negotiate a truce.

No, we weren't best buddies again, not yet. But there was something I could finally bring myself to do. Since the whole kiss incident, I hadn't even looked at the footage we had taken that day. Now I decided to upload it onto the computer, maybe fool around with editing it a bit.

I watched those few recorded minutes over and over. I could never get tired of seeing Nell's face, listening to her voice. I watched it so many times, I think I fell into a trance, because I nearly jumped out of my chair when Megan came up behind me.

"I told you. Camp's great!" Megan had put a little Girl Scout enthusiasm into her voice as she talked into her cell. Who was she trying to kid? Oh, that's right. Mom. It seemed to be working. "No, the food's not bad and my bunkmates are really nice."

I twisted around to look at her. The little kid in me felt the urge to grab the phone from Megan and compete for one-on-one time with Mom. When I caught her attention, she rolled her eyes at whatever Mom was saying. "Okay. I'll talk to you again next week. Love you too." She ended the call. "That's done. Morning, bro."

Her eyes were still puffy from sleep, but they locked on the monitor, on the segment of the video where Nell went tumbling out of view. Then it was Megan on the screen, walking in front of me on the trail.

"Hey! You promised to delete that!" Megan tried reaching over my shoulder for the mouse.

I shrugged her away, laughing. "No, Megs. I'm keeping this. I need all the ammunition I can get."

"I look terrible. Am I actually that fat?" She tried lunging over me.

"Yes, you actually are. Look at that ass on you. It's the size of Texas."

"Very funny." She pushed me and we began tussling. Seeing as I'm about a foot taller, she didn't stand much of a chance.

We really got into it for a while. She'd almost gained control of the mouse and edged me off the chair, when something on the screen grabbed my attention. I shouted, "Cut it out! Stop!" I threw my arms around her in a bear hug and tossed her onto the couch.

She leapt back up on her feet, but I held my arm up, holding her back. My eyes were riveted on the monitor. "Oh my God," I breathed. "What the hell is that?"

Megan looked over my shoulder. "What? What is it?"

"See that? In the background?"

I turned down the audio, not wanting the sound of Megan's nagging voice to distract me from the image I had glimpsed on the screen. I rewound, Megan quickly walking backward in jerky steps. As she moved away from the camera, her angry face getting smaller, over her shoulder, back in the woods, was a large, indistinct figure.

I froze the frame. "There," I said. "See that?"

Megan studied the image for a second. "Hey!" she said. "Someone was spying on us."

"Someone?" I asked. "Or some*thing*?" It was just a dark form, contrasted against the even darker green shadows of the mountain laurel. But it was big. It was peering down at us from behind a huge tree.

"Oh, come on, Jakey," Megan said. "It's a man—hiding behind a tree. Maybe it's that Samuel guy."

I enlarged the picture, but it was out of focus. The resolution sucked. Too blurry to be able to really make out what was there. But something was there. "It can't be Samuel. Samuel's pretty tall, but he's really thin. Look at the shoulders on that thing."

"We were on our way to the swimming hole. Nell told me last night that everybody goes there. It could be anybody."

I couldn't take my eyes off the screen. My brain was racing. How could I make the image clearer? I was surprised when my voice came out in a whisper. "Look at it, Megs. It's all one dark, uniform color."

"So? You can't really see anything."

"If it was a person, you would be able to make out a shirt color or a difference for the skin. You would be able to figure out where the face ended and the scalp started. Whatever this is, it's all one color."

"It could be just the way the light's hitting him."

"Maybe. Or maybe it's something covered with brown fur from head to foot." I opened the browser. "Wait a sec." I followed a couple of links. A freeze-frame picture from the famous Patterson-Gimlin film appeared. "This is probably the best shot of a Bigfoot anybody's ever gotten."

"Or a bad shot of a guy in a monkey suit," scoffed Megan.

"No one's ever proved it's really a Bigfoot." I turned to look at her. "But no one's ever exposed it as a hoax, either. And believe me, they've been trying since 1967."

"I don't know." She sounded skeptical.

"I *do* know." I turned back to the computer, returning to my own film. "I've seen the thing, up close and personal." Frustrated, I pushed back away from the desk. "I've seen it and heard it. And smelled it. I know it's real. And it was right there! I had the camera trained on it—and I didn't get a clear shot!"

"So? You'll get a better shot next time."

"God! It was right there, watching *us*. And I was too busy fooling around to even notice." I was disgusted with myself. "Some kind of documentarian I'm turning out to be."

"How were you supposed to know what might be lurking in the woods?"

"That's the whole trick of filming a documentary. You never know when the moment's going to happen. The key is to be ready for *anything* all the time. And I wasn't ready. I missed it, and it might never happen again."

Megan placed her hands on my shoulders, bending over a little bit to get a closer look at the blurry image. "I don't know, bro, considering how many times you've run across this thing—he seems to be as interested in you as you are in him. You'll find each other again." She sounded a little scared.

"And next time, I'll be ready."

CHAPTER 21

Later that morning, Megan and I set out with the camera. But within a couple of hours, things started to fall apart. The air was close and muggy. Megan did a terrible job as on-camera talent—more like on-camera no-talent. She couldn't read a sentence of Nell's copy without flubbing the words. When ominous-looking clouds started rolling in, we were both ready to pack it in for the day. What had become obvious to me as we hiked—aimlessly, I'll admit—was that we needed a plan. And I knew that planning was something that Nell was really good at. I had to get her back on the team, which meant smoothing things over with her dad—a scarier prospect than running into an eight-foot monster in the middle of the night.

We weren't too far from home. Megan was trudging alongside me, texting as she walked.

"I can't believe you're even getting a signal out here. Who're you talking to?" I asked.

"Barry." She didn't take her eyes off the screen as her thumbs moved at warp speed.

"Barry?" I groaned. "What are you talking to him for?"

"He asked me if I wanted to go to a movie tonight, and I said yes."

I stopped in my tracks, grabbing her elbow so that she came to a halt too. "No way. You can't date Barry. He's too old for you. Not to mention the fact he's an idiot."

"Yeah, Grandma? Who's going to stop me?" She yanked her arm out of my grip. "It's not a date, anyway. At least I don't think so." Her brow crinkled. She looked disappointed. "A bunch of kids are going."

"The same bunch of stoners who were at the carnival?"

"Yeah, probably. Including Nell. I think she's going." She gave me a sly smile. "Want me to ask if you can come too?"

Sometimes I wish she didn't know me so well. "Fine. Tell him I'm coming too. But tell him we'll meet them there. I'm not letting you get into a car with that guy." It was better she drive around with her unlicensed brother.

Okay. I confess. The film was great. When was the last time I saw a movie the way a movie is supposed to be seen? Months. I didn't care that it was a low-rent rip-off of the Batman franchise. There was pounding music, rocking car chases, fantastic special effects. And I was in a crowd full of other teenagers sitting in a dark theater on a Saturday night eating popcorn and yelling through the action. I wasn't sitting with Nell, but she was only three seats down with the other girls, including my sister, who was out of Barry's immediate reach. As a matter of fact, it didn't seem like anybody was hooked up with anyone.

Nobody was high that night, either. Not yet, anyway. And as long as they were sober, the other guys were friendly enough. Even Barry was a normal human being.

Once the movie was over, we all stood in the bright lobby, looking out at the dark, rain-soaked parking lot. After a general discussion, everyone decided to grab a bite to eat at the diner on Route 202.

It seemed half the people in the county had the same idea, because the place was packed. Michael moved fast, grabbing the one open booth, and the rest of the guys piled in with a little bit of roughhousing. Megan slid in right next to Barry, who treated her to a hefty arm around her shoulders. Katie and a red-haired girl moved in a little more gracefully, then another guy pulled up a couple of chairs for Nell and himself. That's right. That left me the odd man out. I felt like walking back out into the rain, but I couldn't just leave Megan there with Barry. And I was hungry. I simply turned around and grabbed a stool at the counter, staring at my own sorry face in the long mirror that lined the wall. I was determined to concentrate on a brownie deluxe covered in hot fudge and vanilla ice cream, topped with walnuts and whipped cream. I prepared myself for the fight I was going to have with Megan when she wanted Barry to take her home.

After I placed my order, I leafed through a newspaper that had been left on the counter. When I felt someone glide onto the stool next to me, I didn't look up until I recognized the scent of mangos, and found myself staring into Nell's chocolate eyes.

"Hi, mind if I join you?"

"That's okay. Go back to the party." I looked down at the paper again, but I wasn't really reading anything. My heart was thudding.

"If you don't mind, I'd rather sit here." She pretended to read the paper too. Was I crazy, or did she sound shy all of a sudden?

"Fine by me. Can I order you something?"

"I'm not really hungry. I'll just have a cup of tea."

Nell's eyes widened with amazement when the mountainous dessert arrived, and I immediately asked for an extra spoon. We moaned with happiness as we dug in.

When we finally came up for air, Nell was looking at me again. "So, I gather that you've got Megan helping you out with the movie these days."

I finished licking my spoon. "Yeah, but we haven't gotten anywhere."

"That's too bad."

"We lack organizational skills."

"I'm good at that."

"I know."

"Do you think I could come back on board?" There was apology in her eyes again, and a sadness that I didn't understand.

"I never wanted you to leave."

"I know." She took a deep breath. "I'm not even going to try to explain anything. But, for reasons I don't want to go into, can we just keep this a secret from my parents for a while?"

"I guess." The idea of that made me uncomfortable. But at that point, I was going to go along with anything Nell wanted. And at the end of the day, what was one more secret?

Then Megan plopped down onto the empty stool on my other side. "Hey, bro—I'm going for a ride to some lake with Barry and—"

"Oh. No. You. Are. Not." I clasped my left hand tightly on the back of her neck, the way our dad did when we were little kids.

"But—"

"Forget it." With my free hand, I picked up my check from the counter and, still gripping Megan, started steering her toward the cashier and the exit. On the way out, we passed the booth, where the guys were having a loud discussion about those *Jackass* movies and the stunts they wanted to try. With any luck, Barry might kill himself before he got a chance to ask Megan out on a real date. Moving fast, I tossed a twenty on the table. "That's for my little sister's share of the bill. We have to get going. Our dad always waits up for Megan. Thanks. It was a really fun night. See you."

Luckily, Megan was so stunned by my swift and decisive action, she didn't put up much of a struggle. Thank God I still owned the older-sibling advantage—a remnant from the days when my mom used to put me in charge while she was at work. Just then I realized that Nell was trailing behind us, with a kind of lost expression on her face. I wouldn't have believed it was possible, but I was so intent on getting Megan safely away from Barry's clutches, I actually forgot about Nell for a second.

I turned to her and asked, "Can we give you a lift?"

"Yes," she said. "We need to finish our conversation."

CHAPTER 22

Megan stomped out of the diner in a major huff. Just to be mean, she snagged the front seat so I couldn't talk to Nell. Then she switched on the radio, finding some sappy emo ballad she knew I'd hate and cranking up the volume. If that was all the acting out she was going to do to get back at me for dragging her away from Barry, I could live with that.

We drove along and Megan finally thawed out some. She'd never let on, but I think she was secretly relieved that I'd gotten her out of a potentially risky situation. She turned to hang over the back of her seat and talk with Nell. I just wished she'd put on her seat belt. A fine, drizzling rain was falling, and a cool breeze blew in the open windows. Girls are amazing. I think they were yakking away about an author they both liked, but I could hardly follow their conversation. When some rap song about beating up girls and shooting cops came on, Megan blasted it even louder. That's where I drew the line. That pounding bass was giving me a headache. I snapped the radio off.

The abrupt silence in the car was strange. Megan immediately started to protest, but I cut her short. "Forget it. Can't we just have a little quiet?"

"Fine." Megan crossed her arms and slumped down in her seat. For a while, the only sounds were the rubbery rhythm of windshield wipers and the hiss of tires on wet pavement.

A deep, hollow note sounded somewhere in the distance. At first, I figured it was the distant rumble of thunder, but there wasn't enough crash in it. I thought it must be a foghorn, before I realized that was impossible. The closest ocean beach was more than a hundred miles away.

Then I knew what it was.

I pulled the Jeep onto the shoulder of the road and slammed on the brakes. The girls slid in their seats, each one crying out.

"Shut up!" I said, turning off the engine. "Listen!"

There it was again. That hollow, booming howl—a desperate, lonely cry in the night. I could feel it echo in my skull and bones, prickling fear and excitement through me like tiny needles. It was really happening, and this time I wasn't alone.

"What the hell...?" Megan breathed, looking at me, her eyes wide.

"What is that? A moose or something?" Nell's voice was shaky.

"It's something all right." I opened the car door.

"Where are you going?" demanded Nell anxiously.

"I have to get the camera. It's in the back."

"There's nothing to film!" Megan was on the hysterical side.

"The camera records audio too," I reminded her, trying to stay calm and in control of myself. "And if I can get that sound down, we'll really have something." Dashing to the back of the Jeep, I yanked open the rear door and grabbed the camera bag. I also retrieved the big flashlight I'd stowed back there the morning after my first nocturnal roadside encounter. Both girls had swiveled in their seats to watch me. I could just catch the glint of their eyes in the dark interior. Before I closed the door again, I said, "I'm sure we'll hear it better outside."

As I stepped around to the side of the car, the girls were whispering—loudly—as they spilled out. I didn't pay attention to what they were saying because I was straining to hear another roar. The rain had stopped, but there was still cloud cover, making for a moonless night. Nell and Megan tripped over each other in the dark, and Megan was giggling.

"*Ssshhhh!*" I hissed, worried that their fuss might scare off whatever was out there.

"Oh, fine, Mr. Librarian," Megan snarked back at me.

"Ouch!" cried Nell.

Megan mumbled an apology; she must have stepped on Nell's foot or something.

"Come on," I urged in a low voice. "Be quiet, or we won't hear anything." I pressed the camera's Power button and started scanning the horizon.

"All right, all right," Megan muttered, annoyed but willing to cooperate.

Nell moved next to me.

For several moments the three of us stood rooted in the scruffy weeds on the side of the road, listening, only to be serenaded by the usual sounds—the clicks and whirring of insects, the soft whisper of stirring leaves. Nell's shallow breathing near my ear. My own heartbeat.

I could feel the building tension in the girls. And the restlessness. "I guess that's it," I said. "But you did hear it, right?"

"We heard something," Nell said. "Something weird."

"It must be gone," said Megan.

"Yeah," I admitted. "The show's over for tonight." I was just about to suggest we get back in the Jeep, when we heard it again. And I say *we*, because when the howl started I looked at Megan and Nell, and as dark as it was, I saw the amazement and fear in their faces.

We turned our heads in the direction the sound was coming from. The wild, eerie wail rose up from the dense woods covering the steep ridge looming over the roadway. It seemed to hover over us before blowing away on the moist wind. As the sound faded, only silence was left in its wake, as if even the insects and small night creatures were listening for more.

None of us moved until finally Megan said, "Okay. That is officially the most bizarre thing I have ever heard in my entire life."

Nell touched my arm, sending a chill up my spine. "Did you record it?"

I looked down at the camera still in my hand. The red Power light winked at me. "Yes." I breathed out with relief. "But the power's getting low. Let's go back to the house and see what we've got."

The girls tumbled back into the car. I turned off the camera as I headed to the rear of the Jeep to stow away the gear. I'd hoped for a little more, but it was a start. That indistinct image I'd taped the other day was a blur, but it could prove to be a convincing blur. And I was fairly sure I'd managed to record that second cry. It had come from pretty far away—maybe a half a mile or so—but the camera was sensitive to sound.

I slid in the driver's side door. "Whoo!" I said with a grin. Nell was sitting up front and returned my smile, eyes shining. She looked as excited as I felt. Our eyes locked for a second— and I smelled it before I felt it.

Something tried to rip my arm off.

I lost my balance, hanging half-in, half-out of the Jeep, kicking as I struggled to pull away from the powerful force. The girls were screaming. I think I screamed. One second I had been looking deep into Nell's eyes. The next, searing pain stabbed through my neck, arm, and shoulder. The thing's stench moved around us like a fog; even as I yelled and gasped for breath, it filled my nostrils and mouth like poison gas.

I was aware of both Nell and Megan's weights as they threw themselves on me, clutching, pulling against the monster. We were all fighting together. I couldn't see what, exactly, had a death grip on me, beyond a solid wall of dark fur.

Suddenly, a metallic flash gleamed near my face, moving with a pounding regularity. Megan wielded the flashlight like a club, beating the creature that gripped my arm, while Nell was hanging on to me around the waist, hauling me toward her with all her strength.

Between my own cries and the girls' shouts, I made out the heavy breathing of the creature. As Megan struck at it, the breathing turned to grunts of pain and anger.

I saw stars for a second when one of Megan's blows accidentally cracked me in the temple. Nell plopped her butt on my stomach and leaned on the horn.

The surprise of the horn must have startled the thing enough to loosen its hold on me, because all at once I was free and able to curl back into the Jeep, the weight of Nell on my lap anchoring me.

Nell turned the ignition, hit the gas, and gunned it.

The Jeep lurched forward, tires squealing and spraying gravel.

We sped away, hooting and shouting in both terror and triumph. Nell still leaned on the horn; the driver's-side door swung freely. I don't know how she managed to keep driving, but after a few hundred yards or so, Nell pulled over long enough to move her butt off my stomach so I could slam and lock the door and take the wheel again. Then we continued to Uncle Horace's house, safe for the moment behind that weird fence of his.

CHAPTER 23

Running from the Jeep to the house, we burst in, making all kinds of racket, flipping on every light. The door slammed so hard against the wall, a small shower of plaster hit the floor. We were hooting and hollering, when suddenly, Nell stopped and said in a hushed voice, "*Hey, sshhhh!* Hey! We're going to wake up your dad."

Megan and I just sort of froze in our spots and our eyes locked. Next thing you know, the two of us were laughing like lunatics—like someone had given us both a hit of some powerful laughing gas. Finally, while I was trying to get some air, I caught the expression on Nell's face. She was looking at us like we'd lost our minds, which I guess, in a way, we had.

"No worries there," Megan gasped. "Our dad's AWOL."

Nell's face got all serious. "What do you mean?"

"We mean he's away. Out of town. Has been for weeks. Haven't heard from him in days," I said.

"Where is he?"

"Nicaragua," Megan said.

"No, Megs. Guatemala."

"Nicaragua, Guatemala, Kuala Lumpur, Oompa-Loompa Land." Megan flopped down on the sofa. "What difference does it make?"

"You mean you guys have been living here on your own?" Nell asked.

"Yep," said Megan. "Just us chickens."

Nell was amazed. "That's cool. My parents would never let me stay on my own."

"That's because they're responsible adults who actually make sure you're safe and taken care of." What would Dad think of what just happened? Mom would've flipped, that's for sure—especially because Megan was there.

A dark look came over Nell's face—for a second I thought she might cry—before she said in a low voice, "My parents aren't so great. Not always. And they work overtime to make up for it."

I was just about to ask her what she meant, when Megan said, "I don't know about you guys, but I have to pee. I can't believe I didn't pee my pants back there."

"I was scared enough to," said Nell.

"I've never been so scared in my life," agreed Megan.

"Same here. My heart's still pounding." Nell patted her chest with the flat of her hand, as if to calm her palpitations.

"You know what, Jake?" Megan turned to me. "Tomorrow, you have to find that Samuel guy."

My stomach did a flop. I was losing my crack team. But after all, it made sense. We had just come face-to-face with the fact that we were dealing with a genuinely dangerous situation. I couldn't expect the girls to take that risk.

"I understand." It was hard to talk around the lump that was forming in my throat.

Megan was staring at me. I was trying to hide it, but I knew she could read the disappointment in my face. "Understand what?"

"Why you guys wouldn't want to go on. I don't blame you for being scared."

"Scared? Who's scared?" Nell was indignant.

I shrugged. "You are. You just said so."

"Weren't you?" Nell demanded.

"Well, yes, but—"

"We said 'scared,' not 'scared off,'" Megan pointed out. "Of course we were scared. So were you, bro. A big, stinky monster just tried to rip you apart."

Nell crossed her arms and glared at me. "Don't forget—*we* rescued *you*."

"Yeah," growled Megan, mimicking Nell's stance. "You'd have been a McDonald's Monster Meal if it wasn't for us. If you think you're doing this without us, you're crazy."

I shook my head. "Frankly, at this point I think we're all crazy." I grabbed the camera bag. "But what's even crazier is that we haven't listened to the recording yet." I pulled out the camera, and because the battery was pretty much dead and I had to plug it in anyway, I connected it right to the computer. The girls stood behind me, looking over my shoulders. Nell's dark hair brushed my right arm like a whisper of silk. Megan's impatient breath puffed loudly into my left ear. Apparently, she'd forgotten she'd needed to pee. While we waited, I asked, "So, why do I have to find Samuel?"

"Because he knows what's what. Enough of all these random encounters," Megan said. "The only way to catch this thing is to be prepared. We have to get to where it goes before it does. We have to be there ahead of it and ready to roll."

"And Samuel's the one who knows where to go," Nell added.

"Right," I said. "But it's not like I haven't been looking for him." We all fell silent as tonight's images showed up on the monitor. Not that there was really anything you could call an image—just dark blurs and flashy smears of headlights as my shaky camera work panned the area. We listened to our Three Stooges routine, tripping and shushing and cursing in the dark.

Then all was silent. We shut right up as soon as the wild, eerie yowling began. Coming from the speakers, it sounded even stranger and more remote than when we'd heard it in the open. As the sound of it filled the room, it chilled the air.

No one spoke while I played it back three times, until finally Megan said, "Well, bro. I think you got it."

"My question is—" Nell began. Her voice was low and thoughtful. "If we thought that first call was about half a mile away…"

Instantly, I knew where she was going with this.

Megan burst in—her eyes lighting up with realization. "Then how the hell did it jump on us so fast?"

I turned to the girls. "Because there are two of them. The one screaming its head off up on the ridge…"

"And the one it was calling to." Nell said.

CHAPTER 24

Considering all the excitement the night before, it was a wonder I fell asleep. But after I'd taken Nell home, I crashed, dead to the world. The first shafts of morning sunlight hitting my face woke me right up, and I was dressed and downstairs before six. Imagine my surprise when I found Megan hard at work, sifting through the papers on Horace's beat-up old desk.

"Have you even been to bed yet?"

Megan didn't look up from the papers in front of her. "Couple of hours, maybe."

"What are you doing?"

"Well, I could tell that you've been going through this stuff, but it's such a mess. I thought I'd try to organize it some. Maybe it'd all make more sense."

That's my little sister. She might come across as an airhead slacker, but when she gets something in her head, she pursues it like a relentless ferret. (Come to think of it, she even looks a little like one.) Usually it's something stupid—like learning lyrics to some dopey song, but there's a reason why she's a straight-A student.

"Good luck." I yawned. "You want some coffee?"

"Sure," said Megan.

"You're going to need it." I knew what a mess those notes were in. I turned to head into the kitchen, but she stopped me.

"Hey, wait a second," she said. "I wanted to ask you— when the heck was this taken?" She held up a photograph. I stepped over to get a better look at it. Taking it in my hand, I peered at the picture. It was creased and yellowed, and the shot was out of focus. A kid stood on a dock wearing a plaid shirt and blue jeans, holding a fishing pole, squinting into the sun. The boy looked oddly familiar.

"I don't know," I said. "It's pretty old. Looks like it dates back to the 1950s."

"Very funny," Megan snapped, snatching the picture out of my hand.

"What?" I asked. What was she snarling about?

"How could it be that old?" She gazed at the photo. "It's a picture of you, isn't it?"

I snorted. "You're nuts."

"I am not," Megan protested. "I swear to God." She looked closer again, her nose practically touching the picture. "Well, maybe it's not you, but it sure could be you." She looked up at me. "Hey! What did old Horace look like?"

"I have no idea. Never met the man."

"My guess? It's a picture of Horace when he was about your age."

That wasn't such a nutty thought.

"I bet Samuel could tell us."

"Well, we'd better get a move on." I turned back up the stairs.

"Hey!" Megan protested. "I thought you were going to make coffee."

"No time if we're going to find Samuel this morning," I called down over my shoulder. "I have to be at work by nine. See if you can find some cookies in the kitchen."

"What for?" said Megan.

"Samuel has a sweet tooth. I don't want to visit him empty-handed."

As we drove up the old logging road, it was a relief to see the plywood door pulled away from the entrance to Samuel's wreck of a cabin. And there he was—right out front—heating something up in a battered saucepan over an open fire. He was wearing a pair of hiking boots, grubby long johns, and a too-big flannel shirt. He looked up at the approaching Jeep with eyes like a scared rabbit. I quickly stuck my head out of the open window and called out, "Hey, Samuel. It's me, Jake. Remember—Horace's kin?" I was afraid he was going to bolt into the woods.

"'Kin'?" Megan muttered. "What is this, *The Beverly Hillbillies*?"

"Shut up, Megs." I pulled the Jeep to a stop. "That's just the way he talks."

As we got out of the car Samuel visibly relaxed and stood to greet us, hands on his hips, a big gap-toothed smile on his face. "Well, lookee here. I got company."

I reached out to shake his dirt-caked hand. "Hey there," I said. "It's good to see you. I want you to meet my sister, Megan. She's come to spend the summer."

"Hello there, young lady." Samuel dropped my hand to pump Megan's. "It's a real pleasure."

"Same here." Megan smiled at him like she was meeting the Prince of Wales. "It's an honor. I've heard so much about you."

"Well, what have you heard, Miss Megan?" Samuel dropped her hand and gave her a quizzical look.

"I've heard all about your fascinating work, studying the Sasquatch."

Samuel folded his arms across his chest. "Heard about that, have you?"

"Yes, sir," Megan said. "Heard about it—and last night we had an encounter."

"Really?" Samuel's eyes went from Megan's to mine to confirm she was telling the truth.

"Yes," I said. "That's why we're here. We've come to ask if you'll help us keep tradition going. We want to follow in your footsteps—and Horace's. We want to learn everything you can teach us about Sasquatch."

"Well now. That's a mighty big request. You think you're up to it?" He squinted at us critically.

"Yes, sir," Megan said.

Samuel shook his head. "But you're just a little girl."

"I'm tough."

"She is," I assured him.

"Share my breakfast, and we can talk about it." Samuel stepped over to the fire to stir his meal with a stick.

"That would be great, Samuel." Megan held up a box of sugar wafers. "We brought dessert."

"Well, come on, then."

I peered into the saucepan with apprehension. I wouldn't put it past Samuel to be serving up possum stew or braised swamp weed. But in the pot were the contents of a can of baked beans, simmering gently. Phew.

"Excuse me, Samuel?" Megan asked.

"Yes, young lady?"

"Before we eat, can I ask you a question?"

"Of course, darlin'."

Megan pulled the old snapshot out of the back pocket of her shorts. "Can you tell me who this is?"

Samuel pulled a bent pair of wire-framed reading glasses out of his shirt pocket and perched them on the end of his beaky nose. He studied the photo. "Well, of course I didn't know him back in those days, but this sure looks like your Uncle Horace."

"Told you!" Megan beamed at me.

"Why didn't you tell me I looked so much like Horace?" I asked him.

He took off the specs, tucked them away again, and handed me the snapshot. "Well, it's self-evident, isn't it? Since when do

I need to tell a family member that he looks like somebody he was related to?"

"You have a point there." How was Samuel to know that my great-uncle had been a complete stranger to me?

"Well, I think our meal's just about ready. Let me just pop in the house and grab a couple of extra plates."

Megan and I settled down on one of two logs that were set up in classic campground formation, listening as Samuel clanged and banged in the shadowed interior of the little cabin. When he finally emerged, he was clutching a couple of tin plates straight out of a cowboy movie. Under his arm, he carried something big and white.

He put the plates down on an old card table he'd set up under a big oak tree. When he turned around, he held the white object in both his hands, presenting it to us like it was a treasure.

"I thought you two might be interested in taking a look at this." Samuel stooped slightly to show us what he was holding.

It took me a second to realize what it was. "Oh, my God! It's a footprint!"

"Huh?" Megan asked. Samuel's eyes were glowing with excitement.

"It's a plaster cast of a footprint," I explained. Samuel nodded. I looked into his eager face. "And I'm guessing it was made somewhere around here?"

"That's right, son," Samuel said. "Horace and I made it, about ten years ago—from a print we found at the reservoir."

I reached for it, and Samuel passed it to me like he was bestowing me with the Crown Jewels. The plaster felt rough and cool in my hands. The cast was at least eighteen inches in length, maybe ten in width—the contours of five toes, the ball of the foot, and the heel clearly defined. Megan murmured an appreciative, "Cool."

"Let me tell you," Samuel continued. I could hear the pride in his voice. "Prints like these? They are not easy to come by. I don't know what it's like in the Pacific Northwest—never been there—but in New England? To get proof with a print like this? It takes some doing."

"Why is that?" Megan asked respectfully.

"New England woodlands are tricky. Rocky, for one thing. And all the deciduous trees dropping leaves. You get a layer of debris always falling on a trail, obscures any tracks you might be looking for. But I got this one right after a big storm. Beautiful, isn't it?"

"I'll say," I said. "May I keep it?"

I could see the reluctance in Samuel's face. He reached to take the cast back from me, then withdrew his hands. His face was grave. "Sure. Guess it really is time to pass the baton. But you got to take good care of it. It's the only one left. Horace had a couple at his house, but they were wrecked one year when a pipe burst and flooded his study."

"I promise," I said, my expression as solemn as his. "I'll take good care of it."

He crossed his arms and nodded. "I believe you will. Now. Let's get down to business." As he served up the beans, he started sharing everything he knew. "First thing you got to know about Sassy? He's always hungry. The thing that drives him—day in and day out—is food. He's an omnivore. Eats everything, like us. Got a sweet tooth too." He winked at Megan as he crammed in a mouthful of cookies.

CHAPTER 25

"That's some bruise you got on your ear there," Nell remarked when I joined her at the register. It was her morning to ring and mine to bag. She looked remarkably bright-eyed and bushy-tailed.

I touched where Megan had cracked me in the head with the flashlight last night. It was sore, all right. "I forgot about that." After a night's sleep and having the meeting with Samuel already, it was hard to believe the attack was less than twelve hours ago. Rubbing the tender spot, I said, "This one is Megan-inflicted. But you should see the bruises on my upper arm." I lifted the sleeve of my shirt a tiny bit—just enough to give her a hint of the deep purple welts that had blossomed from elbow to shoulder overnight.

"Whoa," she breathed. "That looks bad. What are you going to tell everybody?"

"That's why I'm wearing this stupid football jersey," I explained. "The sleeves are long enough to cover most of it. Hopefully nobody will notice."

Nell gave me that evil little smile that makes me go all light-headed. "All dressed up like a real jock. Maybe you'll get invited to try out for the team."

"God, I hope not." My face went red. I loved and hated it when she teased me.

She eyed me critically, wrinkling her nose a bit. "Nah. I guess you're too skinny."

"Lucky me," I said.

"They still might ask you about that ear," Nell reminded me.

"I'll just have to tell them my sister hit me in the head with a flashlight." I grinned, and the conversation had to stop there, as shoppers started lining up. It got so busy we didn't really get a chance to talk again until our lunch break. Over Nell's meatball grinder and my tuna sub, we decided to meet at my house after our shift so that I could fill her in on the meeting with Samuel and how we were going to proceed.

When I got home around six, there was no sign of Megan. By the appearance of the neat piles on Horace's desk, she had made good on her promise to organize the Sasquatch material. It looked like she'd spent hours sorting through all the stuff. The computer was still on in the living room. The kitchen was tidy, and I could tell by the smear of purple on the knife tossed in the sink that she'd had a PB&J for lunch.

When Nell got to the house, I was just coming down the stairs after making sure Megan wasn't taking a nap. I'd already checked the backyard. I'd even looked in the woodshed and the cellar.

Worry must have shown on my face, because when I answered the door, Nell said right away, "What's wrong?"

I stepped aside to let her in. "Megan's not here."

"So?"

"So—she doesn't have a car. She's out there somewhere by herself."

Nell got what I was saying. "Right. And we know what else is out there."

"Right. And I didn't specifically tell her not to go out by herself, but you'd think she would be smart enough to know it's not a good idea."

"Have you tried her cell phone?"

"Sure. But either she's not getting a signal or it's turned off. The calls go straight to voice mail."

"It's really warm today. Maybe she just went for a swim. Want me to take a run up to the swimming hole and check?"

"No!" Maybe I was a little too emphatic. Nell took a step backward and looked startled. "No," I insisted, but in a softer voice. "It's not any more safe for you than her out there—I think now's a good time to start using the buddy system. Nobody goes wandering around the woods alone."

Nell protested. "I've been hiking these trails most of my life, and nothing's ever happened to me."

"Something happened last night," I reminded her.

She went pale, and her eyes got big. "You've got a point."

"But I'm sure you're right. She probably went for a swim. Let's go get her."

Megan wasn't at the swimming hole. As far as we could tell, she wasn't anywhere. We followed trail after trail, calling her name until it started to get dark, and then we had no choice but to head back to the house. I was so worried I felt nauseous, but I tried not to show it.

As we made our way back, I said, "You know, I've been doing a lot of research online. There's a lot of Native American folklore about Sasquatch."

"That's really interesting," said Nell. "What are the stories?"

"For one thing," I said, feeling the blood pound in my ears, "there are tales about clans of big hairy beasts snatching young Indian maidens for brides."

"Well, if our Bigfoot grabs your sister, he'll get more than he bargained for," Nell said.

"Yeah, he'll probably beg us to take her back." I laughed, but I didn't really think anything was funny at the moment.

There was still no sign of Megan when we walked in through the kitchen door. I turned to Nell. "You might as well go home. I don't want your parents to worry about you."

"No, it's okay," she assured me. "I can wait with you for a while."

I'd wanted to ask before—now seemed the right time. "So, where do your parents think you are?"

Nell blushed. "I told them I was going to Katie's."

"You shouldn't lie to them. It's not like they're exactly in love with me as it is. No sense in making the situation worse. There's nothing more you can do here. You should go home."

"No. I'd rather stay."

"What's the point?" I was really worried. I couldn't stop picturing how it would be—finding Megan all broken and bloody in the woods. What it would be like to tell our parents.

"Maybe we should call someone," said Nell.

"Like who?"

"Mr. Morgan, the sheriff. Or the state police. They could help us find her."

"No one's going to be able to find anything in the dark." I started to panic.

That's when the sweep of headlights lit the living room.

"What the hell?" I yanked open the front door, stepping into the warm night air.

"Bye, Barry," Megan sang as she slammed the passenger door of Barry's Mustang. She was holding a huge pink teddy bear.

If Barry saw me on the porch, he ignored the fact. As soon as the door was closed, he put the car in reverse and peeled out of the driveway.

"Where the hell have you been?" I demanded. Right away, I noticed that Megan swayed as she walked. She was drunk.

She ignored me. Looking at Nell, she shot her a big, goofy smile. "Hey, there, Nelliekins! Barry took me to Lake Compounce. Did you know that it's the oldest amusement park in continuing operation in the whole US of A?"

Nell crossed her arms and stood aside to let Megan pass into the house. "Yeah," she said dryly. "As a matter of fact, I did."

Now I knew how my dad felt when he was so mad he wanted to hit me. It was hard to stop myself from slapping

Megan across her face. I started shaking with rage. Tension pulled my fingers into tight fists. That was no good—I was ready to punch her, pummel her, smash her. I let Nell get between Megan and me as we followed her into the house.

"What have you been drinking?" Nell asked her.

"You ever have a root beer float spiked with Southern Comfort? It is deeelicious!"

"Can't say that I have." Nell watched Megan throw herself on the couch.

"And Barry won me this little cutie pie. He sure can throw a baseball!" She held the stupid bear up over her face, then started kissing it on the nose. That's when I noticed how red and raw the skin around her mouth looked. I knew what that meant. Megan had been doing some heavy making out.

I still wanted to punch Megan—but I wanted to kill Barry. It was bad enough he'd touched her—worse, he was drunk too. Driving my sister around. I was worried about monsters in the woods when I should have been worried about an asshole behind the wheel.

I was so pissed I couldn't speak. Nell seemed to sense how I was feeling because she assumed the role of bad cop, giving me a chance to gain some control of myself. As a matter of fact, my own mother couldn't have done better.

"So," Nell began. She was glaring at Megan with a stern expression. "Do you know what you just put us through?"

"What are you talking about?" Megan looked at Nell with wide, innocent eyes. Her smudged mascara and eyeliner made her look like a demented raccoon.

"We've been worried sick about you," Nell said. "We searched everywhere."

"Geez, I went out and had a little fun. I'm not a prisoner or anything."

"No. But you should be more considerate—especially after what happened to us last night. You should have called Jake—told him where you were going."

"He would've just said no," Megan grumbled.

"You bet your ass," I growled.

"See?" Megan looked to Nell for sympathy. She wasn't going to get any.

"At the very least, you should have left a note so that he wouldn't worry."

"He would have worried no matter what." Megan's gaze shifted to the blank eyes of the stuffed animal.

"Well, anyway," Nell huffed like an old-lady schoolteacher. "This whole evening so far has been a huge waste of time. I came here to talk about Bigfoot. Go jump in the shower and get yourself straight. Jake and I'll throw something together for dinner. Then we can have our meeting."

"Fine," Megan said in an equally huffy voice. Dragging herself and the bear off the sofa, she tramped up the stairs.

Nell turned to me. "So, what have you got to eat?"

My anger simmered down as we got busy in the kitchen. Nell had managed to defuse the situation, and I was beginning to feel relief. At least my sister wasn't dead under a rock somewhere. She was home safe, and I had refrained from beating the living crap out of her. "Thanks." I filled a big pot with water for pasta and showed Nell what we had to make dinner.

"That's okay," Nell said lightly. "I could see how upset you were."

"I wanted to kill her."

"No. I just think you were really scared." Nell looked up from chopping onions. "You really care about her."

I put the pot on the stove and turned on the burner. "It's just…it's always been her and me. My dad was never around. And since I was about eight, Mom left us alone together while she worked at the hospital. I've always been in charge. She's always been my responsibility."

"And you take it seriously. That's a good thing." Nell started sautéing the onions. We stood side by side at the stove for a while, listening to the onions hiss in the hot oil. They smelled good.

I stared down into the water in the big pasta pot. It was nowhere near boiling. Finally I said, "I don't think I can handle this. I think I need to call my mom—tell her to come and get Megan."

"You can't do that," Nell said softly, but somehow adamant.

"That's the only way I can think of to protect her."

"She trusts you. If you call your mom, she won't trust you anymore." I glanced sidelong at her. She looked sad. "You can't do that to your sister."

"I don't know what else to do," I admitted. "She's only fourteen."

"Look, I know you were really freaked out—and it's obvious Barry's not your favorite person, but he's not as bad as you think he is, and Megan's not as stupid. You have to admit, nothing really happened."

"But—"

Nell looked at me with those big, dark eyes. "If you call your mom, she'll take you both back to Norwalk," Nell pointed out. "No more Operation Bigfoot." She turned away to dump ground beef in with the onions, breaking it up with the wooden spoon.

"Right," I said.

We were just putting the plates of spaghetti on the table when Megan shuffled in wearing a huge T-shirt that hung to her knees like a nightgown. Her short hair stood up in damp spikes, and her face was scrubbed clean. She was a little green around the gills, but more with it. She glanced at the food warily. "I don't know if I can eat that."

"You'll feel better once you have something in your stomach," Nell said, and we all took a place at the table.

We slurped up the food for a while in silence. I had already decided to follow Nell's advice and not say anything about Megan's outing with Barry. I'd find another time to lay down the law about running around behind my back. "You know, while we were out in the woods before"—I couldn't resist giving Megan a nasty look—"I started thinking. We've wasted a lot of time searching for this thing. What if we lured it—made it come to us?"

"Like a trap?" Nell looked at me with a spark of interest in her eyes.

"Not necessarily a trap," I said. "Just…leave out some bait, something it won't be able to resist."

"Samuel said it's always looking for food," Megan said, her mouth full of spaghetti. For someone who didn't think she could eat, she was sure shoveling it down. "This is pretty good. Do you think Bigfoot likes pasta?"

"I don't think we can leave out just anything," Nell said. "You know, my mother's always going on about natural foods and the importance of a macrobiotic diet—how it's healthy to eat locally grown food in season. This creature—or creatures—don't get their stuff at the supermarket. They don't eat fruit trucked in from Florida. I think we should use organic food—nothing sprayed with pesticides or covered with wax to look shiny—stuff that grows around here. Otherwise they might get sick."

"Mr. Pelletier buys some locally grown produce, and there's the farmers market," I said.

"And my mom has an organic garden loaded with all kinds of vegetables."

"Samuel told us they're omnivores," Megan said. "They like meat too. He said they eat game when they can catch it, and fish and frogs."

"And eggs," I said to Nell. "The eggs from your mom's hens would probably be all right for them to eat." *And venison*, I thought, remembering the panicked eyes of the deer fleeing from its predator. We could find a locally raised side of beef.

By the end of our spaghetti dinner, we had planned a regular banquet for our big-footed friends.

CHAPTER 26

Megan was supposed to come with me to the farmers market, but I let her sleep in. I'd heard her in the bathroom in the middle of the night, and from the way it sounded I figured the spaghetti hadn't stayed down. Before I left, I checked my email, hoping there would be a message from my dad miraculously telling me that he was on his way home—let *him* figure out what to do about Megan—but no such luck. I scrolled through pages of old messages, looking for the last one I'd received from him. Almost two weeks ago. I should've been worried about him too, but how much worrying can one guy do? It wasn't the first time my father had disappeared into the deepest wilds of unknown lands without sending any word home— just ask my mother. His vanishing acts were a big problem in their marriage.

I made a little detour on my way to the farmers market. Barry's Mustang was the last car to pull into the employees' parking lot with only minutes to spare before the store opened. I'd have to conduct my business with him in record time.

As Barry stumbled from the car, I slid out of the Jeep and crossed to him in two strides. Before he knew what was happening, I'd pushed him against the side of the Mustang. I hoped his sorry butt left a dent. His hands flew up defensively, his eyes wide with surprise. "Whoa!"

Crazy adrenaline was pounding through my head and muscles. "Listen," I hissed, seeing my spit splatter his face. My grip twisted the front of his shirt and I could smell stale alcohol on his breath. "You keep away from my sister. She's just a kid!" I released him, flinging him back against the car again.

"Hey, dude. Easy," Barry said, his hands still up, palms facing me. "You don't get it."

"Oh, I get it." My fists balled into weapons; I wanted to kill him all over again. "A drunk fourteen-year-old is an easy piece of ass for a shithead like you."

"No man, it's not like that." Barry put on this wide-eyed, innocent face. "I really like Megan. And she likes me. I would never hurt her."

"Hurt her? You were driving drunk—you could have killed her!" I poked him in the chest, hard, like Nell's father had poked me. "I'm not going to give you another chance." On any other day, Barry might have been able to cream me, but I was so crazy mad at him at that minute that if he'd tried to fight me, I would have ripped him to shreds.

"Jake, man, you got to believe me."

"No, I don't." I backed away, leaving Barry staring at me, mouth open as I jumped into the Jeep. Just before I drove away, I called to him. "Keep away from my sister!"

Just when he was sure I was really on my way out of the parking lot, but still close enough to hear him, Barry shouted, "Only if she tells me to, douchebag."

I wasn't shaking anymore by the time I got back to the house. As a matter of fact, I was feeling more relaxed than I had in days. I almost felt good. I found some great stuff at the farmers' market—peaches, watermelon, and local honey. I almost bought a couple of chickens, but I wasn't ready to feed old Bigboy any dead things. I didn't want to stimulate his appetite for fresh meat; let him keep hunting those frogs.

By ten o'clock Megan was ready to go, and Nell had arrived with a basket of eggs, some green beans, a zucchini, and a tub of strawberries. We spent the rest of the morning setting up what we called "feeding stations," where we placed a variety of food, keeping track of what we left where. The plan was to check back in a couple of days and see if we got any activity.

Of course, we knew that Bigfoot wasn't the only animal roaming the woods in search of food. And when we returned to the feeding stations as scheduled, there was plenty of evidence of animal interest. Each site was crawling with insects. White droppings marked where birds had picked over the piles of gnawed detritus left by squirrels and other rodents. But when we visited the place where we'd left the eggs, they were just gone—along with the jar of honey. We'd left them alongside the trail where I'd had my first experience, near the barricade of slender trunks that was now no more than a pile of sticks. A nearby tree stump had made a nice buffet table, providing a flat enough surface so that the eggs wouldn't roll off.

"Are you sure this is where we left the eggs?" Megan asked.

"Positive," Nell said as she wrote her observations in a spiral-bound notebook.

"Maybe it was a raccoon or something." Megan circled the stump, eyeing the ground around it with interest.

"A raccoon would have left a mess." I remembered what it was like to clean up after the annoying critters. "There'd be broken shells all over the place. And a raccoon would have probably just dumped out the honey and licked the jar clean right here. It wouldn't have taken everything away."

"It wouldn't have been able to," Nell agreed. "Even if it could hold stuff in its little hands, they run on all fours."

"I think this is the spot," I said. "This is where we should set up surveillance."

CHAPTER 27

Considering what we knew about Sasquatch activity, we figured the best time for our stakeout was late afternoon. I brought the tripod, and we took care setting everything up so that the camera was concealed in the foliage but still able to get a clear shot of the area around the stump. After the food was laid out and the camera positioned, we burrowed our way into a dense bramble thicket several yards away from the buffet stump. Once we settled in as comfortably as possible, there was nothing else to do but wait.

And wait.

And wait.

"God, my foot's asleep," Nell complained. Megan had been going on for some time about the ants that were trying to crawl up her pant legs. Me? I had been wishing that I'd remembered to spray on mosquito repellent. They'd been feasting on my neck from the minute I'd hunkered down. We got so squirrelly in our cramped little Bigfoot blind that one minute we were griping and poking each other trying to get comfortable, and the next minute we were giggling over nothing like little kids in church. We took turns shushing each other. Nothing was going to come close to us if we kept making such a racket.

As we sat and waited, the light filtering through the canopy changed from bright yellow-green to golden, then deepened to a burning reddish-orange as the early-evening shadows deepened. By then the three of us had fallen into a drowsy inertia, too bored and stiff to even complain anymore. I think

Megan even fell asleep for a while, lucky enough to be able to lean against the base of a tree.

My own eyelids were growing heavy, my leg muscles were cramping, and my stomach had been rumbling for at least an hour. But the need to take a whiz was the most urgent problem. Then I caught a whiff of that foul, wet-dog-dipped-in-poop smell, and before I even realized what that meant, I heard a twig snap and the rustle of dried leaves. Blood rushed to my ears, and the skin all over my body prickled in goose bumps. I touched Megan's shoulder, then Nell's, putting a finger to my lips to signal silence. Rising to a crouched stance behind the camera, I lined up the viewfinder.

As the creature moved into our line of vision, I was so excited I could barely breathe. Its massive bulk filled the camera frame—but it had come up from behind where we were hidden, so all I could see were its broad shoulders and the back of its fur-covered head. It moved with a heavy, plodding gait, and I could feel the impact of each of its steps as it moved to the stump. It was definitely going after those eggs.

"Holy shit," I heard Megan breathe, and I would've pinched her, but I was afraid that would make her yelp. I couldn't even shoot her a dirty look, because I didn't want to glance away from what I was observing, afraid that if I broke my gaze, the creature might fade away like smoke. I grabbed her wrist and squeezed, a soundless, urgent plea for silence.

"What's that lump coming out of its shoulder?" I heard Nell whisper. The creature was hunkered over the stump, gathering up the eggs, and I noticed what Nell was talking about. In the space where the head and shoulders met, there seemed to be a domed growth, covered in the same pelt of reddish-brown fur. It wasn't until a glint of reflected light shone from the bulge that we all realized at once what we were seeing.

Eyes.

Staring back at us.

"A baby," Nell gasped in an awed whisper. "It's a female! She's holding a baby!"

At the sound of Nell's voice, the creature straightened her spine, becoming still and alert. I reached to the girls on either side of me, placing a steadying hand on their shoulders, and the three of us froze, not even daring to breathe.

Turn around, turn around, turn around! I was screaming in my head. I needed to get a shot of the female's face and was desperate to get a clear view of the infant.

Brrinnnggg. Brrinnnggg. Brrinnnggg!

The artificial shriek of Megan's cell phone sounded through the quiet clearing like the sudden wail of a police siren. The abrupt noise caused us all to jump and cry out. I totally freaked, knocking over the camera and getting tangled in the tripod.

The creature turned, her huge dark eyes widened with panic. Before I could get a good look at the rest of her face, she took off in a loping run, curling herself protectively around her baby.

"Oh no!" Megan called after the mama Sasquatch. "Come back! We won't hurt you."

"Shut the hell up," I barked angrily. It was her fault I didn't get the shot.

In spite of the thorns tearing at her face and hair, Nell plunged through the brambles. "Let's find out where she's going!"

Megan was right behind her. I was still floundering in the underbrush, trying to recover the camera as I called out, "No! Wait!"

I had no choice but to leave the equipment as I scrambled after the girls. They were both tearing along the trail like deer, legs flying. From where I was bringing up the rear, the Sasquatch was already out of view. I was soon out of breath, but not because I was winded. I had a really bad feeling.

With good reason.

We were running through the narrow trail that led to the swimming hole, where steep inclines rose sharply on either side. I was losing ground and could just make out the brief white flash of the soles of Megan's sneakers in the shadowy woods as she followed the trail that curved to the right.

Then—a howl, a deep, roaring bellow that could crack the sky open.

My head swiveled, instinctively looking for the source of the noise. High up on the ridge to the left, still howling, galloping down the hill at a thunderous pace and threatening to come between the girls and me, was the male.

A jolt of adrenaline shot through me. My legs and lungs burned with it. The girls screamed. I don't know how I did it, but I reached the point in the path where the Sasquatch was headed, putting myself between the creature and the girls.

It was terrifying, watching that thing hurtle down the hill toward me, eyes blazing, huge yellow teeth bared, arms shaking belligerently. All the while its unearthly roar filled my head. I shot a glance over my shoulder and was sickened to see that the girls had stopped a couple of yards up the path, frozen with horror and indecision. I stood my ground, staring up at the beast as it bore down on us, and yelled, "Go! Run! Get the hell out of here! Now!"

Out of the corner of my eye, I spied a fallen branch. Moving swiftly, I picked it up, holding it in front of me. It was reassuringly heavy; I could face the monster.

Somewhere in the mix of the creature's roars, I heard the girls screaming, begging me to run with them. But I stood my ground, never taking my eyes off the monster. "*Go!*" I shouted again. "*Go home!*"

I thought I heard the girls' retreating footsteps crashing through the woods, but it was hard to tell beyond the hollow rasps of air pumping in and out of my own lungs, the sound of the creature's roar, and the pounding beat of its heavy footsteps as it got closer and closer to where I stood.

Just as I braced myself, believing the beast was going to smash into me, use its weight and momentum to break me into pieces, it came to an abrupt halt, almost skidding on the carpet of fallen leaves only a few feet from me.

Time froze.

The roaring stopped, replaced with a buzzing stillness. As seconds elapsed, I became aware of the quick thuds of my heart, the rough bark on the log I gripped as I craned my neck to look up into his face. The Sasquatch's eyes locked on mine. The fiery reflection of the sunset made them burn red. His breaths came in short, guttural pants; his fetid odor filled my nostrils, searing my throat and lungs.

Suddenly, he lifted his huge arms, shaking his fists over his head in a challenge as he grunted a deep, staccato woofing sound.

I fell back a step, holding the limb across my chest, never taking my eyes off his, not backing down.

With his massive fists he beat his broad chest—once with the right hand, once with the left—sending solid, leathery thumps echoing through the woods.

For a moment, I was afraid he was going to lunge forward, use those powerful fists to pummel me, but he just continued to stare. I saw something change in his eyes. Maybe it was only a shift in the early-evening light, but it seemed to me that his gaze softened, as if deciding that I didn't pose an immediate threat to him and his family. But there was something else there too. Was I crazy, or did he search my face as if he recognized me?

Then his gaze broke for a second, looking past me to where his mate had fled. When his eyes met mine again, I could see a warning in them, but I understood he meant me no harm. He was just protecting his family.

And he knew that I was protecting mine.

Then he barked at me again, raising his arms menacingly as he did, but then letting them fall to his sides.

I swear to God—I was being dismissed.

"Jake!" Megan called out.

What the hell? All this time I thought the girls had made it to safety. From the sound of my sister's voice, she was right behind me somewhere.

"Come on, Jake," Nell pleaded. "Run."

I stepped three paces backward before turning and breaking into a run.

They were both calling me now, and I headed in the direction of their voices. At last I saw the tops of their heads peering around the side of a huge boulder. As I got closer, they both stepped out from behind the rock, arms reaching for me. Without breaking stride I grabbed Nell's hand in my right and Megan's in my left and pulled them with me down the trail toward home.

"Wait a second, wait a second." Megan gasped, pulling her hand from my grip, slowing down. "There's something in my shoe."

Skidding to a stop in the middle of the trail, we were all panting deeply, excitement and exertion leaving us struggling to catch a breath.

As Megan plopped on the ground to fix her sneaker, Nell flung her arms around my neck, hugging me hard. "That was amazing," she cried. "*You* were amazing!" Her cheek was hot against mine, her arms clung tightly around my neck. "It's like we're in a dream or something!" I savored the feel of her against me but fought against the impulse to return her embrace. I kept my arms at my sides until she released me. If she sensed my reluctance to reciprocate her spontaneous display of affection, she didn't show it. "I can't believe what we just saw!"

"Did you get any of it on camera?" Megan looked up at me as she shook a pebble out of her sneaker.

"I'm sure I got the back of the female," I said. "But not enough to convince anybody that she wasn't just some joker in a monkey suit."

"We better go back and get the camera," Nell said.

"I'll go," I insisted. "Alone. You girls go back to the house."

"No," said Nell. "We all go. Your rules—no one goes hiking around the woods alone."

"Listen," I said. "Just do what I say. I'm pissed at you guys as it is."

"Why, for God's sake?" asked Megan as she got back on her feet.

"I told you to go home."

"Huh," Megan remarked. "I thought you were yelling at the boogeyman. You know, like in, 'Shoo, bad dog. Go home.'"

"Very funny, sis. You were supposed to get the hell out of there, and you know it. You could have been killed."

"You could have been killed too," Nell pointed out.

"I told you to run," I repeated.

"No way, bro. No way were we going to leave you alone. We have your back. Get used to it." Megan glared at me, her arms crossed stubbornly over her chest, her expression fierce.

I almost got a little misty-eyed, seeing my baby sister looking so tough and determined. She was a good person to have on my side.

CHAPTER 28

The film of Mama Squatch didn't come out very well. We tumbled into Horace's ratty living room dreaming of fame and fortune, and when we saw what the camera had actually recorded, we were extremely disappointed. I hadn't succeeded in framing the shot. The female's broad back came into view all right, but the rust-colored fur filled the frame in such a way that it was impossible to distinguish what the image was. In the brief period we'd caught on tape, so much time was wasted shushing the girls that I'd hardly caught anything of the creature on film. The camera being on a tripod hadn't made much of a difference. My hands must have been shaking like crazy. The erratic, uncontrolled sequence went from the female's hairy back to a jerky pan of the area before the lens swerved up to the sky, then back to catch a shaky glimpse of her brown shoulder and a blur that I think was the top of the baby's head. Then the phone rang and I knocked the camera over and that was that.

"You're right," Nell said glumly. "Anybody looking at this would think that we staged some dopey hoax."

"If only there was such a thing as smell-o-vision." Megan was peering over my shoulder at the computer monitor. "If anyone could catch a whiff of her body odor, they'd know it was the real thing."

"Amen to that," Nell agreed, and the three of us burst into laughter.

"No, but really," Megan continued, "it sucks that we don't have better footage." She looked at me accusingly.

"What?" I exclaimed.

"Well, if you want to be some big-time filmmaker, you're just going to have to do better than this."

"Hey, look," I said, in my defense. "There've been guys trying to get this thing on film for decades. I think I'm doing pretty well."

"But it does have to be definitive," Nell said. "It has to be so convincing that no one can dispute what you have is the real thing."

"Well, all I can say is that I'll keep on working on it." What did these girls want from me? "And," I continued, "it wasn't my cell phone that rang and screwed up everything."

Megan at least had the decency to look ashamed. "Sorry."

"Who was calling you anyway?" I asked.

"I don't know." Megan shrugged.

"It was that jerk, Barry," I said. "Right?"

Megan's face burned red, but she stubbornly denied it was Barry who'd called. I didn't believe it. We might have really started getting heavy into the whole Barry issue if Nell hadn't asked suddenly, "So what did he look like up close?" Her voice was low and thoughtful, but it cut through the tension that was beginning to build between Megan and me.

"Who?" asked Megan.

Nell was looking at me. "The Sasquatch. We couldn't get a good look at him from behind that rock. What was his face like?"

The three of us grew still as I thought for a moment. What did he look like? It was difficult to put into words. At first, all I could recall were those eyes, smoldering red, like live coals, in what I remembered as a dark face—no doubt why we hadn't been able to make out any features when we encountered him at night. "His eyes are as red as anything. His skin is shiny and black, like a gorilla's."

"He looks like a gorilla?" Nell asked.

"No," I said. "Not really. There are similarities, though. He has that heavy brow, like a gorilla or a Neanderthal."

"The supraorbital ridge," Megan said, like she was quoting from Horace's journals.

I shot her a dirty look—sometimes she was such a know-it-all. "Whatever. But that's as far as the resemblance goes. The rest of his face is more—I don't know—human. But not like any human I've ever met."

"Like a caveman kind of thing?" Nell asked.

"No. Well, maybe. I don't think so. He has a more defined jaw and chin, with sharper cheekbones, and his nose was big, but it wasn't flattened down."

"If only you'd had your camera," Megan whined.

"Well, it's your damn fault I didn't," I started in again.

"So? One time I forget to turn off my phone, and you're going to crucify me." Megan's voice grew shrill. She was getting ready for a flat-out fight.

"Enough, you guys," Nell said. "There's no point in arguing." She shot Megan a look. "Just make sure your phone is off the next time." She started gathering her stuff.

"Aren't you staying for dinner?" Megan asked, looking disappointed.

"I can't." Nell backed toward the door. "It's my dad's birthday. I promised my mom I'd be home early."

Her dad. Which dad? The guy who was interesting and welcoming the night she'd brought me home for dinner? Or the guy who nearly drilled a hole through my chest before he threatened to rip my head off? I might have been going home with her, if only I knew what had gone wrong. "I'll walk you to your car."

"That's okay," Nell mumbled.

"No, I want to."

It had started to rain softly, really not more than a mist. The early-evening light was green; the air smelled fresh. Fine droplets caught in Nell's dark hair, and they shone like tiny diamonds. We stood by her car for a moment, looking at each other, and I wanted to take her hand, kiss her.

"I wish…" I said.

"What?"

I hadn't realized I'd said the words out loud. Might as well keep going. "That I knew how to make things right."

"It's not you." Her voice was a croak. I could tell how awkward she felt. That was okay. I wasn't feeling exactly like Mr. Smooth myself. "It's me."

"That line's used too much," I said.

"I know…but it's true. I wish—"

"What?"

"I wish I could explain." Her voice was barely a whisper, her eyes downcast.

"You can."

She raised her eyes, looking into mine. They were gleaming with unshed tears. I felt an ache in my chest. "Maybe," she said, her voice like a soft breeze. "But not now. Not yet."

"I wish you could."

"Me too."

I stood in the driveway until I couldn't hear the funny jingling sound of the Karmann Ghia engine anymore. Only then did I turn and trudge back into the house.

Megan was on the computer, updating her Facebook page.

"You better watch what you post there," I warned her.

"Don't worry. I'm not giving anything away." She turned to look at me, a mischievous smile on her face. "As a matter of fact, Mom keeps a close watch on everything I put up. I just posted how much I love camp." Her expression changed as she looked at me. "Are you okay?"

"Yeah, I'm fine."

"You don't look fine."

I didn't feel fine, either. I flopped down on the sofa. I could have used a big-screen television at that moment. Just turn on the remote and lose myself in a baseball game or some old movie—not think about anything that mattered to me.

Megan had turned from the computer. She was watching me thoughtfully. "She likes you, you know."

"Huh?"

"Huh?" Megan mimicked. "Don't be a dope. Nell. She likes you."

"Great." I sighed. "She has a hard time showing it."

"Well, that's the problem."

"What?"

"She has a hard time showing how she feels. Because something bad happened to her when she was a little kid. It messed her up emotionally."

"How do you know?"

"Barry told me."

"Oh, of course. He knows everything." I snorted.

"I think it's true," Megan said.

"Well, what happened then?"

"I don't know," Megan said. "But whatever it was? It was bad." She yawned, stretching her arms before she clicked to another website. A second later she was laughing at some video on YouTube. "Are you going to start cooking soon? I'm getting kind of hungry."

CHAPTER 29

Megan and I didn't talk much through the meal, though we discussed going back to the feeding station to see if we could gather some DNA evidence, hair samples and the like. I drew the line on looking for Bigfoot turds. I'm not that dedicated a researcher.

We turned in early. I thought I was exhausted—totally wiped out after all that had happened—but I couldn't sleep. The weather was weird. Instead of cooling things down, the rain came with a stifling heat. I managed to doze off a couple of times but woke with bad dreams that I couldn't remember. I stared out the window, making out the inky silhouettes of trees against the navy-blue sky. How many people in the world could say that they had a face-to-face standoff with a mythological creature? I bet only me. And nobody would believe it. That is, except Megan and Nell.

Nell. I thought about how her slender arms felt around my neck. Her breath had smelled like peaches. Her cheek was like warm velvet against mine. I'd wanted to put my hands on her waist, feel her ribs, pull her to me.

But I knew better.

So. What the hell had happened to her? Something bad, Megan had said. How bad? It bothered me that Barry knew more about Nell than I did. If she wasn't ready to tell me, I should respect that, right?

But there were ways to find out. Spending a few minutes on the Internet wouldn't hurt anybody, right? After all, I might not even find out anything.

Walking past my dad's bedroom, I stopped for a second, listening for Megan's moaning breath. There it was, that weird little wheezing that signaled that she was sound asleep. The rest of the house was silent, and there was nothing but blackness beyond the windows. I could hear rain falling steadily outside.

After clicking on the little desk lamp and turning on the computer, I headed into the kitchen, made a cheese sandwich, and poured myself a glass of OJ. By the time I got back to the computer, it was booted up and ready to go.

I didn't go straight to the search, because somehow, I felt guilty and—bizarre as it sounds—kind of scared. I clicked around for a while. Checked my email and—surprise, surprise—there was something from Dad. He was still in Guatemala. I'd wanted to think he'd caught some equatorial fever that made him forget who he was and what he'd left behind, but from what I could tell from the message, he was healthy and busy "exploring other business opportunities" and he didn't know exactly when he'd be heading home, but again he was sure I was getting along just fine.

How was he so sure of that?

Was I fine? I'd figured out how to pay the electric bill—and had become a lunatic about not leaving the lights on—but there was a scary-looking envelope from the town tax department I didn't even want to open. Driving had become second nature—I'd almost forgotten I was breaking the law. I was doing a fair job of keeping an eye on my runaway kid sister, but that could spin out of control at any second. And I'd been tracking down a big hairy monster that could have easily snapped my neck like a twig, just that afternoon. Yeah, I was doing fine. I'd keep things together for my dad, and if everything worked out the way I hoped, by the time he got home, his financial worries would be over.

I stared at the Google homepage for a second before I typed in Nell's father's name. At the speed of light, the first page of hits appeared on the screen. Wow. Tony Awards and Obies galore. Both Nell's dad and mom were big-time designers who did everything from experimental plays to huge Broadway extravaganzas. There was even a review of a production they'd worked on for the Metropolitan Opera.

The first three pages were about the professional reviews and the awards and the accolades. I didn't find the personal stuff until I got to the fourth page. After all, eight years had passed. It was old news.

But it had been big news.

The link I found took me to an old *New York Times* article, brief and to the point. It went something like this: Mr. and Mrs. Davis, well-known in the New York theater world for their set and costume designs, were out of town for the tryout of a new musical. They had left their eight-year-old daughter in the care of a babysitter, a young Barnard student whom the couple believed they knew very well. What they didn't know was that the college girl was a junkie and had a creepy drug-dealer boyfriend. When Nell's parents returned from their four-day trip to Boston, they found the babysitter unconscious in their bed and their traumatized little girl hiding in a closet.

There was plenty more coverage from all kinds of publications, many alluding to suspected sexual assault. I'm sure some went into more graphic detail, but I couldn't read those. Skimming through the pages, I gathered that the police never found the boyfriend and the babysitter pled guilty to negligence charges. End of story. Except it would never end for Nell. My midnight snack turned into a churning mess in my stomach. I shut down the computer, turned off the lights, and sat in the dark for a long time.

CHAPTER 30

The rain continued, not that it mattered much. My work schedule for the week was pretty heavy. There wasn't a lot of time for strategy sessions or stakeouts or showdowns or whatever was going to happen next. And working was fine, because most of the time I hung out with Nell. That was great, except for the day when, over lunch, she caught me looking at her while she wolfed down her Italian sub. I admit it, I was thinking about what I had found out about her, and it must have shown on my face. Ignoring the fact that her mouth was full of salami, ham, hot peppers, and provolone cheese, she managed to say through the thick bread, "What? What are you looking at?"

I felt my face get all hot. "Nothing!"

She swallowed. "Am I grossing you out or something?"

"No!" I protested. *Never!* I thought. She was the only girl in the world who could eat a macho sandwich like that and still look pretty. "No," I repeated, trying to recover some cool. "No, I was just wondering if this rain was ever going to let up."

"I know. It sucks, right?" She took another big bite and chewed for a while before she could say, "But it's supposed to clear up by the weekend, isn't it?"

"I think so."

Lowering her voice, she said, "Maybe we should start planning more surveillance or something."

"Maybe." Honestly, I hadn't decided what our next move should be. I needed time to think.

"What's Megan been up to?"

Megan. That was another worry. I couldn't keep an eye on her while I was at work, and Barry and I had had very different schedules lately. I wondered if that was on purpose. It seemed whenever I was on, he was off—a coincidence? I thought not. "I guess she's been hanging out with Barry."

Nell looked at me. "And that's bothering you."

"Yes, it is," I admitted. "You saw her after a day at the amusement park. You think they've sworn off drinking since then?"

"No," said Nell thoughtfully. "Maybe we should do some stuff together," she continued, keeping her tone casual.

"That wouldn't be a bad idea," I agreed. "'Girls' night out' kind of stuff?"

"Well, yeah. Sure. That would be fine." It was Nell's turn to go pink in the face. "But I was thinking more like the four of us. We could actually do something normal, like see another movie, go on a road trip, something like that."

Was she suggesting a double date? Did that mean she wanted to go out with me? I tried not to blurt out something stupid, but I was breaking into a sweat. "Well, we could." I tried to sound as offhand as she did. "But that would involve actually having to spend time with Barry."

Nell, having polished off her sandwich and a bag of potato chips, was unwrapping a cupcake. "I know how unpleasant the thought of that is for you," she said before taking a bite. "But at least you'd know what they were up to. And maybe if you got to know Barry a little better, you'd feel more comfortable about him and Megan."

"Well, you're right about being able to keep an eye on them, but I doubt I'll ever become a Barry fan," I said. And then I asked, "If we did, say, spend the day together, like you said—what would you tell your parents you were doing?" I couldn't help it. The fact that Nell's parents—her father, at least—thought I was some kind of pervert really bothered me.

Especially now that I was beginning to understand what the problem was.

That pink color blooming in her cheeks deepened to red. "I don't know." She shrugged. "I guess I'd just say I was out with a bunch of friends."

I pushed the rest of my sandwich away, not hungry anymore. "It would be great if you could tell your father the truth. That you were going to be with me."

She tossed the last few bites of her cupcake into the garbage. "I'll work things out with him. I promise."

The next Sunday was the first nice day we all had off, so we decided to make a real day of it and go to Ocean Beach. Megan and I packed a big cooler of food—sandwiches, fruit, chips, and soda—and we agreed that Barry would drive. I was reluctant, but also scared of getting caught without a license and worried that Mr. Davis might recognize the Jeep. Even though Nell said she was going to put things right with her dad, she hadn't gotten around to it yet.

Barry might be an idiot, but I had to admit that he kept his car nice. I was expecting the interior to smell like armpits and stale smoke and to be littered with grease-stained burger wrappers and empty beer cans, but the upholstery and floor of the Mustang were freshly vacuumed and tidy.

When we got to Nell's house, I hunkered down in the backseat, watching as Barry and Megan walked to the front door to call for Nell. We'd already decided that Barry would simply introduce Megan as his girlfriend—no need to complicate things by identifying her with a last name of any kind.

Wouldn't you know it, just as they approached the porch stairs that wacky pack of mini-animals came trotting around from the back of the house, making a crazy din—barking, braying, and clucking. Right away, Megan's face broke out into a huge grin and she bent over, holding her hands out for them to sniff, but Barry looked kind of skittish as the little critters clambered around him. The little dog was yapping and leaping up, jumping against their legs. The miniature donkey and goat both nuzzled Megan with their snouts, but it was that rooster—Chickabod—that was causing the real trouble. I guess old Chickabod didn't like Barry any more than I did, because he went right for Barry's naked shins, pecking away at his ankles like they were corn on the cob.

That's when I cracked up, letting loose a real belly laugh, watching Barry's high-kicking dance as, his eyes widening with terror, he tried to get away from the nutty rooster. But old Chickabod was a persistent little devil and kept at Barry until he tripped, falling on his butt, holding his hands in front of his face to keep the rooster from going after his eyes. Megan ran over to him, trying to shoo Chickabod away and help Barry up all at the same time. His face had gone purple, and he was thrashing his big feet around, obviously hoping to flatten the bird into a feather pancake.

Luckily, that's when Mrs. Davis came to the door, presumably to investigate the source of the ruckus. She calmly trotted over to the battle scene and picked up Chickabod in one easy swoop, tucking the bird under her arm, while Megan pulled Barry to his feet.

I slunk down lower in the backseat, but not so far I couldn't see. I couldn't hear what they were saying, but Mrs. Davis was helping Megan brush dirt off Barry, her face all scrunched in concern. After plopping the chicken back down on the grass, she ushered them inside.

It made me sad, thinking about going into that house. It really sucked that I was banned—at least for the time being.

In a few minutes, Megan and Nell came tumbling out, followed by Barry, who was carrying another whole cooler of food. I couldn't wait to see what Mrs. Davis had packed for us.

"Hey," I said as Barry climbed into the driver seat, "I see you made a new friend."

"Right," Barry growled. "Cute. Puts me in the mood for some fried chicken."

Sliding into the seat next to him, Megan slapped at his shoulder. "Don't be such a baby," she said as we all buckled up for the ride.

It was a long drive, nearly two hours. But I have to say I enjoyed every minute of it. There wasn't too much trouble Megan and Barry could get into up in the front seat, and from where I sat, I could watch every move. And I got to sit next to Nell. For two whole hours we talked and laughed and joked around, and it was nice.

The beach was great too. After the early-morning clouds burned away, the wide sweep of sand, sky, and ocean was awesome. Before now, I'd always lived near the shore, even if it was Long Island Sound. I hadn't realized how much I missed it. That day, as we swam and basked in the sun, we could forget everything else while the freewheeling seagulls circled above and we savored the sensation of sand between our toes. By about five, we were ready to head back home.

When we arrived at Nell's house again, I wished I could walk her to the door, show her parents I could get her home in one piece, but it wasn't time. Before she climbed out of the car, she leaned over and kissed me on the cheek. "'Night," she said softly in my ear. "I had a great time." I knew I should have been grateful for that dry little peck, but I longed for more. She smelled of suntan lotion and sea breezes, and I wanted to pull her to me and taste the salt on her lips. I knew if I was patient and caring enough, I'd get there.

Once we reached our house, Barry made it clear that he wanted to come in. I have to say, the guy hadn't gotten on my nerves too badly, but I was tired and just wanted to turn in. I wasn't in the mood to play chaperone for my baby sister and her hulk of a boyfriend.

Megan, of course, was all for it. "Come on in," she insisted, leading him up the path by his brawny arm. "I want to show you the video my friend sent me from the DMB concert she went to last week."

It was nearly nine o'clock, and Barry apparently noticed that the house was dark, silent. "Where's your old man?" He sounded casual, but I noticed he was looking around like he was casing the joint, maybe wondering if there was anything worth ripping off.

I shot Megan a warning glance, then said, "He had a softball game with some buddies. They probably went out for a beer afterwards. Should be home soon." How the heck did I come up with that one? The only buddies my dad ever had were old business partners that screwed him over—and to my knowledge, he'd never, ever played softball in his life.

Megan rolled her eyes—she knew as well as I did how farfetched that lie was. "You want a cold one?" she asked Barry. Dad had left a six-pack of Coors. I shot Megan another look, and she stuck her tongue out at me before heading into the kitchen.

When just the two of us were in the room, Barry blurted out, "Hey, Jake. Listen." His voice was soft and rushed. Hands in his pockets, he avoided making eye contact with me by pretending to study the titles of the books on the shelf over Horace's desk. "This was a great day. I really appreciate you giving me a chance. With Megan and all." His cheeks looked like someone had drawn bright red lipstick circles on them. He looked and sounded—well—sincere. He picked up an amethyst geode that served as a paperweight on the desk, idly scrutinizing the lavender crystals before putting it down again.

"That's okay," I said, feeling fidgety. "Thanks for driving."

Why was he looking at Horace's old junk like he was interested? I watched, feeling sick as his fingers then moved to the edge of a white cotton dish towel draped over another object I had carelessly left on the desk. Oh shit.

"Hey man," I blurted out. "I'm starving. Let's check out the fridge."

I was too late. Barry lifted the cloth away.

"What the hell is this thing?" Barry asked with a snort of laughter.

My heart sank. "Oh, that?" I shrugged. "Something I made for a school project a couple of years ago."

Megan came back out from the kitchen, a silver can in each hand. When she saw what Barry was examining, she got an "oh crap" expression on her face.

"You're lying." Barry looked up, a crafty smile twisting his lips. "This was part of old Horace's weird science, I bet. What'd he do? Try to pass off this kindergarten craft as evidence of Bigfoot?"

"No." I stepped up to him, taking the cast out of his clumsy paws. Hastily, I stashed it on the floor in the coat closet, feeling Barry's eyes on my back. He had such a sneering look on his face, I had the sudden feeling that he might smash it just for spite. I shut the closet door and faced him. "I made it. It was for a report on how the police create forensic evidence. This was supposed to be a footprint left at a crime scene."

"Right," Barry said with another laugh that sounded like an oink. He was studying me, his eyes all scrunched into slits.

"Yeah, that's right." I was learning a few things about Barry. He might actually seem to be an okay guy for a while, but it was like he couldn't sustain it. The stupid bully in him was always simmering close to the surface, like steam building up in a clogged pipe. And he was about to blow.

Luckily, Megan sensed the growing tension. She thrust her hand out, practically shoving the beer up Barry's nose. "Who cares? Come on." She laughed. "Like Jake said, our dad'll be home soon. Let's drink up and get you out of here before he gets back."

I left them alone—against my better judgment—but I figured that Megan had already given Barry the message that his meter was running out. There wasn't much damage he could do if I backed off and gave them a little privacy. I headed upstairs and threw myself down on the bed without even turning on the light. My window was open, and I heard the squeak of the screen door opening followed by a light slam, the hollow sound of their footsteps on the rotting planks of the sagging front porch, and hushed voices. I would go down and get the cast as soon as Barry was gone and find a safer place to put it.

I must have fallen asleep, because when I woke up, it was completely dark. Megan must have remembered to turn off the porch light after Barry left. A soft breeze wafted in through the window, causing the white curtains to wave like ghostly arms. I was still dressed, even had on my sneakers. Wondering what time it was, I sat up, ready to get a drink of water and change into the gym shorts and T-shirt I slept in.

I froze when the calls began. Maybe they were what woke me up. I heard two distinct voices—the male's cry had the vibrating lower bass notes that made me think of a church organ, while the female's voice was more piercing, plaintive. Hers was the call that carried like sadness on the wind. She sounded as if she were pleading with him to come home.

As I listened, I realized that the lie I'd told Barry might actually come true. Dad might come home any day now—not tonight of course, but there was no telling when. And what was going to happen if he walked right in on the great Sasquatch film project? He might be all for it, but he could also think we were crazy, or putting ourselves in too much danger—and he certainly was going to flip out when he found Megan here. He already held the headliner billing on Mom's shit list. This wasn't going to earn him or me any brownie points. Come to think of it, Mom was the most likely candidate to figure out what was going on—and you could be sure she'd put an end to the whole plan "so fast it'd make your head spin" (one of her favorite phrases).

If this whole scheme had any chance of success, I knew we'd better not waste any more time. Dawn was just beginning to turn the sky a soft, pearly pink as the last calls faded away. I got out of bed to strip off my jeans and brush my teeth. I'd try to grab another couple hours of sleep before the day really started and we could get back to work on Operation Bigfoot.

CHAPTER 31

The three of us were sitting around the kitchen table with cans of soda. Megan looked bored and antsy, but Nell was all ears. I'd been dying to talk to them both all day, but I had to work and Nell had the day off and was running errands with her mother. We couldn't all get together until after dinner. "So, what I've been thinking is this. We have to change the observation strategy in a big way. I think they're too smart to let themselves be caught by an egg sitting on a stump again."

"Do you have any ideas?" Nell asked.

"Around dawn this morning, I heard them calling to each other. It sounded like one of them was near the swimming hole. They need water, and it makes sense that they'd go there at times when they're least likely to be spotted."

"And that's the area we've had the most encounters," Nell pointed out. I could tell by the look on her face, she was remembering that first day, when we thought kids were pelting us with rocks.

Megan looked at her watch. "So, what's the plan?"

"You in a rush or something?" I asked.

She glared at me like I was a lowly study-hall monitor. "As a matter of fact, I am. I've got a date."

Now it was my turn to look at the clock. "Now? It's nearly nine already."

"That's right, Grandma," Megan said. "Barry'll be here any second."

"I don't know about that."

"Just tell me what this big plan of yours is so we can get on with our lives," Megan huffed.

"Well, I was hoping Nell could spend the night," I said. Megan rolled her eyes and Nell looked surprised.

"Not tonight. Tomorrow. I was hoping you could tell your parents you were sleeping over at Katie's," I continued, "but come here instead. We could all turn in early and set the alarm for three AM, then set up another stakeout, this time overlooking the swimming hole. It's going to be a full moon, and the sky starts to brighten up around four-thirty. I figure we might be able to catch them out in the open at their watering spot with enough light to get some footage."

"That's a pretty good idea," Nell said thoughtfully. "I think I can swing it with my folks."

A horn blared outside and we all jumped in our seats. Megan leapt up. "That's my ride."

"Isn't he going to come to the door for you?" I asked.

"No." Megan stood, her hands on her hips. "He says you make him nervous."

"*I* make him nervous," I said. "That's a laugh."

"Yeah, right. Just one big *ha-ha*." She turned to leave.

"Listen you," I called after her. "Be home by midnight. In one piece. And no drinking!"

"Yes, Grandma," she sang before slamming the front door behind her.

Nell stayed a little while longer, using the last dregs of her soda to wash down a couple of Twinkies. We talked about what we would need for tomorrow night and decided that she should come over straight from work so that we'd have a chance to set up the surveillance post in advance. But as we sat there talking, it got to be pretty clear that she was starting to feel a little uncomfortable being alone with me, and soon she was gone.

I was looking forward to the next day, but I had an evening of waiting to get through first. No way was I going to turn in before Megan was safely back in the nest. To kill time, I started acting like a crazy housewife, scrubbing down the kitchen and bathroom like they'd never been scoured before. It made sense, after all, if Nell was going to be a houseguest. She lived in such a nice home, I didn't want her to be grossed out by mine.

I decided not to change the sheets on my bed until morning—I'd be sleeping on the couch so Nell could have a room to herself. I was just finishing the last of the vacuuming when Megan stumbled in. It was nearly one AM. She looked startled and annoyed.

"What the hell's gotten into you?" she yelled over the vacuum's whine, dumping her canvas purse on the floor.

Right away I noticed the dirt she was tracking in. "Hey!" I protested, flipping the switch with my toe. Suddenly, it was quiet in the room. "Leave those muddy flip-flops on the porch. I just cleaned this floor."

She slid her feet out of her flip-flops, but that was as far as she was going to go. Shaking her head, she said, "Bro, I think you have finally gone around the bend."

"There's nothing wrong with keeping the house decent." I unplugged the vacuum cord and coiled it up. "And I'm not the one destroying my brain cells."

"What are you talking about?" she said, crossing her arms defensively.

"You're drunk again. Every time you drink alcohol, you destroy brain cells. Didn't they teach you that in health class?"

She wrinkled her nose. "Well, those cleaning-fluid fumes can't be doing your brain any good. The whole place stinks."

"It doesn't stink. It smells clean. I wish I could say the same for you. You reek like you took a bath in beer." It was true. I could pick up the odor from across the room, over the Lysol and Pledge.

"Whatever," she huffed, starting to march past me to get to the stairs.

"Wait a minute." I put a hand on her arm. "Where've you been? What did you guys do tonight?"

She pulled her arm away from me. With a smirk on her face as she moved to the stairs, she said, "Partied. Talked. Quit worrying."

Like I could I ever do that.

CHAPTER 32

After work, we trekked into the woods to explore the new area of observation. We found a good site to set up camp a few yards away from the most likely spot for our big-footed friends to slurp up some H2O. I didn't want to think about them eating frogs. It was a muggy night, and the mosquitoes were swarming, so the humming in our ears made us cranky. All of us cursed as we swatted them away.

Back at the house, I fried up some burgers, and we scarfed them down. It was only eight-thirty by the time we finished cleaning up, but we all decided to go to bed—had to get a few solid hours of rest before reporting for the dawn patrol, right?

I couldn't sleep. I tossed and turned on the crisp, clean sheets I'd put on my bed for Nell as I thought of her, across the hall. My gallantry had been wasted. The girls decided to bunk in together—that slumber party mentality they all have—and I cringed just thinking about those gray, greasy sheets on Dad's bed. I doubted he'd changed the linens even once since we moved in, and I'm positive that Megan never gave cleanliness a thought.

I listened to them settling into bed. There was muffled conversation and giggling. Thumps, bumps, the squeak of bedsprings, and a little shriek of surprise. Though there were two closed doors and the space of the hallway between us, I could hear the gentle murmurs of their pillow talk. Thinking about Nell's soft voice whispering her deepest, darkest secrets to Megan—feeling close enough to trust her to keep those secrets safe—made me lonely.

At last, the house fell silent except for some dopey beetle that kept banging its dopey beetle head against the window screen, trying to bust in. What could possibly be in this cramped little room that a bug would work so hard to get at? Maybe it liked the smell of freshly laundered sheets.

What is it about the wee hours of the morning that makes everybody so quiet? I was already awake before the alarm rang. I doubted I'd gotten more than four hours of sleep. Slipping out of bed and into my clothes, I brushed my teeth before I woke up the girls.

After tiptoeing into my dad's room, I stood looking at them both, lit softly from the light spilling in from the hallway. Megan was sprawled on her back, her arms flung open wide, her mouth slack, that soft moaning noise escaping with every exhale.

Nell was curled up into a tight little ball under the sheets, scooched over so far away from Megan that it was a wonder she hadn't toppled off the edge of the bed onto the floor.

I tapped Megan's shoulder and whispered, "Hey, Megs. Time to wake up." Why was I whispering like I was afraid to wake the baby?

Megan's moan turned into a groan. As my taps turned into pokes, she started swatting at me with her hands, her eyes still determinedly squeezed shut. "Go away," she croaked. "Sleeping."

"Yeah, yeah. I know. Come on. Get up." I don't know why, but I was reluctant to give Nell's shoulder a nudge. Guess because she seemed to be wound up so tight in dreams, I didn't want to give her any sudden shocks.

Finally, I got Megan to drag herself out of bed by tickling her feet. She started twitching like she had ants crawling up her leg. And it was a double bonus, because Megan's agitated movements roused Nell out of her deep slumber. She sat up abruptly, blinking in confusion until she recognized me, and said, "Oh, right. I guess it's time."

Despite the fact that the three of us were bleary-eyed and still yawning, we were ready to go about twenty minutes later. No one had raised their voice over a whisper yet, even when Meg gave me hell for forgetting to buy more coffee. So much for the steaming Thermos bottle we had planned to bring.

The air was moist and cool as we stumbled outside, the sky a deep navy blue. Tiny bats flitted crazily above our heads, finishing up their night's meal. I sensed the sun was ready to make its appearance. As we picked our way along the trail, the dew dampened our sneakers and the first birdcalls pierced the predawn silence.

By the time we reached the camp we'd set up, the sky had brightened a bit, glowing with swirls of tangerine and raspberry. We settled in, trying to make ourselves as comfortable as possible. I was glad I'd remembered to douse everyone with bug spray, because the air was thick with gnats and mosquitoes. A silvery mist rose from the water as we looked out over the lake, and we heard the plop and splash of fish leaping out of the water to catch flying insects, as well as the croaking of bullfrogs in the reeds.

An hour went by, then two. The warmth of the sun burned away the mist, leaving the water a sparkling blue. A flock of quacking ducks made a splashy landing on the surface, and a swan paddled by. I think both of the girls slept for a while, leaning back to back against each other for support. I managed to stay alert, scanning the edge of the woods for signs of movement, ready to jump to the camera, which I had set up on the tripod.

Every rustle in the underbrush made me hypervigilant, but all that emerged from the tangle of leaves, branches, and ferns was a deer, and later a chipmunk.

By seven, I was stiff, cold, and bored to death. Not to mention the fact that I was suffering from sleep deprivation. I fought it for as long as I could, but I gave in like the girls, letting my heavy eyelids close for a few blissful seconds, then a little longer—

"*Yow wow!*"

The call shattered the early-morning silence, echoing across the expanse of water and sky, seeming to shake the ground.

"*Whooo Hooo!*"

Closer now.

Megan, now wide-awake, raised herself up onto her knees, peering over the cover of brambles. "What the hell is that?"

"Is it them?" Nell asked, breathless with excitement.

Megan started to stand, but I yanked her down.

"Hell, no," I said in a low voice.

Clumsy crashing, the snap of twigs.

"Well, something big is coming this way," Megan said. "Maybe you should get behind the camera."

"No, we don't need the camera for this," I said grimly. "Something big is coming all right. Something big and stupid." I glared at her, getting more pissed by the second.

Megan read my expression. Her eyes went all wide and innocent. "What?"

"What's going on?" Nell looked from me to Megan, not realizing what was happening.

I turned to her. "It's not a what. It's a who."

"Who?" Nell asked, not getting it.

On cue, Barry tumbled out from behind a rock. "Found you!" he crowed. One look at him, and I could see that he was drunker than ever. Great. He looked like he'd never been to bed, partying through the night and into the morning.

I didn't say a word. Didn't trust myself. Shaking with rage, I started to pack up the gear.

"So, where's this boogeyman of yours?" Barry made his way over to us with swaying, clumsy steps.

"You suck, Megan," I hissed in her ear as I unscrewed the camera from the tripod.

"What?" She was trying to maintain her innocence. "I don't know how he knew to come here."

"Bullshit." I glared into her eyes, only inches from mine. She flinched. "The other night when you guys went out— when you were just talking—you came home bombed. You must have told him. You were just too drunk to remember."

Her face crumpled. She looked really upset. I didn't care.

Barry was on us. "So, my man. Your creature feature start yet?"

"No, Barry," I said tightly. "Nothing's going on. Time to go home."

"What are you doing here, Barry?" Nell asked as she stood up.

"Nell, sweetie!" He turned to her, throwing his arm around her shoulders, pulling her close. "You guys have been leaving me out of all the fun."

"What are you talking about?" Nell smiled, trying to make light of the situation.

"You know! The big adventure. The quest for fame and fortune. I want to get me some of that too."

"I still don't know what you mean," Nell said. "We're just making a nature film. For an online class Jake's taking."

Barry furrowed his brow, making him look more like a Neanderthal than usual. And more menacing. "That's a damn lie, Nell." He pulled his arm away from her, somehow giving her a little shove as he did. She stumbled and almost fell.

"Hey," I protested, stepping toward Nell, putting my hand under her elbow to steady her. "Like I said, Barry, we're finished here. Why don't you go home?" If he didn't leave—like, in the next thirty seconds—I thought I might kill him. Then Megan.

"I told you," he continued, his jaw set belligerently. "I want in. The Bigfoot thing."

"Go home, Barry," was all I could think to say.

"But you guys are off the mark." Barry crossed his arms across his chest, like he was ready to give us a lecture, share the wisdom of his pea brain.

"Go home," I repeated and continued to pack up. Nell and Megan helped, working together to fold the blanket.

Barry squatted on a fallen log, making himself comfortable. "This movie idea of yours is jack."

"If you say so." I made sure that the camera was securely in its case and put it carefully into my backpack, then I folded up the tripod and slid it into the pack too.

"They say a picture's worth a thousand words. But really? A picture ain't worth shit. 'Specially when everybody in the damn world's got a computer and a digital camera and Photoshop. Everything looks fake, you know?"

I slid the straps over my shoulders and heaved the weight of the pack onto my back. I caught Nell's eyes. She was ready to go too. I couldn't look at Megan. I was too mad.

I turned to start hiking back to the house, but Barry made a movement that caught my eye. He slid something out of the waistband of his jeans. Something that gleamed and flashed an oily reflection in the thin morning light.

"Like I said," Barry said, "a picture ain't worth shit. You need hard evidence. Physical evidence. DNA, that's the ticket."

I couldn't take my eyes off the gun in his hands. Handgun. He was playing with it, twirling it. Like he was playing Cowboys and Indians. The barrel was weirdly long. It looked wicked heavy, even in Barry's oversized mitts. I couldn't look away from it. Nell and Megan were staring at it too.

"No one's gonna believe you found Bigfoot unless you catch it," Barry went on. "Or kill it."

Megan's face was all mottled and red. Her hands were balled into fists. She looked scared, but fierce. "Put that away," she demanded. "Your dad's going to rip you a new one if he finds out you took his Magnum."

How the hell did Megan know it was a Magnum?

"Please," Nell said softly. "Put it away before someone gets hurt."

Barry looked at her. A goofy smile spread across his face. His eyes were small and mean. "We're on safari, right? Hunting big game? Wusses do it with cameras. Men do it with guns."

I wanted to just walk away from this place and Barry forever, but I got this crazy notion that he might just shoot me in the back if I made a move, so I stayed where I was.

"How does that song go?" Barry said. His eyes were drooping. He was slurring his words. "A-hunting we will go, A-hunting we will go..." He sang that one phrase over and over.

"Why are you being so mean?" Megan demanded shrilly.

Barry just grinned at her, his big, sloppy mouth twisted into an ugly leer.

"Is it because I wouldn't do it with you?" she blurted out. I could hear the tears in her voice. She was angry and hurt. Scared too.

"You're a cocktease," Barry said.

"I'm only fourteen." Her voice was thin.

I wanted to shake Megan until her teeth fell out. It was her fault Barry was here. I wanted to *kill* him. But since he was holding the first honest-to-God real gun I'd ever seen in my life, I held back. For all I knew, it was loaded.

I kept my voice steady. Looking straight into Barry's eyes, I said, "Look, man. We're going home. You should go home too. Get some sleep."

"Screw you," Barry said in a lazy drawl. His right hand, still holding the gun, fell limply into his lap. His head dropped.

Suddenly, the bough of a tree gave way with a snap. We heard a coarse, huffing pant coming from a dense growth of bracken. Barry's head snapped back up, his eyes darting wildly.

The sound was hot and threatening as we all looked over to its source. The early-morning light remained thin, the rays slanting through the foliage at an angle that obscured our vision. I couldn't really make out the huge black form that came crashing through the woods in our direction.

The girls screamed. Barry shouted. The gun went off. The report was like a crack of thunder.

My ears rang from the explosion. My nostrils burned from the hot metallic stink of gunpowder. My heart broke as I heard a shriek of pain. The bullet had found its mark.

The immense creature bolted back into the underbrush.

"What the hell?" I screamed, lunging at Barry and knocking him off his feet. He landed on his back with a *whoof*, a stunned look on his face as he struggled to breathe, the gun still in his hand.

"Oh my God!" Nell and Megan wailed and clutched each other.

Was it the female taking her baby down to the lake for a drink? Or the male—sensing that there was an imminent threat to his family?

Either way, it had managed to turn tail and run, despite the wound. I had to help, if I could. Without thinking about anything else, I started to run after it. Soon, Nell and Megan were right behind me.

At first I ran blindly, but soon discovered that all I had to do was follow the sound of splintering wood, the trail of flattened plants, and the spatters of blood.

Our pursuit of the creature went on for at least a half-mile, until at last I heard a great sigh and a crash not far away. I slowed down, instinctively knowing that my quarry was no longer leading a challenging race.

The girls caught up with me, and we all stopped short as we glimpsed a huge, dark form, lying in the shadow of an enormous hemlock tree. I could hear Megan's whimpering prayer behind me. Nell was moaning, soft and sad. Hot, sticky tears were streaming down my own face as we approached the thing lying beneath the great tree. I was sick with dread.

What had I done? With each wary step I took, it hit me more deeply that this wasn't a game I'd been playing. I'd been shown something wonderful and rare, and all I'd wanted to do was exploit it. I had brought about its destruction.

Megan and Nell each took one of my hands, and the three of us moved silently across the bed of pine needles, hardly daring to breathe as we looked at the fur-covered back of the massive animal.

"It's a damn bear!" Barry's face was twisted into a dismissive sneer.

Nell flew at him, her eyes blazing. "It could have been one of them!" she cried, the veins in her neck popping.

Barry was startled by her vehemence, but he managed to laugh sneeringly. "One of them? Like in Bigfoot? You actually believe his shit?" He jutted his chin in my direction.

"It doesn't matter what I believe." Her voice was still loud, angry. "That was a living creature minding its own business, and you just blew it away for the hell of it!"

"If it was a Bigfoot, the proof would be lying right there at your feet. Case closed." Barry looked down at the bear, which already seemed smaller and forlorn now that it was dead. "But as it is, at least there's one less bear to be a nuisance." He nudged it with the toe of his sneaker. "This guy's raided his last garbage can."

Nell took a step away from Barry, never taking her steely gaze off him. After taking a couple of slow, deep breaths, she spoke again. Her words were razor-sharp. "All this time," she said, "since Jake and Megan moved here, I've defended you, made excuses for your behavior. It's not Jake's fault he has a problem with you. It's yours. From the day you met, you've done nothing but give him a hard time."

"I don't need anyone making excuses for me," Barry said, like a sulky kid.

"No, you don't," Nell agreed. "Because there is no excuse for the way you've been acting." She opened her arms, as if to frame the scene around us. "But this? What you did here, today? It was stupid and cruel. Unforgivable. And it could just as easily have been one of us! We're done!" Her face went red, and it was clear that she was having a hard time fighting back tears. She started heading back the way we'd come.

Barry spun, swaying a moment as she passed, scowling. "So that's it?" Nell didn't turn around. "After all these years? You hook up with some arty faggot and his slut sister, and you just dump all your old pals?"

Searing rage shot through me, but I fought to keep it in check. He still had the gun, and now we all knew it was loaded. "Shut up, Barry," I growled.

He turned and looked at me. "No. I'm not going to shut up. I've put up with that snotty ice princess all these years, and now she's blowing me off? You don't know the half of it. I can say what I want."

I finally looked at Megan. Her face was crumpled by the struggle to hold back tears too. As mad as I was at her, she was my sister. Those harsh words gushed like a stream of diarrhea out of his mouth. "Come on," I said to her. "Let's leave this shithead to clean up his mess." As much as I wanted to pound Barry, I needed to protect Megan. I needed to get her away from him.

Giving me that stubborn, pig-eyed, bully-challenge stare, Barry raised his voice to a shout, to make sure that Nell could hear every word. "Maybe that's the kind of boyfriend you need, Miss Priss *Eleanor*. After all that childhood trauma, the only guy you would go for would be a dickless wonder like old Jakey-boy here. Or maybe it's his little sister you really like. Maybe that's why I couldn't get her to put out. Maybe she's a dyke too. I can just picture you two little lesbos going at it."

Gun or no gun, I wound up and smashed his face. The moment before the punch hit, he turned his head so my fist landed in the valley between his nose and left cheekbone. The impact jammed my arm into my shoulder socket. I didn't know I could punch so hard. Maybe it was because he was extra-slow and thick from the booze and no sleep, but he fell like a ton of bricks. His eyeballs rolled up under their lids before they snapped shut, and a spurt of blood gushed out of his left nostril, flowing down over his mouth as his knees buckled out from under him.

And he dropped the gun.

While I stood there, stunned at the effect my blow had had, Megan had the presence of mind to snatch the gun up off the ground. Barry moaned and made a feeble attempt to sit up, but Megan gave him a foot to the chest and knocked him back down. Before he could make another try, we both broke into a run, chasing down the trail after Nell.

When Megan and I finally caught up with Nell, she wasn't exactly crying, but you could tell by the tear tracks running through the dirt on her cheeks that she'd only just stopped.

Megan and I fell into step on either side of her, but it was a while before she asked, "So what happened?"

"Jake decked him," Megan answered, her voice a mix of pride and disbelief.

I sort of felt the same way. I'd actually flattened the big, bad bully. As a reminder of my heroic feat, my hand was killing me.

"Good," said Nell. "Then what happened?"

I shrugged. "Nothing. I made sure he wasn't dead, then we left him there."

"Fine," Nell said.

"I got this." Megan held the gun up so she could see.

"Good," said Nell.

For the most part, we didn't talk anymore. Our headlong plunge through the woods caused us to stray so far from the trail, picking our way back to the campsite was slow going. We lost our bearings over and over, circling around for a long time. More than two hours had passed before we finally stumbled onto the shore of the lake.

With relief, I collected my backpack. Thank God all hell didn't break loose until *after* I'd stowed my camera safely away. The girls set to work picking up the rest of the stuff scattered around the site until Megan turned to me and Nell and said, "Ready?"

Nell got a funny look on her face. "Just one minute."

"What?" I asked.

"Give me that thing," Nell said to Megan.

Megan knew what she meant right away and handed her the gun. For a moment Nell held the Magnum, weighing it in her hand, staring at it like she couldn't quite believe it was real. Then she took three long strides to the water's edge and, swinging her arm wide, heaved the gun. It flew over the lake in a soaring arc, splashing down a good distance away from shore, where the water was likely to be so deep and murky it could never be found. I'd never even touched the thing and was glad it was gone, but I hated the thought of the oily metal forever polluting the water as it rusted away.

CHAPTER 33

"You left the door open, Megan," I said when the house came into view, looking hunched and gray under the overcast sky. The promise of early-morning sunshine hadn't lived up to expectations. A clammy drizzle had started falling, making us feel even more miserable, if that was possible.

"I did not!" she protested automatically, but maybe still feeling guilty about the whole Barry mess, conceded in a grumble, "At least I don't think so. Who can remember what happened at four AM?"

I dropped it. It wasn't a big deal, really. Most of the time I never bothered to lock up anyway. We were so far off the main road, it didn't seem to matter. Besides my camera, which I had on me, the only thing worth stealing was the computer.

The morning's events had left a smothering dark cloud over us. After trudging in and dumping our gear, the girls threw themselves on the couch and I headed into the kitchen. I was as exhausted as they were, but I was starving too. The dank chilliness that settled in with the rain gave me a craving for grilled cheese and a pot of Campbell's tomato soup.

I served the girls at the kitchen table. They must have been as hungry as me because I didn't even have to call them; they were led by their noses. We wolfed down the sandwiches and slurped up the soup. It wasn't until we were all digging into a communal half-gallon of Rocky Road that Nell said, "So what's next?"

Dropping my spoon, I pushed back from the table, my stomach uncomfortably full. "Nothing."

"What do you mean?" Megan asked.

"I mean nothing. No 'next.' No plans."

"That might be a good idea," Nell said, a thoughtful look on her face. "Give us some time to regroup."

"I don't think so," I said. "We're done. Operation Sasquatch is over."

"So that's it?" Nell crossed her arms, giving me a wide-eyed stare.

"Yep."

"You're going to let Barry win," Nell asserted.

"Funny," I said, "it really doesn't have anything to do with Barry."

"But he was the one who messed everything up today," Megan chimed in.

"Maybe that wasn't such a bad thing."

"I don't get it." Megan shook her head.

I thought for a moment before I said, "I think we're messing with something that should be left alone." Neither girl replied. And there was nothing left for me to say. All of a sudden I was so tired I could barely keep my eyes open. I was a little queasy, too, from all the heavy food I'd just inhaled. Without another word, I got up from the table and went to my room, where I fell asleep.

It must have been the middle of the night when I finally woke up. I was about to roll over and go back to sleep when I heard snuffling from across the hall. I got up and tiptoed to Megan's door, listening. Sure enough, she was crying into her pillow, great heaving sobs. Nell must have left a long time ago. Megan would never have carried on like that if she thought anyone could hear her. I put my hand on the knob and started to turn it, then stopped.

Maybe I should just turn around and go back to bed— leave her to it, spare her the embarrassment. Spare myself the embarrassment. But she sounded so pitiful. I wished my mother were around; she'd know what to do.

And then I knew what I had to do. It was pretty simple—I could be like my father and just walk away, pretend I didn't hear a thing. Or I could go in there and talk to my sister.

I turned the knob. The door hinges squeaked, and she stopped crying right away. "Hey," I called softly.

"Go away." I could hardly hear her rudely ordering me out, the words all muffled into her pillow.

"Oh, come on." I walked up to the edge of the bed. "It's all right. I'm not mad at you anymore."

"I screwed everything up," she wailed, again into the pillow, so it sounded like she'd screwed everything up in a land far, far away.

"Well, let's just agree that you're never going out with that shithead again."

"No problem."

I sat down on the edge of the bed beside her. Her head and hands were completely buried under the pillow. Gradually, her breathing evened out, and she grew calmer. "Hey, Megs?" I said. "The other night... Why didn't you tell me Barry gave you a hard time?"

Finally, she pulled her head out from under the pillows. It was very dark in the room, but I could see the glint of tears in her eyes. She said in a baby voice, "Because you'd just say 'I told you so.' I didn't want to hear it." She rolled over onto her back and sighed. "And I was scared if you got mad, you'd do something stupid..."

"Like deck him?" I smiled a little, flexing my right hand. Damn, but my knuckles were still throbbing.

"Well, yeah," she admitted. "And I was afraid if you guys got into it, you might get hurt."

"Ouch. Thanks for your confidence in my ability to defend your honor."

"Oh, you know what I mean. Barry's such a shithead."

"Tell me about it."

"The other night?" Her voice got very small, and she curled over onto her side. I had to lean in closer to hear what she said. "Everything started out okay, you know? And we were fooling around, in his car, but he started to get pushy. Tried to do things I didn't want to do."

"Christ, Megs," I muttered, running my hands through my hair. The heat was turning up on the fury that now simmered every time the subject of Barry came up. But what could I say? She'd known how I felt about him from the start. All I could do was listen.

"So that's when I started talking. Like if I talked enough, I could get him to stop pawing me. I kept yakking away—about anything I could think of. I don't even know what I was saying. I was just trying to talk my way out of a bad situation."

"All right, I get it."

"And that's when I must have told him about our plans. Like I said, I don't even remember what I was blabbering about. I just remember this desperate need to keep talking, like that was going to keep me safe. What a dope."

"Not so stupid, Megs. It worked, I hope. I mean, he got you home okay?"

"Yes," she said, almost whispering. "Whatever I said distracted him from the—the other thing. He hardly said a word on the way home, but he got me here okay."

The fury was now at a near-boil. I should call the police. He'd tried to force himself on my fourteen-year-old sister. But listening to her trembling voice in the dark, full of hurt and fear, I didn't want to expose her to what that accusation might bring unless she wanted to take it on. "Then it was worth it. Spilling the beans to Barry. So stop worrying about that. Just let me know if you want me to kill him, because I would love to."

Suddenly uncurling from her fetal position, Megan sat up and threw her arms around my neck. We held each other tight for a few moments before I pulled away, giving her a kiss on her damp cheek. "Get some sleep now."

"Okay, Jake," she murmured, settling back down onto her pillow. "I love you, you know. And you were great today."

"Whatever, Megs. I love you too."

CHAPTER 34

My shift didn't start until noon, so I slept late the next morning. When I came downstairs to grab some breakfast, I found Megan sitting on that saggy couch, her nose stuck in an old book she held in her left hand. She was wiggling her right hand into funny positions, her gaze darting between the pages of the book and whatever she was trying to do with her hand.

Frankly, I was more interested in the contents of the fridge than in what she was doing. I was just glad she wasn't crying. But when I came back out from the kitchen after my bowl of cereal, she was still at it, this intense look of concentration on her face.

"What the heck are you doing?" I had to ask.

She looked up from the book, noticing me for the first time. "Oh, hi," she said before turning her attention back to the book and splaying her fingers around in weird ways.

"What are you doing?" I repeated.

"Huh?" She raised her eyes again and held up the book, like it would explain everything. "I found it when I was going through Horace's notebooks and stuff."

"Megan, the book doesn't have a jacket and the title's worn off the spine. What are you reading?"

"Oh, right." She lowered it onto her lap. "It's a book on American Sign Language."

"So? Why's that so fascinating?"

"Why?" She shrugged. "I don't know. Now that Operation Bigfoot is dead in the water, I thought I needed a new project. God knows there's nothing else to do around here."

Especially when you're done with your boyfriend. "You're weird."

"No, I'm not," Megan said. "It's cool. Like learning a new language. Silent communication. If I learn how to sign and teach my friends, think how useful it could be in school."

"Well, don't let me keep you from your new diabolical plot."

"Are you going to work?" Her voice was small again, like it was last night.

"That's the plan," I said. "Soon as I wash up."

"But what if...?"

"If I run into Barry? Nothing," I assured her. "As far as I'm concerned, we're done. If he tries to start something again, I'll deal with it. We do work in the same place. I'm just hoping all I'll ever have to say to him is 'cleanup in aisle six.'"

By the time I came back downstairs, showered and ready for work, Megan was standing by the door, her canvas bag slung over her shoulders, a pair of little granny sunglasses perched on her nose.

"Where are you going?" I asked.

"It's supposed to get really hot today," Megan said. "I thought maybe you could drop me at the library."

"You're kidding, right?" I marveled.

"Well, what else am I supposed to do?" she whined. "At least the library's air-conditioned."

I sighed. "Okay, come on."

It wasn't until we were well on our way that I finally asked, "What time did Nell leave?" I'd been thinking about it nonstop since I got up, but I was feeling like a dope. After all the nasty things Barry had said, how could I not have asked Nell if she was all right? Sure, I was going through my own crisis, but it was selfish not to offer her a few words of sympathy. After all, no matter how big an idiot Barry might be, she had considered him a friend. I didn't know what the pecking order was in that little clique of theirs, but it couldn't be good that Nell was on the outs with Barry.

Megan shrugged. "She took off right after you went to bed. She said she was tired too."

"It was a rough day."

"I'll say," Megan agreed.

It turned out I didn't need to worry about dealing with Barry—not that morning anyway. Because the first thing Mr. Pelletier told me was how pissed he was that Barry had called in to say he was grounded for a week—meaning he wouldn't be able to work. I tried to find out what he was being punished for without seeming too interested. I didn't get more info than that Barry had to learn to respect other people's property. I gathered the property in question was the gone-forever Magnum. I also managed to get out of Mr. Pelletier that it was, in fact, Barry who'd phoned, not his father. That was some kind of relief—dead men don't make telephone calls. I wouldn't be arrested on murder charges. Added bonus—Barry was knee-deep in crap with his old man for losing the gun.

The only thing that bummed me out was when Mr. Pelletier added, "Looks like you're going to have it doubly rough this afternoon."

"Why?" I asked.

"Because Nell called in too," said Mr. Pelletier. "Seems that she's going to be late as well."

"How come?" I tried to sound casual, but right away I was worried. Had she somehow gotten caught up in Barry's problems?

Mr. Pelletier shook his head. "Don't exactly know. Guess there was some trouble up at their place this morning. Vandalism of some kind. I didn't press her for information—she was too upset—but she did say the police were there."

My heart pounded. It was hard to tie my apron on because my hands started to shake.

"So, anyway, Jake," Mr. Pelletier continued, "I'm going to need you on the register, but if you get the chance, see if you can stock the can aisle during the lulls."

"Sure thing." Waiting for Nell was going to be excruciating.

Nell was a mess when she finally showed up a couple of hours later. Her face was blotchy, and her usually shiny, dark hair was pulled back into a lumpy snarl of a ponytail. She was dressed in a pair of sloppy sweatpants and an oversized T-shirt. Luckily there weren't too many customers around. I rushed over to her.

"What happened?" I asked. "Are you okay?"

Those big brown eyes of hers were swollen and bloodshot, and before she could say anything, they filled with tears. "Let me punch in," she said, her voice thick with emotion, "then I'll tell you." She turned abruptly and headed off.

Just then, old Myrna came shuffling out of the back room. "Boss says I'm taking over on the register. Wants you to get going on those canned goods."

"Sure thing." I practically leaped over the counter to follow Nell.

When I caught up with her, she was putting her stuff in her locker, her head bowed so I couldn't read the expression on her face. "Nell…" I stood close, afraid to even pat her on the shoulder. "Nell, tell me what's wrong."

"Oh, Jake!" she exclaimed with a sob, turning to me. "It's Chickabod. Somebody killed Chickabod!"

"That crazy little rooster?" Of course it was that weird minichicken. How many Chickabods did I know? "I'm sorry. That's terrible. So, what happened? A coyote get him or something?"

"No, it wasn't a coyote!" Nell wailed.

"Are you sure? I mean…"

"Not unless a coyote is capable of wringing a bird's neck without taking a bite or breaking the skin. Not unless a coyote would throw the poor little corpse onto the front porch!"

"A coyote wouldn't. But I can think of someone who might."

Our eyes met. Nell knew who'd done it too. Then her face went all red. "It was terrible. It was really early, and I was on my way to feed the goats, and I walked out the door, and I stepped on something, and I looked down…" A shudder ran through her, and she buried her face in her hands. That's when—what the hell—I put my arms around her and pulled her close. She didn't shy away from me. I could feel her shaking, her warm breath against my chest as she cried. Poor Nell.

When she seemed a little calmer, I said softly, "Mr. Pelletier said the police came. How did they get involved?"

Nell lifted her face. For a second, we were nose to nose— and it was crazy, considering we were talking about stepping on a dead chicken—but I had to fight the urge to kiss her. She must have sensed how I felt, because she stepped away, wiping the tears from her cheeks with her palms.

"Well, you can guess. I screamed my head off," she said. "My parents were there in two seconds. Right away, they knew someone did it to be mean, so they called the police."

"So? What did they say?"

Nell plopped down on one of the folding chairs at the lunch table. "They agreed that it was a malicious act. They asked us if we knew anybody who might be that mad at us."

"What did you tell them?"

"I told them yes. I told them who I thought it could be." She slumped down, folding her arms on the table and cradling her head in them. "I told them I thought it might be Barry."

"Did they, you know, arrest him?" I asked.

"They called his house," Nell said. "They talked to his dad. His dad said he wasn't home—that he'd gone down to Ansonia to do some stuff around his grandparents' house for a week. That he'd left the night before."

"His father gave him an alibi?"

"Guess so," Nell said.

"So that's it?"

"No." Nell lifted her head and looked at me. "The police said they'd continue to investigate. They were going to leave, but one officer decided to take another look around, and…" Her face went all blotchy again.

"And what?"

"He found a footprint."

"Well, that's good, right?" I said. "Can't they match the impression of a tread to a shoe?"

"He found a big footprint—unnaturally big. A weirdly big, bare footprint."

"Oh," I said, thinking that over for a few seconds. "You don't think…?"

"Honestly, Jake? I don't know."

The swinging door burst open, and Mr. Pelletier stuck his head in. "Oh, Nell. You *are* here. I need you at the other register." He glanced at me. "And Jake, let's get going on those cans."

How many ways can someone put corn in a can? Or yams, for that matter? An even bigger question is, why would anyone want to? And who buys this stuff? Creamed corn, whole baby corns, Niblets (whatever they are), yellow kernels, white kernels—I'll bet if you closed your eyes and ate each one, they'd all taste exactly the same. They all would taste exactly like that soggy, lukewarm spoonful the cafeteria ladies plopped into the little section of my lunch tray in second grade.

One good thing about a boring job—it gives you time to think. Not that thinking was doing me any good, because all I could think about was that stupid footprint—that singular, stupid footprint. Come on—wouldn't there be more than one print? Shouldn't there be a trail of footprints leading back and forth to the woods?

It had to have been Barry. He was the only person in the world that would have it in for poor Chickabod. It wasn't even worth considering any other possibility. But I had to hand it to him...who would have believed that Barry was capable of pulling off a prank that would leave the police scratching their heads?

And considering Barry was MIA, I couldn't even confront the son of a bitch.

I was still puzzling it out as I finished up for the day. No chance of talking it over with Nell—by the time I was ready to go, she was tied up behind the register.

Megan was already waiting for me in the Jeep. "What took you so long?" I could tell right away she was cranky. She looked hot and tired.

"I was working, remember?" I slid into the driver's seat, popping the key into the ignition. "What did you do all day?"

"I've been at that damn library the whole time," she whined.

"Don't you have to be quiet at the library?" I snorted. "I can't imagine you pulling that off for such a long time."

"Well, if you must know," she sniffed, "I actually volunteered. Some nutty old lady took me up on the offer. I spent the day shelving books."

"No way." I gave her a sidelong glance.

She had her elbow up against the passenger-side window. Her chin was resting in her hand. Shrugging, she sighed. "I'm going to keep doing it for the next couple of weeks. I need to do something to kill time before I have to go home."

Home. That word hit me like a bag of wet cement. "When's that?" I croaked out.

"When's what?"

"When do you have to go home?"

"Dude. It's August. Soccer camp ends in less than two weeks."

How did the time go so fast? Next thing I knew, it would be September and I'd be starting my junior year in a new school. And it would just be Dad and me again. That is, if Dad ever came back. "Hey, genius," I said. "How do you plan on getting back home without Mom killing you?"

"Um, funny you should ask," Megan said, giving me a sly smile. "Easy-peasy-lemon-squeezy. I'm going to tell her about this great girl I met at camp who just happens to live in Westport, whose parents just happened to have offered me a ride home. And then my best, beloved, big brother is going to do me a solid and drive me down, hopefully in the middle of the night so we don't get caught."

That's my Megan. Always thinking. I felt a grin coming on, just in appreciation of her devious mind, but a sinking feeling squashed it before it really got going.

Home. I imagined the two-hour trip to Norwalk, pictured pulling into the long driveway that led to my mother's fancy new house, saw Megan hopping out and waving good-bye to me with her little backpack over her shoulders, dragging the big one along by her side. Then, as she slipped inside the warm welcome of the house, I was supposed to turn around and speed away without seeing my mother. The thought of that made the roof of my mouth ache.

Ridiculous. What did I care, right? I was mad at Mom. Didn't want to see her anyway.

I had to change the subject. "You didn't hear what happened at Nell's house, did you?"

"No." Megan turned to face me, her eyes bright with curiosity.

I told her about Nell's gruesome discovery, and how the cops found the footprint. I let her draw her own conclusion.

She didn't say anything at first, just looked thoughtful— and glum. She sighed a few times and shifted uncomfortably in her seat. Finally she said, "You don't think...?"

"Yeah, as a matter of fact I do," I replied, keeping my eyes on the road.

I heard the tears in her voice. "But, why? Why would anyone do such a horrible thing?"

I ticked the most obvious reasons off on the fingers of my right hand as I continued to drive. "Because he wanted to hurt Nell. Because he wanted to ruin the Bigfoot thing for us. Because he had it in for Chickabod." I glanced over. Her brow was furrowed, her mouth set in a hard line.

"What he did to Chickabod?" she finally said. "I'd like to do that to him."

"Me too."

"But we can't," she said. "So what can we do?"

"Not much. Seems his dad shipped him off to Grandma's." I shrugged. "I just hope he stays there for good."

"I'm sorry," Megan whispered. I barely heard her over the sound of the engine.

"I know." I was pulling into the driveway. Though it was only the beginning of August, the days were getting shorter. Dusk already and the bats were out, flitting over our heads in their frenzied hunt for mosquitoes. Horace's house looked like an old man hunkered down for a long wait. The windows reflected the early-evening light in their dark, blank stare, and the fence closed around us in a bony embrace.

It should have blown over. There was really nothing to go on. As far as crime investigations go, it wasn't a huge case. After all, chickens get knocked off by the millions every day, right?

So I wondered for a long time how the story broke. Maybe some kid had a part-time job at the police station for the summer and peeked at the incident report. He could've called his buddy who was interning at the local paper. I don't know for sure. But somehow, the media got wind of that stupid footprint.

Nell hadn't mentioned that one of the cops had taken a picture of the footprint. I didn't know anything about it until Mr. Pelletier showed me the front page of the *Gazette*. The *Gazette* wasn't much—six pages of smudgy newsprint that reported on all the events in the county, like bingo games and antique car shows. It also listed births, deaths, and marriages, and a few ads for local businesses. So I was surprised when Mr. Pelletier practically pushed the latest edition into my face.

"Do you know anything about this, young man?" He was stern, giving me one of those looks that teachers give you in study hall when they think you might have been the one who threw the spitball.

I took the paper from his hands, studying the grainy, indistinct black-and-white photo. It showed what definitely looked like a footprint in the muddy edge of a puddle, but nothing in the picture gave an indication of scale. "I heard something about it," I said. "Nell told me about the dead rooster."

"Is that all you know?" Mr. Pelletier crossed his big arms.

Oh, geez. He suspected it was staged and he thought I had done it. I looked straight at him and held his gaze. "Yes, sir. That's all I know, and I hope the police get to the bottom of it soon."

He took the paper back from me. "Well, all right, then. If you're sure. I just thought with all that crazy nonsense your uncle used to go on about, you might have gotten some ideas."

"No, sir."

Just then, Barry emerged from the baking aisle. While Mr. Pelletier's back was turned, Barry flipped me the bird. As soon as our boss glanced around, Barry was all smiles again. "Hey there, Mr. Pelletier," he exclaimed in a hearty voice. "Back in town and reporting for duty!"

"Glad to see you," Mr. Pelletier said. "There's a delivery due any minute now. I'm going to need both you boys to help unload the truck."

I stifled a groan. I was doomed to spend a good part of the day with the last person on Earth I wanted to spend time with.

Barry threw another 3x3 carton of cake mix into my arms with undue force. "So, Jakey-boy," he said as he watched me stagger in an effort to regain my balance, "you guys ever find that boogeyman?"

"Nope. Turns out you were right all along." I stacked the box on the metal storage shelf and braced myself for the next cardboard-covered missile to fly through the storeroom.

"Me? Right about something? I can't believe you'd admit it."

"Turns out my dad's uncle was just a kook and there's nothing out there. We've given up the search. The movie project's all washed up."

"Too bad." He had a quizzical look on his face as he picked up the next box and threw it at me. "From what your sister blabbed to me, it sounded like you guys thought you were really on to something."

"Nope. You must have been drunk and misunderstood her."

Barry snorted. "*Someone* was drunk."

"Don't go there," I warned in a low voice.

Barry held up his arms in a gesture of truce. "Hey, buddy, forget I said anything. Let's let bygones be bygones. Fresh start and all that bullshit, okay?"

I looked him in the eye. "Sure, Barry. Let's be pals. Why don't you start by taking it easy with those cartons? Pelletier will have both our asses if we bust one of these open."

His eyes went all wide and innocent. "Gee, pal! Am I going too fast for you? Why didn't you say so?"

"Just leave those boxes there and go get the next load," I said wearily.

We worked for a while, moving on to other dry goods without much more conversation until, out of the blue, Barry said, "Yep, I'm surprised you guys gave up on that Bigfoot movie." I looked at him, wondering why he cared. "The way you acted about the gun and all, it was like you really believed you were protecting something."

"I just didn't want anyone to get hurt," I grumbled.

"Maybe, but it felt like something else was going on."

"Think what you want. Let's just say that as far as I'm concerned, whatever secrets might be in those woods can stay secret." I shelved the last box of Rice-A-Roni. "I think we're done here."

CHAPTER 35

It was midnight. I was lying in bed, listening to crickets and straining to hear the eerie duet of the Sasquatch mates calling to one another. But they were silent, and—I knew it was crazy—I wondered if they missed me as much as I missed them. Ridiculous. They were probably relieved to be living their big, stinky lives undisturbed by nosy teenagers.

Megan was quiet too—no moaning snores tonight. After the long, stressful day of working alongside Barry, you'd think I'd be able to conk right out. But I tossed and turned, questioning whether I should have told him I believed he was responsible for Chickabod's death, thinking about how empty the days seemed now that the great Bigfoot project had been scrapped—and how awkward I felt around Nell. With no movie to work on, if I called and invited her to just hang, it would feel too much like I was asking her out on a date. We'd been getting along so well, I didn't want to rock the boat.

The next morning, I dropped Megan off at the library and was so out of it when I pulled into the grocery store parking lot, I almost drove right through the police tape blocking the entrance. But there was no way I could miss the news truck parked at the curb—one of those panel jobs with a satellite dish on the roof. The big white number three painted on the side told me it was from the Hartford station. There was a lot of activity around it. A bunch of guys were running around with headsets draped around their necks.

Now what?

After parking the Jeep down the street, I walked back to the store. I knew that there was no point in asking the TV crew anything—they were sure to feel too important to talk to some kid. It would have been nice to watch them at work, though—observe the real deal, professionals in action and all that. But I might as well have been invisible as I strolled past them, craning my neck to see what was going on.

There seemed to be a big hubbub around the Dumpster.

I made my way to the front entrance of the building. The store was quiet, and even though we were open for business, the place looked abandoned. I finally found the entire morning shift gathered in the back room, crowded around the window that looked out onto the back lot.

Peering around Zack, the deli guy, I could see Mr. Pelletier standing in a pool of artificially bright light with a young woman who appeared to be jabbering away into a microphone. I guessed she was a reporter interviewing Mr. Pelletier, but she seemed to be doing all the talking.

"What the heck is going on?" I blurted out.

"Someone vandalized the parking lot—made a big mess around the Dumpster, smashed up the storage shed, broke the windshield on the delivery van." Myrna looked back at me, twisting her wrinkled face over her shoulder. She was lit up with excitement. "The cops were here for hours. Left one guy to keep an eye on the scene."

"Was anyone murdered?"

"Not so's they found yet," Myrna said in an ominous tone that sounded almost hopeful, her mouth clamping down into a grim line before she turned her attention back to the surreal scene outside.

"Then why the big deal?" Since when did some kids fooling around in a parking lot become worthy of a featured spot on the five o'clock news?

"There's another one of those big footprints," Zack said, shrugging my hand off his shoulder. "Like at Nell's place."

"Bullshit!"

"Watch your mouth there!" Zack said, as if I could offend Myrna's delicate sensibilities. But I wasn't really listening to him anymore. I was pushing through the employee huddle to get to the back door.

I burst out and marched toward the corner by the garbage enclosures, where there was more yellow police tape and a couple of guys with cameras. It looked like they'd wrapped up the interview; the reporter wasn't anywhere around. Out of the corner of my eye, I saw Mr. Pelletier scowling at me, having noticed my dramatic appearance on the scene, but I didn't care. I wanted to see for myself.

Aware of hands grabbing at me, I shook them off and pulled away. I found myself staring down at a soft patch of ground right where the blacktop ended. Sure as hell, it looked as if someone had left a huge, distinct footprint in the scruffy grass.

For a few dizzying seconds, I stood transfixed, thinking all the time, *No way!* I mean, why, after all this time, would the ever-elusive Sasquatch go on a rampage in a downtown parking lot?

Forceful hands kept tugging at me, and blathering voices were yelling, but I couldn't take my eyes off that one print. Again, one print. Only one print. But it sure looked like the real thing—like a real Bigfoot.

In that swirling moment, while there was nothing but angry chaos around me, it struck me—I had never actually seen a Bigfoot print. Like Samuel had said, it was hard to find any animal tracks in the kind of debris that litters the New England woodland floor. So why did I think this one looked so convincing? So familiar, like I'd seen it before? Because I had.

Because it was made from Samuel's precious plaster cast— the one he had given to me. The day Barry had killed the bear, the day we'd gotten so stupidly lost for hours, the day we came back to find the door wide open—it was starting to make sense.

Now Mr. Pelletier was on me, yanking insistently on my arm. "Jake, son," he was saying, "I know you're curious." He stopped, eyeing me with extra-close scrutiny. "Not *too* curious, are you?"

I shook my head in denial. I wasn't going around making footprints or causing trouble, and I started to say as much. Mr. Pelletier cut me off, "All right, all right, but there's an investigation going on here. You have to go back into the store. It's time everyone got to work."

I stood my ground, stubbornly refusing to move. "Where's Barry?"

Mr. Pelletier seemed surprised by my question but answered right away. "He called in sick this morning."

"Right." I shook his hand off my arm. As soon as I was free, I broke into a run.

A quick stop at the house confirmed my suspicions. The plaster cast was gone from the bottom of the coat closet.

I pulled into the driveway of the little ranch, noting that the lawn chair we'd dumped Barry on all those weeks ago was right where we'd left it, a shaggy clump of weeds growing up around it. Two cars were in the driveway—Barry's Mustang and a big old Cadillac.

Somehow, I hadn't expected a woman to come to the door. She was small and timid-looking, wearing faded jeans and a nondescript T-shirt, her graying hair pulled severely away from her haggard face. She eyed me suspiciously while wiping her hands on a dingy dish towel. "Yes?" she said. "Can I help you?" Funny, I'd heard so much about Barry's badass dad that I'd never considered that he might actually have a mother.

Right away I switched gears from kick-butt confrontation into nice-young-man mode. "Excuse me, Mrs…Ma'am?" I said politely. What the hell was Barry's last name? "Sorry to disturb you, but is Barry home?"

She was shrewder than I'd thought. Her eyes narrowed to slits, and she crossed her arms. "That depends," she said. "Who's asking?"

"Oh, I'm sorry." I smiled sheepishly. "My name's Jake Oliver. I'm a friend of Barry's. We work together at the market."

"Is that so?" It didn't look like she had any intention of budging from the doorway. "I never heard of you. What do you want with Barry?"

"I heard he wasn't feeling well," I said. "Just thought I'd stop by and see if he needed anything."

"No, he doesn't need anything." She started to retreat into the house.

Like a desperate door-to-door salesman, I stuck my foot out to stop the door from banging closed. I think my big toe was permanently dented, but I tried not to let the pain show on my face. "Well, actually, there *is* something else." I spoke in a rush, not so nice anymore. "I have to see him for a second. He borrowed something from me, and I need it back."

Weird, but I'd gotten through to her. Politely claim you were a concerned friend? She was a bulldog of a gatekeeper who wouldn't let you pass if you lit dynamite under her. But accuse her kid of being in possession of property that didn't belong to him—that was an "open sesame." Go figure.

She hollered, "Barry!" over her shoulder, so loudly I actually jumped. Then she turned back to me and ordered, "You wait here," before slamming the door in my face.

Standing on the little front porch, I could hear muffled conversation, some bumping around, and more door-slamming, until Barry finally burst out of the house. He looked like he'd just rolled out of bed, puffy-eyed and wrinkled, his hair standing up in spikes.

When he realized it was me waiting for him, he pulled himself together a bit and smiled at me lazily, scratching his stomach through his T-shirt. "Dude," he drawled. "What brings you here?"

I willed all my anger and tension into my balled fists before I answered with clenched jaws, "You have something that belongs to me."

Barry plopped himself down onto a beat-up old rocking chair, eyeing me thoughtfully. "Is that so? Now what might that be?"

I wanted to smash him in the face but knew that wasn't going to get me anywhere. How many times had I punched this dude already? He was the only guy I'd ever hit, and even though it was beginning to become a habit, it obviously hadn't left a lasting impression. The yellowing bruise on his cheek from the last time would disappear soon. I'd already hurt my foot—no need to reinjure my hand. But just in case I needed to pummel him again, I curled up my fingers so tight into my palms that I thought they might break. "Let's just say I figured out where those bogus footprints are coming from."

"Hmmmm." He looked up to the sky. "I think I might have read something about that in the newspaper."

"Yeah, and now there's a TV film crew at the market."

At that piece of information, Barry threw his head back, letting out a whoop of triumphant laughter. "Awesome!"

"No one else seems to have figured out who's causing all this trouble," I said, ignoring his amusement. "So why don't you just give me back the cast, and I won't tell the police you're to blame."

Barry's laughter stopped abruptly, his face collapsing into a scowl of anger. "Don't you have something to give back to me first, asshole?"

For a couple of seconds, I was genuinely at a loss. What did I have that he thought belonged to him? All I could think of was Nell, but that couldn't be what he meant.

And then I remembered—the oily glint of the gun as it arced through the air before splashing into the reservoir. I looked him in the eye. "I don't have it, man," I said in a low voice. "It's gone."

"That's bullshit, Jakey-boy." He straightened up, glaring at me, the muscles of his jaw flexing. When I didn't answer, he went on, "You keeping it under your pillow? Or did you sell it?"

"Trust me, Barry, it's just gone. I threw it in the reservoir." Better that he blame me than Nell. As I spoke, I watched him, kind of like you might watch a rattlesnake, caught in the suspense of wondering when it was going to stop hissing and finally strike.

I'd braced myself for an assault, but to my surprise, Barry slouched again, seeming to relax. He let that lazy smile ooze over his beefy face again, and he crossed his arms. "Then let's just say I don't have anything of yours, either."

"Why, man?" I said. "What's the game?"

"No game, Jakey-boy." He uncrossed his arms and started examining his fingernails. "When you stole that gun, you brought a ton of shit down on me. I just want to return the favor."

"Barry," I said in a reasonable tone, as if he was a reasonable person. "We were just afraid someone was going to get hurt. And no one did."

"I'm not hurting anybody, am I?"

"I don't think Mr. Pelletier is too happy about the van's windshield," I pointed out, "and you hurt Nell, that's for sure."

Barry shrugged. "Collateral damage," he said in an offhand drawl, "and that damn bird had it coming."

"I still don't get it," I said, truly baffled. "You ripped the plaster cast to get back at me for the gun—but what's with the footprints?"

He looked at me, a mean, icy fire burning in his eyes. His voice was low and menacing. "Thought it was time I forced your hand, man."

"You'll have to explain." It was my turn to shrug.

"You show up here, out of the blue, with all your bullshit about being a movie director, making big money." He stood up, thrusting his big-jawed face into mine. It took all my willpower not to back away. "So, here it is, asshole. Here's your big chance to show what you got. The world is watching. Time to put up or shut up."

I tried not to flinch from his hot, stale breath. "I told you, dude. There's nothing out there."

"To be honest with you, asshole?" Barry grabbed the neckband of my T-shirt tight around my throat, pulling me up onto my toes "I think you're right. I think you made the whole thing up. But Nell believes you. And now Nell will see what a lying piece of shit you really are." Then he shoved me backward, sprawling off the porch. I flew wildly through the air, my arms and legs flailing before I thudded down painfully on my butt in the dust at the bottom of the stairs.

Before I could scramble back to my feet, expecting him to land on me in a full body-slam, Barry disappeared back into the house, the door crashing behind him.

Gasping for air, I stood in the stillness of the deserted yard for a second, hardly aware of my aching butt.

So, all this time, what was going on between us and between him and Megan—it was all about Nell.

CHAPTER 36

Due to our lack of television, Megan and I never saw the story that hit the local evening news. But it must have been a good one.

It was around ten o'clock when the first carload roared through.

Megan was sitting on the couch, her hair still wet from the shower, curled up with the sign-language book. I was watching the last fifteen minutes of *Butch Cassidy and the Sundance Kid* on DVD. The sound of tires squealing and drunken whoops sent us both flying to our feet. Our eyes locked.

"What the hell's going on?" Megan asked, her eyes wide.

Instinctively, I shut down the monitor and told Megan to turn off the lamp. As soon as the room was dark, we crept to the window at the front of the house. I was especially glad the porch light wasn't on. A car had pulled onto the shoulder of the road. The scene was dimly lit from the headlights and interior lamp. From what we could make out, a bunch of people were piling out from every door. Flashlight beams bounced against the dense trees. We heard wild laughter and glass breaking. Someone let out a howling war cry that sent a chill up my spine.

"Did you tell Barry that Dad's away?" I couldn't keep the accusation out of my voice. It was bad enough Barry had the balls to break in to steal the plaster footprint. Last thing we needed was for that crowd to storm the house. I figured they wouldn't dare if they thought an adult was on the premises.

"I swear! I didn't! You don't think they're coming here?"

"I don't think so," I said grimly. "I think they're heading into the woods."

Even from where we sat, huddled against the wall in the dingy, darkened room, we could feel the overheated excitement of the group. The laughter and shouting had a hysterical edge.

When the second car pulled up, the atmosphere felt downright dangerous. From the size of the guys spilling onto the side of the road, it looked like the football team had showed up. A deep voice yelled, "Let's go find that Bigfoot!" More bellowing and apelike howls echoed in the night.

"Oh no!" Megan gasped, turning to look at me, her eyes wide with alarm.

"How much you want to bet Barry's out there someplace?" I said.

"I'm not going to take that bet." Her voice was shaky. "Shouldn't we do something? Call the police?"

"We could," I said, considering. "But then we'd have a whole lot of questions to answer ourselves. I don't think we want to do that."

"Do you think they're going to find anything?"

"Doubt it. They're making a lot of noise. If they got anywhere close, the Sasquatch would hear them and move away."

"There they go," Megan said as the crowd formed a loose column, following the trail that led into the preserve.

"It's like watching the villagers march off in search of Frankenstein's monster. All they need are pitchforks."

"Thank God for flashlights," Megan said. "Imagine if they had torches! The idiots would set the woods on fire."

We watched the action outside until we lost sight of the last beam behind the black cover of trees. As they moved farther and farther along the path, the sound of their voices receded. Within minutes, all we could hear were the crickets again.

"I hope they don't get too scared," Megan said eventually, and I knew she'd been picturing the same scene that was playing in my head. I could see our big hairy family hunkered down in the back of a cave, listening to the strange, threatening noises disrupting the nighttime forest. Would they know it was a new species of predator—stupid, but dangerous—coming after them?

CHAPTER 37

Neither Megan nor I slept too well that night. After the gang of idiots piled into the woods, there was nothing left to do but wait for them to come out. Determined not to be too ruffled, we both agreed to go to bed. I'm sure Megan lay as alert and anxious in her bed as I did in mine, until at last, sometime around three AM, the hunting party found their way back to their cars. This time the sound of gunning engines and squealing tires was a lullaby. Exhausted and relieved, I finally managed to drop off to sleep.

But the alarm that woke me up at dawn was even weirder—a thumping, whirring, rhythmic thunder.

Megan was in my room before I could plant my feet on the floor. "Now what?" she shouted over the deafening roar.

"How should I know?" I pulled a T-shirt over my head before I stuck my head out the window.

A helicopter—flying so low over the house it shook the frame and rattled the windows. I had to twist my neck awkwardly to catch a glimpse of it. "Holy shit!" I exclaimed. It left me in a cold shadow as it passed over.

"What? What?" Megan was thumping on my back impatiently. "What is it?"

I pulled myself back into the room. My head was spinning. "It's a helicopter. There's a guy with a video camera hanging out of the door." In fact, the way the man was dangling, for a dizzying second I thought he had a gun and was getting ready to strafe the house.

"Shit!" Megan exclaimed. It was her turn to stick her head out of the window at a crazy angle.

I tugged the back of her shirt. "If you don't want to end up on TV, you better pull your head back in."

CHAPTER 38

We searched for local news online, but it was hard to grasp what was really going on from what we could find. It was important to remain informed if we wanted to keep ahead of what was happening. Before I could even walk into work, Nell rushed out into the parking lot, stopping just short of running into my arms. "Oh my God, they've been calling the store like crazy, but all Mr. Pelletier would say was, 'No comment'! Then he couldn't stand it anymore and let the machine pick up for a while. Finally, he just pulled the plug from the wall."

"Who's calling?" I asked stupidly. Stupidly, because I'd seen the helicopter—I knew what she was talking about.

"The network-news people. All of them! They must have picked up on the local news segment last night. All of a sudden, it's a big story. It was on all the morning shows—the national shows!"

I couldn't tell if Nell was wild with dismay or excitement. I suspected it was a little of both.

My stomach tightened.

Then Megan came running around the corner of the building. She was all lit up too. "Did you hear?" she called as she approached. I'd just dropped her off at the library. I didn't know she was capable of moving that fast.

"Shut up," I hissed, looking around to see if anyone was watching us. And it was very possible that someone *was* watching—a cop or a reporter. We were standing right in the middle of a crime scene. "Look, it must have been an incredibly slow news day yesterday. Remember, no one has actually seen a Bigfoot, right? The three of us, standing right here, know this is all bullshit, a hoax. Just stupid Barry making trouble. And as soon as the media figures that out, it will all die down." I looked at Nell. "Have they talked to your parents?"

She shook her head. "No. I guess they haven't discovered the Chickabod incident yet."

"Hopefully they won't." I looked at my watch. If I didn't hustle, I was going to be late. Mr. Pelletier had been pretty cool about my disappearing act yesterday—the last thing I wanted to do was piss him off today.

"Yeah, right," Nell agreed, taking a deep breath. "We just have to be cool."

"Sure," Megan said. "No one but the three of us and Samuel know for sure that there's anything behind all this."

"Right," I said firmly, "and we're going to keep it that way, right?"

"Right," the girls said in unison.

So we all went to work and got through the day as best we could. Pretty soon it became obvious that the excitement wasn't going to die down anytime soon. The day went by fast, because it was crazy busy in the store. I guess the few local diners and fast-food joints were so backed up, people were piling into the market, looking for sandwiches and drinks, grabbing every kind of snack. We were working double-time to restock. Who knew you could run out of bologna?

Once again Barry was a no-show, which was a relief. It would have been okay if he slipped up and said something that would incriminate him, reveal the truth behind the damage in the back lot. But he was more likely to open that big, stupid mouth of his and say something that would put me in an awkward position.

That night, it seemed like Megan and I would never make it back to the house. Two days earlier, we wouldn't have seen any other cars on the road home. Now we were caught in a traffic jam. There's only the one road that leads out of town toward Horace's shack, and it was bumper-to-bumper with vehicles. There were pickup trucks and minivans, old broken-down jalopies, and shiny new cars. Who knew there were so many Bigfoot hunters in the world? And how did they make it to this remote corner of Connecticut so fast?

When we finally pulled into the driveway, I was glad for that weird fence. It made the house hard to spot from the road. I couldn't stand the thought of anyone pulling out of that steady stream of sensation hunters to ask for directions or beg to use the facilities. It wouldn't hurt to keep the lights low again. The hinges on the front gate creaked when I swung it closed for the first time.

CHAPTER 39

Another sleepless night. It was beginning to be a regular thing. When Megan joined me in the Jeep, she was looking the worse for wear too. We'd been up half the night, listening to the traffic going by, desperately surfing the net for scraps of information. Nell had promised to keep a lookout for any more stories appearing on TV, but she hadn't called. We could only hope that all the Bigfoot-hunting nuts that were going to show up were already here.

There were still hordes of strange customers at the store, but it's weird how quickly the unusual becomes the norm. Nell had the day off, and once again Barry wasn't around, so I pretty much kept to myself. By three in the afternoon, I don't think I'd spoken more than a few sentences to anyone, so I nearly jumped out of my skin when someone struck up a conversation with me while I was restocking the cookie aisle.

"Fig Newtons," a female voice said, somewhere over my head. I was squatting down, stocking a low shelf.

"Huh?" was my stupid response. Whoever it was, she was standing behind me. Glancing over my shoulder, all I saw were slender, jean-covered legs that I guessed went with the silvery voice. She must be talking about the box I was putting on the shelf.

"Fig Newtons," she repeated cheerfully, plucking the box out of my hand. When she bent over, a whisper of silky hair brushed my cheek. She smelled like peppermint and freshly ironed clothes, warm and clean. I felt like some weird troll, hunched awkwardly on the floor, twisting in a mad contortion to see more of her. Her feet were what I saw next—white sandals and tanned toes with nails polished a pearly pink. She kept talking, seeming unaware of the clumsy way I was groveling around. "I mean, whoever thought to put figs in a cookie? Because really, who eats figs?"

"I don't know," I mumbled. Honestly, I'd never given it a thought.

"I loved them when I was a kid," she continued. "They were all soft and sweet, but I can't remember the last time I ate one."

Grabbing the last couple of boxes, I shoved them onto the shelf, eager to get on my feet. As soon as I was standing, I found myself face-to-face with an angel.

She smiled at me with dewy lips. "It's Jake, right?"

I was knocked out. How did she know my name? Had I met her before? She was older than me, but not by much—maybe in college? "Uh, yeah," was all I could say.

"And you're Horace Oliver's nephew, right? You live in his house?"

"Um, grandnephew." My eyes were caught in the high beams of her big baby-blues. She knew me, but why couldn't I place her? Did she run with Barry's gang? That didn't seem possible. Had I met her the night of the carnival, or at the movies? Wouldn't I have remembered her?

Her laugh was musical, like tinkling chimes. "Of course, that's what I meant." I remained trapped in her bright gaze for a moment that seemed to last forever, until finally she said, "So—what do you think of all this?" She wrinkled her nose as she spoke.

"All of what?" I asked.

"All the Bigfoot excitement—what do you know about it?"

For a second, I couldn't look away from her hair. It was like a hundred different colors of blonde were all woven together, styled in wavy layers. It was perfect. She was perfect. *Too* perfect. "Um, know? Me? What do I know?" I stepped away from her. "Nothing."

She gave a little schoolgirl pout. "That's not what I heard," she purred. "I heard you were the go-to guy around here."

I felt my face go hot and red. "Well, I don't know where you got that idea." I bent down to pick up the empty carton.

"Oh," said Angel Face in a cooing voice, "I've been asking around. From what I hear, Horace was a knowledgeable guy."

"Yeah?" I ran my thumbnail along the top seam of the carton to slit the tape open and felt a burning slice in my thumb. Damn. Paper cut. Great. I had no choice but to suck my thumb. Either that or bleed all over the place.

"Yes, and from what I gather, you might have access to some useful information." She reached around me, shelving the package of cookies into place. Her bare arm brushed my bare arm, causing an electric prickling. As she straightened back up, we were standing practically nose-to-nose. I wished my thumb wasn't in my mouth. "I'd love to meet with you somewhere to talk about it. When are you finished here?"

"Well, I don't know…," I began to say. "I get off in an hour, but I have to give my sister a ride…" Hey! Wait a minute! She was fishing for information. God, was I an idiot. All I could do was blame sleep-deprivation for dropping my guard. That, and blatant seduction. "Who are you?"

Her manner briskly shifted into the brightly polished attitude of a grown-up, professional woman. Holding out her hand, she said, "Courtney Braxton. I'm a producer for *Another Day, USA!*"

Oh shit. I wanted to run away, but she held my hand in her iron grip, pumping it in such a vigorous handshake that my shoulder started to ache.

Twisting my hand free, I said, "Got to get back to work." I tried to run, but she kept hot on my heels.

"No, really, Jake, please," she called after me. "Please sit down with me! I just want to ask you a few questions."

I managed to get the swinging steel door closed behind me, sliding the bolt home so that she couldn't follow me into the employee area.

I had walked right into that one. But I hadn't told her anything, had I?

CHAPTER 40

I tried to find busywork in the storeroom to get myself through the last couple of hours. But I was so desperate to get out of the store that when Mr. Pelletier came through, I told him I had a stomachache so that he'd let me leave early. Darting out the back door like a fugitive, I made it to the Jeep before Courtney could find me again. I had the feeling that I hadn't seen the last of her. She'd pegged me as someone in the know. And it freaked me out.

Megan was surprised to see me walk into the children's section of the library. I found her in a back corner shelving history books. "What are you doing here?" she asked in a loud whisper. "I was going to meet you at the market in an hour."

"I'm a nervous wreck," I admitted. "I feel like they're closing in on us and we're at a real disadvantage. We have to find someplace to watch the news tonight...somewhere public, so we can hear what people are talking about." I told her about Courtney and was glad when Megan's eyes grew wide with concern.

"Holy shit!" she said in full voice, setting off a chorus of harsh shushing and angry glares from a small gathering of mothers with their little kids. She cringed a silent apology, then grabbed my arm and dragged me right out of the library. She led me over to a stone bench, and we both plopped down.

"So," I said. "We need to find a Best Buy or Walmart or something. One of those places that has a big bank of television sets."

"And what? Ask the kid working there if he wouldn't mind switching from the *Harry Potter* DVD to the news? That wouldn't be too obvious." She snorted. "Besides..." She checked her phone for the time. "It's quarter to six now. We need to find someplace closer. And I'm getting hungry." She punched in a number. After a few rings, I heard the soft, husky tones of Nell's voice, faint but distinct, through the phone's tiny earpiece. "Yeah, hi, it's me," Megan said. "Look, is there some old-man bar around here that has a TV? We want to catch the news and pick up some gossip." She listened to whatever Nell had to say, then said, "Yeah, I think I know where that is. Can you get a burger there?"

I gestured in annoyance at her. Was she worried about the national news media machine descending on us, or about stuffing her face?

She shrugged me off. "Yeah, that sounds perfect. Why don't you come with us?" My mood lifted when Megan said, "Great, meet you there in ten."

Smart girl, my sister—I was finally going to see Nell, but I tried not to show my eagerness. "An old-man bar?"

"Sure." She stood, stowing her phone back into the bottomless pit of her purse. "This is like the biggest thing to happen around here since the Revolutionary War. The regulars will skip a few innings of the ball game to catch the news tonight. Every old geezer in town's going to belly up to that bar. We'll see what the media's saying, and we'll also get an idea what the local take on it all is."

Like I said—smart girl, my sister.

It wasn't surprising that McTavish's was a dump, complete with a tacky linoleum floor that sucked at the soles of your shoes with each step and red, vinyl-covered chairs that dated to the 1950s. Smoking in bars might have been banned in

Connecticut years ago, but the dark paneled walls seemed to exude a half-century's worth of stale cigarette smoke.

Just as Megan predicted, guys that looked like they'd just come in from a long day working outdoors sat on every barstool. Wearing heavy work boots and trucker caps, they reached for their frosty mugs with thick, calloused hands as their attention was focused on the flat screen suspended from the ceiling. Surprisingly, the tables were filling up as well, and we quickly snagged one with a good view of the television.

Minutes after our arrival, Nell walked in. Only then were the eyes of the men at the bar diverted from the television. They watched her move across to us with her long-legged stride, her dark hair flowing down her back. I felt a strange mix of emotions welling up in me—pride that this amazing girl was coming to sit with me, anger at the obviously pervy appreciation in the older men's faces, and a big walloping stab of insecurity.

We ordered burgers from a waitress old enough to be our great-grandmother. I couldn't take my eyes off her bright orange, curly hair.

After Ancient Orphan Annie left, Nell asked, "What are we really doing here, anyway?"

I pointed to the television set. "We're here to see this." And sure enough, the room fell silent as we all watched the young reporter, who I recognized as the girl who had interviewed Mr. Pelletier, give a brief update on the story. There were a few shots of Main Street to show the number of out-of-state cars that were clogging the town. The segment ended with a couple of brief, man-on-the-street Q&As before the local girl signed off.

"Well, that was weird," said Megan.

Nell only sighed with happiness as the aged waitress shuffled over to serve us our plates loaded with enormous cheeseburgers and mountains of fries.

"Go on and tell Nell about the producer from *Another Day, USA!*" said Megan.

So I did, leaving out being so dazzled by how pretty Courtney was that it took me some time to figure out she was trying to pump me for information.

"Wild, huh?" Megan reached for the ketchup. "Too bad we can't call Mom and tell her about it."

"Why's that?" Nell asked through a mouthful of meat and bread.

"Our mom's crazy about that show," I said as I sprinkled salt on my fries. "She watches it every morning—when she's not at work or sleeping, that is. There was a time she was putting in so many hours at work, she said it was the only way she could keep up with what was happening in the world. When she pulled the graveyard shift, she'd stay up to watch before she crawled into bed."

"It became a habit with all of us," Megan chimed in. "It got so that, even if Mom wasn't home, we'd put it on every day. Like we couldn't get through the morning routine without it."

"It's true," I agreed. "We'd get up with the morning lead story, eat our breakfast while watching the international headlines. If we didn't leave the house by the 7:35 Sensation, we'd be in danger of missing the bus."

"The 7:35 Sensation?" Nell asked.

"Yeah, you know," said Megan, "all those stories about grooms falling overboard on their honeymoon cruises, chimp attacks, dead celebrities... You know, the tabloid stories—"

"Shhhhh, look!" I pointed to the TV.

The local newscast was over, and the network news was droning on. I'd been watching with half an eye as we ate. Then on the screen there was an aerial view of a densely wooded expanse broken by a clearing where I saw the roof of our dilapidated house surrounded by the outline of the irregular fence.

"Holy crap!" Megan breathed.

Everyone watched in silence as the little town in the middle of nowhere, in the third smallest state in the country, was featured on the national news because of a stupid-ass stunt perpetrated by the biggest asshole I've ever had the misfortune to meet. Unbelievable.

The story didn't say anything new, really, and nothing even remotely substantial. But the correspondent tried to make himself sound all interesting and mysterious, talking about secrets lurking in primeval forests, the truths that may lie at the heart of ancient legends—all that kind of crap.

After the piece ended and the show went to commercial, the room came alive in a buzz of conversation. I swear I heard the names "Horace" and "Samuel" mentioned.

I pushed my plate away, my appetite gone. "This is bad," I said, "and it's only going to get worse. Wait and see what happens tomorrow. Every nut in the country is going to descend on this town in the next twenty-four hours. It's going to be a nightmare."

"What can we do?" Nell asked, her voice low, her expression solemn.

"I don't know," I said, "but we better come up with something fast." We were all silent for a while, considering what we could do to protect the Sasquatch from the overexcited, media-incited hordes that were about to invade their sanctuary.

"Well," said Megan, "there's one good thing."

"What's that?" I asked.

"At least none of the national-news guys have picked up on what happened to Chickabod. That would be awkward."

"What do you mean?" Nell said, looking puzzled.

I wish to God I'd been able to anticipate what Megan was about to say. If I had only shut her up—kicked her hard enough in the shin to break her leg so that she'd be in so much pain she wouldn't be able to talk. Then she wouldn't have said to Nell, "Well, if they knew about what happened to Chickabod and the footprint in your yard, and then did a little background check, you could have been tomorrow's 7:35 Sensation—young woman traumatized in childhood revisited by tragedy…"

Silence again. Dead silence. Nell's face went white. "What do you mean?" she said again, this time her voice tight and hoarse.

Megan's expression registered horror as she realized the enormity of the slip she'd made. I could have killed her. I could tell that she was struggling with what she should say next. She didn't make a good choice. Her voice faltering, she said, "You know. I'm just glad they're not going to dig up what happened to you when you were a little girl."

Nell seemed to be studying the faux woodgrain of the Formica tabletop, so I couldn't read her face. She spoke in such a low voice we could barely hear her. "You know about that."

"Yes," I admitted.

She looked up at me, her dark eyes full of pain, swimming with tears. "Because of what Barry said…in the woods that day…about my *trauma*?"

"Before that, but I don't know much. Just that something bad happened with a babysitter a long time ago."

"Why didn't you tell me that you knew?" Her voice rose, edged with anger. She met my eyes first in an accusing glare, then shifted to Megan.

"Barry told me a while ago," Megan said, shrugging her shoulders in a limp gesture of apology.

"And you told him?" Nell nodded to indicate me.

"Yes." Megan bowed her head.

Nell looked at me, square in the face, her eyes blazing. "Why didn't you tell me you knew?"

I wanted to reach across the table and take her hand, but I'd learned my lesson—if Nell wanted to be touched, she did the touching. Instead, I folded my hands in front of me on the table and said, "I was hoping you would tell me yourself— when you were ready to tell me, like you said."

Nell shot up, sending her chair toppling over with a crash. "You can both do me a favor and leave me alone!"

Before I could react, Nell spun on her heel and dashed out of McTavish's.

I locked eyes with my sister before jumping up in pursuit of Nell. Not wanting to waste a second, I sprinted between tables toward the door. Just a few tantalizing yards away from grabbing the doorknob, I caught a glimpse of Nell running toward her little Karmann Ghia. Then I suddenly landed face-flat on the sticky, gray floor. If that wasn't bad enough, my sudden tumble caused a domino effect as Megan, right behind me, somersaulted over me.

Dazed and confused, still anxious to catch up with Nell but wondering what the hell just happened, I looked up to find that crone of a waitress glaring down at me. Ancient Orphan Annie had stuck her orthopedic shoe out to trip me up before I could get to the door.

"Not so fast, pal," she growled, baring her yellow teeth in a snarling grimace. Her fisted hands were on her hips as she took a quick sidestep to get between the door and us. "You're not going anywhere until you pay your bill—plus tip!"

As I tried to get to my feet, I said, "I wasn't going to stiff you, I swear! I was just trying to catch up with my—"

"Easy to prove," she said. "Just show me the money."

A basso voice behind me said, "Yeah, show my ma the money, punk."

I twisted my head around to find the bartender, all six foot six of him, standing menacingly over me. The flat overhead light reflected off his bald head.

Megan and I scrambled to our feet, digging in our pockets for money. Within seconds, both of us held our hands out, offering wads of bills to buy our freedom.

Ancient Orphan Annie snatched the money from us and carefully counted. Only when she was satisfied with the amount did she give the nod to Junior. He stomped his huge booted foot to the floor with a deafening thud, just millimeters from my foot.

"All right, you two," he said. "You can go. But don't show your faces here again. Got it?"

"Got it."

"Yes, sir!" Megan barked, already at the door, clawing to get it open.

It was no surprise that Nell was nowhere in sight when we finally made it outside. We could hear a roaring chorus of laughter coming from inside the restaurant as we plodded to the Jeep.

Getting in and slamming the door, I rested my head on the steering wheel for a moment before I started the engine.

"What should we do now?" Megan asked, her voice a tentative whine. "Should we go after Nell?"

I lifted my head and glared at her. "Too late now, big mouth. What the hell were you thinking?" I felt like slapping her.

Tears welled in Megan's eyes, and her cheeks got all red and splotchy. "I forgot!" she cried. "I forgot that we're not supposed to know!"

"Well, we may never be able to make things right with Nell now," I said miserably, turning the key in the ignition and putting the Jeep in reverse. I tore out of the parking lot.

"Are we going home?" Megan asked over the roar of the engine.

"Not yet," I said.

CHAPTER 41

My heart sank when we pulled up to Samuel's old shed. I had expected him to be sitting outside in the last light of the day, maybe heating up a can of chili over a campfire. But the scruffy clearing was absolutely still, the little log cabin boarded up tight.

"Damn," I breathed, putting the Jeep in park but letting it idle as I thought.

"Where do you think he could be?" Megan asked meekly. She'd been quiet on the ride out, no doubt feeling guilty about Nell and scared I'd yell at her some more.

"I don't know." All this crap was bearing down on us. I needed someone to talk to. Someone who knew more than I did. Someone who might be able to help.

Megan and I continued to sit in silence for a few more minutes, and it was just that time of the evening when dusk seems to fall with a thud.

My indecision was paying off. As the sky went from a deep blue to a velvety black, I could just barely make out a tiny glint of light between the slats of Samuel's little cabin.

I turned off the ignition, jumped out of the car, and ran to the door, resisting the impulse to pound on it. Taking a deep breath, I rapped lightly and called in a soft voice, "Samuel? It's me, Jake Oliver—Horace's grandnephew. I need to talk to you."

Megan had followed me. I could feel her listening intently for Samuel's response.

"Go away!"

"Hi, Samuel. I'm here too," Megan called, managing to keep her voice gentle. "We need to ask your advice."

"No. Go away!" The old man's voice was muffled, but emphatic.

"But we don't know who else to talk to," she pleaded truthfully. "Please come out and talk to us."

"Can't," Samuel replied, his voice less harsh. "There're too many out there."

"Too many what?" I asked.

"People," he said in a hoarse whisper. "Strangers. All over the place. Haven't you seen? The woods are crawling with them. These are my woods. I like it here because there aren't too many people. Now there're too many people."

"Yes, Samuel," I said. "We know about that. That's why we're here."

"Are you here to make them go away?" he asked, his voice hopeful.

"I don't know if I can do that," I said.

"Oh." He sounded miserably disappointed. "Then why did you come?"

"How long have you been shut up in there?" said Megan.

"Days." We could hear him sigh.

"Are you all right?" she crooned, like she was talking to a little kid. "Have you got enough to eat?"

"I got enough beans, water, and Beefaroni to get me through for a while."

"How about something sweet?" she asked. "You got anything sweet to eat in there?"

"No," he admitted, forlorn.

"Hold on one sec," Megan whispered to me.

Now what? I was getting frustrated by the big waste of time this trip was turning out to be. If Samuel wouldn't or couldn't help us, we had to come up with a different strategy, pronto.

Megan furiously rummaged around in the bottom of her bag. Finally, a big grin brightened her face as she pulled out a battered Kit Kat. "Hey, Samuel? I got a treat for you—something to satisfy that sweet tooth of yours," she sang, "but you have to come out here and talk to us if you want it."

"What you got?"

"A Kit Kat bar," Megan answered.

We both held our breath until we heard the rattle of metal as Samuel unhooked the latch. The door creaked open, and I was shocked by the wild look of fear on Samuel's face. He was painfully thin and extremely dirty.

"Where's the candy?" he demanded.

Megan took a step back. "Right here in my hand, but you have to come out." She held up the bait in clear view.

The temptation was raw in Samuel's face, and I could see how torn he was between venturing out of the security of his lair and the desire to cram that candy bar into his mouth.

"Come on, Samuel," Megan continued to coax. "There's no one out here but Jake and me, and you know us; we're not strangers. Come on and get some fresh air and dessert."

"All right," he finally agreed, taking a full step out. It had gotten very dark, but the moon was rising, bathing us in a milky light.

Walking with stiff, jerky steps, Samuel made his way to the fallen log he used as a bench. We cautiously followed him over. As soon as he was settled, Megan handed him his reward.

Just as I knew he would, Samuel practically inhaled the candy, and it wasn't until he'd swallowed every morsel and finally came up for air that he asked, "What the hell's going on around here, anyway?"

"That's why we're here," I reminded him.

Megan cut in. "We knew that this all would be really strange to you, and we wanted to explain what's going on."

"Well, go ahead." Samuel, bolstered by a sugar fix and somewhat restored to his old self, prompted her with a nod. I was itching to blurt out exactly what we wanted from him but decided to follow Megan's lead.

"They've heard about the Sasquatch. They're all out looking for them," she began.

"And we're afraid someone will find them. Try to take them away from here or worse. We're afraid the Sasquatch are going to get hurt," I said. "That's why we need your help."

Samuel rubbed the whiskers on his face thoughtfully. "Heck, that *is* a problem. You're going have to get them to the house."

"To the house?" I asked. "What house?"

"Horace's house, of course."

"Why?"

Samuel shrugged. "That's what Horace did when things got bad. Like that year we had the big blizzard. He gave them shelter from the storm."

"Horace brought them into his house?" I asked, totally confused.

"Well, not in the house, so much as the cellar."

"But we thought Horace was afraid of the Bigfoot," Megan said.

"What in the world made you think that? Horace wasn't afraid of them. And they weren't afraid of him, either," Samuel said.

"Then I don't get it," Megan said. "Why build that big fence if he wasn't afraid of them?"

He looked her in the eye. "Fences are useful things, young lady. They're good at keeping things out. But they're just as good for hiding behind, just as good at keeping the things you want to keep private, private."

All of a sudden, that crazy fence made all the sense in the world. "How did you get them to come down from the ridge?" I asked.

Samuel looked at me like I was nuts. "You asking me? I don't know! It was your uncle who really understood them. Oh, they know I keep an eye on them, put up with me tracking them—but they don't let me get too close. It was old Horace they tolerated. And I don't know how he did it."

"Well, we're just going to have to figure it out. Can you at least help us find them?"

"Sure," he said, but I could hear the doubt in his voice. "I think I know where they're holing up these days."

"It's too late and too dark to do anything about it tonight. We'll get an early start tomorrow." I stood up.

"Why don't you come on with us now, Samuel," Megan said, "spend the night at the house?"

Fear crept back into the old man's eyes. "No." His voice went all quavery again. "I can't. Can't leave my stuff unguarded. Too many strangers around."

I was too tired to point out that not a single person had come anywhere near us during our visit. Besides, the prospect of having that smelly old man hanging around wasn't very pleasant—especially if we were getting ready to entertain a bunch of stink bombs in the cellar. "All right," I agreed, "but you have to promise to help us track them down tomorrow."

"Oh sure, oh sure," Samuel agreed, nodding emphatically. He stood and started edging back toward the safety of the shack.

"First light, Samuel," I called as he darted back into his hidey-hole and slammed the door. "We'll be back at dawn."

CHAPTER 42

I didn't need a television to know how bad things had gotten overnight. It was only four when I crawled out of bed, deciding to let Megan sleep for another half-hour or so. Tiptoeing down the stairs, I headed into the kitchen to make coffee. While it brewed I turned on the computer. No point checking the local papers, since they only published once a week. I went straight to the *New York Times* homepage, but never expected to see what I saw.

It was a front-page story—the stream of traffic heading up Route 7. Our little town was drawing a crowd—a huge one. The woods would be crawling with them.

We had to get those Sasquatch to safety, and we had to do it quick.

I'd only been down the cellar stairs once before. It was a dank, dark place that smelled of mildew and damp stone. Cobwebs hung everywhere in dusky gray swaths. Grabbing a broom, I swept each step as I headed down. Once I made it to the bottom, I found a pull chain to light the one grimy bulb that hung from the low ceiling.

Just as I'd suspected, it was a depressing little space. Stains on the concrete floor showed where groundwater had seeped in. Even in the dimness, you could see the small speckled piles of mouse turds in the corners. Shelves full of dusty junk covered one wall. The water heater and the furnace stood side by side near the steps up to the Bilco door that led to the backyard.

I felt bad, thinking about the Sasquatch having to hide in here, but then told myself I was being silly. Those guys lived in the woods, right? This cellar was probably the Grand Hyatt of the Bigfoot world. And if I brought some blankets and pillows down, it wouldn't be so bad, right? The fact of the matter was that it would have to do—if I could even get them there.

Coffee. Coffee was what I needed then. Heading back up the stairs, I shut the door behind me, wanting to contain the mildew as best I could. While I was on my way to the kitchen, I was stopped in my tracks by what I could swear was a soft tapping at the front door.

I froze in the dark living room, listening intently for a few moments, until I decided that it must have been a mouse—stirred up by my unprecedented visit to his domain in the basement. I resumed my mission. Before I'd gone two steps, the knocking started again, more emphatic and definitely coming from the front door. What the hell? My heart started pounding. Who could it be? I glanced toward the window and saw the first rosy hues of dawn. Of course—first light. Samuel must've gotten mixed up and thought he was supposed to meet us here. No problem. I strode to the door, swinging it open wide.

"I saw the light." Courtney's big, toothy smile gleamed brightly in the dimness. It struck me as kind of creepy, like a jack-o'-lantern. "I guessed you might be up."

Totally thrown by seeing her standing there on the doorstep, I said, "What are you doing—stalking me?"

Not exactly stepping over the threshold, she leaned casually against the doorframe and smiled sweetly. "Let's just say I'm keeping my eye on the prize."

Oh brother. "I don't know what you're talking about."

She crossed her arms, smile still in place. "As far as I can tell, we're the only news crew that's got a line on your uncle's... eccentric field of study. We think you might be able to give us a different angle."

"He was my dad's uncle, and he passed away." I stepped away from the sweet scent of her perfume. The smell was tickling my nose, which hadn't yet recovered from inhaling decades of cellar mold. I was feeling a little dizzy.

"Oh, we know that," Courtney dismissed. "But we figured that you'd know a little bit about his research, that you'd be able to give our story a little, well, depth."

I shrugged. "All I know is that Horace was the local nut job. I don't really know why, and it's not something I like to talk about. Sorry." I tried to swing the door closed, but Courtney managed to slither into the room with the grace and determination of a python. She was standing close, forcing me to back away from her. When she spoke, I could feel the warmth of her breath.

Her voice was low. "Maybe you could ask your dad to come down for a minute."

I didn't like the emphasis she put on the word *dad*. "Are you nuts? The sun's not even up yet. My dad would rip us both a new one if I woke him up now."

"Is that so?" she purred. I never knew a purr could sound so ominous.

"Yeah, that's so," I countered, trying to put on a tough front.

"What are you doing up so early?" she said. Her eyes narrowed, and her lips curled into a smile of cruel amusement.

"Work. I'm going in early. Big truckload coming in that needs to be unloaded."

"Really?" She cocked her head to look at me thoughtfully. "And how are you getting there? In that Jeep of yours?"

"Well, yeah, sure," I stuttered, unsure of where she was going.

She ran her fingers through her golden hair, looking thoughtfully off into the distance behind my right shoulder. "Huh. Funny."

"What's funny?" I was really getting fed up with being the mouse in this game.

"Well," she said, that big smile beaming again. "I have connections in all sorts of places. Like the Connecticut

Department of Motor Vehicles. I had a friend of mine in the department run your name. And you don't seem to have a driver's license. From what I could find out, you don't even have a learner's permit."

"Your friend is mistaken," I blustered.

"Maybe. People do make mistakes. But still…I think it may very well be my civic duty to inform the local authorities of the discrepancy."

That was all I needed—to get busted for driving without a license. *Thanks a lot, Dad.* I took a deep breath. "Listen, what do you want from me?"

"It's not so much what I want," said Courtney, pouting her plump lips, "but I work in a very competitive business. I need you to help me shine."

"Well, how do I do that?" I asked, resigned.

She snapped to attention, turning off the sex-kitten pleading and said, "My boss wants to interview you. You have to be honest, and it has to be exclusive."

"I told you—I don't know anything!"

"That's beside the point. My boss thinks you do. He wants to interview you, and he wants to be the only one. And it's my job to deliver. Have we got a deal?"

"When is this all going to happen?"

"Soon." Courtney's megawatt smile fired up extra bright, lighting up Horace's dreary living room. "I'll be in touch."

CHAPTER 43

I'd just shut the door behind Courtney when Megan came clattering down the stairs. "How come you didn't wake me up?"

"For God's sake, Megan," I yelled at her. "We're not going to the mall! Put on some real shoes and a pair of jeans, will you?"

"What bug wormed its way up your ass?" she shot back, though she did look down at her short-shorts and flip-flops with a thoughtful expression.

"The Courtney bug," I answered, shoving a couple of water bottles, some apples, and a can of bug spray into my backpack. My camera was stashed at the back of the closet in my room. Whatever happened today, I had no intention of capturing it on film. I didn't even want to be tempted.

"What?" Megan gasped.

"You heard me," I said. "*Another Day, USA!* seems to have us under surveillance or something. The second I turned the lights on this morning, Courtney was on the doorstep."

"That's crazy! It's still practically the middle of the night."

"She's a vampire for all I know. Believe me—Courtney was here."

"What did she want?"

"She wants to know what we know," I said grimly. "And she's not above using blackmail to get what she wants."

"Oh, come on," Megan scoffed. "What has she got on us?"

In a mock-German accent, I said, "Belief me. Courtney has vays of making us talk." I was trying to make light of the little encounter I'd just had with Miss Courtney, but the truth was...she scared the heck out of me.

"Oh, come on, like what?"

"Let's just say she knows a little too much about us. I think she even might have figured out that Dad's AWOL."

"How could she know that?"

A shiver went down my spine as I recalled the sinister way Courtney had asked if I could get my dad to come down. "I don't know, Megan! She's just good at her job! Which is more than I can say for the rest of us." I glared at her, hands on my hips. "Now hurry up and change your damn clothes. God knows how far we're going to have to hike today, so get on some good sturdy shoes and a pair of long pants, and let's get going. We're late."

"All right, all right, Grandma," Megan grumbled. "Can I get a cup of coffee first?"

"No!"

"What about Nell? Should we call Nell?"

I'd been thinking about Nell, about how she would want to be a part of Mission Sasquatch Rescue, but I didn't know how to bridge the abyss that had opened up between us. "We don't have the time."

Turned out we were going to have to hike even more than anticipated. After being careful that no helicopters or news vans were following us, we turned into the entrance of the old logging road, only to find it blocked by a wooden barrier. A stone-faced state trooper stood on duty, and as I brought the Jeep to a stop, he called out, "You have to turn around. This road's closed, sir. Authorized vehicles only."

Megan started to call out, "But our friend—"

I shut her up with a swift jab to the thigh. Megan stifled a yelp but stopped talking. Samuel was squatting on state property. Now that the place was swarming with all kinds of law enforcement, someone might try to evict the old geezer. I also didn't want to bring any particular attention to myself and my no-driver's-license status. "Okay, Officer." I slammed the gearshift into reverse, getting out of there fast. There was nothing left to do but go back to the house, park the car, and trudge on foot through the woods to Samuel's shack.

Needless to say, it was well past dawn when we got there. Worse yet—we encountered dozens of people on the trails along the way. Family groups and gangs of teenagers, some crew-cut idiots that were all tricked out in camouflage following their stupid GPS devices. There was an excitement in the air that was almost festive.

It would be a disaster if one of these groups got to the end of this search before we did.

Again, there were no signs of life around the shack, but I strode up to the door and knocked softly. "Samuel?" I called, putting my mouth right next to a crack. "It's us. Jake and Megan."

"I brought more cookies," Megan said over my shoulder. "I thought you might want to eat something before we got started."

No response. Not a sound. I knocked again. Maybe it was my imagination, but I swore I could feel him breathing, knew he was listening all crouched down and wired up on the other side of the thin plank door.

"Come on," I said, my voice a little louder. "I know you're in there, Samuel. It's too late to change your mind. We have to get going and we have to go now."

"You're late!" His voice came through the door, muffled and raspy.

"We know," said Megan, "and we're very sorry. We couldn't help it."

"Those strangers," he hissed, "they're all out there, worse than yesterday."

"We know." Megan's voice was soothing. "We'll have to be careful. Try not to let anyone see us. But if anyone comes close, I promise—we'll do all the talking. We won't let anyone get near you. Please, Samuel," she continued, revealing a little of the impatience we were both feeling, "you have to come. We can't do this without you."

"And if you think the woods are crowded now?" I added. "Just wait and see what happens if they find the Sasquatch before we do. Thousands more will show up, I guarantee."

That did it. The door creaked open and Samuel peered out, his face pale and anxious. He scanned the clearing around us, and when his gaze focused back on us, his expression became more determined. "Where are those cookies?"

"Right here." Megan yanked off her pack to retrieve the box.

"I'll eat while we travel," Samuel said, his voice steady. "We got a long way to go."

He wasn't kidding. Miles. And it felt like every step was uphill over rough terrain. As far as I could tell, the temperature had risen to around ninety. That pack strapped across my shoulders felt like it weighed a hundred pounds and was generating heat. Megan glared at me with sweat streaming down her face. I'm sure she was wishing she was still in those shorts and flip-flops.

The good news was, as soon as we left the well-blazed trails behind us, we didn't encounter a single soul. The bad news was that Samuel kept marching along in front of us at a grueling pace, never slowing up and never looking back. He might have been old and skinny, but he was tough, and it soon became obvious that he was in much better hiking shape than we were.

Every once in a while, I worried about what would happen if we lost sight of him. We had traveled so far from anything familiar, I could never find my way back. We marched through meadows and along streambeds, through densely wooded areas and clambering up rocky ledges, always following an upward incline.

And then, suddenly, we were standing out in the open on the top of a high ridge, struck by the full glare of the hot sun. Samuel led us to the edge, where far below lay a sweeping view of the countryside we had covered. The dense canopy of the treetops stretched out as far as we could see, giving the impression of a vast, green ocean, ancient and infinite. In the brilliant sky above, a red-tailed hawk spiraled and swooped lazily on the thermals.

Megan stood silently beside me, taking in the endless vista. She had been weirdly quiet throughout the whole trip. At that moment, it was like we both forgot that somewhere beyond the wilderness were towns and cities, factories, airports, and malls—all strung together by endless, snarling networks of concrete highways and steel railroad tracks.

"Nice view, right?" Samuel's creaky voice broke our reverent silence. "We're almost there, but I thought we should take a breather. Fortify ourselves with a little food and water."

Sighing with relief, I wiggled out of the backpack, zipping it open to rummage around for the water and fruit I'd stashed in there. I went to offer Samuel a bottle, but he was already taking a swig out of an old-fashioned round canteen—one of those green-canvas-covered things with a screw-on cap attached by a little metal chain. I guessed it was Boy Scout standard issue circa 1950.

Megan eagerly reached for her bottle and with a groan plopped herself right down on the ground. "Are we almost there yet?"

"Yes," said Samuel, munching on a cookie, "only another half-mile or so."

"Are you thinking of setting up a campsite for the night?" she asked.

Samuel looked at her like she was crazy. "Why would I do that?"

"Well," she said, "we've come so far already. It'll be dark by the time we head back, won't it?"

"It's only a little after noon now, young lady," he said, shaking his head. "We haven't hiked more than two...maybe two and a half miles."

I didn't say anything, but I thought he must have been kidding. It felt like we were halfway to Canada.

"That's impossible!" Megan protested.

"It's the truth," Samuel insisted firmly, "and I'll tell you something—I'd have been there and back home again by now if it weren't for you two. You move like snails." He tipped his head back, and we watched his Adam's apple bobbing as he drained the last of the water out of his canteen. "City kids." He shook his head again. "Let's get going." He barked a laugh. "Don't want to be out after dark."

"What the hell?" Megan breathed, when, twenty minutes later, we came upon an obstruction in the path.

I knew right away what it was—a crude barrier made up of a tangled pile of heavy tree limbs, just like the one I'd seen a few weeks earlier.

"We're here." My eyes trained uphill, following the path that led up to a bulging outcrop of granite. I caught Samuel's eye. "There's a cave up there, right?"

"That'd be my guess," Samuel agreed.

"Do you think they're here?"

"I'm fairly sure."

"How can you tell?"

"Sniff the air," Samuel said.

I lifted my chin and breathed the muggy breeze through my nostrils like a weird wind connoisseur. There was the top note of green things—leaves and pine resin, layered with the spicy scent of fallen leaves. Mixed in were the deeper odors of moist earth, decaying vegetation and mold. But there was more—traces of rank meat, wet dog, sweat, and a tang of salty ammonia that stung your eyes.

Oh, yes. They were close by.

The three of us took in the steep pile of boulders that rose in front of us. Megan posed the obvious question: "Now what?"

Damned if I knew.

"Got to let them know we're here," Samuel said.

"How do we do that?" asked Megan.

"Well, guess I'll give them the old Sasquatch yoo-hoo," said Samuel. He cupped his hands around his mouth and inhaled a great lungful of air.

"No!" I pulled his arms back down. "If you let out that Yeti yodel, every nut in the woods will be here in ten minutes."

"Then what do you suggest?" Megan looked at me with annoyance, obviously questioning my credentials as Sasquatch know-it-all.

"Well, let's at least get a little closer."

"We don't even know if they're really up there," she pointed out.

"True," I agreed, "but if you have a better idea, please share with the group."

"Fine." With an ungracious sigh, she swept her arms ahead of us. "Lead the way."

Samuel stepped forward, his expression determined. "No. I'll go first."

CHAPTER 44

"*Youch!*"

We hadn't clambered a hundred yards up the steep trail before Samuel's yelp of pain convinced me that we were heading in the right direction.

"Damned beast," Samuel complained, rubbing a livid welt on his forehead. Looking up the hill, he yelled, "What the hell did you do that for?"

From behind me, Megan asked, "What happened?"

"My guess is he just took a rock to the head," I answered over my shoulder. "Is that right, Samuel?" I called up to him. "You all right?"

"Yeah, I'm fine. But you guessed it…"

Before Samuel could finish his sentence, we all ducked as another missile zinged over our heads. Samuel jumped up to his feet and yelled, "Cut that out! It's just me!"

His call was answered with a hit to the shoulder. Rubbing the spot, he dropped back to where Megan and I remained hunkered down.

The three of us crouched low, and Samuel said in a hoarse whisper, "I don't get it. They're indifferent to me, but they know me. They've never been out-and-out hostile before. I figure they must be real riled up."

"What can we do?" asked Megan.

"We don't have a choice," I said. "We have to get them to safety. We have to find a way to get them to come with us."

"What about our safety?" Megan looked worried.

"Let's face it, Megs," I said, "we're expendable."

"What the hell does that mean?"

"As far as we know, those guys up there just might be the only three of their kind on the whole planet. The world is full of teenaged humans."

"So?" Megan whined. "That doesn't mean I want to get conked with a rock."

"Neither do I," I admitted. "We just have to push through and take our chances. It's the only thing we can do."

"I agree," Samuel chimed in. "But if you're scared, young lady, I wouldn't blame you if you stayed here."

"No, if you guys are going, I'm going," Megan grumbled.

"Brave girl." Samuel patted her head.

"Okay, then," I said, "but take off your packs. We'll use them like shields."

We started making our way up the hill again, backpacks over our heads where they deflected a steady rain of rocks. After a while, Samuel started letting out a funny barking noise every tenth step or so. At first, we let the sounds go by without commenting on them, but finally, Megan couldn't stand it anymore. "Samuel, what's with the woofing?"

"It's one of their vocalizations," he answered. "Sort of like saying, 'How ya doin'? I'm on my way' in Sasquatch."

Despite the weight of the big red pack on her cranium, Megan managed to shake her head in amazement. "You're an interesting guy."

He started up again. "Arf...arrrRRRGGH!" His "vocalization" turned into a scream of pain as Samuel fell to his knees. A rock fell next to my foot with a heavy thud.

As Megan and I went to him, he shouted out, "Goddammit, you big skunk! That one really hurt!"

We squatted down on either side of him. He was rubbing his thigh briskly, and there were tears in his eyes. "He's playing a little too rough now."

"Are you okay?" Megan asked.

"That was a big one." I went back and picked up the rock from where it had landed. It was the size of a softball, and by hefting it on my palm, I knew it weighed at least two pounds.

Samuel was still wincing with pain when I showed the rock to him. He measured its size with an assessing eye. "Yeah, he means business all right. I'd say his warning volleys have escalated to a serious threat." He took a deep breath, bracing himself to stand. Struggling to his feet, he swayed unsteadily before taking a couple of test steps. Both Megan and I were on either side of him, ready to keep him upright.

"I don't know about this." Megan's voice shook.

"I'm fine, I'm fine," Samuel insisted, waving us away. "But like I said, they're acting strange. It's normal for them to try and scare off intruders, but it's not like them to really try and hurt someone." He tried to peer through the impenetrable mountain laurel and prickly bushes that hid the Sasquatch, then looked back at us, blue eyes clear, mouth set in a line of determination. Pointing to a huge boulder a little ways back into the woods, he ordered, "Now, I want the two of you to take cover behind that big rock over there."

Right away, we protested, but he cut us off. "I won't take no for an answer. It just isn't safe. I'm going to go on ahead— see if I can't get them to calm down. Show them we mean no harm and are here to help. I'll give a shout if I need you."

"No," I insisted. "We go together."

"Son," Samuel said, "I'd never forgive myself if anything happened to you youngsters. If you don't do like I say...then I'm out. Right now. I'll just turn around and go back home."

I met Megan's eyes. She gave a little nod. "Okay," I said, "but we have your back."

"I know that, Jake." Samuel put a firm hand on my shoulder. "Now get behind that big rock over there, and don't come out until I say so."

We *kind of* got behind the boulder—at least we retreated a bit to stand by it—as we watched Samuel forge ahead. Right away, stones started whizzing through the air again, and without slowing his pace, Samuel lifted his arms to protect his head as he continued up the incline.

He was close to the crest of the hill when a deafening bellow shook the earth. Megan and I clasped hands, and I was positive that fear squeezed the breath out of my sister's lungs as surely as it did mine.

"Oh my God!" Megan gasped.

"Come on," I cried, "we can't just sit here!"

We took off, tracing Samuel's footsteps up the hill. At the summit the ground leveled off and Samuel was on his knees with his head bowed, looking as if he had tripped and was struggling to get back to his feet.

The huge male Sasquatch was striding toward him, holding in both hands a heavy log, which he was swinging in powerful, wide arcs. The violent force of the moving club forced a searing rush of air in our direction. His long, yellow teeth were bared in a jagged grimace, those fiery eyes burning like red-hot coals.

It was one of those desperate moments when, all in an instant, time seemed to simultaneously come to a dead stop and race ahead at a dizzying speed. I was certain Samuel was about to have his skull crushed by that huge hunk of lumber—and that I would do anything to stop it.

"*Stop!*" I screamed, hurtling myself across the open space to catch Samuel in a low tackle and rolling us away from the vicious, arcing swing of the log.

In the eerie quiet that followed, we came to rest under a bush. Samuel was stunned and motionless in my arms. The Sasquatch was frozen in place, the tree limb still raised menacingly over his head, but the terrifying grimace that had contorted his face changed into an expression of comical astonishment.

I disengaged from Samuel and whispered in his ear, "Are you all right?"

With a tight intake of breath, Samuel wheezed, "Not sure. You knocked the wind out of me."

"Sorry." Never taking my eyes off the Sasquatch, I helped him sit up, and once he seemed steady enough, I pulled him to his feet as I stood myself.

As we cautiously moved, I realized the Sasquatch was watching me with equal intensity, and with, well, something else in his eyes. "Samuel," I said, keeping my voice low and level, "walk over there and stand with Megan."

To my surprise, he didn't argue, just stepped briskly over to where Megan was standing by a huge oak.

I took a few steps closer to the Sasquatch until I was only a few yards away, facing him squarely, my shoulders thrown back, my eyes meeting his in a dead-on stare.

Crracck! Without warning, the male lowered the club down with a great slam against the hard-packed ground, sending a shuddering vibration through the earth we stood on. I tried not to flinch. We continued to hold each other's eyes, but I saw that something had changed again in the Sasquatch's expression. His head was cocked to one side, as if he were considering something.

A strange calm surrounded us, as if the Sasquatch had decided that we weren't a threat after all, though there was still wariness in his attitude. Okay. That was good. But how long could we hold this standoff? How was I going to get him and his family to come with us? My brain started skittering all over the place—like how in hell had the Pilgrims gotten that first recipe for pumpkin pie out of the Indians?

"You have to come with us." I flapped my hand to beckon him in our direction, hoping he'd get it.

His eyes still locked on mine, he tilted his head the other way, as if that might help him to understand, but he didn't move. What could I do? Leave a trail of Reese's Pieces? I suspected tricks like that only worked in the movies. I half-turned, making big, plodding steps, waving my arm for him to follow.

He didn't move.

"Hey, Jake. Can I try something?" Megan's voice was shaky. I could tell she was frightened but trying to handle the situation.

"No," I called softly over my shoulder, "stay where you are." Sassy was still holding that big tree limb, and we were still very close to him.

"But—"

"No."

"I think I can communicate with him." Without waiting for permission, she walked slowly but steadily to stand next to me.

Her first attempt was a swift beckoning motion, not unlike my first try, but with less flapping. As she moved her hands she said, "Come," in a firm, clear voice.

Next, she brought her fingertips together at a pointed angle, drawing her hands down in a diagonal movement, then vertically squaring off. "House," she said.

Then, her hands moving in a rapid sequence that involved a circular motion that I didn't quite get, she said, "Danger."

Finally she repeated the "come" and "house" parts.

My eyes darted between the Bigfoot and Megan, and I saw that somehow Megan had made some kind of connection. Not that the big guy had moved from his spot or anything, but he was watching her intently, looking like he was not only surprised by what she was doing, but—I don't why I thought this—relieved. The expression on his face had relaxed, and he was looking at Megan like he was thinking, "Finally, someone around here knows what they're doing."

Megan started the sequence again, and I could sense she was getting a little frustrated, like she thought she could speak Sasquatch on the first try, but to her credit she stuck with it. Still, Sassy couldn't seem to make up his mind what to do.

Who knows how long we might have stood there like that? At last, though, something amazing happened. From out of the shadowy undergrowth, the female emerged, cautiously moving to stand by her mate. For a moment that made me breathless, her eyes, a deep garnet color, locked on my face and she smiled softly at me, like she knew me. It was only then that

I saw the two wiry little arms wrapped around her neck and the smaller set of wide-set, dark eyes curiously peering over her shoulder at us.

Gently, Mama Squatch thumped her mate on the arm to let him know she was there. She only came up to his shoulder, and he stopped studying us and turned his gaze down to meet hers. Something must have passed between them beyond our comprehension, because there was a change in the male's attitude. He returned his attention to us as he took a firm stride in our direction, placing himself between his family and us. Then he raised that great big stick he was clutching. Holding it over his head, he shook it vigorously three times, then let his arms fall back to his sides.

There was no mistaking what he was saying. He was saying that they would come with us, but he didn't exactly trust us—and if anyone messed with the wife and kid there would be hell to pay.

I nodded, telling him I understood. Still holding the Sasquatch's eyes, I called over my shoulder, "Samuel, are you okay to walk?"

"Yes."

"Good. Because you're going to lead us out of here."

"Ready when you are."

I looked at Megan, who was still standing at my side, an expression of amazement on her face. "You did good." I winked at her, and she answered with a little smile and a huge sigh. "Now, tell them to come with us again," I said. "See if you can get them to follow you, then go and stand behind Samuel. We'll have to keep a tight formation. I'll bring up the rear."

And that's how we began our trek back to the house. I tried to maneuver us into a single file, but the big guy made it clear that there was no way he was going to let me out of his sight. The two of us ended up walking side by side behind Mama Squatch and the baby. I was aware with each step how massive the male was, how he shortened each heavy stride so that he didn't outpace the rest of us. His huge arms, long and heavily muscled, swung in a wide sweep with every step. He still held that thick branch in his right fist.

The first mile or so went smoothly. As we traveled, the surrounding woods were still and calm, but even the sound of a chipmunk scrabbling through dead leaves set our hearts pounding. The sun continued to burn during the afternoon and sweat streamed down my back as we walked, but a sense of urgency propelled us at a brisk trot, never taking a break for water, never stopping to rest.

As we got closer to the house, not one of us, neither man nor beast, forgot for a moment that the woods were crawling with strangers whose only goal was to find us. By now the surroundings were familiar and we were hiking along a clearly defined trail.

"*Ho!* Whitey!" a deep male voice sounded, echoing through the woods. "Did you hear that?"

When we heard the man call out, we all froze, eyes locking then shifting one to another, and seeming to move as one unit we all dove into a dense stand of mountain laurel.

We'd been traveling in a steadily downhill direction, and the voice was coming from somewhere below us. Desperately, I peered out from between the branches and leaves but I couldn't see anybody.

"I heard something all right! Something big!" Another excited voice, thinner and creaky, and much closer. Again, I strained to see where the men were hiding as we huddled close together. Whatever hesitation the Sasquatch might have felt about us seemed to evaporate, as they were piled up right with us, just one big happy family. I could feel their coarse fur tickling my bare arms.

"See anything?" First Voice called out.

"Nothing," Second Voice cried, "but do you smell that?"

My heart sank—dead giveaway. Funny how you get used to an odor when you're in the middle of it. I had forgotten that potent Bigfoot stench, hadn't thought about how strong it was.

"Smell what?" said First.

"All of a sudden, it stinks over here," Second complained, "like an elephant just walked by and took a dump."

That's when I saw it—a rustling of leaves about two hundred yards away. I realized it was one of those artificial blinds—green netting camouflaged with fake leaves. That's where Second was—and he was camped out right between us and where we were headed. How the hell was I going to get us out of there?

I looked over my shoulder at our strange group of travelers. Everyone looked back at me with worried eyes, except for the male. He was glowering; the jutting ridge of his brow lowered so that all you could see of his eyes was a glimmer of dark ruby. I realized his right hand was probing the ground as his intent gaze concentrated on finding the source of the voices. He was getting ready to lob a rock.

"No!" My order came out a hoarse croak. I couldn't believe it, but I had grabbed his arm, stopping him from lifting the jagged stone he'd just found. Beneath his rough fur, I felt the taut strength of his muscles, the density of his bones. He could snap my neck like a twig, and I had the nerve to be ordering him around. With relief, I felt his arm relax as he dropped the rock, and he gave a low, throaty growl that sounded like he wasn't sure he approved of my opinion

Now I had to maintain whatever authority I seemed to have in the moment. First I put a finger to my lips to signal silence, then I held my hands up and mouthed the words, *stay here…don't move.* Megan and Samuel responded by nodding solemnly in agreement—I could only hope the Sasquatch got what I meant.

I scuttled low through the cover of brush and tree trunks until I was a pretty good distance from our hiding place, before shooting up to a standing position. Then I ran full steam down the hill, screaming all the way, "Over there! Did you see that? I saw him! I saw him! A bigass mother! Oh my God! Did you see him?"

Second Voice jumped out from behind his blind. "No! I didn't see nothing! Where is he?"

Gesturing wildly as I ran, I pointed in a westerly direction. "He was running that way! Come on, let's go!"

First Voice emerged from behind a huge rock. "Lead the way, kid!"

And I did. Honest to God, I had no idea that I could run that fast. I could hear the two men lumbering after me. They were both middle-aged, and I could tell by their heavy breathing and muttered curses that they weren't in very good shape. First Voice, especially, was having a hard time. He was burly to the extreme and kept tripping over his clumsy work boots.

Now, I knew where I was—a distinct advantage. I was sure that I would be able to lose these guys pretty soon. What I hadn't figured on was encountering other Sasquatch search parties. First a group of three teenagers joined in, then a family of five—mom and dad and three little kids—and another group of four older guys that looked like they would be more likely to hunt deer than imaginary creatures.

There was no choice but to keep running. I felt like a fox being chased by hounds, and real fear motivated me to run faster. As the number of pounding feet increased behind me, I could feel a frenzy building, a bloodlust, and I became afraid that if I didn't deliver their prey at the end of the chase, the crowd pursuing me was likely to tear me apart with their bare hands.

But at least I was leading them away from the Sasquatch and my sister and Samuel.

"He must be heading to the reservoir!" I shouted in an attempt to keep the parade behind me fired up. I didn't see the fallen tree trunk across the trail. I had been looking over my shoulder, trying to gauge how far I could take those guys. I was still sprinting at full speed when my left shin hit the low-lying obstacle with a solid full-force crack that dropped me to the ground, bright flashes of light dancing in front of my eyes.

Feeling nothing but the pain vibrating through me, I curled up the side of the trail, clutching my leg with both hands.

No one stopped to help me up. Maybe they didn't see me. The mom, dad, and kids were too busy helping each other over the log that had taken me down. The deer hunters and teenagers jumped over it and past me. Second Voice trotted by, limping a little bit and holding his side like he had a stitch. First Voice noticed me in surprise, and because of that he tripped too. He landed on his big beer belly with a *whump*. His surprised eyes met mine.

"Yeah," I said. "That step is a doozy."

Second Voice doubled back to help his friend to his feet. Once First Voice was up, he bent over, offering me his hairy-knuckled hand.

"No, thanks man, I'm good. Taking a break," I assured him. The two looked at each other, shrugged, then continued on.

Waiting until they were out of sight, I got to my feet slowly, wincing as fiery shots of agony flashed up my left shin. My leg was in bad shape, no doubt about it. But when I tried putting some weight on it, it didn't buckle. Okay. Fractured? Maybe. But not broken. I could make my way back to where everyone was waiting for me.

But would they all still be there?

CHAPTER 45

As I hobbled back the way I'd come, more and more people trotted past me. They were all on cell phones and walkie-talkies, and by the excited chatter that clouded the air like the whine of mosquitoes, I knew the word was out.

I continued on in the opposite direction.

By then it was afternoon, and the steamy humidity of the day was cooking. I don't think I've ever been so tired in my life. My leg was killing me. I found a good, sturdy stick to use as a cane, but it wasn't much help. I was actually glad that my stomach was empty. With the pain came nausea, and I would have puked up anything I'd eaten.

I don't know how much time had passed when at last I reached the spot where we'd hidden. After making sure no strangers were watching, I called softly, "Megs, are you still here?"

Megan's loud whisper was hoarse with tension and relief. "Oh my God. Jake? Is that really you?"

"Yes." I sighed and leaned against a big beech tree in an effort to take some weight off my leg. I closed my eyes to stop the woods from spinning, and when I opened them again, Megan was crawling out from under a bush.

"Where the hell have you been?" she squawked. "It's been nearly an hour. We've been going crazy."

"I led a big gang of people as far away from here as I could get them before I practically broke my leg." I blinked back tears, feeling my own anger rise. It wasn't fair that she was yelling at me.

"We were going to give you ten more minutes before we went on without you." She rose to her feet, slapping the dirt off her palms.

"Is everybody still back there?" I asked.

"Yes," said Megan, "but they're getting antsy. I think the Sasquatch are getting ready to bolt."

It was weird, how I wasn't moving but the ground beneath me felt unsteady. I closed my eyes again. "I started a wild-goose chase to the reservoir, but I don't know how long the distraction's going to hold up. We better move fast."

When I opened my eyes this time, Megan was staring at me with a concerned look on her face. "Bro? Are you all right?"

"Yeah, I'm fine. I told you, I tripped and hurt my leg... I'm fine."

A few minutes later, the weird group was assembled around me. "We're almost home, and I think we'll make it if we stay clear of the trails. I don't know why, but every person we've run into out here has been walking along a trail, like it's a law or something."

"City kids," Samuel sneered.

"Probably so," I agreed, "but let's make sure it works to our advantage. Ready?" All eyes were on me. "Let's go."

So, with Samuel leading the way, we set off again. Plowing through the woods off-trail was extra slow going. Samuel was hardly speeding, but I was having a hard time keeping up. It seemed that under every step there was a rock or a stick or a dip in the ground to throw me off-balance. Every time I stumbled, a fresh jolt of pain shot through my leg. I wasn't the only one having a tough time. Something was bothering Baby Big. He or she, or whatever it was, was getting cranky and had started making a pathetic whining sound, like an unhappy cat. I was worried that if we had to hide, Mama Squatch wouldn't be able to keep the puppy quiet and it'd give us away.

Twice, we heard voices, forcing us to duck for cover, huddling close together until we were sure the coast was clear. The second time it happened, I was the first one to crawl out of our hiding place. I thought I was favoring my left leg, but I somehow bumped it on a big rock—and it hurt like a mother.

I couldn't help it. I let out a howl.

Seconds later, a shot rang out, and as I fought to control my panic, I felt a bullet zip right over my head.

"Did you hit it?" a voice called out. Another asshole hidden behind a hunting blind, but this was a bigger asshole—an asshole with a gun. Great.

"Don't know," came the response, "but I sure saw something."

Had they seen the Sasquatch? Luckily, nobody had followed me out yet, but I could hear the baby starting to fret again. What could we do? Lying on my stomach, arms crossed over my head, my nose buried in the brown, dank leaves, I almost felt like giving up. Only about a quarter-mile left to go, but it seemed like we were never going to make it. I was thinking about what to do next when I felt Samuel burst out of the hiding place, and standing up in the open, he called out, "Hey! Idiot! Quit shooting! There's no Bigfoot here! Just an old man." He was stomping his feet angrily and waving his arms high over his head.

"Oh Christ!" one of the men said. "Sorry, man!"

"Didn't you hear?" Samuel called out. "What kind of idiots are you? Someone saw the creature a couple of miles due west of here. And here you sit on your big fat butts shooting at people. You better get going, or you'll miss all the action."

"Yeah? Is that true?"

"That's what I heard," said Samuel, "but either way, you can tell I ain't no damn Sasquatch, so put down your weapon."

"Come on, Carmine, let's go."

"Now hold on," said Carmine. "We got to make sure the old dude's okay! I could have killed him!" He called to Samuel, "Are you okay, mister?"

"Oh, now no worries, fellas. Luckily, I'm fine. But if you don't hurry up, you'll lose the trail. You go along now," Samuel assured them.

"You sure, pal?"

"Yep, hurry on now."

"Thanks for the tip, dude. Sorry again that I shot at you. I need to remember there are more than just Bigfoot out here."

"Thank the Lord you're such a lousy shot," Samuel said.

Still lying low, we listened to the sounds of the two men gathering up their gear and marching off in double time toward the reservoir.

We waited to make sure those guys were really gone before we resumed our hike. The baby started to cry full out. Mama Squatch was making funny grunts to soothe it, but it wasn't working.

Samuel came over to help me up. "We're running out of time and luck. We better hightail it quick."

"You're right, Samuel." As I got to my feet to run, my leg refused to cooperate, and I collapsed back down. "Damn!" I cried. "You guys go on without me."

Before anyone could agree or protest, I felt myself floating—weightless, my arms and legs dangling, the ground falling away. Disoriented and dizzy, it took me a few moments to comprehend that I was in the male's enormous arms. Wild exhilaration pulsed through me, while at the same time, I fought against a primal urge to struggle out of his grasp and flee. Somehow, though, I knew I could trust him as he tossed me over his shoulder like I was a sack of feathers before he set off at a brisk trot.

Why was I surprised that he knew the way? Of course he did. He knew every inch of these woods—probably a hundred square miles' worth—and he was setting the pace. We'd be at Horace's house in no time—as long as we didn't run into any more trouble. I was bent at the waist over his broad, muscular shoulder with my head dangling somewhere halfway toward his ass. I hate to say it—after all, the guy was doing me a favor—but he smelled even worse back there.

When we reached the edge of the woods, we came to a stop. With surprising gentleness, he eased me down and stepped away from me. Landing on my good leg, I kept myself upright by putting a steadying hand on Megan's shoulder. Still behind the cover of trees, we scanned the last stretch of open meadow that stood between us and Horace's fenced-in backyard. I looked up at the blue sky. Not only would we be visible from the road as we raced to the sanctuary protected by that fence, but we would be sitting ducks if a helicopter happened to fly by.

For several tense moments, we all listened intently. Birds were calling, and insects whirred and clicked in the tall meadow grass. The wind rustled through the leaves behind us. But we didn't hear a human voice or an engine of any kind.

"Let's do it," I said.

"Quick like a bunny," Samuel said cheerfully.

Without hesitating, the big guy heaved me up again and took off at a furious pace. We leaped and jostled and pounded over the last few hundred yards, and while the male was holding me securely over his shoulder with his right arm, he was clasping his mate's hand with his left, making sure she and the baby were not left behind.

CHAPTER 46

There was really a family of Sasquatch in my basement.

It was crazy. The real deal was right at the bottom of my cellar stairs—the subject of debate and conjecture and scientific expeditions. I could prove to the whole world that the Sasquatch was real. I could put an end to the mystery once and for all. Funny thing was, now that the opportunity had arrived, I didn't, for even a second, consider getting my camera out of the closet. It was like the whole plan I'd cooked up that summer was made by some other guy. It wasn't me. Not anymore.

After taking a couple of Advil, I was resting on the living room couch, an ice pack balanced on my left shin. There was a livid bruise, and it still hurt; it was likely I had a hairline fracture. I hoped once the Advil kicked in, I'd be fine.

Megan and Samuel were down in the cellar with our guests, settling them in. I couldn't manage the stairs yet. Megan had brought them a bucket of water and some old blankets and towels. We figured they might want to make a nest of some kind. As soon as Megan and Samuel came back upstairs, I was going to discuss the food issue with them.

The doorbell rang.

Damn. We'd forgotten to lock up the front gate.

Struggling to my feet, I hobbled to the door and opened it. "Courtney."

"Well, don't look so happy to see me." She leaned casually against the doorjamb.

My heart pounded. Had she been watching the house? I looked over her shoulder, and instead of a news van, a long black limousine with tinted windows was idling in front of the house. I breathed a little easier. I'm sure I would've noticed that thing from the woods. "What do you want, Courtney?" I tried not to show how rattled I was.

She crossed her arms and smooshed her face into her annoying, little-girl pout. "I've been looking all over for you."

"Congratulations. You found me."

"I went to see you at work."

"I didn't go to work today."

"But when I spoke with you this morning, you said you were. Big delivery to unload and all that."

"Got a call from my boss after you left. The shipment was rescheduled."

"When you weren't at work, I came back here. The Jeep was in the driveway. I knocked and knocked, but, nobody answered."

"I'm here now." I shrugged. "What do you want?"

"Aren't you going to ask me in?"

"No."

She craned her neck, trying to peer into the room. I wasn't much taller than her, but I still tried to block her view. "Could I talk to your dad? I'd like to ask him something."

"He's not here," I said.

"Where is he?"

"None of your business."

She looked insulted. "Geez, Jake, I was just wondering. I've been asking around, and it seems no one has seen him for a while."

I shrugged again. She was a TV person—they feed on talk, don't they? Maybe if I just refused to say anything, she'd starve and go away.

"But your little sister's here, isn't she? Everybody in town seems to know her—must be that crazy pink hair. Kind of unusual in these parts, I guess. She stands out—has people talking, about the two of you. In fact, they've been saying that, as far as anyone can tell, the two of you are living alone out here. Two minor children without any adult supervision." She gave one of those *tsk-tsk* sounds and shook her head. "You're so isolated, without any means of transportation—you not having a driver's license or anything. I wonder if the authorities would be interested in a situation like that. I mean, I'd hate to think what could happen if there was an emergency." She smiled at me, a big, toothy, white smile of phony kindness and fake concern.

Her threats chilled me to the bone. "What do you want, Courtney?"

"There's someone in the car who wants to meet you." She straightened, suddenly all business.

"Gee, I was told never to talk to strangers."

"Oh, this is no stranger."

"Who is it?"

"My boss. And my boss expects me to make things easy for him. He would like to speak with you, and I'm asking you nicely if you will meet with him."

"I've got nothing to say to him."

"He thinks you do." She gave me this hard, don't-mess-with-me glare.

I was beginning to feel desperate. I had to get rid of her. "Let me think about it."

"No."

"I'm kind of busy right now."

She laughed harshly. It sounded like the caw of a crow. "Yeah? Doing what?"

"Well, I don't want to talk with him here. The house is a mess."

She rolled her eyes, put her hands to her hips. "Then come on out to the car."

"Now?"

"Yes, now!"

I took a deep breath. "All right, then."

"All right." She sounded a little surprised that I'd actually agreed, but I had to if I was going to get rid of her. And I was desperate to get rid of her. I stepped out onto the little porch, and before she spun around to lead the way to the car, she stood practically nose-to-nose with me, and said in a growl, "Don't make me look bad—got it?"

CHAPTER  47

That short walk out to the car felt like I was marching to meet a firing squad. I tried not to limp—no point giving Courtney reason to ask any more questions. Praying that Megan and Samuel would stay inside the house, I wouldn't even let myself think about what the Sasquatch might do.

We had almost reached the car when the driver jumped out, wearing a *Men in Black* kind of suit and sunglasses. He was a big guy with a shaved head, thick neck, and broad shoulders; I wouldn't be surprised if he did double-duty as a bodyguard. Who was he guarding—Courtney? He didn't say a word as he swung open the passenger door and, with a sweep of his arm, gestured for me to get in.

I was expecting some old guy in his shirtsleeves, maybe with a cigar stuck in his mouth, talking on the telephone and ordering people around. I didn't expect to find myself face-to-face with Rick Morris, the lead anchor and undisputed star of *Another Day, USA!,* America's most popular national morning news show.

Not everything was a surprise. He was talking on the phone. He gave me a once-over with his gunmetal-gray eyes and held up his index finger, stopping me.

I was so stunned, I couldn't move for a second. Then the driver gave me a small but definitely insistent nudge with his burly hand.

Making sure that I closed my mouth, which I realized was hanging open in astonishment, I crawled in to sit opposite

Rick…Mr. Morris…that guy my mom watched on television every freaking morning of her life. Once I was in, the driver shut the door. Morris's focus returned to his telephone conversation, and he was taking notes on a yellow legal pad. I noticed that his nails were perfectly manicured, looking pinker and shinier than a guy's should. He was wearing a pale blue polo shirt and khaki trousers. I couldn't help peeking at his feet—topsiders, no socks. His long face and square chin were freshly shaven. His dark hair was perfectly cut and neatly combed, but I swear I could tell where the plugs had gone into his scalp to hide the fact that he was going bald. I'd never seen anyone in my life who looked so, well, *clean*. He smelled clean too, like expensive soap and laundry detergent.

After trekking through the woods on one of the doggiest dog days of summer and getting a piggyback ride on a walking stink bomb, God only knew what I smelled like.

"Sure thing, Ken," Morris was saying in his weirdly familiar voice. "Let's schedule that trip to Laos for next week… Yeah, yeah, I'm sure it'll make a great story too." It crossed my mind at that moment that living with Rick Morris would be a lot like living with my dad—but with money. "I'll give you a call tomorrow. Bye." He pressed a button to end his call and hit me with the full intensity of his big eyes and his even bigger and brighter teeth. I couldn't help it—meeting this really famous guy gave me a genuine thrill. Leaning forward and offering me his hand, he said, "Jake Oliver, nice to meet you. Do you know who I am?"

Did I know who he was? I knew so much about him it was ridiculous. Embarrassing. It was my mother's fault, I guess, that I knew about those hair plugs, and that he was married to some famous supermodel and that he didn't like cheese. But I tried to act cool, like he didn't impress me. I also couldn't help thinking what a kick this would be for old Mom—if she could see me now. "Sure," I mumbled, returning his firm shake, conscious of how hot and sticky my own hand was.

"So," Morris said, "let's cut right to the chase. I know you were reluctant to speak with me, so I really appreciate this meeting. You probably think I'm just a talking head you see on TV, but let me tell you something: You don't get to where I am in this business unless you've got instincts. And my instincts are telling me there's really something behind all the hype and hysteria going on around here." He looked at me like he expected a comment; I didn't trust myself to say a word.

"So, anyway," he continued, "I sent Courtney out here ahead of me to follow some leads. You've probably figured out by now, she's pretty good at what she does. I only work with the best." Now he leaned forward again, his hands on his knees, looking square into my eyes in a way that made me feel like he could see how my brain worked. "And you know what she found out? No matter where any lead starts…no matter what direction it takes off in…it ends up with you." He leaned back into the deep, padded leather seat, regarding me with a thoughtful look. "How do you figure that, Jake?"

Knowing I would have to say something, eventually, and not wanting him to think I was a complete idiot, I said in a voice that came out all squeaky and weird, "Because of my Uncle Horace?"

Morris banged the armrest with his hand, causing me to jump. "That's right! I hear your Uncle Horace was an extraordinary man."

I shrugged. The guy was a little overenthusiastic. "Granduncle. And I wouldn't know. Never met him."

Again he leaned forward, holding my gaze like a rattlesnake. "But we both know that his life's work was studying the Sasquatch. And I believe you've picked up right where he left off."

"Not really." In the chilly interior of that limo, across from bigger-than-life Rick Morris who was oozing his charm and charisma all over me, I felt like I was losing a grip on reality. It was like being in a dream. And the most surreal part of it all was—I had what he was looking for! I could deliver those

ANDREA SCHICKE HIRSCH

Sasquatch to him right that minute. But I would never do that.
I could never betray them. All I wanted to do was get rid of
Rick Morris ASAP. He was, literally, too close for comfort. If I
didn't get rid of him quick, it might be too late.

Morris's eyes were still holding mine like burning lasers. I
cleared my throat. "Mr. Morris—"

"Jake, please! Call me Rick."

"Um, Rick. Say I *did* know something—what would be in
it for me?"

"Just think of it, Jake." A weird radiance came into his eyes.
"By sharing what you know, you'll shed light on an age-old
mystery. You'll be bestowing the gift of wonder on a jaded
world."

What a load. I gave my head a little shake. "Like I said,
Rick, what's in it for me?"

Rick sat up straight, looking offended. "I don't know what
you mean."

"There might be a few things I know—a few things I've
heard and seen. But why should I tell you?"

Morris turned down the thermostat on the warm and fuzzy
moment we'd been sharing. "Jake, if you're asking me if there's
any monetary compensation for your cooperation, the answer
is absolutely no. *Another Day, USA!* never pays for an interview.
It would mean compromising our journalistic integrity."

Yeah, right. They got people to spill their guts and expose
every dark corner of their lives and those people didn't get paid
a dime? Meanwhile Morris's show got the ratings and sponsors,
then raked in the dough. What a racket. I'd been pretty naïve to
think that coming up with real Sasquatch footage could make
me rich. They would've found a way to steal it from me.

I didn't say anything. Honestly, I didn't know how to play
this situation.

Morris must have sensed that I was getting ready to bolt. He
turned on the touchy-feely furnace again, and I had to admit,
he was hard to resist. "I know it doesn't seem fair, but," he said,
creepily intimate, "have you ever heard of Andy Warhol?"

252

"Sure, pop artist, 1960s."

"You know what he said, right? Everybody gets fifteen minutes of fame. Well, if you and I sit down, and you give me a good interview, you'll have your fifteen minutes. It's for you to decide how to use it."

"What do you mean?"

"This is strictly off the record—and I'll deny it if you quote me—but it's not unusual for our guests to walk away from an appearance on our show with a movie deal, or a book deal, sometimes worth, oh, five…six, sometimes seven figures. You just have to work the angles. My staff might be able to help you with, you know, making the right connections afterwards."

From the first moment I met him, I had to admit that I'd thought I'd liked Rick Morris, but the longer I sat in his limo, the more I suspected that I was the victim of a good cop/bad cop routine. Courtney played the bad cop part very well. But this year's Academy Award for best leading actor was going to Rick Morris—creepy good cop extraordinaire. I'd reached the point where I didn't want to have anything to do with Rick Morris or his staff—I never wanted to see Courtney again, that was for sure—but he was right. I did have to decide what I wanted to achieve with those crucial fifteen minutes. An idea was beginning to form. "So, how do you want to do this?"

With a full-blown gleaming white smile of triumph, Morris said, "You agree to grant me an interview?"

Lucky me, apparently Rick Morris was my best friend again. "Sure." I shrugged. "Fire away."

"Not now," he said with a laugh, and he held up a hand, "and don't say another word. Save it for tomorrow. I want to keep everything fresh."

"Tomorrow?"

"Yes, tomorrow morning, if that's all right with you."

"Where? What time?"

"We could do it here, in the house—"

"No. No. Not here." Shit. That was all I needed.

Morris could see my obvious agitation. "No problem. We're staying at the Days Inn. I'm sure they have a room we could use. I'll be on a live feed through nine AM—I do have a show to do," he said with an "aw shucks I'm just a humble guy" chuckle. "So let's say, oh, nine thirty?"

"Okay," I agreed and added quickly, "but Rick...one thing."

"What's that?"

"I don't want anyone to be able to recognize me. I want to be in shadow, my voice altered. You know. I want my identity protected."

"Really? Why?" Morris asked.

"Everyone already thinks my uncle's a kook. I don't want to be tagged as the next village idiot."

"You sure?"

"Yes. I won't do it otherwise."

Morris sighed and shrugged. "Fine. Have it your way. But it's too bad. You're a nice-looking kid. The audience would love you."

"Whatever. Not my problem. That's the condition."

"Okay with me. I'll send the car for you." He gave me a wink and added broadly, "Because you don't drive, right?"

"Uh, right." Okay, Rick, old buddy, I get the threat. A chill ran down my spine that had nothing to do with the AC. I clutched the door handle.

Morris reached out and grabbed my wrist. "Jake," he said. His eyes were cold, glittering like chunks of ice. "I expect you to be straight with me. No bullshit. If you lie to me—or decide not to cooperate—there will be consequences."

"Look, Rick," I said, making my eyes all wide and innocent, "I said I'd do it. And I'd never lie to you." I tried to twist my arm out of his grasp, but he continued to hold it in a vise-like grip.

"And Jake," he continued, "make sure you take a long, hot shower, man. And put on some clean clothes. I hate to be the one who tells you, but you smell kind of funky."

CHAPTER 48

The heat of the day hit me like a brick when I tumbled out of the limo. The extreme change of temperature actually made me feel light-headed. Courtney and the driver were leaning on the car smoking cigarettes, deep in conversation. I rushed past them, not saying anything.

Still struggling to disguise my limp, I reached the safety of the front porch. I couldn't think about the fact that I'd just agreed to do an interview on national television. If I did, I would freak out, and frankly, I had more pressing matters to worry about. I ducked into the house, slammed the door, and shot the bolt home.

Turning in the shadowy room, I found Megan and Samuel looking at me with wide-eyed stares.

"Who were you talking to?" Megan asked.

"You wouldn't believe me if I told you."

"Try me." She crossed her arms, giving me a challenging glare.

I almost did tell her, right then, when a deafening *clang* started booming through the house.

Samuel clapped his hands over his ears, looking stricken. I saw Megan mouth the words, *What the hell?*

My heart started pounding, seeming in rhythm to the banging coming from the cellar. I knew right away what was making the racket. That's not what scared me. The question was, did the banging start before or after the long black car managed to slide out of hearing distance? I didn't have time to look out the window to find out.

Ignoring the pain in my leg, I reached the cellar door and was down the steps in seconds. The room was dimly lit. I first saw the female huddled up in a corner, cradling the baby in her arms. My eyes followed the sound. The male was halfway up the concrete cellar steps that led to the backyard, his fists beating against the metal doors that stood as his barrier to the outside world.

"Stop! Stop!" I shouted uselessly.

He couldn't hear me over the deafening booms. I had to get him to stop. Reluctant but determined, I approached his side, reached out, and put a hand on his arm.

The male swung around and glared at me, his eyes wild and glowing red. I could tell that he was holding back an impulse to attack.

Keeping my left hand on him, I tried holding his eyes with my gaze, hoping to calm him. Trying to give the impression I was cool and in charge, I raised my right hand slowly and said, "Watch," like he would know what that meant. With my right hand, I reached up to grasp the lever that secured the cellar door closed, and slowly—so as to clearly demonstrate how to do it—I turned the lever and slid the bolt down, then pushed the door up and open.

"That's how you do it." I stepped into the open air. I wanted to show him that he was here for his own protection, for the safety of his family. They weren't prisoners. They could leave any time they wanted to.

The male pushed past me, rushing up the last few steps. Once in the backyard, he threw back his head and breathed deeply, closing his eyes for a moment, as if savoring the fresh air. But the air wasn't fresh—it was still really muggy, especially compared to the cool dampness of the cellar. I was surprised that he preferred the humidity and heat. But then I closed my eyes and lifted my nose. I could smell the richness of the soil, the scent of pine, and the tickly smell of dried grass. The aroma of honeysuckle sweetened the air.

When I opened my eyes, I saw that Mama Squatch had crept out, and with Baby still on her lap, she had seated herself just high enough on the steps to be in the daylight.

"Okay, you guys," I said. "I get it. I'll leave the door open. But I just hope you're smart enough to stay close to the house. Now I've got to go and find you something to eat."

CHAPTER 49

I rushed out of the house, only stopping long enough to tell Megan and Samuel to keep an eye on the Sasquatch while I went out for food. And to close the front gate after I'd pulled out.

"But we've got plenty of food," Megan protested, a hint of panic in her voice.

"Megs," I said, "we can't just feed them tuna casserole and peanut butter sandwiches. They'll get sick. I've got to get fresh food."

"Can I come with you?" she asked, sounding scared, like a little girl.

"Somebody's got to stay in charge here," I said, lowering my voice and looking over her shoulder at Samuel, who was sitting at the kitchen table, munching his way through a package of Oreos and a quart of milk. "I think you're more qualified for the job than he is."

It was strange, pulling into the grocery parking lot. It was full of cars and people coming and going. I yawned, feeling beat to hell. I was still somewhere in the middle of the longest day of my life, and it wasn't over yet.

Driving around to the rear lot, I parked as close to the back door as I could get. I figured I'd be hauling out a bunch of heavy cartons. Those were big critters I had to feed, and who knew how long they'd be staying. I glanced around before ducking in the building. The windshield on the delivery van had been repaired, but there was still a big dent in the storage shed. All the trouble that Barry's staged rampage had caused. Where the hell *was* he?

If I remembered correctly, there was a ton of good stuff in the walk-in that was going to work just fine. Lots of local berries—strawberries, blueberries, and raspberries—were pulled from the shelves because they were just a little too ripe or starting to mold. There was a case of eggs, a couple of bushels of corn, green beans that were past their prime, and plenty of leafy greens. A little light in the protein department, but there was enough nutritious stuff to keep them going for a few days.

Starting a pile of what I knew I would take, I kept looking around for other ideas. I also grabbed some past-due-date orange juice and yogurt for Megan and me—and Samuel too. He was going to be another mouth to feed for a while.

I was so busy getting everything sorted and ready to go that I didn't hear Mr. Pelletier enter the walk-in. He harrumphed so loudly, I nearly jumped out of my skin.

Putting my hand on my chest to steady my thumping heart, I smiled and said, "Mr. Pelletier! You scared me!"

He didn't smile back. In fact, he looked pretty grim. "Jake, what are you doing back here?" His voice was dead calm.

"Um, just getting some stuff together for Samuel...you know."

He eyed the carton of raspberries I was holding. "I don't think Samuel will appreciate moldy fruit."

I looked down at them. They did look pretty furry, but I was guessing that the Sasquatch digestive system could handle more than the average human. "I figured I could pick through them and find what was edible."

"Tell you what, Jake," Mr. Pelletier said, "no need to put together a delivery for Samuel. I'll go back to doing it myself."

"Oh," I said, "but I don't mind."

"Nevertheless—I'll take it from here."

"Okay," I said, starting to feel like a ton of bricks was about to fall on my head, "but why?"

Mr. Pelletier dropped the load. "Because you don't work here anymore."

I couldn't help it—a lump formed in my throat. I choked out, "You're firing me?"

"Yes. You're welcome to shop here as a regular customer, but your employment is terminated. Effective immediately. If you need to clear out your locker, please do so now."

"Can I ask why?" I said, my throat tight.

Mr. Pelletier sighed. "Really, Jake. This shouldn't be such a surprise. Where were you supposed to be at nine o'clock this morning?"

"This morning?" I echoed, genuinely confused.

"Yes, this morning," said Mr. Pelletier. "You were scheduled to work this morning. You didn't show up. We were short-handed. That hurts business—especially when it's busy like it's been."

I felt my face going red. With everything else that'd been going on, I'd completely forgotten my work schedule. "I'm so sorry, Mr. Pelletier. I promise—I won't let it happen again."

"You don't seem to understand. Today was your third strike. You've become too unreliable, Jake. I'm sorry, but this just isn't working out."

"*Third* strike?" I asked, genuinely confused.

"Yes. You don't even remember," he said, shaking his head. "The day after the back lot was vandalized? You were supposed to work, but left the premises and didn't come back. And then there was another afternoon that you just up and disappeared—said you were sick but didn't clock out."

"I can explain everything!" I burst out, even though I couldn't.

"I'm afraid it's too late." He looked down at the floor, thinking about what he was going to say next. "It's not just that you've been playing loose with your schedule. I've had complaints."

"Complaints?" Now I was really confused. Who complained about me? Did I squish someone's tomatoes? Make the wrong change? "What did I do?"

"You're not getting along with your coworkers. Frankly, I've never had a problem like this before—I even got a call from a parent."

That must have been Nell's father.

"But the one thing I really can't get past," Mr. Pelletier added, "is the simple fact that none of this Bigfoot nonsense was going on until you showed up in town."

Judging by the stern look on his face, I saw there was no point in trying to defend myself. But I also hadn't lost sight of why I was standing in the walk-in at that very moment. "Okay, Mr. Pelletier. I'm really sorry it didn't work out. Just let me take this last delivery up to Samuel."

"No, Jake. Please, put the box down and leave."

There was nothing else for me to do but what he asked. I put down the box of moldy berries and rushed past Mr. Pelletier to get out of the door. Whatever I had left behind in my locker could just stay there. I was too rattled to fiddle with the combination on the lock.

Fired.

What was even worse? I was leaving without the food.

I was grateful that no one was in the back room as I stormed through. I had almost made it to the door when I heard Nell ask, "Jake? Where are you going?"

CHAPTER 50

"**I** can't talk to you now," I called over my shoulder, not breaking stride as I raced toward the door. I could sense her trotting after me, smelled her fruity shampoo. Who'd've thought I'd ever be running away from Nell Davis? But I was, because I couldn't deal with her—not right then—and it was killing me.

She wasn't the kind of girl who gave up, though.

I made it through the heavy back door. I could feel it about to swing shut behind me, locking me out for good.

Then Nell caught up and lunged forward, grabbing the tail end of my T-shirt and yanking me back as hard as she could. She jerked so hard, she yanked me right off my feet and onto my butt.

At least she had the decency to be shocked at her own strength. "Oh my God!" she gasped, falling to her knees beside me. "Are you okay?"

Wincing a little bit, I eased the pressure off my right butt cheek, which seemed to have taken the brunt of the fall, though the impact had sent a fresh shock of pain through my leg. "I'm fine." I looked up into her face, only inches from mine. Her dark eyes were wide with concern. I fought the impulse to smooth away the hair that had fallen across her eyes, catching in her dense lashes. It hurt too much to be so close to her. "Got to go," I mumbled, shrugging her helping hand off my arm. I couldn't help it, I looked at her again. Her face had crumpled with hurt.

"What's the matter?" she asked, her voice thin. "Are you mad at me because of the other night? I'm not mad at you. Not anymore. I overreacted."

"No." I got to my feet, though my throbbing leg didn't make it easy. "It's not that. Look, I got to go."

"You *are* mad at me. I'm sorry. I just get upset when… It's just hard for me to talk sometimes…"

"Look, I'm not mad at you!" I practically yelled. "I just got fired."

She grabbed my arm. "Tell me what happened!"

I stopped, spun around, put my hands on her shoulders. "Nell, please. We'll talk later! I can't do this right now!" I started running for the car again, then came to an abrupt halt. "Shit!"

She practically ran into me. "What?"

I turned to face her again. "Do you have any cash on you?"

"Not on me. My wallet's in my locker. Why?"

I had rushed out of the house without money, because I'd fully expected to walk away with free food. "Could you get it? I need money for groceries. Isn't there a Stop & Shop on Route 7? I don't have time to go back home."

"Sure, but what's the emergency?"

I took a deep breath before I spoke. Now that the shock of being fired was wearing off, I couldn't believe I hadn't told her what was going on right away. After all, she had been in on it from the beginning. She cared as much as I did. "The Sasquatch." I enunciated each word. "The Sasquatch are in my cellar. And they need food."

"No way!" Nell punched me in the shoulder, her eyes bright with excitement. "Why? How?"

"I'll tell you everything, but—" I stopped talking. Something caught my eye. Someone was standing by the Jeep, leaning against the driver's-side door.

Courtney. Luckily, she was facing in the other direction, as if she expected me to come around from the front of the building. "Damn."

"What?"

"Do you have your car?" I asked, ducking to hide behind the air-conditioning unit, pulling Nell down with me.

"Yes."

"Where is it?"

"Right over there." She pointed behind us. I eyed the little green car, figuring whether or not we could get to it without attracting Courtney's attention.

"Is it locked?"

"No." She snorted as if I'd asked the most ridiculous question.

"Come on." I grabbed her hand and pulled her along. Keeping low to the ground like we were dodging sniper fire, we scuttled to the Karmann Ghia, ducking in as quietly as possible.

I scrunched down in the passenger seat. Peering over the dashboard, I was relieved to see that Courtney was still staring off in the wrong direction, seeming oblivious.

Nell followed my gaze. "Is she the problem?" she asked, jutting her chin at Courtney. Her eyes were fierce.

I nodded. "Could you get your money? Can I borrow your car?" I asked in a panicked rush.

Nell sat erect. Only then did I notice that the key was already dangling in the ignition. "No need for money." The engine turned over with a *vroom* and that happy little jingling sound that only old Volkswagens make. "My mom's got everything we need—organic and locally grown. I seem to remember that they liked our eggs in particular. Let's go."

CHAPTER 51

So, like a couple of foxes, we raided Mrs. Davis's henhouse and made off with about a dozen eggs. Then we hit the gardening shed where the produce was packed up to take to the farmers market. For good measure, we did a quick run through the vegetable patch and grabbed whatever looked ripe enough. It was a good haul—plenty of fresh corn, zucchini, watermelon, cucumber, and peas. The tomatoes were at their peak—firm and sun-warmed. Mrs. Davis grew a ton of herbs, and I thought to grab a handful of fragrant basil with the thought of tossing a few of those tomatoes with pasta for our own dinner. I must have been getting hungry.

Luckily, Mr. and Mrs. Davis were out—Nell wasn't sure, but thought they might have gone into Hartford for the day. We had no idea when they might come back, so we worked fast.

Back in the Karmann Ghia, I finished telling Nell about the morning's adventure in the woods, how we had persuaded the Sasquatch to come back with us. Was it really only that morning? It was still light out, that lingering August dusk. I didn't tell her about the impending interview—I hadn't even told Megan yet. Maybe because just the idea of it still freaked me out. I didn't want to think about it, let alone discuss it with anybody.

By the time we got to the house, the moon was rising over the trees, a half-circle of silver in a lavender sky. Before we got to the driveway, I asked Nell, "Do me a favor? Keep going. Just drive right past the house." I slumped in the passenger seat, peering out, scanning the sides of the road for any signs of news-related vehicles. Once I was sure the coast was clear, Nell doubled back, and I jumped out of the car to open the gate before she could make a full stop. After she drove through, I closed it securely behind us, keeping our secrets safe behind the jagged edges of the fence.

Giddy with excitement, we unloaded the car and, with our arms full, walked around to the back of the house.

There we found Mama Squatch sitting serenely on the weedy grass, watching fondly as Baby and Megan rolled a ball back and forth between them, like it was the most normal thing in the world. At our approach, Mama looked up. When she noticed Nell, she quickly rose and grabbed the baby before moving toward the cellar door. Then we heard a low, menacing growl. The male emerged from the shadows under the eaves where he must have been standing, watching over his family. He stepped forward, the fur on his wide shoulders bristling, making him appear even huger than he was. His eyes burned like molten steel.

With a crash, Nell dropped the carton she was holding, her mouth open in amazement.

Megan was alert to the defensive reaction to our sudden appearance and sat still.

"It's okay," I said calmly. As I hoped, the sound of my voice diverted the male's attention from Nell. I caught his eye, and holding his hot glare, I slowly put down my bags. As I straightened, I held up my open hands, palms facing him to gesture there was no threat. Then Megan, just as slowly and deliberately, stood and moved in a measured pace to stand next to Nell, who remained rooted to her spot. I noticed that as Nell stared at the Sasquatch, she stood with her spine straight, chin high, her shoulders thrown back, as if to prove to the male and to herself that she was determined to be brave.

Megan put her hand on Nell's shoulder, then said, "Friend," making what I assumed was the sign with her hands.

The male huffed out a great exhalation of air, sending the scent of rotting meat wafting on the summer breeze. He still looked pissed off, but he seemed to relax.

"Megan," I muttered. "Tell him we have food." Out of the corner of my eye, I watched as she made a gesture that obviously signified eating.

He came over to us. Megan, Nell, and I stood our ground in a row, trying not to recoil as he came closer and closer. He was coming to investigate what we had in the bags and the carton. He picked up a sack at my feet and stuck his nose into it, his wide nostrils flaring as he inhaled. Seeming satisfied, he dumped the contents onto the ground. Zucchini and ears of corn rolled into the grass. As soon as she saw them, Mama Squatch, with Baby riding her piggyback, moved forward and started gathering the vegetables.

The male then stepped away from us, as if to show that the confrontation was over. I let out a huge sigh of relief, and I could feel Nell, still standing beside me, breathing easier too. She picked up the carton she had dropped and, keeping her head meekly down, carried it over to the open cellar door, like an offering. I watched the Sasquatch and he watched me as she delivered the box.

As soon as she moved away, in a sudden movement, the male thumped me on the chest with both fists—not as hard as he could, but hard enough to send me flying on my ass. Again! How many times had I landed on my butt today?

Maybe I should have been scared at his sudden display of force, but as I scrambled back to my feet, I could feel right away all the tension had dissipated. I looked into his eyes and saw humor there, like if he could, he would say, "She's your female; I get it! I just wasn't expecting company."

Mama Squatch moved to the carton and was pawing through the contents, making purring sounds of approval. The male looked at her over his shoulder, then joined his mate as she took inventory of their food supply.

Night was falling, the only light coming from the pale glow of the moon.

Megan looked at me. "I don't know about you, but I'm starving."

We left the Sasquatch to their dinner and went inside to rustle up something for ourselves.

We pitched in to make the meal, laughing and joking as we worked. Below us, in the cellar, our visitors seemed to be settling down for a quiet night, safe in their sanctuary.

To my amazement, while I was out, Megan had gotten Samuel to clean up. When we sat down to dinner, he was sitting across from me, all pink-skinned and shiny, wearing a clean shirt and sweatpants that Megan had pulled out of our dad's dresser. The pasta tasted great with the sauce I made from the tomatoes and basil with a little bit of garlic, olive oil, and Parmesan cheese.

It was about the best night of my life until around eleven o'clock, when I got a sinking feeling, like that moment in the story when Cinderella realizes it's pumpkin time. "Hey, Nell."

"Yeah?" she answered, smiling.

I didn't want to break the spell. It was a perfect moment. The Sasquatch were safe in the cellar. Nell and I were clearing the table. Megan was helping Samuel navigate through the newly discovered wonder of the Internet. But I had to say it. "Shouldn't you be thinking about going home?"

She was rinsing a plate in the sink, but she shrugged. "I was thinking of crashing here for the night. I'll bunk in with Megan like I did before."

I put the stack of plates I was holding on the counter. "I don't think that's a good idea."

"It's okay." She scraped away at something stuck on the serving spoon. "I left a message on my mom's phone. I told her I was sleeping over at Katie's."

I sighed. "Really, Nell, I don't think that's a good idea—"

"Don't you want me here?" She gave me a look with those big, dark eyes that made me weak at the knees.

"Of course I do," I said, my voice going all raspy. "It's just… Well, you know what I'm worried about."

"I do." She took her hands out of the soapy water, drying them on a dish towel. "And it's all my fault. You've been asking me to talk to my dad—make things right—and I haven't done it. I'm sorry."

"It's just—" I repeated.

"Please let me stay. I've missed so much already."

"But—"

"I know." She took a step toward me.

Before I could say anything else, Nell Davis kissed me. Right on the lips. Not a long kiss or a wet kiss or a kiss with tongue or anything—but a sweet kiss, a warm kiss, a real kiss, not a sisterly, I-like-you-like-a-friend kiss. A kiss full of promise. Her lips parted from mine with a moist, tiny *pop* as our mouths disengaged. "So, can I stay? Please?"

"It's just—"

"Just what?" Megan asked, clomping into the room. She had left Samuel engrossed at the computer. She opened the freezer and took out a pint of ice cream.

The spell was broken. I could move away from Nell. "It's just—I need to get to bed. I have to get up real early in the morning."

"Why?" Megan spooned a big mouthful of Phish Food into her mouth. "I thought you said you got fired."

"I have to be ready when the car comes for me."

"Car? What car?" asked Nell.

Then I told them both about how I'd been coerced into giving Rick Morris an interview.

"Get out!" Megan exclaimed, her mouth hanging open wide enough to show the slimy coating of ice cream on her tongue.

"What are you going to tell him?" Nell asked anxiously.

I'd been thinking about that, all afternoon. "The truth. As long as I can get it to work for me, I'm going to tell the truth."

CHAPTER 52

The sound of the blaring car horn nearly made me jump out of my skin. Thank God I'd woken up early. It wasn't exactly like I could sleep anyway. *It must be the driver,* I thought, *coming to collect me and finding the gate closed.*

Not just closed, but secured with a heavy chain and padlock I'd found in the cellar.

Rick Morris had said he was going to send a car for me, but he didn't say what time, so I was ready before it was light. I needed some quiet time to work out a strategy and make some notes to self.

Quiet time was over. Whoever was honking meant it as an assault.

"All right, all right," I said under my breath as I ran down the stairs. The girls had stumbled out of their room and were following me. "Make sure everything's okay in the cellar," I ordered before unlocking the front door.

The horn blower hadn't let up for a second. I flung the door open and marched down the walk.

It took me a while to work the lock and chain loose, and during the struggle the honking stopped. I got the front gate open wide enough to peer out, squinting against the harsh glare of headlights.

The edge of the gate crashed into my face, smashing my brow and cheekbone. Pain burst in my skull, and I fell to my knees, my arms crossing defensively over my head as I tried to see past the alternating pulses of light and blackness.

"Get my daughter out here right now!"

Daughter. Damn. I dared to look up.

Mr. Davis was glaring down at me, a wildness in his eyes that made me think of the Sasquatch. Anger and heat and fear.

"Mr. Davis!"

"Get my daughter!"

"Okay, okay," I repeated. "Can I stand?"

"Yes, get up," he said. "I didn't mean to knock you down. I was just trying to get in."

Keeping a wary eye on him, I got to my feet. "Mr. Davis, I'll get Nell," I said, "but I just want to say…I never hurt her. We're friends."

"Just go get her," he growled.

"Please let me finish," I said, looking him in the eye. "I understand why you're here. You're protecting your daughter. I respect you for that."

"Frankly, kid, I don't give a shit."

"*Daddy!*" Nell had appeared and was glaring at her father with a horrified expression. "What are you doing here?"

Mr. Davis looked surprised at her sudden appearance, and oddly deflated, like somehow he'd been looking forward to staging a more aggressive offensive. "What am I doing here?" he echoed. "Well, let's see. Oh yeah. Your mother and I were getting ready to pack up for the farmers market at four AM when we discovered that all the stuff had somehow disappeared. And when we called Katie's house to find out if you knew anything about it—guess what?"

"I wasn't there?" Nell said.

"No, honey. You weren't there. You lied to us. We didn't know what to think."

"I guess you figured out you could find me here."

"That's right. This is the first place I thought of, and here you are."

"And see? I'm okay, so calm down, all right?"

"No, Nell. It's not all right."

"But it is, Daddy."

"No, it's not." He pointed at me, his eyes steely. "You bring this boy into our home and tell us he's your friend, and that's fine. But almost every time you spend a couple of hours with him, you come home a wreck—"

"It's not his fault. It's mine. I like being with him. He makes me feel normal. But because I'm so weird, I don't know how to handle feeling normal. So I run away from it and lock myself in my room for a while. Does that make sense?"

I started to smile—because, well, it did. And Nell liked me. She said so. But the smile ended in a wince. Moving the muscles in my cheek made my eye hurt. It was swelling up pretty bad. Nell moved to me, touching my face gently. Her eyes were full of concern. "God, Dad, what did you do to him?" she exclaimed. "Who knew you were such a bully?"

"Hey! What the heck's going on out here?" Megan slipped out from behind the gate. I could see that she recognized Mr. Davis from the day we all went to the beach. Her face brightened. "Oh, hi!" she said with a little wave.

"Daddy, do you remember Megan? She's Jake's sister. If it makes you feel any better, I was sleeping in her room."

"Nell…" Mr. Davis started to say, showing his discomfort.

"Jake's a nice guy, Dad. I trust him. And I'm telling you that you can trust him too."

"Oh, Nell." Mr. Davis sighed. "We've built our whole lives around keeping you safe."

"I know, Daddy. And I love you for it. But I'm okay."

"Let's finish this discussion at home," Mr. Davis said. "Your mother is going crazy."

"You can tell her I'm fine. You can tell her I'll be home later."

"Sweetheart…," Mr. Davis said.

"Please, Daddy. I. Am. Fine. And I can't come home because we've made plans for the day, and I want to keep them. You have to trust me."

"All right," he said reluctantly, "I'll go. But this subject is *not* closed." Mr. Davis heaved a great sigh, seeming to clear his head. He didn't look at Megan or me. His eyes, bright with tears, stayed on his daughter as he retreated into the still-running Range Rover. He held his gaze until he pulled away and took off down the road.

As soon as he disappeared around a bend, Nell said, "Well, at least I've had *that* talk with my dad. I'll have to come up with a story when he asks about the missing veggies." She turned to me. "We'd better get some ice on that eye and clean you up. You look terrible."

CHAPTER 53

Thankfully, I had a chance to clean up before the *Another Day, USA!* car picked me up. I was delivered to the motel and shown into a room that had been set up for the interview. A lot of time was spent positioning lights in relation to where I'd be sitting during the taping, and on the placement of Morris's chair. For some reason, I had to physically inhabit my spot through the long, tedious process, but no one seemed to care where Morris was. Every once in a while, Courtney flitted through the room, tagging different members of the crew for serious discussion. She never once looked in my direction, or acted like I was even there. Guess once she had me where she wanted me, I wasn't worthy of any more of her precious attention.

I probably should have found the whole process fascinating. After all, this was the world I was interested in, right? But within a couple of hours, the combination of high-strung nerves and screaming boredom made my brain shut down. Two hours turned to three, morning became afternoon, and still Morris didn't show up. Along the way, somebody offered me a bottle of water. The only time I left that damn room was to pee.

There was no clock, and I didn't have my cell phone or a watch with me, so I could only guess it was about one-thirty by the time Rick Morris finally breezed in with a great flurry of excitement. "Whoa! Jake!" He slapped me on the back. "Walk into a door?"

"Something like that," I mumbled.

After sitting around for so long, all of a sudden everybody was in a huge rush. The director plopped me back down in that chair again. The makeup girl came along and put a bib around Morris's neck so she could dab him with powder while he looked over some notes on a clipboard. Final adjustments were made to the lights, and at last, the director called out, "Quiet on the set!"

Immediately, everyone on the crew seemed to melt away so that it was only Morris and me.

Morris looked up from his notes and smiled—that warm, gooey, fake-best-friend smile. "You ready for this, Jake?"

My hands were sweaty and it felt like there was a big cotton ball caught in my throat. For hours, I'd been sitting there, planning how I was going to play this, and now I didn't have a thought in my head. I just wanted to run. I cleared my throat. "Um," I began, "are you sure this is okay? Don't you need to get permission from my parents or something?"

Morris laughed. "Why? There's not going to be any sexual content in our discussion, is there?"

"Huh?" was all I could say.

"You're sixteen, right?"

"Yes."

"Well, unless we're going to broach an adult subject—which usually means sex—we're cool. You don't need a permission slip. But," he hastily added, "I'd be happy to talk to your mom or dad before we begin—if they have any questions."

"No, no. That's okay. They're fine with everything," I assured him.

He looked at me, his eyes all soft with concern. "Would you like to tell me who hit you?"

"Nobody hit me," I said. "I fell out of bed this morning."

"Sure, Jake," Morris said broadly. Then he shrugged. "Doesn't matter. Audience isn't going to see your face. Good thing, though, right? Otherwise I'd have to ask you on camera— for the sake of the audience."

"But you don't, so let's drop it," I said. "Can we just start?"

So we did. Just like that. An intense silence came over the room. Rick Morris started with this little prepared statement about the alleged Bigfoot incidents that had occurred in town—the vandalism and the footprints found on the scene. He explained that I had personal reasons to protect my identity. Then he started in on the questions.

I can't repeat the whole experience word for word. I never watched the broadcast, and the whole interview unfolded like a dream, with my memory of it as sketchy and elusive as dreams are.

What do I remember? I remember answering questions about Horace, described moving into the house and finding all his research material. I remember Morris asking me about my first experiences. I told him about that first day in the woods, coming across the strange barrier of stripped trees, the feeling that someone was watching me. I went on from there, telling about the eerie cries in the night, my certainty that there was something real but unexplained out there, that my granduncle wasn't crazy. I told him about the day Nell and I had rocks thrown at us on the way to the swimming hole. When I described that first nighttime encounter on the road, when I cut off the male from his pursuit of the buck, I knew that I had Rick Morris in the palm of my hand.

I swear to God, he believed me. After I finished telling him about the night the male tried to drag me out of the car, I thought Morris was going to swoon in ecstasy.

There were two things that I carefully left out of my narrative. I had two thoughts running through my head the whole time so I wouldn't mess up.

Note to self—do not tell him about the pungent aroma of the Sasquatch.

Note to self—do not mention that I own a camera.

The room remained absolutely silent. I could tell even the guys on the crew were hanging on every word.

Morris paused for a moment, letting the nightmare image of an enraged monster attacking a car parked by the side of the road sink in. He was good at his job. He knew how to build suspense in a story. But I had a pretty good idea of how to do it too.

"So, Billy." Billy was the alias I'd chosen. Morris sat back in his chair, gazing hard at me with a thoughtful expression on his face. I'd seen him do this a million times. After drawing plenty of sensational stuff out of me, he was going into hard-nosed-journalist mode. He needed to show the audience that he wasn't gullible, that he was getting ready to ask some tough questions, challenge me.

I was ready for him.

"You really expect me—and all of America—to believe that you saw the creature you described and that it assaulted you and your companions on the side of a road in Connecticut?"

"I know it sounds crazy," I said, keeping my voice steady. "I couldn't believe it myself. But I wasn't alone. My friends saw it too."

"The friends who refuse to come forward."

"Do you blame them?" I countered. We'd established early on in the taping that I hadn't experienced everything alone, but I wasn't going to divulge anybody's identity. "They're afraid that everyone will think they're nuts."

"Are they?" Morris asked. "Could it have been some kind of shared hallucination? Or did you really see something extraordinary out there?"

"That was my question. And I was determined to find out."

"And how did you do that?"

"We set up a stakeout. We were going to get proof."

Morris leaned forward in his chair, eager again. "Tell me about that."

And I did. I took him down to the edge of the reservoir in the early-morning mist. Kept him crouching uncomfortably in the bushes with my unnamed companions and me. But in this version of the story, I knew there was a gun, so when that great, lumbering beast plunged out of the woods, I made it sound like we were being attacked and the shot was fired was in self-defense.

"You shot it?" Now Morris looked really skeptical. I was losing him again.

"I didn't shoot it," I said, "my friend did."

"Oh, right."

"But the thing is," I continued, "there were two of them."

"Go on," Morris urged, but he had this look on his face, like he thought I was bullshitting him, like he was getting ready to pull the plug.

"Yes, there were two! And they were huge. And as soon as the first one was hit, the other one went over to it. It wasn't dead. It let out this horrible scream, but it didn't fall down or anything. My friend shot at them again, but I guess he was nervous and his shot went wild, didn't hit anything. But it scared them, because they turned tail and ran back into the woods."

"So then what did you do?"

"We chased them," I said, like that's what anybody else would do. "It was easy to follow their trail. They made a lot of noise and flattened everything down as they ran. There was a trail of blood to follow too. We went after them for about a half a mile or so. And then we saw."

"Saw what?"

"The one that was shot had collapsed. It was lying down under a big tree. The other one was standing over it." I was picturing the fictional scene I was weaving so clearly in my mind that I actually teared up. After all, that could have happened. Barry was such a jackass. What if we had found the Sasquatch that day? I could imagine the female finding her mate under that big hemlock tree, hear her howls of grief.

Morris responded to the emotion in my voice. "Go on," he urged. "What happened next?"

"It looked at us. The one standing. It saw us, watching." My voice broke. I'd worked myself up to the point where I was actually choking back a sob. I used it. "It was terrible. It rushed us, roaring like a lion. Its eyes were blazing red and it was baring its long yellow teeth. I was sure it was going to kill us."

"What did you do?"

"Ran the hell out of there."

"Did you ever go back?"

"No. We were too scared."

"How long ago did this happen?"

"A few days ago."

"Do you think the body of the dead one's still there?"

"I guess." I shrugged. "It'd be pretty gross, though."

"Would you be able to take us to the spot where it died?"

"Sure, I think so. But the one that's still alive is still mad. I think that's why it's been storming around town. It's looking for revenge."

"Okay, cut," Morris said, breaking the mood. Right away, I was aware from the buzz of conversation and shuffling that there were maybe a dozen other people in the small room with us. He looked around until he found the person he sought. "Tom," he called, "could you come over here a second? And somebody find Courtney." He unclipped the microphone from his shirt.

The director showed up at Morris's side. "Yeah, Rick?"

"I want to finish this in the field. Can we do that?"

"What'd you have in mind?"

"Billy here is going to take us on safari."

Courtney entered the room, striding briskly while talking on a cell phone. "What's up?" she asked Morris.

"We're going to finish this in the woods," Morris said, rubbing his hands together. "I think we can play this out to be a prime-time piece. Show a teaser tomorrow morning, but save the whole thing for *USA Amazing Magazine* tomorrow night. Really max out the ratings." He looked at me, his eyes hard. "That is, if you can deliver. Can you?"

"Yes," I said, my voice thin.

"But we can't do it now!" Courtney protested.

"Why not?" Morris was annoyed.

"There's a helicopter waiting to take you back to New York. You've got an interview with the Italian prime minister at five."

"Damn," said Morris. "Can't Heather do it?"

"No. He insisted on you. And anyway, Heather's on location too. She's in Iowa covering some corn festival."

"Tom, can we keep the crew here one more night? I'll come back."

"Sure, I guess so."

"And Courtney," Morris said. "See if you can line up an expert. What do they call them?"

Courtney and Tom blankly stared back at Morris.

"Cryptozoologist," I said.

Morris slapped me on the back. "That's it!" he cried. "Call the Discovery Channel and see if they can hook us up with one of those kooks. We're going to need someone with credentials to authenticate our find."

CHAPTER 54

They finally released me around four in the afternoon, and I found Nell waiting for me in her little green car. She'd figured that the fewer times a limo pulled up to the house, the less chance there was for them to discover the Sasquatch were on the premises. Smart girl. By then I was starving, but I insisted on going straight home. I wanted to make sure the family was doing okay.

When we walked in the door, the strong odor of Bigfoot musk hit us—it had permeated the house. I'd expected that would happen, which is why I'd been careful not to mention their distinctive stench in the interview. The first time Rick met me, he commented on how bad I smelled. I didn't want anyone to put two and two together.

While I gulped down a couple of PB&Js, I filled the girls and Samuel in on how the interview went, but I didn't tell them about finishing it up in the woods tomorrow. I only told them that I would be meeting with Morris again, that he wanted to ask me a few follow-up questions.

Then I went out to check on the Sasquatch. They were in the backyard again, Mama and Baby cuddled up together in the shade, napping. The male stood over them, alert and tense. We looked at each other, and while we stood there, we could hear the sounds of traffic moving along the road beyond the fence. The area had continued to fill up with thrill-seekers and creature hunters. The television crews had attracted even more curious strangers. A crowd had formed outside the Days Inn, hoping for a glimpse of Rick Morris. No one had so much as glanced at me. If all went according to plan, tomorrow they would begin to leave, and our quiet corner of rural Connecticut would return to normal.

We spent another tense evening surfing the net for any information or leaks about the interview. Finally, around ten, Nell announced that she was leaving for home. "I have to deal with my parents sooner or later. Might as well get it over with. I'll watch the show in the morning so I can report back." She slipped her feet into her sandals and picked up her keys. "Why don't you guys come over and watch?"

"Can't. My meeting with Morris is at eight," I said, "and Megan has to stay here to keep an eye on our buddies."

"Well, I'll make sure I record it," Nell said. After wishing "'Night," to Samuel and Megan, she turned to me. "Walk me out?"

We stepped out into the night. The air held the chilly bite of autumn. The sting of cool air on my cheeks sent a melancholy shiver through me. The summer was coming to an end. An amazing summer. The summer I found the Sasquatch. The summer I met Nell.

I walked ahead of Nell to open the gate. When I finished, she was waiting for me by the side of her car. We stood looking at each other in the soft amber light spilling from the living room windows. She was smiling at me, but shyness had come over both of us.

After a few moments, she spoke. "I just wanted to say thank you again. And sorry about the whole scene with my dad."

"It's okay."

"No, it's not. But it will be. I'm going to fix everything tonight, I promise. I want my parents to like you. And they did, at first, before I messed everything up."

"You didn't mess anything up. We're still here, together, right?" I wanted to put my arms around her. Instead, I put my hands in my pockets. "Once we get the Sasquatch through all this safely, we'll work it out, okay?"

I could hear the tears in her voice. "Okay. And then I'll explain to you why my parents freak out every time I stub a toe."

"Only when you're ready," I said. "But thank you." I knew she was telling me she trusted me.

Then she threw her arms around my neck, and it took my breath away. Nell was warm and solid against me, her breath tickling my neck, and I felt brave enough to finally hold her tight. A few moments later, as she eased herself out of my embrace, she kissed me again.

After Nell drove off, I secured the gate with the chain and padlock. Not ready to go back into the stuffy house, I walked around back. The basement doors stood wide open to the night sky, but Mama and Baby were nowhere in sight. I guessed they'd retired into the basement for the night. But the male was still there, standing vigil in the middle of the backyard, his face turned upward. I sensed how he felt—edgy and pent-up, worried. Watchful. Lonely. Resolute. I scuffed my feet loudly as I walked, to alert him to my presence. He turned toward me. The moonlight reflected in his eyes.

I raised my hand. "Good night."

He raised his hand to me in return and then resumed gazing up into the star-filled vista above him.

CHAPTER 55

Rick Morris greeted me in the Days Inn parking lot. He was all tricked out in hunting gear—cargo pants and a khaki vest with an amazing amount of pockets, like he was some kind of Great White Hunter. The manly-man effect he was going for was ruined by the fact that everything he wore was crisp and new.

"You ready to go, 'Billy?'" he asked, a broad grin on his face. I was surprised by his buoyant friendliness—that is, until I realized a cameraman was standing beside him, recording his greeting. Not wanting to have any of the news vehicles near the house, I'd taken the risk of driving the Jeep into town. Now I was glad I had also taken the precaution of parking at the back of the lot.

I shielded my face with my arm. "Hey!" I protested. "Protecting my identity—remember?"

"Oh, it's okay, we'll remove your face digitally before we air this," Morris assured me.

"Sure," I said. "But the less I'm on camera, the better—okay?"

"Fine, fine." Morris looked at me funny. "What's with the coat? Kind of hot for that, isn't it?"

I had put on my dad's old army surplus jacket. It was huge on me. "Oh, this?" I said. "My mom freaks about Lyme disease. I made a standing promise to her that I'd never go into the woods without completely covering up."

Before Morris could comment, a member of the crew pulled him away. A crowd of fans had gathered around, like they do outside the show's studio in New York City. Some people had big posters that said "Hi Mom!" and stuff. A bunch of teenagers messed around along the fringes of the gathering.

Of course Barry was there. He was easy to pick out because that big volleyball head of his loomed over everybody else. My eyes locked on his. His mouth opened wide in a braying grin as he flipped me the bird.

Then Morris was back without the cameraman, talking to me. "This is our driver, Craig." I shook some guy's hand, turning my attention away from Barry. "You're going to ride up front with him, give him directions."

"We're going now?" I asked.

"Yes, right away," Morris said.

"But what about the rest of the show?" I asked. "It's only eight-fifteen."

Morris laughed. "Thanks for your concern, but I got people to cover for me, Jake. I want to get this done as soon as possible so everything can be edited and polished to air tonight."

"So you haven't shown anything yet?"

"Are you kidding me?" Morris squeezed my shoulder. "You were one of the lead stories this morning. We showed the first few minutes of your interview at 7:10. And I understand we're getting quite a response. This is going to be big, Jake."

I gave the driver directions to the old logging road. It would make the hike I had planned a good twenty minutes longer than if we'd taken the trail that started near the house, but I wanted to keep them as far away from home as possible. The network had gotten clearance from the state police to access any part of the preserve. The white van traveled as far down the rutted old trail as it could go, and then we all clambered out and got organized at the head of the path that led to the reservoir.

Besides Morris and me, the Discovery Channel had delivered on the cryptozoologist—a skinny, short guy with a long beard and round glasses who seemed very nervous and didn't say anything. There were two cameramen, the director and several assistants and lighting guys, and one other producer besides Courtney. Oh yeah. Courtney had to come along too. And she didn't look happy about it. She was definitely what Samuel would call a "city kid." I couldn't wait to see how she was going to do in those little gold sandals of hers when we had to hike off-trail.

I'd decided before we started that I was going to drag this out for as long as I could, but I had to keep them interested. I showed them some of the places I'd talked about in the interview, like what was left of the barrier and the rock lean-to. When we got to the path that led to the swimming hole, I took a long time describing where my "friend" and I were when the rocks started pelting down on us. I even managed to get Morris and a cameraman to hike up the hill with me to get a stone-thrower's perspective.

Along the way, the crypto guy corroborated my story, stating nervously that what I'd been showing them and what I was describing was similar to other documented Bigfoot eyewitness accounts. But then it started to get hotter and later, and I knew I had to deliver something bigger pretty soon.

We reached the place where Megan, Nell, and I had camped out, where Barry had crashed the party. We'd left some stuff behind—a couple of water bottles and the old plaid blanket we'd sat on. It was a nice touch. Finding that junk got Morris all excited, like he'd found archaeological evidence of some past civilization, not some litter left behind by a bunch of kids.

I went over the tale of the encounter and shooting again, pointing out where we were hiding and where the creatures had jumped out of the bushes. I made sure to emphasize how misty it was that morning, how confusing that made everything.

Once I was done, Morris said, "Can you take us to where you found the dead one?"

I took a deep breath, made sure I looked a little scared. It wasn't too hard; I *was* scared. Not of the Sasquatch, but of these people and what might happen if I didn't play this right. All morning long, I'd been spinning a tale of red-eyed giants with long fangs running around throwing rocks. It made a good story, but what effect would it have on the hundreds of people roaming around looking for Sasquatch? "Yes, I think so," I finally said, "but it'll be rough going. There's no trail."

Morris gave a smug little laugh, as if to remind the audience and me what an intrepid kind of guy he was, that he'd faced more dangerous situations than this before. "I think we can handle it, Billy. Lead on."

I kind of enjoyed the last leg of the journey. We had to slog through swampy areas and thorny underbrush. Then we climbed a steep, rocky incline. Mosquitoes swarmed, and I had to stifle a chuckle when Morris got slapped in the face by a springy branch. I did laugh out loud, a little, when the strap on Courtney's sandal broke and she had to hobble across the rocks and roots as best she could. As the afternoon wore on, the weather got muggier, and Courtney's perfect blonde hairdo was turning into a frizzy puffball. Sweat was making her once-flawless makeup melt away, leaving behind a red, swollen face that wasn't so pretty.

Finally, we reached the clearing marked by the enormous hemlock, and I could see right away that there was still a mound beneath it.

I stopped dead in my tracks. My words came out in a hoarse whisper. "There it is." I pointed. Then I added truthfully, "I can't go any closer."

"Why not?" Morris asked.

Why not? First of all, the thought of getting close to that dead thing was just, well, disgusting. Second of all, I still felt bad that it was dead. And I didn't want to be standing too close to Morris or Courtney at the moment of the big reveal. But what I said was, "I'm too scared."

There was eagerness in Morris's voice when he said, "Never mind. You stay here. You…" he spun around and grabbed the arm of the crypto guy, who looked as enthusiastic as I felt about checking out a pile of rotting flesh. "Come with me."

I watched from a distance as the news crew approached the hemlock and the thing underneath it. I could imagine the flies and the smell—a stink even worse than a living Sasquatch—and waited until I heard what I was expecting.

"Turn off the camera!" Morris's howl was a high-pitched squeal of anger. "Where's that kid? *Sonofabitch!*"

That's when I reached into the pocket of my coat and pressed the Record button of my camera.

In a flash, Morris covered the ground that separated us and was right up into my face. "You little shit!" he hissed, his spit spattering my face. "It's nothing but a stupid bear! And you knew that—didn't you?" He grabbed me by the coat, pulled me off my feet.

"No! No, Mr. Morris!" I said, stuttering, now really afraid. "I swear to God! I thought it was a Bigfoot—but I told you the other one chased us off before we could get close enough to really see."

"Liar!" Courtney screeched. She was standing next to Morris now, hands on hips, the angry expression on her face causing her eyes to go all buggy.

I don't know how that meek little guy mustered the courage, but the cryptozoologist felt the need to interject. "These sort of troublesome incidents happen frequently—a bear being mistaken for a Bigfoot. It's frustrating, but bound to happen as both species typically populate the same habitats. But we must endeavor to persevere in our research and never waver in our dedication to find the evidence that will prove the truth."

"Oh, shut up," Morris said, turning his back on the man. "I don't know how I'm going to do it, kid. But I'm going to ruin you." Morris's voice was low and menacing. I could smell coffee on his breath.

"Honestly, Mr. Morris," I said, "I haven't told you a single lie. I'll take a polygraph test."

He let go of me with a little shove of contempt. "I'm not going to waste any more time on you."

While Morris was all in my face and contemplating killing me, the film crew had maintained their distance, shuffling their feet and averting their eyes. Now Morris gave a broad wave of his arms and called over, "We're done here, guys. Let's get the hell out of here."

When Morris turned away, a weird emotional wave washed over me. I felt dizzy and nauseous and my knees went all watery. I sank to the ground. Folding my legs up, I rested my head on my knees and covered my head with my arms. Only then, when I was sure no one could see my face, did I allow myself to grin. Who knows how long I might have stayed there? My hope was to remain until the film crew packed up and headed back to the van. Then I figured I could hike the ten minutes or so back to the house. The Jeep was still parked in the motel lot—I'd worry about picking that up later. Maybe Nell could give me a ride, or I could pedal down on my bike. I wondered how long it would take, once the word got out that there was no dead Bigfoot after all, before all the idiots running around the woods started to clear out. How long would it be before the Sasquatch could reclaim their kingdom?

I was looking too far ahead. A shadow loomed over me. "Get up!" a voice barked. "We have to get out of here."

Courtney.

She was spitting mad. It was a wonder she hadn't kicked me to get my attention. Then I remembered she was having a hard enough time keeping those stupid sandals on her feet. "That's okay," I said. "You guys go on without me."

She nudged me with her big toe. "We can't," she said. "We don't know where we are. You have to lead us out of here."

The next half-hour or so was pretty uncomfortable. Everyone who had a cell phone was trying to get someone from the network on the line to start damage control. They all found out what I'd learned weeks earlier—spotty service in these great wide woods. It didn't stop them from trying, which was kind of a relief. It kept them busy. The crypto guy was the only person who seemed unaffected by the disappointing outcome of the safari. For a while, he trotted along beside me, cheerfully telling me about other expeditions he'd been on, asking me a ton of questions about my experiences. I couldn't take it, though, and sped up my pace. Eventually, he fell back into the pack and let me lead the way alone.

When we got to the van, I was as exhausted as everyone else. I suspected that Morris and Courtney would have liked to abandon me there, so I jumped into the front with the driver before they could object.

The van had barely come to a full stop in the motel parking lot when I jumped out and started heading for the Jeep. Morris didn't waste any time, either, and before I could go twenty steps, he'd grabbed me by the arm and pulled me back, dragging me to the far side of the van, out of hearing distance of anyone else.

"I just want you to understand that this isn't over," he said, his mouth to my ear. He was looking over my head, making sure no one else was within earshot. "There will be repercussions. I will ruin your life."

"I'm sorry about what happened, Mr. Morris," I said, "but everything I told you was the truth."

"Come on, kid," Morris growled. "You played me. You play—you pay. And you're going to pay, big-time. Watch your back. I won't forget this."

I yanked my arm out of his grip. "Again, Mr. Morris, I'm sorry. But you know you can spin this your way. I figure you've got a week's worth of good material. You'll be starting up a new series tomorrow morning—*The Greatest Hoaxes of the Century*—right?"

"Just get the hell out of here," he sneered. "I'm sick of the sight of you."

"Okay, I'm going." I took a few steps backward to put some distance between us. "But just so you know—ever since the corpse under the tree was identified as a bear? I've taped everything you've said to me."

"What?"

"I have a video camera in my pocket. I didn't get any visuals, but the audio should be pretty clear. I wonder how your audience will respond to America's most trusted newscaster threatening some kid who was just trying to help him on a story."

I almost made it to the Jeep. There was still a big crowd of gawkers trying to catch a glimpse of their beloved star, Rick Morris. They could have him. I just wanted to get out of there. When I made it to the driver's door, I made the mistake of looking over my shoulder.

What I saw made my heart sink.

Courtney was deep in conversation with a state trooper. State troopers were all over the place. I'd even heard rumors that the governor was considering calling in the National Guard. Guess the authorities were worried that all those Bigfoot hunters might start shooting at each other out there in the woods with nothing else to do.

Courtney was talking fast with a serious look on her face. The trooper was listening closely, his brow furrowed. She stuck her arm out, pointing in my direction. The trooper looked at me.

Courtney remained where she was standing, a mean smile on her face as the trooper started marching in my direction.

I stood my ground with what I imagined was an open expression on my face. I was just an innocent kid, minding my own business, right? The trooper stopped right in front of the car, his legs planted in a wide stance, his arms crossed over his broad chest. I couldn't see his eyes behind his sunglasses. I'd seen enough movies with evil state troopers to be sufficiently intimidated, but I was going to do my damnedest to talk my way out of whatever shit was about to hit the fan.

CHAPTER 56

"Good afternoon, young man," said the state trooper, his voice serious but not threatening.

"Hi," I said.

"Where are you off to?"

"Me?" I shrugged. "Nowhere."

"Looked to me like you were about to go somewhere."

"No, sir," I said.

"This your car?"

"No, sir. It's my dad's car." I should have focused my entire attention on the trooper, but I couldn't help being distracted. The fans around the entrance of the motel were buzzing with reenergized excitement.

"Is your dad around, son?" the trooper asked.

"No, sir. He's out of town." My glance darted over the officer's shoulder in an attempt to catch a glimpse of what was going on. While most people's backs were turned, one woman was pushing the other way through the mob with a familiar impatience. She was pretty far off, but there was something about the confidence of her stride and the gleam of gold in her brown hair that hit me hard in the gut.

"Please pull out your driver's license," said the trooper.

"My driver's license?" I echoed like an idiot.

"Yes, your driver's license."

"Why do you want to see my driver's license?" I felt my face grow hot. I'd told him my dad was out of town. How could I have made such a stupid slip?

"Just a routine request. May I see it, please?"

I gulped, just like a character in a cartoon. "I don't have one, sir," I admitted. Even though I couldn't see the trooper's eyes, I could feel his glare boring into my brain, seeing my fear and growing desperation. And *she* was still coming our way, fast—jogging almost.

"You don't have a driver's license?"

"No, sir." I watched her approach. Anything was better than looking into the darkly reflective blank of the officer's sunglasses.

The trooper bowed his head and started rubbing his chin, like he was thinking deeply. "Hmmm, interesting. Where do you live?"

I gave him the address, trying to keep my voice even.

"Why, that's nowhere near here, is it?"

"A few miles. Not too far."

She was a hundred feet away. I hoped she wasn't going to yell at me. I'd had enough of that. For that matter, I hoped the trooper wasn't going to yell at me.

"So, tell me then," the trooper continued. "If you don't have a license, and your dad's out of town—how did this Jeep come to be parked here?"

I opened my mouth to speak as my imagination began spinning a wildly complicated tale involving friends and favors that I knew wasn't going to be convincing. But before I could say anything, she reached us.

"I drove," she said, her voice sending a *gong* vibrating in my brain. My heart pounded harder, if that was possible. I felt dizzy with a wild riot of emotions.

The state trooper pivoted his head in response to her declaration.

"You drove?" he asked her.

"Yes, officer," she said. "I drove."

"And you are?"

"His mother."

Mom. It really was my mom. Thinner than the last time I'd seen her, and really tan. When she pushed her big sunglasses off her nose and onto the top of her head, she gave me a look with her hazel eyes that said, "Let me handle it from here." She smiled at the trooper.

"Is this your husband's car?" he asked, a little ruffled now.

"My ex-husband's car. Is my son in some kind of trouble, officer?"

"Not exactly, ma'am," the trooper said.

"Then we're free to go?" she asked.

"Not exactly." The cop's mouth set in a stern line as he regrouped. He spoke directly to her. "There's been a lot of trouble around here that cost a lot of money and manpower. Now it looks like it was all a big prank. I'd like to know what your son here knows about it."

I wondered what Courtney had told him.

Mom stepped to my side, putting her arm through mine, pulling me close. She smelled kind of briny, like she'd come straight from the beach. She probably had. "Jake, sweetie, please tell the officer—did you have anything to do with some kind of practical joke?"

"No." I could have passed a lie-detector test.

She turned from me and spoke to the trooper. "Well, there you go. He doesn't know anything about it."

"Ma'am—"

"If you have any more questions for my son, sir, let me know and we'll make arrangements with my lawyer." Her tone was firm.

"Well, there is one thing…" I added. My mother pinched my thigh—her signature shut-up move. I tried not to wince.

"What's that?" said the trooper, crossing his arms again.

"I do know this one kid," I continued. "His name is Barry. The other day, he was goofing around with this huge plaster model of a foot. He was making all kinds of Bigfoot jokes."

"Where can I find him?" the cop asked.

I gave him Barry's address.

My mother looked at me like she thought I was crazy. As far as she was concerned, we were good to go. She'd gotten us out of a sticky situation. Now I was complicating things. Maybe I *was* nuts. I'm not usually the kind of person to snitch on someone. She knows that. But Barry did start all this nonsense, and maybe the only way to have it finally blow over was to give him up to the authorities. Once the proof of a hoax was out there, everyone would give up and go home. The memory of Barry's ugly laughter that morning made me surer that it was the right thing to do. I just wished I could be there when the cops knocked on his door and prayed that he still had the plaster cast he'd stolen from me.

The trooper was still writing Barry's address in his little notebook when a state police car pulled up.

"Hey, Mike!" the driver called. "Accident on Route 8. We gotta go!"

The cop looked up. "Sure. I'm coming." He slipped the notebook into his back pocket and turned to my mother. "Ma'am?"

"Yes, Officer?" She lowered her sunglasses back onto her nose, signaling to him she considered the conversation over.

"You might want to contact that lawyer of yours." Having gotten in the last word, the trooper turned and got into the car.

I looked at my mom, and just when a million questions were about to spill out of my mouth, a howling chorus of cheers rose out of the crowd that was still milling around the motel entrance.

My mother grabbed my arm. "Jake! Look! It's Rick Morris!" She started pulling me along. "Come on! You know him. Introduce me!"

"Mom! No!" I protested, desperately trying to dig my heels into the ground.

"Oh, please," she snorted. "Don't pull that embarrassed-teenager act now. I want to meet Rick Morris!"

"Mom, I can't." Oh, this really sucked. It looked like Morris was getting ready to jump into an idling limo. He was spending a few last minutes working the crowd—shaking hands and signing autographs. A slick, professional nice-guy smile was plastered on his face. Oh geez. My mother was about to turn that smile around to a frown. That's what I was afraid of, anyway.

I wasn't moving fast enough for her, so she stopped and grabbed my arm. She said, low in my ear, "Look, you, you have a lot of explaining to do. If you want to live to see tomorrow, you will make your mother happy with this one little request."

She pulled me through the crowd without caring if she was rude or stepped on anybody's feet. I'd never seen her quite so crazed. To my great relief, when we finally got within Morris's earshot, she cried out like they were best friends, "Oh, Rick? Hi!" She let go and left me to fend for myself in the seething ocean of desperate fans, all of whom were pissed at her for shoving her way to the front. She grabbed his hand, pumping it up and down as she introduced herself as my mother. That's when I cringed, feeling like I might puke. But she went on and on, still shaking his hand, telling him how much she loved the show and what a great job he did interviewing her son.

He was responding to what she was saying pleasantly enough, but his eyes were as cold and sharp as razorblades. I matched him with an equally harsh glare that I hoped conveyed the message: *Remember the recording! Be nice to my mom, or else!*

He must have got it, because he flashed that slick grin at her one more time as he disengaged his hand and excused himself before he climbed into the backseat, the tinted windows hiding him from view as the big car slowly pulled away.

Mom came rushing back over to me and gave me a big hug. "Oh my God. Jake! I can't believe I just met Rick Morris!" At that moment, with her arms around me like that, it was like I'd never been mad at her in my life.

"Terrific, Mom," I said, falling in step beside her.

"And he was so nice," my mother exclaimed.

"Right," I agreed. "He's a great guy." We were working our way back to the Jeep. By now, my feet hurt and a hunger headache was beginning a dull throb.

"And to think you weren't going to tell me about being on *Another Day, USA!*" She shook her head.

"I was too!" I protested feebly.

"Oh no you weren't," she countered. "And by the way— who hit you?"

I touched my cheek. The swelling had gone down, but it was still tender to the touch. "Oh. Nobody. I'll tell you later. I'll explain everything."

"You bet you will."

Having my mother show up like she did was a surreal, miraculously well-timed event. I tried really hard not to limp. If she noticed another injury, she'd have me in the emergency room for a full work-up. The words "What are you doing here, anyway?" came out of my mouth. I wished right away I hadn't said them.

She came to a sudden halt, put her hands on her hips, and said so emphatically it was almost yelling, "Because I saw you on TV! What did you think?" The switch had been flipped. The elation my mother felt at meeting Morris morphed directly into something very different. She was mad at me. The signs were there. She was emitting that bristly electric force field that triggers the impulse to run. After successfully protecting me from the cop and meeting America's most trusted newscaster, she could unleash Mad Mom.

"You were on the show I watch every morning! I knew what town in Connecticut Rick Morris was in. I know where you are. Do you think I'm an idiot? Just because they filmed you in shadow and they made your voice sound funny—I know the way you talk, how you sit forward in a chair with your shoulders hunched. Christ Almighty, did you think I wouldn't know my own child!" She let out a huge sound—not so much a sigh, but a releasing growl of pent-up…something. Then she continued stomping her way to the car. We hadn't gone twenty steps when she stopped again. "And where's your father in all this?"

I stopped too, mutely facing her with a fearful stare.

"He's not here, is he?" she hissed. "He's pulled his famous disappearing act, right?" She didn't wait for a response but walked on with me trailing behind. When we got to the Jeep, she said, "Well, I guess I'm driving. We'll figure out how to pick up my rental car later." As we strapped into our seats, she barked, "And why don't you have your driver's license yet?"

My face was now paralyzed in a pop-eyed expression. She was on a rant. When my mom's on a rant, there's no point answering or trying to argue. All you can do is sit tight until she calms down enough to engage in a real dialogue. "So, there I am at seven AM, having a cup of coffee and getting ready for my morning walk along the beach—and next thing I know, my very own son is on television, being interviewed by Rick Morris. For a minute, I thought I was hallucinating—or having a stroke—or still in bed, dreaming—I didn't know what to think or how to react!" She turned the key in the ignition. "So, anyway, where am I going?"

"Take a left out of here, then turn right onto Main Street," I answered.

"Okay." For a minute, she concentrated on her driving. Then she started up again. "So, then I started shouting. Jim was still upstairs, but he came rushing down. As soon as I told him, he was great, didn't waste a minute. He chartered a flight off Nantucket and set up the car rental."

"Is he with you?" I prayed he wasn't.

"No. We both thought it best if I handled this on my own."

Good decision. By then I could tell that she was talking herself down—I wasn't home free, but we were getting closer to a two-way conversation.

After I gave her some more driving directions, she asked, "So where is your father—Asia, Africa, the North Pole?" Before I could answer, she said, "Never mind, I don't care. It doesn't matter." She clamped her mouth shut like her jaws were steel hinges. That's what happened whenever she wanted to say something critical about my dad. She'd made us a promise after the divorce to never say anything bad about my dad, no matter how mad she got.

Her silence lasted until we pulled into the driveway and I jumped out to open the gate. I was glad the tirade had wound down. It gave me a chance to think. Not that I came up with anything. I had no idea what I was going to tell her, how I was going to explain.

"This is it, huh?" she said as she got out of the parked car. She was looking at the house and lawn curiously. "Not bad," she said, "kind of cute." Her gaze landed on the little green Karmann Ghia. "Who does that belong to?"

"My friend, Nell."

"So, I presume she's here?"

"Oh, yeah. I guess she's around somewhere."

"Do her parents know there isn't any parental supervision?"

"Her parents have an idea of what's going on," I said cautiously. Walking down the driveway, I busied myself with securing the chain and padlock. When I turned back, my mother was scrutinizing me with a hairy eyeball.

"I'm not in any danger of becoming a premature grandmother, am I?" she asked. That's another thing about my mom. She's a nurse, so she never shies away from uncomfortable questions. She's not squeamish about anything—bowel movements, masturbation, or the color of your pee. As far as my mom is concerned, every topic—no matter how excruciatingly embarrassing—is an open forum.

"No!" I said. "Come inside," I added with a resigned sigh.

"How much trouble are you in?"

It was a fair question. "Some. But not that bad."

"Are we going to need that lawyer?"

"No," I said. "I don't think so."

"Well, at least your sister's safe at camp and out of this mess." Still looking around, she sniffed the air. "I can tell you one thing about this place."

"What's that?"

"Take a whiff," she ordered. "Smell that?"

I dutifully smelled the air. "So?"

"It stinks! The septic system's probably failing. Who knows when the last time was that anyone pumped out the tank? I suppose that'll be another thing I'll have to take care of." She looked at me, shaking her head. "Okay, lead on. Let's see what you've got inside."

CHAPTER 57

I held my breath as we stepped through the front door. I had no idea what was waiting for us inside. Samuel must have finally gotten sick of the computer, because no one was in the living room. Everybody must be out back with the Sasquatch.

Mom walked around the room, taking it all in with a critical eye. "Everything looks very tidy," she said with an approving nod. "How long has your dad been away?"

There was no point in lying. "Weeks," I said. "Four or five."

She shook her head and spit out the classic *tsk-tsk.* She started flipping through the unopened mail that had accumulated on the little table by the door. "Looks like he's been paying the bills, for the most part." No need to tell her I'd been taking care of those. She picked up one envelope and looked at it more closely. "This looks like the property tax bill, though. It was probably due in July. My guess is he'll forget to pay it all together and he'll lose everything to the town before you know it."

I plucked the bill out of her hand. "I'll take care of it." The thought of losing my little house in the woods sent a stab of fear through me. I'd learned to love this place.

She raised her eyebrows. "Okay. Work it out with your dad." She entered the kitchen. I trailed after her, watching as she opened cabinets, checked the stock of cleaning supplies under the sink, and inspected the contents of the refrigerator. She straightened up. "Pretty good," she said. "Will I be horrified by the state of the bathroom?"

"Nope." If she'd seen me scrubbing everything the night before Nell first stayed over, she never would have asked that question. Worse things than a ring in the bathtub were about to be revealed.

"I have to admit," she said, "I'm very impressed. You've done a good job of handling things on your own."

"Thanks."

"So, where's this Nell?" she asked with a little smile. I felt my face redden.

"It's about time you got back!" Before I could stop her, Megan plowed through the swinging kitchen door. "We're going stir-crazy sitting around here…"

For a second, the three of us froze in place, our faces each broadcasting some variation of shock.

"Mom!" Megan gasped.

In a flat voice, Mom said, "Well, you're not Nell." She crossed her arms and let out a deep breath. Megan started backing away. Fight-or-flight had kicked in—and she was going with the flee option. Mom lunged forward and grabbed her arm, saying, "Oh no you don't."

"Mom, Mom! I can explain," Megan started babbling.

"That's what your cohort in crime here promised, but obviously he hasn't even skimmed the surface." My mother gave me a withering look.

Clang! A reverberating metal crash sounded behind the house, followed by a wild "*Aaaaiyiiii!*" I rushed to the back door as *oh, no* and *careful there* and *what happened?* added to the confusion. I picked out Samuel's voice. And Nell's. But there were guttural grunts and a high-pitched keening, and underneath it all, heartbreaking little whimpers of pain.

Bursting outside to find a chaotic scene, I could tell in a moment what had happened. Somehow the Bilco door had slammed down and injured Baby Squatch. Mama Squatch was holding her offspring in her arms, looking down at it, moaning with concern. Samuel stood a distance away, looking worried. Nell was trying to get close enough to assess the damage, but not too close. The male, in true dad fashion, was pacing back and forth, looking angry and upset, but clueless about what to do.

I was aware of Megan and my mother flying down the concrete steps behind me. Predictably, as soon the male saw my mother, he went all aggressive—the whole display—baring his teeth, his fur all bristling, and this time he added pounding his chest to the act. What was he going to do—attack my one-hundred-ten-pound mother?

Already a few paces ahead of Mom, I immediately jumped in front of her, shouting, "No!" from the deepest depths of my lungs. Then I pounded my chest too—in rhythmic thuds that felt like a bass drum echoing through me.

The male seemed so surprised by my forceful mimicry of his behavior that he backed off, his brow still lowered in a menacing scowl, still breathing deeply, but now I was sure he was rethinking his attack on my mother.

I held my ground, and I was pissed. When the hell was this big, hairy idiot going to trust me? Did he really think I'd bring someone here who'd hurt him? Did we have to go through this big macho showdown every time someone new showed up? I took a breath and said in an even voice, "Megan, tell him it's safe, explain she's our mom. Whatever. Do your stuff."

My poor mother—she must have been having a heart attack. Had she screamed? Maybe she'd passed out. I glanced over my shoulder at her.

What had I been thinking? This was my mother, the nurse that had seen every kind of horror that passes through emergency rooms on a regular basis, dealt with every kind of freakazoid imaginable. My "poor" mother was standing as cool and in control as anything. I could imagine that she hadn't so much as flinched when coming face-to-face with a stressed-out monster. Right away, I could see she was assessing the situation. She was looking over at Mama Squatch, who was still curled protectively over her baby, appearing oblivious to our little interspecies drama. "Megan," she said, her voice level and matter-of-fact, "you can communicate with them?"

"A little," Megan said.

"See if you can tell him I can help the infant. See if he'll let me get close enough to look."

Megan started on a series of signs that didn't make any sense to me but held the attention of the male.

Meanwhile my mom looked at Nell. "Are you Nell?" she asked, in the same briskly professional voice. Nell nodded, her eyes wide. "Go get my bag. It's a big, white leather thing. I left it in the living room."

"Walk slowly until you get in the house," I added, keeping my eye on the male, who was definitely still on edge.

"And who's this?" my mother asked, looking at Samuel. His mouth wide open, he was staring at her in wonder as if she were an angel straight from heaven.

"Mom, this is Samuel. Samuel, this is my mom." The formal introduction felt absurd under the circumstances.

"Samuel?" said my mother. "Do me a favor and get me a big bowl of warm water. And see if you can find some soft, clean cloth. A couple of T-shirts will do, anything."

"Sure thing." Both Nell and Samuel jumped carefully to action, leaving my family and me alone with the Sasquatch.

"How are you doing?" Mom asked Megan.

"I'm not sure. I think he understands that you're okay," Megan said, sounding a little iffy. I could understand why. The male still looked pretty upset.

"I don't think he's going to let you near the baby," I said.

My mother stepped a few paces closer to the male. She held up her hands. Her voice was soothing. "I know you can't understand me, fella. But you should let me take a look at your baby." Now she tried her hand at sign language. She pointed to Mama Squatch and made a cradling movement with her arms. Then she pointed to me, again motioning with her arms as if she were holding an infant. "See?" she said, looking into the male's eyes. "I get it. That's your baby. This is my baby. I'm a mom too. I know how you feel. Your baby is hurt. I think I can help." Never taking her eyes off the male, she started slowly sidling toward where Mama was still bent over the baby, both of them whimpering.

I stayed by her side. I never took my eyes off the male, either. Megan edged along with us.

Miraculously, the male seemed to relax a little bit. At least his breathing slowed down and the tension in his arms and shoulders seemed to lessen. The expression on his face looked more curious than suspicious.

By the time we reached the female and her baby, Nell came out with my mother's purse. Mom was famous for always carrying around a huge sack crammed full of weird stuff— sewing kits, water bottles, duct tape, and always, always a first aid kit. Taking the purse from Nell, she started rooting around in it, all the time making these cooing, sympathetic sounds. Mama Squatch shied away from my mom, letting out a little cry of fear. I just hoped she didn't rile up the big guy again.

My mother didn't let up on her clucking sounds. Then she took hold of my hand and pulled me down with her as she sat on the ground near Mama and Baby, but not too close. Making sure Mama Squatch could see what she was doing, she started examining the bruise beneath my eye, cooing and exclaiming over it. When she saw Samuel come out of the house, she waved him over, and as soon as he placed the bowl of water and T-shirts beside her, she got right to work, tenderly bathing my face with a warm, damp cloth.

It was clear that Mama Squatch understood, because when my mother finished her show of nursing me, she let Mom get close to her baby.

"Let me see the poor thing," my mother crooned. Gently, she unfolded Baby Squatch's limbs, quickly scanning its little body—which was about the size of a human three-year-old—for injuries. "There's the problem," she said. I saw it the moment she did—a small gash on the right ankle. "Looks like her foot got caught in the door and the metal edge took off some flesh." My mother held the not-so-small, furry foot in her hand, tenderly flexing the joints, expertly running her fingers over it, feeling for broken bones. "It's a little mooshed— swollen, but no fractures. The laceration needs to be cleaned out, though."

She washed out the wound with the warm water, smeared in a good dose of antibiotic ointment, and wrapped the baby's ankle in gauze. "No Band-Aids," my mother said as she tied off the dressing. "Could you imagine the pain of ripping adhesive off this fur?" When she was finished, she laid her hand on Mama Squatch's arm. "She'll be fine." Baby was a girl. Of course she was. I'd have to stop referring to her as *it*. With her usual efficiency, Mom packed up her kit, stood, and without another word, walked steadily toward the house.

The rest of us humans followed her, leaving the Squatch family to comfort one another. My mother marched briskly ahead of us, and she was rushing, nearly breaking into a run. She pushed the back door open, and we trailed behind her like ducklings, through the kitchen and into the living room, where she collapsed onto the couch. "Holy hell!" she exclaimed. There were tears in her eyes, and her hands were shaking. "I've never been so scared in my life!"

CHAPTER 58

Megan ran and got Mom a glass of water. I sat down next to her, holding her hand. She was really shaken. I'd never seen her so upset. When Megan came back with the water, she grabbed the glass and swallowed some down, closed her eyes, and made a visible effort to try and slow her breathing. After a few moments, her eyes popped open wide again and she exclaimed, "That's some 'hoax' you guys have going."

We didn't know how to respond.

She looked at us all, her eyes questioning. "They're real, aren't they? Please tell me I'm not seeing things. Or smelling things. That stink could revive a coma patient."

"They're real, Mom," I said. The girls and Samuel nodded in agreement.

"And they live—here?" my mother asked.

"No," I said, "they're only here until all this craziness dies down. Then they'll go back into the woods."

"But the police have all but accused you of vandalism and fraud. You could get in a lot of trouble. Why don't you tell them the truth?"

"Because the truth is the Sasquatch didn't do anything," Megan said.

"Yeah! What happened downtown? It really *was* a case of juvenile delinquency," I said. "Some asshole we know did it."

Mom gave me a look. I'd have to watch my language. Then she shook her head. "So you didn't lie to Rick Morris."

"No," I said.

"But you weren't completely honest, either," Mom pointed out.

"No, I wasn't. I gave him as much of the truth as I could to get him to the bear carcass. I figured if I strung him along that far, he'd get mad, give up, and go away."

"Bear carcass?" she asked with an added level of distress. "Never mind…tell me later." She closed her eyes for a moment, collecting herself. "The whole Bigfoot myth is not a myth."

"Right," Nell said.

"So, your father's Uncle Horace wasn't so crazy after all." Mom opened her eyes and looked at me.

"Apparently not," I said. "He dedicated his whole life to studying them and protecting them from the outside world. Samuel, here, was working with him all along." Samuel gave my mother a bashful little smile. I think he was a little scared of her. He'd barely said two words since her arrival. I looked at Nell, then Megan. "The three of us have decided to follow in their footsteps."

"And we have to keep it a secret," Nell said.

"Could you imagine what would happen to them if they were exposed to the media?" I said.

"Or if hunters had a chance to take a shot at them?" Megan added.

"And now I guess it's my secret too," said Mom. "So, what do we do from here?"

"I don't know about you guys," Megan chimed in, "but I'm getting hungry."

Mom sent the girls out to buy some groceries. "Use your credit card," she ordered Megan, and then gave her a funny look. "I noticed you hadn't used it all summer. And here I thought you were being good. What a dope."

Megan shrugged. "I couldn't disclose my true whereabouts."

"You've been here all the time?"

"I told you I didn't want to go to soccer camp."

My mother's eyes narrowed. "I'm going to have to implant one of those computer-chip tracking-device thingies under your skin."

"Well, we better get going," Megan sang out. "Come on, Nell." She hastily darted out the front door with Nell following close behind. We could hear their laughter as they tripped down the steps.

My mother's face crumpled with anxiety. "Is it safe to be outside with…them?"

"Yes, once the male gets used to you, it's okay."

"What if he decides he doesn't like you?"

"Luckily, I haven't seen that happen yet."

She shook her head again, like if she rattled her brain enough, all of this might start making sense. "I think I need to lie down for a little while."

"Sure thing. Just pick a room and crash."

She stood up, looking pale and a little unsteady on her feet. "They don't come inside, do they?"

"No, Mom. You're safe. They're mostly outdoor pets. Just keep out of the basement."

"Very funny."

"You were amazing, Mom."

"Just kicked into work mode," she said. "Every family gets overwrought when a child's been injured. You just have to be firm and work fast."

"Not every father is eight feet tall and can rip your head off in one swipe."

"Yep, that was a first. Those red eyes of his are pretty freaky. I'm going to have nightmares for a while."

"You can handle it, Mom. You can handle pretty much anything."

"It's beginning to look like it runs in the family." She ruffled my hair. "I'm going to lie down before I faint."

CHAPTER 59

Megan and Nell were full of news when they came back a couple of hours later. "Barry was arrested," Nell announced as she put a shopping bag on the counter. "The cops went to his house. They searched his room and found the plaster footprint."

"Serves him right," Megan said in a low voice. Her cheeks had flamed red. I thought I saw tears of anger in her eyes.

"And somebody got shot in the woods by some idiot who thought he saw a Bigfoot," Nell went on, "so the state police have ordered the public out of the preserve."

"Was the person killed?" I asked, thinking how Samuel had been close to being a gunshot victim a few days ago.

"I think the guy was hit in the shoulder and he's going to be okay. But it was enough. They're doing a sweep right now, marching out everybody they can find, no exceptions."

I smiled at Nell. "The Family Squatch can go back home soon. Maybe tomorrow."

She smiled back. "I know! Cool, right?" Stepping closer, she said in a soft tone, "And I saw Mr. Pelletier. He heard about Barry and was pretty upset. He told me to tell you he'd like to talk to you."

I felt a pang of discomfort—getting fired still hurt. "Cool."

"Well, you guys look busy," my mother said as she came through the kitchen door. She'd taken a shower, pulled her hair back in a wet ponytail, and was wearing one of Megan's sweat suits. The country-club façade was gone. With no makeup on, somehow she looked older, but younger at the same time. I felt a lump rise in my throat.

Mom jumped right in, pulling stuff out of bags. "Good work, girls. Looks like there's everything I need to make a nice dinner."

And she did. Roast chicken with herbed potatoes and a warm salad of cauliflower and red peppers. Crusty bread. It was all delicious and homey, the food I'd loved since before I could remember. My mother was talking to Nell like they'd known each other for years and drawing Samuel out of the shell he'd crawled into the minute he'd met her. She was good at putting everyone at ease.

After we'd eaten, the girls went out to make sure the Sasquatch had everything they needed for the night. Samuel was drawn back to the computer, leaving my mother and me alone to clean up. We'd just finished clearing the table when the shrill beep of my mother's cell phone went off. She dug around in her purse and pulled it out. "It's Jim. I better talk to him."

"Mom!" I said, before she could take the call.

She looked at me. "Yes?"

"Are you going to tell him?"

She paused for a second, thinking. "No," she said decisively. "Not now. It's our secret, right?"

I let out a sigh of relief.

She answered the phone. "Hi, Jim—could you hold on one sec?" She placed the phone against her chest, gazing at me. "Are you going to tell your father?"

Now I needed a second to think. "I don't know." That was a tough question. I didn't see how to avoid telling him, but I sure didn't look forward to dealing with his reaction.

She stepped into the living room to continue the call. She wasn't gone long, but when she came back, something had changed. For the last few hours, it had felt like the old days when it was Megan, Mom, and me—just the three of us against the world, because Dad had been away so much. But that phone call brought it back to both of us how much had changed—how Megan and I had a stepfather to get used to and an unreliable father to contend with.

She started drying the dishes.

"What did you tell him?" I asked. I couldn't call the guy by his real name. I don't think I'd ever said it out loud.

"Just that everything was fine here and I'd call him tomorrow." She put the dish in the cupboard. "And that it's been great to finally spend time with you." I could tell she was on the verge of crying. "I miss you, honey."

"I miss you too, Mom." I bent over the roasting pan in the sink. No matter how hard I scrubbed, I couldn't get the crud off the sides.

She moved to stand next to me and reached for the pan. "Here, let me work on that," she said, her voice shaky.

I looked into her face. She was blinking back tears. The tip of her nose had reddened. I let go of the pan, opened my arms wide, and hugged her. I wanted to say, "I'm sorry."

But then all hell broke loose.

CHAPTER 60

A car roared by the house, horn blaring, a howling chorus of shouts and curses shattering the quiet night. Not just teenagers on a joyride. They sounded out of control and hostile. Then it sounded like a second car sped past, and a third. I ran into the living room. My mother followed. The girls and Samuel joined us at the window where we were peering out, trying to see what was going on.

But the high gate was closed, locked up tight. We couldn't see anything beyond the fence.

Now it sounded like a drag race—gravel popping, tires squealing, a girl's high-pitched laughter, and the horns sounding like a shrieking chorus of demons.

The cars kept whizzing back and forth, doubling around and back again until we could hear one car, at least, come to a stop, brakes screeching. Then a voice shouted, clearly recognizable, "Hey, Oliver! You asshole! You shithead, tattletale baby! You sicced the cops on me! I'm going to make you pay! You think you can hide behind that shitty fence?"

"I'm calling the police," said my mother, her face grim.

"No!" I said. "We can't let the cops come now. What if they decide to take a look around?"

Megan was at the front door. She flung it wide open. "Go away, Barry!" she yelled. "Leave us alone!"

"Samuel—quick," I said, "make sure the Sasquatch are safe in the cellar." He nodded, his eyes wide with fear as he turned to go.

Suddenly, Nell was outside too. She was calling out, trying to reason with him. "Barry, go home. You're already in trouble. Don't make it worse."

"Is that you, Nellie?" Barry brayed like a jackass.

"Yes, Barry, it's me. Go home before the police get here."

"What difference does it make? I'm already screwed. The ticket's as good as stamped. They're sending me to jail. Might as well get even before I go, right?"

"It's probably not as bad as you think—" Nell started.

"You know what?" Barry's voice had risen to a hoarse scream, shouting over the racket of the other two cars that continued the noisy parade back and forth. "I hate talking through this goddamned fence!"

"Hey, Barry! Hey, man!" another voice called. "Why don't we burn the piece of shit down? I got a gas can in my trunk!"

"I got a lighter!" Barry cried. "Let's do it!"

On our side of the fence, we looked at each other in horror.

"Barry, don't be an asshole!" Even as I shouted, we heard the *chunk* of a car trunk closing and could already smell the thick, oily odor of gasoline.

"This is already out of control. I'm calling 911 right now," my mother said, reentering the house.

"I'll get the hose." I headed to the backyard.

"We'll fill pots with water," Nell cried.

It took me a few moments to find the rusty valve in the dark. I turned it and said a prayer of thanks when I felt the coiled length of hose jump and grow cool as the water started to gush through it. By the time I returned to the front of the house, I couldn't see the fire yet, but I could smell it. I searched for a glow and smoke so I'd know where to aim the spray. At the center of the gate, the first lick of flame leapt above the fence. The air filled with wild yelps of approval from the kids in the cars. They sounded like a pack of bloodthirsty coyotes celebrating a kill.

I opened the nozzle full blast, but while I was trying to put out that blaze, a bright object soared in an arc and caught on the top of the fence. It took me a moment to realize that it was a burning T-shirt that had probably been doused with gasoline. As I rushed to soak that one, another flaming ball of fabric—a towel or rag—was lofted toward the top of the fence farther along. And then there was another one. First Nell, then Megan dashed out of the house, hauling full pots of water. Now three fires were blazing in different sections of the tinder-dry fence that they had splashed with gasoline. As we desperately tried to put out the flames, the crowd on the other side cheered as the fire took hold.

Above the yells and through the smoke, I heard Barry's voice. "Damn! This is taking too long! And what the hell, I got nothing to lose."

My mother came out with a blanket. "They're on their way." She took in the sight of the growing conflagration with shock. She grabbed my arm. "Water can make a gasoline fire worse. Don't aim at the flames. Just get the wood on this side as wet as you can."

A car door slammed and an engine revved with a growl. It sounded like one car, at least, was driving away at high speed. For a wild moment I thought they might be leaving, until I heard it roaring back again. The mob began shouting, "No! No! Stop! No!"

"Get away from there!" Nell was on me, pulling me away from where I had been hosing down the gate. We watched in disbelief as Barry's Mustang crashed into the fence. I don't know who was screaming—it was probably all of us—as we dashed from the front porch to the car, which had come to a full stop under a flaming pile of boards. The horn was blaring. The windshield was shattered. A blazing plank was wedged into the open passenger window, and a huge section of burning plywood and a pile of other boards obstructed access to the driver's-side door. Peering through a web of broken glass, I could see Barry slumped over the wheel. The interior of the car was filling with smoke, and I recognized the acrid stink of burning vinyl.

The girls were pulling the boards away from the car and my mother was beating at the flames with the blanket. Now that the gate was breached, I could see headlights. I couldn't make out who the others were through the smoke, but I knew they were still there.

"What's the matter with you?" I yelled at them over the horn and the crackling fire. Yanking at the passenger door handle was futile. It was locked and searing hot.

"We have to get him out of there!" I tugged and twisted at the burning board jammed into the car until at last I got it loose and flung it aside. At least then I could pop the lock and get to Barry.

We heard the faint wail of sirens getting closer.

"What the hell are you doing, man?" I heard a voice shout.

"Helping Barry!" another guy answered.

"Get in your car! We gotta go—can't you hear them coming? Let the cops get him out."

"But Barry—"

"Screw Barry! I ain't sharing a jail cell with him! Let's go!"

Car doors slammed, engines revved. Two sets of headlights pulled back and swerved away as the cars sped from the scene.

The girls and I leaned over licking flames into the smoke-filled interior of the car, struggling to pull Barry's heavy, inert form out of the driver's seat. We couldn't budge him, and were soon driven back by the heat and the smoke. I saw that the girls' faces were blackened with soot as we looked at each other, all of us wide-eyed and coughing.

My mother's voice was hoarse, but she managed to shout over the horn's persistent blare. "Don't give up. He might not make it otherwise." The sirens were definitely closer, but not close enough. Nell was back in the car with the blanket, trying to smother the wicked, flickering flames that were burning the passenger seat and dancing along the carpet, licking at the cuff of Barry's jeans.

Then I felt him approaching. Rhythmic tremors. Small earthquakes as his great stride rapidly covered the ground.

Huge and formidable, the male emerged from his hiding place to see what was threatening the safety of his family. He took in the scene at once. Alarm sparked in his red eyes at the sight of fire. Without hesitation, he moved to the driver's side and heaved the weighty, burning pieces of lumber, tossing them away as if they were light as cardboard. Finally he got to the door itself and yanked it off with a great shriek of metal.

He reached around Barry's waist and pulled him out. As he lifted him, the horn was finally silenced and we could hear the emergency vehicles only moments away.

The male bore Barry's weight easily in his arms, carrying him to the backyard, a safe distance from the car and smoke. We all followed.

Megan helped the male ease Barry to the ground in a pool of light spilling from the kitchen windows. She cradled his head in her lap.

Barry opened his eyes and started coughing. He looked up into Megan's worried face. "Megan, hi. Am I dead?" he asked in a frightened whisper.

"No, just an idiot."

The sirens, now deafening, came to a stop. I turned to the Sasquatch. "You have to get back in the cellar." He met my eyes with a hard, resistant glare, like he was tired of being ordered around. "Megan," I said, turning to her. "You have to tell him to hide."

Samuel had emerged from the cellar and was at the male's side, trying to coax him down the steps. Megan shifted Barry's weight so her hands were free, then started to sign to the male that he was in danger and had to flee.

Barry sat up, growing more alert. "What's going on?" he asked. He looked over Megan's head and saw the Sasquatch, towering over us, a hulking shadow in the darkness. The only visible part of his face was the burning glow of his crimson eyes.

"Holy shit!" Barry squealed in panic, trying to writhe away. I could tell something was wrong with his leg. Besides the gash on his head, there were also burns on his face and arms. "What is that? What *is* that?" he whimpered.

"He saved your life," I said.

"Get him the hell away from me," Barry pleaded.

I looked at the male again and said, "Please. Go to your family."

I could hear the rescuers' shouts and calls as they clambered out of their vehicles. There was nothing more I could do to convince the Sasquatch to go, so I rushed back to the front yard to meet the firemen and police. When I got there, the firemen were already dousing the flames with chemical foam. Barry's once-cherry Mustang was reduced to a charred heap. I ran to the ambulance so I could lead the EMTs to Barry. It was only then that I felt the searing pain radiating from my palms, and the raw burning in my throat. No doubt we all needed first aid. I hoped the male had had enough time to get back in the cellar and that he hadn't been injured.

It was hours before the cops and firemen left. After a rapid assessment and a consultation with my mother, the paramedics didn't insist that we go to the hospital. Unlike Barry, our burns weren't serious, and they treated them before taking Barry away in an ambulance. My mother made Nell go home. After we walked her out to her car with the promise that she'd call when she got there, we walked back into the house, which reeked of smoke.

I waited about half an hour after the last cop car pulled away before I checked on the Sasquatch. I wanted to make sure the police were gone for good—that they weren't going to ask me to make another statement, explain what happened one more time. Though we couldn't absolutely identify them because of the smoke and confusion, I was sure Barry's pals were going to be questioned.

Samuel was out back, sitting on a lawn chair, dozing. I lifted the handle on the Bilco door and stepped into the darkness of the cellar. It was eerily silent. The smoke had not filtered in. The odor of mildew and dust prickled my nose, but not much else.

"Hello?" I called, softly. "Are you guys okay?" I listened. Nothing. No movement. No breathing. Nothing. I waved my hand in front of me in the darkness. I knew the pull chain was dangling from the ceiling somewhere. Feeling the coolness of the little linked metal balls against my fingertips, I tugged. The bulb lit. I looked around the cellar.

The Sasquatch were gone.

CHAPTER 61

When I woke the next morning, the house was already buzzing with activity. Nell handed me a cup of coffee as I came down the stairs, still groggy with sleep. "Morning."

"You're here early," I mumbled, taking a sip from the mug, hoping the coffee would mask my morning breath. I hadn't brushed my hair or my teeth. I had been too exhausted to take a shower the night before.

"I'm here to give your mom a ride into town. She needs to pick up her car."

Megan, wearing a pair of old work boots and heavy gloves, was outside cleaning up the yard. My mother was on her cell phone, making some kind of arrangements. She was back to being the country-club lady. Her face was carefully made up, and her hair was styled. She was wearing the unfamiliar clothes she'd arrived in.

"Where's Samuel?" I asked.

"He's out back. He wants to talk to you."

Samuel was still sitting in the same chair, in the same position, as he had the night before. He must have spent the night there.

"Hey, Samuel," I called as I came down the steps. "Good morning. Can I get you a cup of coffee?"

He stood. I could see that he looked a little unsteady and stiff—I could practically hear his joints creak. How old was he—seventy, eighty? It couldn't have been comfortable for him, sitting out in the damp all night. "No, Jake. I'm okay." He held his hand out to me. I shook it. "I'm heading out. My guess is that the Sasquatch are fine, but I think I ought to check and make sure."

"I wish we'd had one more day before they went back out there."

"I wouldn't worry too much. After all, they've been hiding in these woods for centuries, right? If they don't know anything else, they know how to avoid us humans. I bet they went right back to their old haunts. They didn't like being all pent up here." A wistful look came over Samuel's face. "Come to think of it—it's time for me to go back home too. I'm going to hike on out and see that they got home safe. I'm only going to come back here if I have bad news, understand?"

"Sure, Samuel," I said. "But you're welcome to stay here as long as you like—whenever you like."

He nodded. "I appreciate that, Jake. But you got your family here, and it's time for me to go back to where I belong."

"I understand," I said. "I'll come and visit you—soon—if that's all right?"

Samuel smiled. "Look forward to it." Without another word, he turned and marched out the back gate. I watched him cross the meadow as far as the tree line, and then he disappeared out of view.

Instead of going straight back into the house, I walked around to the front yard to assess the damage. A tow truck and a flatbed were idling by the Mustang's blackened remains, and several guys were standing around, trying to figure out how to load it. I had no idea who'd sent them. It could have been Barry's dad, but it might have been the cops. After all, Barry'd used that car as a weapon—it was evidence. We were just lucky he hadn't hurt anyone but himself. The grass beneath the car was singed. A good portion of Horace's crazy fence had been knocked down, and what remained standing was burnt a few hundred feet in either direction. Our first line of defense had been seriously penetrated by the assault.

I turned. The house was standing, solid and dependable. I walked up the front porch and stepped inside.

"There you are," my mother said. "I was looking for you." To Nell she said, "Ready?"

"Sure," Nell said.

Mom looked back at me. "Come on—we're going for a ride."

"Can I come?" Megan asked.

"No!" said Mom. "You're grounded! Maybe forever, but at least until the yard is presentable. Get back out there."

"Awww!" Megan griped.

We left her hard at work while Nell gave my mother and me a ride into town. When she found the rented Lexus, my mother jumped out, leaving Nell and me alone for a minute.

"You okay?" I asked.

"Yeah, I'm good." Nell smiled at me. Those dark eyes of hers were sparkling. And damn. She smelled like peaches and cream today. Maybe it was her shampoo. But maybe she just smelled delicious all by herself. "I wish I could help with the cleanup, but I have to go to work."

"That's cool," I said. Mom impatiently honked the rental car's horn. I wanted to kiss Nell, badly, but not with my mother watching. "I'll call you later."

"You better," Nell said, smiling.

"Where're we going?" I asked as I got in the car.

My mother kept her eyes on the road. "There's a fence company around here somewhere. I talked to someone there this morning. They have inexpensive stockade fencing that should do the trick."

I thought about how much money I had in the bank. The tax bill was going to take up a big chunk of the cash I'd saved this summer. "I don't think I can afford to fix the fence."

My mother's voice was soft and had that warm tone that always kind of choked me up. "Samuel explained to me why the fence was there. I'm in on this nutty project, remember? What should we call it—'Save the Sasquatch?'" She reached over and squeezed my hand. "I'll pay to install the fence, sweetie— and we'll do it right, hire a surveyor—my contribution to the cause."

I felt a weight lift off me.

"On one condition," she added.

Uh-oh.

"You have to come home with me."

I pulled my hand away. "I can't! I'm all signed up for school!" With Nell! "And what about the Sasquatch? What about Dad?"

"Your father is the least of my concerns." Taking her eyes off the road, she looked at me. "You are my greatest concern." I could see she was serious.

"I'm fine, Mom, really."

"Jake, I'm so proud of you. But you're sixteen! You shouldn't have to handle all this adult responsibility."

The fence place was up ahead. We didn't say anything more while my mother pulled into the lot and parked the car. She switched off the ignition and turned to me. "Sweetie, I want you to come home. I want you to get your driver's license. I want you to work hard in school so you can get into a good college and grow up to be whoever you're supposed to be. I want you to come home because, obviously, your sister loves you and needs you and misses you horribly. I could kill her for running away, but I get why she did it. I want you to come home because I love you and miss you too."

I didn't say anything. I didn't know what to say. I wasn't sure how I felt.

"I know you love your father," Mom went on. "Hell! I still love your father, believe it or not. But you can't sacrifice your future for him."

"If I go back with you," I said, my voice a whisper, "then Dad will be all alone. He won't have anybody."

Mom sighed. "Oh, Jake. He left *you* alone. That wasn't fair. That wasn't right. It was totally irresponsible. I could go to court and fight for custody—force you to live with me. You can be damned sure I'd win. But I don't want to do that. We don't need to go through that as a family. We've been through enough."

"I know." I looked down at my hands, studied the bandages.

"I'm not asking you to abandon your father, or the Sasquatch," my mother said. "Or leave Nell." She smiled a little. "It's only a two-hour drive from home to here. I'll buy you a car! You'll be able to pick your dad up at the airport whenever he decides to breeze in. Take him back to the airport whenever he bugs out again. You can visit him every weekend. Spend your summers here! I'm not asking you to give up on your father. I'm just asking you to continue the life I've worked so hard to give you."

"I don't like to take anything from him."

"Oh, for God's sake," my mother said with a huff. "Are we going to start this again?" She turned to me, put both of her bandaged hands on my face, forcing me to look into her eyes. "If it makes you feel any better, I'm going back to work. Turns out, playing tennis every day is a bore. I hate it. I need to be a nurse again. I've taken a job working at a free clinic. Doesn't pay much, but I'll be helping people who need help, and every dime I make will go into those college funds for you and Megan. Just like before, but we live in a nicer house. Okay?"

I couldn't argue anymore.

Later that night, after dinner, once I was sure that Megan and Mom were asleep, I crept downstairs and turned on the computer. With everything that had been going on, I hadn't done anything as normal as check my email for a long time. I logged into my account and found pages and pages of unopened messages. I decided to go through them in chronological order, oldest first. There was one from Kendall. It made me smile. Turns out she'd been visiting her grandparents, staying in a cabin on a lake in Middle-of-Nowhere, Wisconsin. She said they were lucky to have running water, never mind that there was no WiFi. Both Kyle and Andrew came through with a couple of jokey messages. Wait until they found out I was coming back.

The message I was really looking for was there too. Seeing it—sandwiched in the list with ads from Amazon and notices of Facebook activity—made my heart race.

Don't let me down, Dad.

I clicked on the little envelope icon. As usual, the tone was terse, to-the-point:

Jake,

Need another couple of weeks. Should be back before school starts, but I know you're a big boy and can get there on your own if I don't make it.

Dad

I checked the date. He'd sent the message nearly three weeks ago. Nothing since. I wrote him one back:

Dad,

Hope you're well. Everything here is fine. Bills are paid and the Jeep's running great. Decided to go live with Mom. But weekends and summers with you, okay? Long story. I'll fill you in when I see you.

Love, Jake

I hit the Send button and shut down the computer, sitting quietly in the dark as the screen dimmed to black.

CHAPTER 62

It was my last day with Nell. For now, anyway.

My mom dropped me off at the market so I could meet Nell coming off her shift. While I was waiting for her at the back door, Mr. Pelletier came out. He was so upset, I almost felt sorry for him. Bottom line? He felt bad that he'd misjudged me and promised me a job next summer. That was good. I was planning on coming back.

Once Nell finished, we went to visit Barry in the hospital. He was pretty messed up. Besides smoke inhalation and third-degree burns, he'd broken his leg. Turned out his parents had gotten him a pretty good lawyer. The lawyer figured he could keep Barry out of jail, but he'd be on probation for a pretty long time.

I asked Barry why the hell he drove his car into the fence.

"Thought I was in so much trouble, it'd be easier for everyone if I checked out. Glad now it didn't work out that way."

Nell gently touched his shoulder. "We're glad too."

"What are you telling everyone about what happened?" I asked.

"Nothing!" he said. "No one would believe me. What's that story—'The Boy Who Cried Wolf?' I don't want everyone to think I'm crazy too!" He thought for a second. "But I *did* see what I saw, right?" He sounded like he was ten.

"You sure did," I said. "And he saw you, don't forget."

"You owe him your life," Nell said.

"I know," Barry said.

"You put his life in danger more than once," I said. "You better not do it again."

"I won't," Barry said. "And Jake?"

"What?"

"Tell Megan I'm sorry. She's great. I shouldn't have messed things up with her like I did."

"I'll tell her."

Nell drove us back home. When we walked into the house, Megan was coming down the stairs with her duffel bag. We were leaving tomorrow. "You ready?" I asked her.

"Sure," she said, "just let me put on my sneakers."

As we set off on the trail, the leaves stirred in the breeze. They were already touched with yellow and red. The summer was at an end. I'd brought Samuel a supply of cookies the day before, and he'd told me where he thought the Sasquatch were living those days. Megan was ahead of us on the path where Nell and I, walking hand-in-hand, had come upon that weird hollow where we'd both taken a tumble—the place where I'd given her that first disastrous kiss. As Megan disappeared around a bend, I stopped, and Nell stopped too. I could tell by the way she looked at me that she was remembering that kiss too. She kissed me, long and slow. When she finally pulled away, she was smiling. We continued down the trail.

Before long, we came upon that weird, Flintstone-style stone lean-to. We could see Mama Squatch and Baby resting in the shade of the rock overhang. Megan was almost there. As Nell and I watched, Baby caught sight of Megan, left her mother's lap, and stood. On her shaky baby legs, she toddled in a rush toward Megan, her long, furry arms outstretched, the expression on her face open and eager. When the two met,

Megan caught Baby in her arms and heaved her up, staggering a little under the infant's considerable weight. She managed to stay upright, though, and the two held each other in a fierce embrace while Mama Squatch calmly looked on.

Then Mama Squatch saw Nell and me, and she stood. I went to her. She gently stroked my face with her leathery fingertips, and I knew she wasn't just showing me affection but thinking about Horace too. Baby Squatch was examining the gifts Nell was taking out of her backpack—honey, blueberries, fresh eggs, and a brightly striped rubber ball—when the earth started to shake and an odor more strongly pungent than Mama's filled the air. The male emerged at the top of the ridge and when he saw us, started to descend the incline. He stood by his mate. Megan lowered the baby to the ground, and the little one waddled back to her mother.

The male and I locked eyes. He was calm, and I could see the strength and courage in his steady red gaze. I wondered what he read in mine. He raised his right fist and thumped his chest once, then did the same with his left. Not in anger or in challenge—in greeting, recognition, respect, one adult male to another. I returned the gesture. Nell and Megan came to stand on either side of me, and the two families faced each other, as friends. It was time for us to go. As I raised my hand in farewell, I felt a bond as strong as blood with the Sasquatch.

It was dusk when we emerged from the woods. The full moon was low in the sky, a huge golden disk illuminating the path to the house. Megan, Nell, and I walked across the field slowly, enjoying our last few moments of quiet companionship before we went inside to sit down to dinner with Mom.

Just before we entered the house and closed the door against the chill evening breeze, a chorus of eerie cries filled the air, carrying on the currents of the wind—three voices singing their ancient song.

ACKNOWLEDGMENTS

My heartfelt thanks to the wonderful writers and excellent readers of the Crow's Nest gang for their unique perspectives and invaluable critiques—Robert Mayette, Lauren Simpson, Bob Gulian, and Kristi Petersen Schoonover, who was my bridge to Spencer Hill Press. To Greg Logsted and Lauren Baratz-Logsted, thank you for opening your home to us. My infinite gratitude to Lauren Baratz-Logsted for your constant enthusiasm, encouragement and generosity, this book would never have made it to print without you—ours is a friendship I will cherish forever.

Many thanks to everyone at Spencer Hill Press, especially my editor, Trisha Wooldridge, for your mad editing skills, guidance, and patience.

All my love and appreciation to my amazing family for the time, space and support they give me so I can write on.

ABOUT THE AUTHOR

Andrea Schicke Hirsch has been a bookseller, editor and copywriter, teacher and paralegal. She studied theatre and English at Fordham University and has a Master's degree in Education from the University of Bridgeport. A Connecticut native, she lives in Wilton with her family. This is her first YA novel.

CPSIA information can be obtained at www.ICGtesting.com
Printed in the USA
LVOW01s0141090715

445415LV00004B/7/P

3 1901 03908 3540

9 781939 392473